Praise for L. Timmel Duchamp

"L. Timmel Duchamp has become a major voice as an editor, publisher, and critic."

—Karen Joy Fowler, author of
The Jane Austen Book Club, and
We Are All Completely Beside Ourselves

"Duchamp writes some of the most rewarding science fiction stories you can read today; she is simply and unarguably among the best."

—Samuel R. Delany, author of *Dhalgren* and *Nova*

"...a unique, essential voice."

—Jeff VanderMeer, author of
the The Southern Reach Trilogy

,

Books by L. Timmel Duchamp

Novels

The Waterdancer's World

The Marq'ssan Cycle

Alanya to Alanya

Renegade

Tsunami

Blood in the Fruit

Stretto

Novellas

The Red Rose Rages (Bleeding)

De Secretis Mulierum

Fiction Collections

Love's Body, Dancing in Time

Never at Home

Edited Fiction and Nonfiction

Missing Links and Secret Histories: A Selection of Wikipedia Entries from Across the Known Multiverse

Narrative Power: Encounters, Celebrations, Struggles

Talking Back: Epistolary Fantasies

The WisCon Chronicles, Volume 1

The WisCon Chronicles, Vol. 2: Provocative Essays on Feminism, Race, Revolution, and the Future, with Eileen Gunn

Chercher La Femme

L. Timmel Duchamp

Aqueduct Press

Seattle

Aqueduct Press
PO Box 95787
Seattle, WA 98145-2787
www.aqueductpress.com

ISBN: 978-1-61976-147-6

Library of Congress Control Number: 2018903995

Cover and Book Design by Kathryn Wilham
Cover Illustrations: Background © Can Stock Photo Inc. / jarenwicklund; Front cover illustration © Can Stock Photo Inc. / dmark3; Back cover illustration © Can Stock Photo Inc. / niki16

10 9 8 7 6 5 4 3 2 1

This book was set in a digital version of Monotype Walbaum, available through AGFA Monotype. The original typeface was designed by Justus Erich Walbaum.

Printed in the USA by Thomson Shore, Inc.

To all the mentors I've had, who
taught me about becoming

Recognition, as a product of memory, is what we learn to rely on as proof of identity and existence. But it is a misleading proof since it does not involve us in what is happening but only in what has happened or a re-presentation of it. "These days," [Gertrude] Stein says, people don't experience but only know what happens "by radios cinemas newspapers biographies autobiographies until what is happening does not thrill any one" (*What Are Masterpieces*, 87). We have learned, one might say, to know without being there. That is how we can mistake cultural ideology for the truth of our experiences.

    —Nancy Gray, *Language Unbound: On Experimental Writing by Women*

1.

A SERIES OF gentle chimes penetrated the fog of deep delta-wave sleep. <<Julia, wake up now.>> Her implant used a soft, coaxing voice for its first iteration of the command, then, after five seconds, repeated it in a firmer, louder voice.

When her eyes opened, revealing the gray tinted plexiglass half a meter from her face, the ship's AI, interfacing with her implant, bombarded Julia with information. <<Your sedative medication has been withdrawn. A vessel is hailing us. Fuyuko is the only other crew member awake.>>

Julia muttered the usual scatological expletives but resisted the impulse to dive into a soothing c-space surround from which she could ease herself into consciousness. The memory of where she was filled her mind, and she ordered her body released from the caretaker's functions. Then, as the information that a vessel was hailing them sank in, she requested the position of *Pax III* and the identity of the vessel hailing them.

<<*Pax III* is at the transudation point in the Cygnus system, approximately 750,000 miles from the planet known as "La Femme" and approximately 1 billion miles from the star Albireo.>>

Julia heard the decoupling of the gastric intake valve an instant before she felt the pinch caused by the removal of the urinary catheter. She wondered for the thousandth time why the caretaker did not perform these operations before waking her. The lid to the caretaker swung away from her. Julia blinked as the onslaught of light struck her retinas, and she shrank from the touch of dry cool air on her skin. For a few breaths it smelled thin and stale. After the silence of being shut away in her caretaker, the collective noise of the many caretakers' fans, individually minor, felt like an assault on her ears.

<<The vessel hailing us is *Leopard*, a shuttle subsidiary to *Pax I*.>>

<Is anyone on board *Leopard*?> Julia queried as the caretaker honked to inform her that her body was now fully disengaged from it.

<<Solita, *Pax I*'s word processor, is on board *Leopard*.>> A dull ache throbbed in her head. Though Velcro straps held her to the pallet, her stomach lurched in sudden panic that her body might drift away, out of control. Softly, half under her breath, she told herself that they had returned to real-spacetime, that she and the ship and everything else on it now enjoyed a location and were therefore no longer in any sense of the word *lost*.

"AI: where is Fuyuko?" Julia said aloud, her voice nearly unintelligible for the thick glob of phlegm coating her long-unused larynx.

"Fuyuko is on the bridge," the AI said, also aloud, using the caretaker's speaker.

Julia cleared her throat and swallowed several times more to get her salivary glands working. Her stomach pitched in a sick wash of acid. "Caretaker," she said hoarsely. "Release the Velcro restraints holding my arms and legs."

"Julia?" Fuyuko's voice said through the caretaker's speaker.

Julia clung to the caretaker's frame with her left hand as she flexed her right hand and ankles. It would be hard walking. Her muscles had presumably been kept exercised, but whenever she spent more than a few days in a caretaker she inevitably found walking and other routine physical activity difficult. It always took her a while not only to reacquire motor coordination, but also to adapt to the sudden demands of meat-space weight. Though of course the latter would be little problem in zero-gee... "Julia, if you are awake, and the AI informs me that you are, respond at once, please. We are being hailed by a shuttle from *Pax I*."

Still clinging to its frame, she stepped out of the caretaker. Unaccustomed effort made her breath come hard. She said, "AI: transmit my voice to Fuyuko." She hoped she wasn't going to vomit. Her body was floating just out of the caretaker, and as had happened the few other times she'd let herself loose in zero-gee, her mind was constructing dissociated images of her body—in this case, of her body floating without control, thinly anchored. "Fuyuko, Julia." Hearing the phlegm still furring her voice, Julia made another effort to clear her throat. "I suggest we instruct the AI to acknowledge the other vessel and ask its crew to stand by."

In the brief pause before Fuyuko answered, Julia imagined the psyche-synthesist wondering why she, Julia, hadn't already done so. "Is there a problem, Julia?" Fuyuko's voice sounded...careful. "Is there something I should know about, or that you could use help with?"

Julia bit the insides of her cheeks to keep back the retort sizzling on her tongue. "I haven't been awake for more than ten minutes," she said evenly. "Would you mind giving me another ten before dumping such an asinine question on me?"

"Very well, Julia," Fuyuko said. "I'll get back to you in ten."

"AI: end transmission," Julia said. Her nausea was getting worse, though she was still holding on to the caretaker's frame. Perhaps she should reconnect with the caretaker and interface with the ship and crew through v-space? Except that the protocol called for her making a personal, meat inspection of both the ship and crew, now that they'd emerged from the transudation shifts. And if she didn't follow the protocol, she'd have Fuyuko on her back, and Vance ready to—

"AI: why of all the crew are only Fuyuko and I awake?"

"The priority order still in effect specifies that first Fuyuko and then you should be released from sedation following the ship's emergence from transudation."

"AI: what priority order are you talking about? Who gave this priority order, and when?"

"The priority order was given by Fuyuko, according to standard emergency protocol. There is no record of when it was given."

In addition to urging crew members to follow the suggestions to be found in the briefing for the *Pax I*'s mission, we are also equipping the mission's psyche-synthesist with emergency protocols to be available during the ship's period of transudation should the crew suffer disturbances the psyche-synthesist or lead diplo believe might result in violence. We are also directing the ship's AI to make interim reports to the First Council at reasonable intervals, which the word processor will transmit via transudation. We urge that crew members throughout the period of transudation use the skin patches prescribed and spend as much time as possible in v-space. As far as it's possible to determine from the unreliable reports from Pax I, no one was attacked while in their caretaker. (Few crew members spent much time in their caretakers because they were briefed to do otherwise, in order to prepare them for fulltime meat-space life on arrival.)

—from the Briefing for the *Pax III* Mission to La Femme

Julia stopped her calisthenics and sucked in a deep breath. She glanced around the ward at the many caretakers in their all-too-unsynchronized positions and non-uniform lengths. Most were upright, but some were canted at a variety of angles, the sight of which could only be exacerbating her nausea. If she looked hard, she could just make out the unconscious faces behind the tinted plexiglass faceplates. "AI: which emergency protocol did Fuyuko invoke?"

"Fuyuko invoked emergency protocol 6C."

"AI: describe the character of the emergency situation."

"There is no record of the situation in which the emergency protocol was invoked."

Julia swallowed repeatedly, but her mouth produced almost no saliva. She needed water, she realized. It could have been a long time since she'd taken anything by mouth. "AI: are any crew members injured?"

"Glory, a member of the Science Section, is deceased. The injuries of other crew members are healing. Do you wish an itemized list of the injuries?"

Deceased. Scratching an itch on her thigh, Julia broke the skin. The itches crawling her body were getting to be nearly unbearable, and her nails, untended for all the time she had been in the caretaker, had grown into dagger-like instruments of threat. "I'll request an itemized list later," Julia said. Not only did the considerable ambient noise and the disturbing visual messiness and poor lighting of meat-space bother her, but she needed a shower to get rid of the stench of her sweat and the filthy, itching slough of dead skin, not to mention a haircut and nail-trim to clear away the animal excrescences that were even more annoying than dirty or dead epidermal cells.

"Julia, may we talk now?" said Fuyuko's voice over the cabin's speaker.

It couldn't have been ten minutes already. "AI: transmit my speech to Fuyuko." Julia worked her way hand-over-hand along the long chrome bar that would get her (eventually) to the personal hygiene box. "So what's the fucking hurry?" she said, resisting the urge to pause for another dagger-sharp scratch. "The AI hasn't mentioned anything about *Leopard* calling for help, or the potential of a serious threat. Is there a problem of which I've yet to be informed?" Her voice, though hoarse, was a trifle savage in tone, she thought, especially for speaking to a psyche-synthesist. Still, the conditions of zero-gee meat-space sufficiently irritated her that she drew considerable satisfaction from slamming Fuyuko with essentially the same question she'd hit her, Julia, with a few minutes earlier.

"No, there's no problem," Fuyuko said. "But I am anxious to get a report from Solita on exactly what did happen on *Pax I*—as I assume you must be, too."

The muscles in Julia's upper arms trembled. "We've waited this long, I presume it won't kill you to wait until I've scrubbed off the layers of dead cells that have accumulated on my body while I was in the caretaker."

"Well no, of course not. But if it's merely a matter of your getting cleaned up, wouldn't it be possible for me to open communications—"

"No," Julia said, "it wouldn't. You see, I will be wanting a report from you first, as to why—for starters—the entire ship was put to sleep on your order and second, as to why you and I are now the only ones awake."

During the long pause that ensued, Julia managed to reach the row of personal hygiene boxes lining the far end of the cabin. "I've already filed a report, Julia. If you'd like to access it while you're getting cleansed—"

"No, Fuyuko, I would not. I'll let you know when I'm ready for it. In the meantime, stay out of my space for at least the next half-hour, will you?" Julia thumbed the door control. "AI: discontinue transmission of my speech."

So Fuyuko had already made a report. That suggested she'd been awake for some time. Which raised a whole other set of questions and problems. As if there weren't enough already to sink a battleship (as people once liked to say).

2.

"MY COMING-OF-AGE WAS the happiest time of my life," Hendrix, one of Julia's grandparents, told her a few days before Julia's coming-of-age. Though the declaration had been inspired by the occasion, it recurred to Julia many times after. At the time she had regarded it as a proper sentiment, reflecting life as it was and should be. Her coming-of-age filled her with joy and pleasure and excitement: joy at knowing herself to be so well-loved by her family, pleasure at the many gifts family members bestowed on her, and excitement at the prospects that now lay open before her, from apprenticeship in the family's eutopic group to exploration of v-space with a freedom limited only by her own imagination. Later, though, the grandparent's words haunted her. Suppose it's true? she asked herself. Suppose the best is now behind me. Suppose I'll never again be as happy as I was then?

Still later, she wondered if "happiness" weren't simply a childish idea. She never ceased to experience sharp, brief moments of elation. And though excitement grew harder to come by, she continued to experience it, too. But if "happiness" implied not a momentary state, but a sort of

V-space (virtual-space) is used to refer to virtual space generally, but is specifically used to denote the shell open to all adult members of the Pax and to adult residents of the Pax's merging zones. The default visualization of the shell is a courtyard on which face as many doorways as the user wishes, though v-space can be (but seldom is) customized by individual users with environments that are not visible to other users; the doorways serve as portals into the user's preferred c-spaces.

C-space, known variously as constructed-space, created-space, consensual-space, and— among eutopians—Cockayne-space, designates a specific site in v-space that has been furnished with its own particular environment and usually requires an invitation or password to enter. The term "consensual-space" usually denotes a site that has been constructed for more than one individual, for either workplace, commercial, social, or familial purposes. "Created-space" tends to be applied to sites constructed for entirely aesthetic purposes, while "constructed-space" most often refers to a private space providing an environment tailored to individual desires and needs. When establishing c-spaces, most individual users tend to use boilerplate forms they can tweak at will.

—from *The Quick and Dirty Guide to Everything of Significance*

semi-permanent consciousness of satisfaction… Now at fifty biological years, she could no longer imagine such a condition as likely
to be again within her grasp. And she wasn't sure she would want
it to be. Continuous satisfaction with one's self, one's life, and with
the state of the world, seemed immature to her now. Desirable,
because it eluded her. But dubiously so.

Perhaps, yes, the pinnacle of her joy, pleasure, and excitement
had come when the family stood around her as she stepped naked
into the caretaker and submitted her body for the first time to total
physical connection. All her parents had been there, cheering her
on, kissing her face, welcoming her to adulthood. "We trust you to
heed the guardian's advice, to keep your body fit for meat-space,"
Lanna said, squeezing her shoulder.

She had not then known embarrassment at being seen to enter
or leave the caretaker. She had not then known the things that
could happen to her body by staying too long in v-space. She had
been informed of them, but the worst physical disorder she had
theretofore suffered had been a sprained ankle, and her clearest
notion of physical malady was of headache or butterflies in her
stomach or a skinned knee or a scratch from a careless attack on an
itch. The caretaker would massage her muscles, void her bladder
and bowels, and nourish and hydrate her as necessary. It would
even regulate her hormonal secretions and monitor her brain
chemistry and deliver corrective medication when necessary. She
knew the rest could not be that important since most adults of her
acquaintance spent the majority of their lives in caretakers.

True, her great-grandparents and other contemporaries of
their generation could not leave their caretakers now, even if they
wanted to, but then they were old and probably wouldn't want to
deal with the degeneration inevitably afflicting their bodies. That
was nothing to do with her. She wouldn't have to face their kind of
problems (and she wasn't sure if they were real "problems") until
she was old herself.

Oh to be "grown-up!" What more could anyone ask for?

And of course, Julia thought at fifty, it was the minimum of what one could ask for. Not being grown-up would have been intolerable if it had lasted any longer than it had. Only of course, like everyone else, she had eventually learned that being grown up wasn't what she had expected. And so just what, she had queried herself at forty, does one look forward to next? Retirement, after which one lives permanently in v-space?

It had been her family's fault, she thought with malicious irony. They had inculcated the ideals of eutopia in her. They had made her expect "happiness" and yet had made it her life's work to seek...more. And not only that, they hadn't warned her that ambitious undertakings inevitably entailed ugly compromises that subtly, often imperceptibly, changed who you could in the future be.

And so here she was, a wreck from who-knew-how-long in the caretaker, five hundred light years from Earth, facing the unknown in the shape of the known.

For most humans outside the Pax, the Delta Pavonians, an intelligent avian species from Delta Pavonis, are mythical creatures, more plausible than fairies, less plausible than angels.... Their movements and vocal communications cannot be intuitively understood in any sense by humans. Nor is it possible to say with any clarity what Delta Pavonians get out of their relations with the Pax, a situation that creates a continual sense of unease in humans, particularly since the Delta Pavonians have occasionally bestowed lavish gifts of technology on the Pax, even as they decline to engage in commercial trade. Though the Pax's diplos make use of AI translation of Delta Pavonian speech, the Delta Pavonians consistently refuse to understand AI vocalizations, thus requiring humans to be altered and trained in performing the necessary vocalizations. Such humans have come to be called "word processors."

Among the Delta Pavonians' most generous gifts have been three ships in orbit around Earth's moon, which they helped the Pax adapt for human use. Numerous word processors have insisted that the Delta Pavonians consider these educational tools that

3.

SUCKING DOWN A bulb of water, Julia debated tactics. She knew she wanted to question Fuyuko before reading or listening to the latter's report. But should she insist on a meeting in c-space or put herself at a disadvantage by undertaking a meat-space meeting on the bridge? Ordinarily there would be no question. But under the circumstances, with communications about to be established with a crew member of *Pax I* and the prospect of meat-space dominance for the rest of the mission, it was probably wisest to begin reaccustoming oneself to doing business in meat-space.

She didn't have far to go to reach the bridge from the caretaker ward, but her body was out of shape, and so, edging hand-over-hand along one of the hold-bars lining the passage, she was soon out of breath and drenched in sweat. To distract herself from the discomfort, Julia mused on the Delta Pavonians' notions of utility. The Paxans had added a few of the hold-bars—distinctive because they were made of smooth, shiny chrome, unlike the dull gray material, roughly textured, used by the Delta Pavonians, and lacked the small platforms that extended at intervals from them. The hold-bars already in the ship must have served as perches, since presumably creatures that will enrich human understanding. flew could manage to get about quite easily in low- and zero-gee. Obviously the bridge, like the caretaker ward (which must have been something else entirely for the Delta

will enrich human understanding. No AI translator has confirmed this belief.

—from *The Quick and Dirty Guide to Everything of Significance*

Pavonians, who did not use caretakers), placed as they were in the hub, rated low on their list of priority spaces. Had they even had a bridge? Julia wondered. Could it be that the bridge had been something else, too? The periphery, which when under spin provided at least some gravity, held technical work areas and relatively large open spaces human crews used for exercise. Perhaps, Julia mused, the Delta Pavonians used the open spaces for singing.

How could her crewmates not be aware of the Delta Pavonians, and the Pax's decades-long failure to achieve real communication with them, every moment they spent in the ship's meat-environs? Creeping through the corridors along the hold-bars, Julia found it impossible to avoid the sick sensation she got whenever she thought of how the Pax had botched their only Contact with an exo intelligent species. Only the word processors had the faintest notion of what the Delta Pavonians were like, but since their contact was strictly limited by the Pax, even they had to eke out the little they knew with imaginative extrapolations.

It would not be the same with the species inhabiting La Femme, Julia promised herself. Whatever *Pax I* had been doing, she would see to it that *this* exo Contact would be different.

Julia lingered for a minute or two outside the bridge to catch her breath. The smell of her sweat nauseated her. And the constant hum of ambient noise in her ears and the many smells permeating the ship's meat-space were not exactly soothing, either. But so. She would have to get used to the messiness of meat-life. According to Paul 22423's interstellar transmission to the Pax, the La Femmeans, like the Delta Pavonians, lived in it full-time.

Entering the cavernous, visually barren bridge, Julia found her orientation opposite Fuyuko's, who appeared to be hanging upside down from the ceiling. This was exactly what she hated about the meat-spaces of the ship. Certain people did, of course, find such anomalous conditions charming, for otherwise there would be no one living in the Pax's orbital arcologies. Certain dancers, graphic artists, and other aesthetically oriented types enjoyed the sense of "truly living in three dimensions" (as Julia once heard it put in a discussion of spacetime aesthetics). Well she wasn't about to turn herself upside down, especially since it was for Fuyuko they were holding this interview in meat-space at all. "Fuyuko!" Julia called. "Come down from the ceiling, will you?"

The psyche-synthesist complied. Then, holding her head in her hands—obviously reeling with dizziness—she groaned a command to the AI to give them recliners to sit on.

Two puddles of bright green plastic, parallel and closely adjacent, extruded from the "floor" and inflated into recliners. Julia eyed them with misgiving. Not only weren't they facing one another, but they were in the center of the "floor," a good distance from all the hold-bars, including the one to which Julia clung. It was a weakness of hers, she knew, but she hated making a fool of herself.

Vanity makes even brilliant people foolish. Of which you've been warned many times, Julia.

Floundering and flailing she got herself to one of the recliners and strapped in. She drew several breaths and tried to recover her sense of personal dignity before looking at Fuyuko. "So," she said, "tell me—" but fell silent when she saw the other's face. A raw red crater gaped beneath the left eye. And on closer scrutiny, a fierce twitch of a muscle there became apparent. Julia struggled to keep her gaze directed at the psyche-synthesist's narrowly set, small brown eyes.

Julia swallowed. And tried again: "The AI tells me that Glory is dead. And that others are injured." Julia noticed Fuyuko's hands writhing finger-to-finger, as though in a contest of wills, one against the other, and her stomach lurched. Ordinarily Fuyuko offered a preternaturally calm and quiet presence in both meat- and v-space, a vibe reassuring to some people and irritating to others. Julia forced herself to continue. "Would you tell me, please, how she came to…die?"

Fuyuko's head jerked sideways, puppet-stiff, to meet Julia's gaze full-face. Her lips trembled visibly, and her right index finger hovered at the edge of the crater under her eye. Her pleasant face, graced with delicate, symmetrical features, had become a rigid mask of tension and—fear, perhaps? Julia watched, sickened and fascinated, as the psyche-synthesist slowly lost her ability to keep the finger from rubbing the bright, shiny meat. The twitch, Julia thought, must be driving her to distraction.

She reached over and tapped Fuyuko's elbow. "Stop picking at your wound," she said, scolding gently as a milk-parent. "When we've finished our business on the bridge, you should get your personal program to help keep your picking under control." Fuyuko's hand jerked back into her lap and, like its mate, clenched into a tight fist. "So tell me about how Glory died. Please."

"My throat's so dry."

"Surely there must be water bubbles available on the bridge," Julia said.

"Yeah," Fuyuko said. "I guess so." Her eyes, frowning and worried, darted about. "The AI said that using caretakers was dangerous. So even though we were briefed to the contrary, I advised everyone to stay in meat-space." Her slight, dainty fingers were writhing again. "I didn't like doing that, though, because almost everyone was showing signs of psychosis. I had to worry about potential suicides on the one hand, and extreme aggression on the other. And Vance…" Fuyuko's gaze swerved to Julia's face and then quickly away.

"And Vance," Julia said softly.

Fuyuko swallowed. "Please, Julia. I think you should read my report. Or else question Vance first."

A thick wave of underarm odor wafted about them, overriding the ever-present faint smell of ozone. *Ah, meat space.* "This isn't a disciplinary hearing," Julia said gently. She extended her right palm. "Just tell me what you know—or rather what you deem important for me to know—before we answer *Leopard* or wake the rest of the crew."

Fuyuko glanced sidelong. "All right," she said hoarsely. She averted her gaze. "But...as I said, virtually all of the crew were experiencing personality disorders. You need to remember that when you're making judgments, Julia."

Julia nodded. "All right. We'll take that as a given. That some problem was afflicting all of us, albeit in different ways. And so, Vance...?"

Fuyuko cleared her throat. "Vance, ah, Vance was upset with Nadia. Because we seemed to be stuck...out there. And because Nadia could not be reached. The word processor was...totally *away*. Inaccessible. And behaving...oddly. Perhaps as the Birds do?" She coughed. "Sorry. I mean Delta Pavonians. As the Delta Pavonians do. And the ship seemed to be responding to her with bizarre sprays of light, and she'd loaded herself with a jet-pack, so that she could achieve a sort of approximation of flying. All the while she was making those strange sounds they call *singing*, really really intense sound that you could feel vibrating in your bones." Fuyuko shivered. "It was horrible, Julia, believe me. There we were, apparently lost, at Nadia's mercy, outside, nowhere, and the clocks weren't working, the AI presenting symptoms of psychosis, and Nadia was flying about, totally unaware when anyone else entered the bridge."

Julia leaned back in the recliner and stared "up" at the "ceiling." "And this, I take it, upset Vance," she said.

"Tremendously." Fuyuko giggled—with nervousness, Julia supposed. "She developed a full-blown case of paranoia. With Nadia and the B—I mean, the Delta Pavonians—at the heart of it, and you—"

Fuyuko hesitated. Julia could feel her stare, but did not turn her head to return it. She let the silence beat on.

After perhaps half a minute, Fuyuko continued. "As her paranoiac delusions grew more elaborate, she wove you and what she called a faction of the Council into the conspiracy." Fuyuko's voice had grown almost breathless. She rushed on in a torrent, as though afraid she might not otherwise be able to get all the words out. "Sometimes she argued that it was just that you were foolishly trusting. At other times she held that you were in league with the...Delta Pavonians."

"Vance is a Do-or-Die Protector of the SQ," Julia said. "So it's really quite natural that her manifestation of psychosis involved inventing that sort of scenario." She rolled her head to the right and caught a look of bewilderment cruising the psyche-synthesist's face.

"SQ? Do-or-Die Protector?" she said. "I don't understand, Julia."

Julia made her a *nice* smile. "Just a little diplo terminology. Vance's faction is called—by others than themselves, I hasten to add—Do-or-Die Protectors of the Status Quo. 'SQ' is status quo. But please, don't let me distract you."

Fuyuko's hand crept toward her eye, then pulled back in sudden consciousness. "Yes. Well. Vance called me to a meeting with her and Loren and Golden. In a c-space bunker." Her nose wrinkled. "She said something about *Pax III* having brought...weapons? Because her faction on the Council seem to think *Pax I* was sabotaged, by the Birds, and—sorry, I mean the Delta Pavonians... where was I, oh yes. She said that her c-space bunker would be the perfect command center. And..." Fuyuko hesitated.

"Excuse me, Fuyuko," Julia said pleasantly into the pause. "But was all this an invention of the moment, or was there some sort of premeditated...plot, shall we say, for want of a better word quickly to hand... And if so, just how did Vance and her, ah, lieutenants, plan on getting around my...authority?"

Fuyuko shot Julia a scared look. "Please, Julia, this is just *background*. I thought you wanted a report on the events preceding my invocation of the emergency protocol?"

Julia examined her short, smooth, freshly cut nails. "Come now. You surely don't think it's escaped my notice that you had the AI wake only you and myself. Stop worrying about politics. Just spit it out."

"Very well," the psyche-synthesist said stiffly. "Vance wanted me to declare you unfit. She said she had weapons. And a sizable contingent ready to follow her."

"Continue."

Fuyuko ran her pale pink tongue around her chapped lips. "I'm not exactly certain what happened. But tensions and depression among the crew deepened. There were isolated outbreaks of violence. Nothing organized. But then—" Fuyuko stared down at her writhing hands. "I wasn't in great shape myself," she whispered, almost inaudibly. "So I started patching sedatives. I became so depressed I could hardly move. At some point, the AI woke me, signaling an emergency on the bridge. So I got myself up and floundered my way here. I found the hatch stuck open, and a fight—no, really it was more like a battle, because there were about a dozen people involved—and some of them with knives…"

"I know this is difficult," Julia said. "But please, Fuyuko, could you speak a little louder. I can hardly hear you."

Fuyuko's teeth caught at her lower lip, perhaps to stop it from trembling. "I looked around for Nadia," she said, marginally louder, though hoarse. "I was worried that they might have…harmed her."

"Shit," Julia said softly. She could just about imagine the panic into which the loss of Nadia would put any sane person.

Fuyuko jerked her head in assent. "I was terrified I was too late. There were clumps of blood and feces floating around. The smell was horrible." She swallowed again and cleared her throat. "But then I saw Glory—and knew that Glory was dead. I can't remember much else, except that I finally found Nadia, on the ceiling, behind a shield. She looked oblivious to the fighting. I don't know if it was the ship that protected her, or if she somehow had some kind of awareness of things going on around her. Though I was relieved that she was safe, I still had to figure out what to do about the fighting. I mean, Glory was dead. And it was obvious that..."

"I understand," Julia said. "It's all right." She leaned over to touch the other's arm and stroked it. "You did the best you could in unthinkable circumstances. Please continue."

Fuyuko pressed her hands to her face, covering her eyes. "Sering was wounded before I could figure out what to do. I should have ordered the AI to implement Emergency Procedure 7B, but it occurred to me to do so only after Sering was wounded, by which time it was too late, since it would probably have meant Sering's bleeding to death." Fuyuko's hands were covering her face, but Julia thought from the choked, quavering sound of her voice that she must be crying. "So I had to pull Sering out of there first. And then I implemented EP7B, and once everyone—except Nadia, of course—was in caretakers, invoked EP6C. With special instructions to wake only the head of mission and myself on our reaching real-spacetime."

Julia pressed her hands to her stomach. How had Fuyuko had the strength to cope? It must have been hell. "Thank you, Fuyuko," she said softly, her voice barely steady. And now it was her problem, her responsibility, her culpability. Like a rock inside her weightless body, heavy, sharp-edged, indigestible. But that was tolerable. She could live with the pain and anxiety—as long, that is, as it didn't wreck all promise of the manifold possibilities to come.

The most important point I have to report—and I can't emphasize this with sufficient strength—is that you *must not send anyone to La Femme who identifies as female.* (In fact, it would be best if you were to send only those who identify as unequivocally male.) All the female-identified members of the crew of the *Pax I*, with the exception of the word processor, were dead by the time we arrived in the Albireo system. Those who didn't die during the first period of transudation died during the second. Transudation poses a clear danger to female humans that must in future be avoided.

—from Paul 22423's (Oral) Report to the First Council

4.

THEY TOOK A break, ostensibly to guzzle a half-liter of water apiece. Julia considered a brief dip into v-space to access Fuyuko's report but quickly discarded the idea. The constant ooze of sedative into their capillaries for so long had left them parched in mouth and throat and with skin like paper. Aware that even minimal physical activity would improve her cognitive functions, Julia released herself from the recliner's restraints and determinedly propelled herself toward one of the hold-bars lining the bridge's perimeter. By the time she reached her goal, the bot the AI had summoned was presenting her with a bulb of water.

Fuyuko's twitch was now so violent it pulled at her cheek; and her mouth had not stopped trembling even when she had finished describing the terrible events on the bridge. What Fuyuko needed, Julia thought, was for a deep friend to enfold her in a long, close embrace. But Julia was not a friend, and Fuyuko would resent it if Julia tried to do that. She was already angry at Julia for not having been the one to deal with the mess on the bridge. Accordingly, Julia confined herself to a few remarks on how they had traveled into the unknown and could only hope themselves prepared to face the challenges it would continue to pose.

When they had finished their water and resettled in the recliners, Julia said, "We're both anxious to find out what Solita can tell us about the situation with *Pax I*. But we've got to prepare a strategy before we contact her. I have a few ideas, but I need your expert input and guidance. Do you feel up to it now?"

Fuyuko's lips, trembling, pressed whitely together. "Yes, of course I feel 'up to it.' But it's not obvious to me why we need to prepare a 'strategy' at all. Surely we should be making contact with

Solita as soon as possible, so that we can find out what has been going on here."

Concern for the psyche-synthesist's stressed state made Julia hold her impatience in check. "But..." Julia paused to consider how best to frame her concerns. "Before we do that, I think we need to have at least some idea about the mental state of our own crew."

Fuyuko frowned at her tightly clasped hands. "You mean...you want me to order full brain-chem workups on...everyone?"

"I'm asking you, Fuyuko," Julia said. "What *you* think. What you think we'll find when we start waking the others. Even whether doing so will be...letting the microbes out of the lab, so to speak."

Fuyuko stared at her. "You mean, out of control?"

"Some of them at least were out of control when you invoked the EP," Julia said.

Fuyuko swallowed. "You're saying you think the psychoses could be...permanent."

"We've no way of knowing," Julia said. "But the strange transmission we got from *Pax I* after they'd reached this system..."

Fuyuko looked away. "After they'd reached the planet, you mean," she said softly.

Julia thought about that. She and Fuyuko, she realized, could be totally fucked-up and not know it. And also, it could very definitely be the case that whatever befell the females on *Pax I* struck not during the transudation shifts but after they'd arrived in the Albireo system.

"You need to run diagnostics on *all* of us," Julia said. "Starting with yourself and me, and then Nadia, before anyone else. AI: how long has Nadia been sleeping?"

"Nadia has been sleeping for three hours and seventeen minutes."

"And was awake before then for who knows how long," Fuyuko said. "We can't wake her now that she's finally getting some sleep. And I don't see anyhow why *she* should be in on it. She's our pilot,

Julia. What possible contribution can she have to make to any other part of the mission?"

Julia debated removing her ankle restraints so that she could cross her legs. The pressure on her bladder was getting to be intolerable. Perhaps a shift in position would mitigate the discomfort? After so long in the caretaker it wasn't surprising her bladder muscles wouldn't function optimally right off.

"But besides all that, checking out the health of the rest of the crew can wait until after we talk to the *Leopard*," Fuyuko said. "This is what we came for, Julia. And the sooner we get some idea of what we will be facing, the better. Think about it. Solita might have positioned herself here in order to warn us against getting any closer to the planet."

Julia offered Fuyuko the most reassuring smile in her repertoire. "I'm as curious and impatient as you are," she said. "But it may be that we have only one chance to get this right." That *Pax I* had already determined the future of Contact with the La Femmeans was Julia's worst fear. "And I believe that we might find Nadia's help useful because she will have a different way of listening to what Solita says than we do." Fuyuko's eyes widened. "Word processors essentially live in another culture," Julia said. "Few of them ever spend enough time in v-space to find caretakers attractive. They have their own city—a meat-space they live in, as children do in kindercities." Or as eutopians lived in Cockayne-spaces. But Julia knew she couldn't say *that*. "As for whether Solita might have an urgent warning for us—I believe she would have signaled an emergency if that were so, instead of passively accepting our request that she stand by."

Fuyuko pressed her hands to her cheeks, exercising obvious care to avoid aggravating her wound. "It will take hours for the AI to assess everybody," she said.

The psyche-synthesist's disappointment, Julia noted, seemed to be overriding her earlier distress. Did she realize how childish she sounded, moaning and groaning about the wait? "Well, start with us, and Nadia, and then do the rest of the Executive Team—Vance, Astra, Blaise, and Candace," Julia said. "We can decide after you've done the Exec whether we should do everyone else besides."

"All right," Fuyuko said. "But you do realize, don't you, that since they've all been in sedated sleep for who-knows-how-long we may not be able to get a meaningful take on what their condition will be once they've been awakened."

"I understand," Julia said. That was something she didn't care to think about unless and until she had to.

5.

JULIA HAD WANTED to be a diplo since early adolescence. Her family provided diverse models for the role, since that was the predominant career of preference among them. Julia was deeply infatuated with one of them, her older cousin Raye, until well into her twenties. Indeed, the family story went that Julia chose to become a diplo in emulation of her cousin. Julia never denied it.

But she had always known herself different. True, her family prided itself on being different. But she was different even from her family, making her difference impossible—and therefore something to be concealed.

The family story had it that she had always been extraordinarily curious. From early childhood the very idea of there being an "Outside" completely apart from the Pax fascinated her. When family members returned from border assignments, Julia would besiege them with questions about what it was like "out there" and about "what people so different from us are like." What did they eat, where did they sleep, and did the children live in kindercities or families? Their answers never satisfied her, since they would inevitably refer her to the usual documentary pieces she had already seen many times over, and so she would press them for personal anecdotes not about encounters with "the leadership, such as it is," but about "everyday persons."

"They live in violence, filth, and pollution," she was always told. "The children grow up physically and mentally stunted. No one receives a proper education. And they are so miserable they are driven by hatred and envy to kill others and to steal and destroy anything that is not their own. Many of the children don't live to see their first birthday." And when she persisted beyond the elder's patience, she would be scolded: "It's ugly, Julia. It's not something a child need concern themselves with." At which point Julia would take her curiosity underground—until the next time a family member returned from duty on the border.

Similarly, Julia often begged to be told what kindercities were like; she wished to meet children who "really lived" in them, to be their friend and get to know them. Kindercities represented the extreme limit of difference for her. And since she never visited or saw even a representation of one, she sometimes suspected they were imaginary, an invention for terrorizing children into the attitudes and behaviors their elders thought appropriate.

"They live without the love of a family, Julia," was the stock characterization she was given of what it was like being a child raised outside of a family. "All the children there were found in merging zones, parentless. It's thought that they're mostly refugees from Outside. They have mentors and the society of others like them, but no parents. It's very different from family life and therefore difficult to comprehend or describe." Julia would anxiously wonder how a child could ever possibly lose *all* their parents. The elder evading her interrogation would sigh. "You'll understand when you're older." Even Antoinette would repeat such platitudes

And then, when Julia was fifteen, the Pax "discovered" the Delta Pavonians. Julia had been excited almost past bearing. She urged her elders to have themselves appointed to the First Contact Commission. Eagerly she pored over every shard and fragment of information on the Delta Pavonians the Commission released. She dreamed of meeting a Delta Pavonian. She dreamed she could fly and sing like a Delta Pavonian. She dreamed of going to Delta Pavonis.

But that had been when she was fifteen—when everything was new and all possibilities fresh and promising. Now the Pax was being given a second chance, and she—a mature adult—had personally been given that chance too. She must not, would not blow this Contact.

6.

WAITING IN THE crew's c-space cafe for Fuyuko, Julia ordered "coffee"—which in her personal protocol happened to be an alias for a stimulus simulating the effects of caffeine, a drug that had been popular for many centuries before the Pax. A tertiary, dressed not in crew uniform but in elaborately and brightly embroidered denim, delivered it with a flourish, in a large, cobalt blue cup, then blinked out. Since Fuyuko had to toggle into v-space to run her tests, and Julia had to return to her caretaker to be tested, the latter saw no reason they could not meet in v-space to discuss the test results.

It would be best, anyway, to acclimate to a full return to meat-space gradually.

It was, frankly, a relief to be in a warmly lit space full of perfect right angles and smelling faintly of citrus. As she sipped, Julia glanced around at the dozen or so tables and, in one corner, the ever-shifting play of holographic figures dancing with an athleticism and flexibility manifesting a kinetic fantasy so wild and extravagant one knew that only the most remarkable imagination and intellect could have conceived it. People liked to keep the most remarkable accomplishments around them in plain sight, wanting, as they did, always always always "the best." But Julia seldom allowed herself even to notice such artistry in simple passing. For one thing, familiarity cheapened it. For another, even a glimpse of it out of the corner of her eye would bring the old misery back up like an esophageal reflux, hot, burning, nauseating, an unpalatable reminder of how she had failed in her deepest and earliest aspiration, that of doing the work people had always called *art. It is not enough, Julia, to imagine the* possible, *as we do in Cockayne-spaces. To do the work of art, one must imagine the* impossible, *one must go beyond anything that has been conceived.* So her great-grandparent

24

Soli had told her, again and again as he rejected everything she did as "trite" and "already in the realm of the thinkable." Not that that had been the whole story, either. Whenever she had gone beyond the "possible" he had scolded her for "indulging in fantasy," most of which, he said, had already been thought of anyway, and so was not beyond "the realm of the thinkable."

It struck her that after all these years, when she finally understood the distinction, it was too late. Why, she now wondered, hadn't she been able to grasp the distinction in time?

The sourness of the metaphorical reflux an unrelenting, burning acid, Julia moved to the chair across the table so that she could sit with her back to the display. She had no time for such personal indulgence. She should be digesting Fuyuko's report and plotting a strategy for dealing with Vance.

"Julia," Fuyuko said, announcing her presence. She dumped a sheaf of printout on the table, pulled out a chair, and sat down.

Julia pointed at the printout. "Is that another report? For me?"

Fuyuko looked past Julia, perhaps to stare at the dancing. "It's not really a report, just the raw data from the first brain chems, collated."

Julia noted how much more pleasant Fuyuko's primary was to look at than the meat-space person she'd talked to on the bridge. There was something to be said for representing oneself as young and pretty (though Julia would never consider doing so herself). "So. What's the lowdown? Are we all officially sane?"

The primary's face remained blank, of course. Julia had long since deduced that Fuyuko allowed it only a set number of expressions. And that blankness, apparently, served most of the time. "The initial tests are...troubling," she said. "To begin with, I had the AI run an analysis of our cerebrospinal fluid. There's much that can be inferred from doing simply that, and it's the kind of procedure that, when an examinee is already connected to a caretaker, doesn't take the AI much longer than a blood test to do." Fuyuko flipped through the printout until she found the page she was apparently interested in. "Here," she said, rotating it and shoving it across to Julia. "This is a graph showing the levels of a serotonin metabolite in each crew member's fluid. The green line represents the level of the metabolite pre-transudation average for each crew member. The black line shows the level actually found in the fluid extracted two hours ago."

The black line, Julia saw, hovered near the bottom of the graph except in two cases. She peered down at the names corresponding to the hashmarks; but the print was too compressed for her to read. "AI: magnify the printout by ten," she said. The AI did so, too fast for her to see the substitution, making the printout overflow the surface of the table. She lifted the bottom corners so that she could run her eye over the names at the foot. Surprised, she looked up at Fuyuko. "What does it mean?" she asked. "That Nadia and I have near-average levels of the metabolite?" Nadia's, actually, was *above* her average level, and her own slightly (but not significantly) below.

Fuyuko folded her hands neatly in her lap. "Well, to simplify—"

Julia interrupted her. "Wait just a moment, please. AI: insert S04 and S07from my personal program." At once S04 and S07 popped into visibility, and Julia indicated the two remaining chairs at the table. S07, all prim and proper, was wearing a tailored white shirt with a black scarf tied in a bow, with its dark, frizzy hair pulled tightly into a bun, while S04, sporting a buzz cut, had clad itself in loose gray sweats.

Fuyuko gasped. "Julia!" She glared first at Julia, and then at each of the secondaries in turn. "They're splits of you, aren't they!" The very idea seemed to enrage her.

Should she have disguised them? "I don't understand your problem," Julia said coldly. "Obviously more narrowly oriented aspects of my self will be better able to focus on particular areas of the problem." The fact was obvious: they needed all the help they could get.

Fuyuko's gaze darted from Julia to each of her secondaries and back again to Julia. "It's not *healthy*," she said. "To deliberately encourage dissociative splits, for *whatever purpose*, is *dangerous*, Julia."

The fragility of the fiction of the self was one of the most precious doctrines of orthodox psyche-synthesis. "I'm perfectly aware of the dogma on the subject," Julia said. "But I've been working with what you call 'splits' for the last thirty or more years, and I'm not about to stop now." Of course one usually didn't let others know one did it. "If they bother you so much, shall I disguise them, or order the AI to conceal them and speak only through my primary?"

"It's sick, Julia," Fuyuko said. "You shouldn't use them at all."

"AI," Julia said (wondering if she should be giving the command subvocally, out of Fuyuko's range of "hearing"). "Conceal S04 and S07 from Fuyuko."

Fuyuko's eyes swiveled from side to side before settling back on Julia. "It gives me the creeps, knowing they're there and I can't see them."

Julia tsked. "They're not *there*, Fuyuko, unless you *see* them. They're simply a partial construction of my consciousness, split off and working temporarily independent of me. They don't exist except as...ideas. And virtual collections of data. Right?"

Fuyuko put her hand over her eyes. "Oh shit," she whispered. "Are you manipulating the lighting without telling me, Julia?"

"That is a rhetorical question, surely," S07 murmured. "Since Fuyuko knows that set elements of consensual-spaces can't be tampered with except by previous notice and consent."

"What is it?" Julia said softly. "Are you getting peripheral distortion?"

Fuyuko held out her other hand in open supplication. "Look, Julia, I can't stay in v-space. Let's toggle out and finish this discussion on the bridge."

If they talked on the bridge, Julia wouldn't be able to use the secondaries on-site. "In a minute," Julia said. "But please, first tell me the significance of the metabolite levels on this graph."

Fuyuko kept her hand over her eyes. "It's hell in here," she said. "The stench of ozone. And flames all around."

"Why are Nadia's and mine around average, and the others' not?" Julia said.

Fuyuko laughed wildly. "You really don't know? To put it simply, the stress we suffered reached such proportions that all of us except for you and Nadia threw out a shit-load of cortisol and burned out our serotonin receptors, which in turn depleted our uptake of serotonin. Which is to say, we've all—except you and Nadia—been damaged by depression. If you'll look carefully at the graph, you'll see that my levels are slightly higher than the others'. But given other test results, it's clear that that's only temporary. In short, if I don't open up new receptors, I'll slide right down with the others."

Julia spoke quickly, aware that Fuyuko might toggle out at any moment. "You mean the entire crew—except for Nadia and me—have taken neural damage?"

Fuyuko now had both hands over her eyes. "Our serotonin receptors have been damaged by overproduction of cortisol. Which ordinarily our caretakers would have prevented. But—shit, Julia I can't stay here. I'll see you on the bridge."

Fuyuko's primary vanished.

Given the psyche-synthesist's current physical state, her inability to function in v-space came as a shock. Julia loathed the idea of leaving the caretaker and resuming total meat-functioning, but that was now the least of her concerns.

7.

BACK ON THE bridge, Julia lay almost flat in the recliner, with her eyes closed. Looking at Fuyuko while they talked would probably not supply the support the psyche-synthesist needed and would definitely distract Julia at a time when she needed to think and was already at a disadvantage having to do so in meat-space, where her "thought assistants" (as she described her special crew of secondaries to herself) could not go. She said, "The AI tells me that the standard method for regenerating receptors is by altering the gene transcription—or rather, restoring it to what it was before the overdose of cortisol."

"Yes, that's correct," Fuyuko said. "I've already ordered the AI to do it in all the cases where it is necessary."

"And in your opinion, will that restore the crew to what it was before we underwent the transudation shift?"

Fuyuko didn't answer at once. After a few seconds, she cleared her throat and sighed (again); she had become, Julia thought irritably, a veritable sigh factory. "I don't know," she said. "There's no way to judge. We don't know if the shutdown of serotonin receptors is the only substantive alteration we're up against."

Julia bit her lower lip. She hated to put it to Fuyuko, but she had to, since only Fuyuko had the expertise to venture an answer. "Have you any idea why Nadia and I were not affected in the way everyone else apparently was? And why you were slightly less affected than the others?"

In the long silence that followed the question, Julia was glad she couldn't see Fuyuko's twitching face and trembling hands even if she couldn't stop imagining them. "I can only speculate, of course," Fuyuko at last replied. "I tend to think it must be because you and Nadia were fully engaged for all the time you were

29

conscious during transudation. Nadia was engaged in 'singing' us through transudation, and you were engaged in your c-space historicals and never once emerged into meat-space for any amount of time. And then, when v-space began to crack, you sedated yourself into unconsciousness. As for me, I began sedating myself as soon as I began suffering certain…symptoms of mental disturbance."

Lying with her eyes shut, her body held down only by the recliner's straps, Julia had the sense that with one false move she might float away with Fuyuko's words, which seemed to be uncoiling like a scarf drifting aimlessly in the zero-gee air. "Could it really be so simple?" Julia said.

"If the problem is an overdose of cortisol caused by the secretion of glucocorticosteroids, then of course it can really be that simple, since neither you nor Nadia experienced the acute degree of stress the rest of us experienced," Fuyuko said.

"So then our theories about the crew of *Pax I* are rendered nonsensical."

An edge rasped in Fuyuko's voice. "Perhaps. If overproduction of cortisol is the only factor."

"Well let's go on then, to more practical questions," Julia said smoothly. "As I see it, we have two sets of problems. The first involves the state of the crew and when we are to waken them. The second concerns Solita and the *Leopard.* If your theory is correct—and I'm provisionally taking it as such—then Solita may well be the only properly functioning crew member on the *Pax I*. One question must be as to why she is out here—whether the crew dumped her here, out of some bizarre paranoiac delusion of the sort you have ascribed to Vance, or whether she escaped in the shuttle because she thought herself in danger. A related question is whether she'll suspect us of being hostile and delusional, too. Which is why Nadia must be present at our first contact with her. You do agree that Solita might well distrust us, particularly if Paul and whoever else is remaining threatened her life?"

"Yes, yes, I agree. That she could be distrustful. But on the other hand, as soon as she talks to us, she'll *know* we're not a threat to her."

Julia opened her eyes and turned her head to stare at her colleague. "Tell me straight out, Fuyuko. Do you have some particular reason you don't want to bring Nadia into it?"

The psyche-synthesist didn't turn her head to meet Julia's demanding gaze, just kept staring "up" at the "ceiling." She took some time before answering. Julia restrained her impatience and waited in silence, just continued to watch her. Finally Fuyuko said, "I don't trust her. She's not one of us, Julia. There's no way of getting around it. In fact, I'd advise we keep her apart from Solita, except under close supervision. Word processors are already... strange. But out here, after who knows how long 'singing' transudation shifts, they could be...changed."

Hmm. Fuyuko hadn't used the more technical term, "altered." "How, 'changed'?" Julia said. "Is there something in her brain chemistry that makes you think—"

"No, no," Fuyuko said, "it's a purely subjective...speculation."

"I see." Julia recognized simple cultural prejudice when she heard it. But then most people on the crew had made it clear they didn't like having Nadia on board from the time they had learned they had no choice but to be sung through transudation by a word processor.

Fuyuko said, "I think the sooner we contact Solita the better. We need to know what's going on. And our delay in responding to her hail must be making her suspicious."

"AI: how long has Nadia been sleeping?"

"Nadia has been asleep for six hours and twenty-three minutes," the AI replied.

"Well, I think she should be woken," Julia said. It occurred to her that Solita might have been expecting Nadia to answer her hail on the presumption that she wouldn't have gone instantly to sleep on hitting real-spacetime.

31

"Very well," Fuyuko said, sighing (yet again). "But to repeat, I advise against it."

The sooner they got the first encounter out of the way, the sooner Fuyuko could be sent back into a caretaker for treatment. She was an irritant when normal, but like *this*...well, there was really only so much of this kind of whiner even a seasoned diplo could take.

8.

"DON'T CALL THEM 'Birds'!" Raye scolded the first (and only) time she heard Julia so designate the Delta Pavonians. "If you can't call them by the name they call themselves—which neither of us, being unmodified, can—then at least call them in reference to the name we give their system. How would you feel if they called us 'primates'?"

Julia had attended carefully because it was Raye who was talking and at that time Raye was the ultimate Magical Adult in Julia's personal universe.

Raye expatiated. "People argue that it doesn't matter what we call them, since the Delta Pavonians won't know it and thus can't be offended by it. But such an argument misses the point entirely. The most important implications of naming haven't to do with the offense the named might take, so much as the restriction it places on the thinking of the namer. If we call them 'Birds,' we'll limit our capacity for knowing anything about them beyond the characteristics we automatically attach to the word *bird*. Which is to say, we'll learn nothing from the Contact and will merely confirm ourselves in the same unchanging, incestuous cast of mind we humans perpetuate, whatever the cost."

Raye had ever been a bold thinker: Julia never stopped granting her that. And Raye's suggestion that offensive names warped the namer's perceptions and ability to think clearly had opened for Julia a vector of thought she'd spent much of her life pursuing.

It had been Raye who had introduced Julia to the pre-Paxans and taught her the concept of "hegemony" and the habit of uncovering the constant struggle for and against hegemony in the Pax, gifting her with a set of ideas too heretical even for eutopians like their own family. Julia understood that this different way of thinking necessarily exposed her to constant if mostly understated conflict. And she had understood enough not to let anyone know that Raye had taught her such a different way of thinking. She couldn't stand the idea of the best part of who she was being attributed to Raye's "insidious influence."

Raye had faltered, though, and she, Julia, had gone past Raye. She had come to associate Raye with the kind of compromise that stinks of corruption. Most notably, when the protocols of Contact with the Delta Pavonians were first being developed, Raye let her greatest opportunity pass her by—all because she had been afraid that if she had the modifications made to her body, her colleagues and superiors would take her for a "translator" (as they first called word processors), and she would be shunted out of the loop. Or so Raye had explained it then.

Sometimes Julia wondered if Raye had simply been afraid to get the modifications, afraid to lose part of her humanity. For all Raye talked about the need to venture Outside, to develop "otherwise," Raye proved just as afraid of drastic difference and change as anyone else. Oh, the family, like all eutopians, prided themselves on their brave challenge to convention, their willingness to try out new practices of living and being, of constructing the self and perceiving the self's relations with others... But just how far did they go? Julia *knew* they never passed what Raye (following a certain modern strain of thought) termed the "invisible limits of the hegemony." They went far enough to scare themselves. But...only just to explore the limits, not to push on them.

Raye explained the family to Julia in the very terms she explained the Pax. It's open and comfortable, she said. Which is the best humans have ever gotten. But there's still a hegemonic pressure working on us all, reiterating and reinforcing the conventional norm that founds absolute knowledge, truth, goodness, and beauty. The family is at the limits of the hegemony, by its very practices challenging its foundational precepts...but still constrained by its invisible limits. While you and I, Julia...*we* are at the margins of the family, constrained by *its* invisible limits, trying to challenge its norms of knowledge, truth, goodness, and beauty, but somehow still relying on them in ways we'll probably never even know. All of us are permeated with the hegemony. But to grow, we need to find the outside, to teach us difference, to stimulate and challenge everything that makes us secure, stable personalities… Raye spoke those words in one of her "letters" to Julia. Of all things Julia still missed, after so many years, their exchange of "letters"—Raye's idea—pricked her with a poignancy touched by distance with nostalgia. The letters had been monologues, recorded each by herself for the other, in which they communicated ideas, thought aloud, and confided more intimately than they ever could face-to-face in either meat- *or* v-space.

Over the years, Julia came to see that because of those letters and conversations with Raye, she had idealized Outsiders as people who experienced a reality so harsh and inescapable that they lived at a level of intensity inconceivable to Paxans, so apparently bland and in thrall to escapist entertainment. Consequently, she'd believed, Outsiders necessarily had a deeper, more immediate understanding of human existence, would live more fully and even wisely (despite the tragically foolish conditions in which the Outside was mired) than those living so easily in a needs-plus system where the provision of subsistence constituted the base from which everyone might or might not pursue the points for doing as they liked in v-space or indulge themselves in the grosser meat-space pleasures some people honestly preferred.

Well, now she was going "outside"—as far outside as she could get. She would be open to and ready for stimulus. And she would not let the hegemony swallow up the challenge posed by exo Contact as it had done with the Delta Pavonians. Not Fuyuko, not Vance, and certainly not Paul would subordinate her (and their!) experience of this "outside" to the foundational norms of the hegemony. Julia was committed to seeing to that. Her sense of self depended on it.

9.

FUYUKO INSISTED ON going to the caretaker ward to be on hand the moment Nadia emerged from her caretaker. Horrified at this invasion of Nadia's privacy, Julia objected, but in the face of her colleague's obduracy, accompanied her. The dimness of the lighting and the sheer visual disorder produced by the seeming randomness of the caretakers' placement and angle of position always made Julia uneasy. She understood, intellectually, that each caretaker had to shift position per the physiological needs of its resident, but her eye could never make sense of it. As for the caretakers' placement, she could find no explanation for their not having been placed in precise, rectilinear rows.

Fuyuko knew exactly where Nadia's caretaker was—as luck would have it, toward the center of the room, where there were no hold-bars. Without any self-consciousness whatsoever, Fuyuko gripped the frame of Nadia's caretaker, which was open. "You need to come to the bridge at once," Fuyuko said without offering even a word of greeting.

"Why the fuck did you put me in this wretched thing?" Nadia, though disconnected from the caretaker, still stood within its frame. She was, Julia realized, furious—well beyond the irritability that came with waking inside a caretaker. "I *hate* caretakers. Except during our next-to-useless training for this mission, I haven't been in one since University—until *now*."

"You needed rest," Fuyuko said. "And you were nodding in and out of sleep, your body drifting about like a corpse on the br—" Fuyuko halted, her eyes, mouth, and jaw exercising modulations of aghast-ness.

Though it felt like some sort of social violation, Julia grabbed onto the edge of the nearest caretaker to keep herself from drifting any further away from Nadia.

Nadia turned a pitiless glare on Fuyuko's facial contortions. But then she did not look so stunning herself. Though she had shaved her head just before beginning the transudation shift, her hair had grown long enough to be matted in some places and wildly thrust out in others. Her pale, anemic-looking skin sported huge patches of dry scales and was dotted with enormous angry pimples. And her bones fairly stuck through the skin, so emaciated had she grown. Julia could not decide which of the two was the least appealing to look at. "So it was *you* who did it to me?" Nadia screeched hoarsely at the psyche-synthesist.

"You were too flaked out even to get yourself to bed." Fuyuko looked at Julia. "You should have seen her—I didn't know if she was sleeping, or unconscious. But I could see that she needed medical attention as soon as possible."

"And *then* there's no *coffee*," Nadia said.

Of course, Julia thought. Living in the meat-environs of the City of Word Processing, Nadia was used to drinking a beverage imitating the beverage from which the c-space stimulant took its name and olfactory simulation.

"Look." Fuyuko's voice was testy, her lips tight with irritation. "I can give you a caffeine stimulant to patch, or you can take the same stimulus in the c-space cafe, where they serve a beverage that simulates coffee. Take your pick."

Fuyuko was offering Nadia a simulation of a simulation, Julia thought, amused.

The offer did not mollify Nadia. "To drink your fucking virtual beverage and get the kick from it," she said, "you have to be in a caretaker—which, as you can see, I'm not."

Fuyuko said to Julia, as though Nadia weren't present, "Is this really worth it? I don't see why we don't just talk to Solita ourselves.

Obviously we should let her go back to sleep in the hope that maybe someday she'll be human again."

Julia fixed Fuyuko's gaze. "Is that some kind of joke?" she said very quietly.

Fuyuko looked away. "Sorry. It was just a figure of speech."

Yes. And maybe a double entendre, too, Julia thought. She looked at Nadia. "You deserve your sleep. There's no question about that. But I'm concerned about the possible reasons Solita might be stationed out here, alone, on a tiny, cramped shuttle, so far from her host ship." Nadia's eyes widened, and Julia nodded. "Accordingly, I think she might be wary of *us*. I'm guessing she hoped to contact you before you went to sleep, before you lost control of the bridge. And now, since we've delayed in answering the hail, it's possible she might believe she's lost the slim chance she had of contacting you before everyone else."

"I'm really, really tired," Nadia said. Her eyes, Julia noticed, never flinched away (as Fuyuko's did every time they tried to meet Julia's). "But if it won't take long, I suppose I can talk to her for you." She frowned. "Though I'm not clear on exactly what it is you want me to say."

Julia smiled. "I want you to let her know in every way you can that we're not out of control on this ship."

Nadia scratched absently at a huge pimple on her neck. "All right," she said— then wrinkled her nose. "But shit, I sure do stink from going so long without bathing."

Fuyuko groaned. "Can't it wait?"

Julia got herself moving toward Fuyuko so that she could clap a hand on her shoulder for emphasis. "Give her a break," she urged the psyche-synthesist. Despite herself, she grabbed hold of the frame of Nadia's caretaker; it was either that or use Fuyuko's body as a hold-bar. "Nadia got us here, which is more than any of us could have done."

That shut Fuyuko up.

10.

HALF AN HOUR later, Julia waylaid the word processor as she approached the hatch to the bridge. "How are you feeling? After who knows how many biological hours working, I know you must be nearly *wiped*." Nadia looked better, as if the shower, shave, and caffeine patch had made up for what must be an enormous sleep deficit.

Nadia gripped the hold-bar about a meter short of Julia. "Actually, I'm not." Her eyes, fixed on Julia's face, looked distinctly sardonic. "I didn't need sleep during transudation." Her eyes narrowed. "Transudation was like...dreaming. Only it was...*active* dreaming, if you know what I mean. Total fascination and ecstasy." Nadia's eyes shone with fiery zeal; Julia caught herself backing off. "I sang in ways I never knew technically possible for me." The word processor's face snapped closed. "Being back in normal space-time is almost unbearable." She looked away. "Like waking up and finding out you've been shut up in a closet, or that you've lost a part of your body. Disabled. Disfigured. Lonely. Mutilated."

Julia slid her hand along the hold-bar, toward Nadia's. "I'm sorry," she said. "I had no idea."

Nadia laughed shortly. "How could you?"

"Then we owe you an especially heavy debt," Julia said. "Without your professional skill and personal sacrifice, we'd never have been able to come here. I only hope—" Julia touched her hand to Nadia's—"that despite the deprivation you now feel, in the long run the richness of the experience will still have been worth having." Even as they left her mouth, the words so sounded like so much stilted bullshit to Julia's ears that she was shamed.

"Yeah. Sure," Nadia muttered without looking at her.

Julia listened to the silence for a few seconds, searching for the rhythm she'd lost. "So," she said briskly. "We don't know what we're getting into now any more than we did when we started transuda-tion. We don't know what went down with *Pax I*, or why Solita is out here on her own. It would be helpful if you could assure Solita we're not...hostile. And if you could read between the lines of whatever she tells us." Julia pressed a little on Nadia's hand. It was always difficult to know about meat-touch with kindercity-raised people. Their affective sensibilities were so different. Still, word processors lived an almost total meat existence and so presumably appreciated meat touch as most normal people did not. As she her-self did not, for instance in this moment, even though she was the one doing the touching...

Nadia frowned. "I haven't got a clue what you're talking about, 'reading between the lines,'" she said. "Since no one has briefed me about anything unusual happening to *Pax I*, I can hardly be the person to help you with any kind of project involving it."

Oh yes. Julia had forgotten. It had been thought best not to cue Nadia to anything strange about *Pax I* lest it interfere with her task of getting them through the transudation shifts. Julia sighed. "It's a long story, Nadia. And very confused. We really don't know what might or might not have happened. Only that we got trun-cated transmissions from the *Pax I* saying some ambiguous things about women not 'surviving' the trip."

Nadia snorted. "Well you must have known *that* wasn't true— unless word processors aren't properly considered to be 'women'?"

Julia's throat tightened. "Excuse me? Have I missed something?"

"How do you think the transmissions reached Earth from Albi-reo space without a word processor to send them back there in the first place?" Nadia said.

Julia stared at the word processor. "You mean...you mean *Solita* sent us those transmissions?"

"Well they sure didn't travel to Earth at simple light speed, did they?"

Julia's head swam with a sudden plunge into lightheadedness. She had assumed the AI had transmitted the reports and, thus, hadn't given a thought to their having arrived at faster than light speed. "I never thought of that," she said. She and the rest of the executive crew of *Pax III* had been called in only after *Pax II* failed to shift out of Sol space. When she'd been briefed on that failure, Julia had wondered what the Council could have been thinking: surely they could not have thought the AI could get the ship through transudation. "Would you know how to send radio transmissions through transudation, without going through it yourself?"

Nadia kicked her legs out and "up" and scissored them. "*I* couldn't do it, but I could get the ship to do it." Nadia did a series of scissor kicks and pulled her hand away from Julia's as she re-configured her body into a squat with her bare feet braced on the hold-bar. Like a monkey, Julia thought as she wondered how Nadia could stand to go bare-footed in meat-space. "I haven't a clue as to *how* it works, only that it does." She grinned down on Julia like a naughty child about to perpetrate adult-irreverent mischief.

Julia thought about grabbing hold of the other's shoulder for friendly emphasis, and then didn't. "We have to go in now, Nadia. But if there's time, let's get together soon and talk. All right?"

Nadia launched into a series of stretches. "Sure. I'm not the one who's going to be busy for this part of the trip."

Julia instructed the AI to open the hatch for them. It was high time they contact Solita.

11.

JULIA CLAIMED A clear, distinct memory of the moment she'd learned some of the more intimate possibilities of interacting with one's own secondaries. At fifty she knew enough of the fallibility of memory to distrust the accuracy of her recollection, but, since one had to have one's own story to tell oneself to oneself, she chose to cherish it as one of the pieces of the puzzle her life represented to her. At a certain point, because the memory involved Raye, she had wanted to wipe it (and all other memories of Raye) from her mind. Not that she could. Strands of Raye twined too intricately with important parts of her psyche to make such recourse practical. Perhaps, more importantly, she had been forced to yield to her knowledge that one had to live with some kinds of pain to survive. Raye had taught her that long before she had had to apply the lesson to the pain Raye caused her.

They were lying on a mat, catching their breath and cooling down after an hour of vigorous exercise. It had been in her early twenties, during that time when she and Raye, in an effort to keep their bodies toned, exercised together every other day, schedules permitting. Julia's body had a tendency to lankiness, which she felt undermined the physical presentation she was building around the freaky opalescent eyes, especially striking against her rich brown skin, she had been implanted with. Exercise, she thought, gave her more solidity and grace. Julia had been performing her professional internship at the time, working as support staff for a senior diplo at Central HQ while Raye happened to be doing a tour at Central herself. Julia had been sunk in feelings of bleak futility. The diplo she worked for was involved in what Julia thought of as a conspiracy but others considered mere power-play. The open cynicism at Central sickened her. And her determination not to play the game either on her own behalf or as the diplo's protégée was endangering her career. Lying beside Raye, their hands touching, their breathing almost synchronous, Julia confessed her pain.

By the precepts of eutopics, one didn't inflict "personal negativity" on one's friends, family, or colleagues. And by diplo rules, written and unwritten, one diplo did not confide professionally in another except to achieve a particular, strategic end. Most diplos would consider telling Raye what her superior was up to blatant, unmitigated treachery. She remembered that even as the words were spilling out of her. But she couldn't stop herself. She had to tell someone. She most especially had to tell Raye. Because Raye, of all persons in the Pax, would understand.

Raye had interrupted her. "Honey, no, stop, because if you don't, you'll regret this," Julia remembered her saying. Could remember, too, her light, cool touch on Julia's hot, sweaty arm. Could remember her voice soft and clear and sympathetic speaking the pointfulness of discretion.

Julia cringed every time she recalled her passionate, demanding response. "Why, Raye? Why are you talking this way to me?" Because of course she had believed she could say anything to Raye when they were alone and in harmony, the way they always were lying on the mats cooling down from exercise. And because she knew that Raye knew her pain, knew exactly what she was talking about, and must herself have suffered through the same thing. (But how many times by then? Julia only later thought to wonder.)

The secondaries the family made for your final exam weren't made simply for producing the Doppelganger Effect, Raye had offered in place of an answer. I know, I know, Julia crossly replied. I use them all the time in my work now. They help me figure out things too complex or emotionally charged for my unaugmented consciousness.

But they are good for more than just work, Julia. Raye spoke ever so gently and softly, her voice as smooth as her fingers stroking Julia's fingers and palm. I use them to help me cope, she said. Who can know me better than my own secondaries? Who can understand and empathize better than they? And who can be more discreet—since they're designed to wipe themselves when tampered with?

And then Raye laughed and pinched the inside of Julia's elbow. I even sex with them, she whispered. Though the ones you have now probably wouldn't be so satisfying, since they were made to different aspects of you and without your direct input. Forget the limits of conventional norms of behavior, she said. Find your own way, Julia. The limits are ideological, not absolute.

There had been more, which Julia later forgot. She remembered, though, that the conversation ended in her lying on Raye's breast, crying. As though, Raye said, she were a little girl again. Raye's voice was gentle, but mocking. Using a tone reminding Julia of work. And *that* Julia remembered so clearly and distinctly it could still make a blush sting her cheeks. But back then, she could take anything from Raye, because Raye loved her and understood her as no one else ever could (or would). What she wanted, lying in Raye's arms, was to climb inside where it was warm and dark and safe, surrounded not only by Raye's love, but also by her total physical self. Raye holding her, stroking her hair...and mocking her.

Oh love. Oh life. And Raye so...*everything*.

12.

WORKING ON THE assumption that Nadia would sing to reassure Solita, and that Solita might be willing to sing what she might not be willing to put into words, Julia gave the AI advance instructions to provide her with a translation (via her implant) of any singing that might pass between *Pax III* and *Leopard*. The Council had long insisted that an AI translation of Delta Pavonian into words achieved as high a degree of precision as a human word processor's interpretation could. Machine translation was, of course, cheaper. And it allowed all those engaged in communication with the Delta Pavonians a sense of not having to depend on word processors (who were considered temperamental and psychologically unstable). Needless to say, they would have used machines to translate words into Delta Pavonian "singing," too—if only they could have persuaded the Delta Pavonians to accept synthetically produced singing. It simply did not occur to the Council that AIs could miss nuances and meanings that human word processors recognized and struggled to understand. But the time Julia had spent in the City of Word Processing had taught her the inadequacy of machine translation. She knew not to trust the AI's interpretation too far. But she also knew that if she didn't order the AI to make such a translation, she'd catch flak, first from Fuyuko, and later from Vance. Besides, it wasn't in her nature or training to keep herself ignorant when an alternative, however inferior, existed.

"I'm going to open a channel to the *Leopard* now," Julia said. She looked at Nadia, who had donned a jet-pack and was drifting with her arms and legs spread wide, "above" the three inflated recliners. "Unless anyone has a last-minute question or statement to make?"

"I think Nadia should strap into a recliner," Fuyuko said. "It's enough to drive a person edge, the way she keeps bobbing about above us, virtually on the ceiling."

Had Fuyuko even noticed the jet-pack on Nadia's back? "Easy, Fuyuko," Julia said. "Let Nadia do what's comfortable. You can always close your eyes if it...*bothers* you...to distraction." The psyche-synthesist presumably had no idea Nadia needed to be free to sing, Julia thought, since if she did, she'd probably be working on Julia to order Nadia not to do it—and would accordingly try to order Nadia to remove the jet-pack.

"All right, all right," Fuyuko said. "Let's just get on with it, shall we? We've waited long enough as it is."

"AI," Julia said, "Open a channel to the *Leopard* and put the incoming transmission on-screen." She stared at the blank flat screen; waiting, she grew aware of Nadia at the periphery of her vision, free-floating.

"Hello, *Pax III*," a voice said as the screen flooded with a visual display of a shuttlecraft interior. The effect was disorienting, for the lighting was nonstandard, and the visible space a long, narrow tube, and so Julia did not immediately locate Solita in the picture. "I'm surprised to see you," she said.

"AI, center on the human figure and magnify by three," Julia said softly, then raised her voice: "And we are surprised to see you so far out from the planet—and apparently alone."

The image on the screen shifted so that Solita's face and body dominated. Her brown eyes, their pupils hugely dilated, looked back at them with almost frightening intensity. Like Nadia, she kept her head shaved smooth.

Two high trills split the air, making Julia jump just about out of her skin. But as suddenly as the attack had begun, the two oscillating notes glissaded into a low gurgling. <<Nadia sends greetings to Solita, and hopes she's as well in body and spirit as she herself is>> the AI said through Julia's implant.

As Solita responded in kind, Fuyuko grabbed Julia's arm. "Julia, stop her—them!"

<<Solita sends greetings to Nadia, and wonders if all is really well with her. She wonders if there is trouble on her ship, and if transudation hasn't altered the self-presentation and representation of her crewmates.>> Julia grabbed hold of Fuyuko's hand, to stop the psyche-synthesist from clawing at her arm. She could actually feel Fuyuko's nails through the heavy fabric of her jumpsuit sleeve. "It's all right," she said soothingly. "I've arranged to get a translation. And I explicitly told Nadia I thought it might be best if she communicated to Solita in Delta Pavonian."

In fact, seeing Nadia in the flesh with Solita's on-screen image looming so immense behind her made the alienness of their abnormally broad shoulders and enormous chest cavities almost intolerable in its wrongness. Julia's eyes kept flinching away from their shoulders and chest to stare in fascination at the word processors' glowing throat stones.

<<Nadia assures Solita that her own crewmates are stable—at least the two who are awake. Nadia wonders whether Solita can tell her why she is so far from the planet and why she voices concern about alterations in her crewmates.>>

Fuyuko was staring rigidly at the screen. "She might as well be one of them!" she said. "Look at her, listen to the noise she's making!"

Julia stared mesmerized at the glowing red stone set in Solita's throat. It flashed in irregular rhythms every time the word processor sang. "Sssh," Julia hissed, wanting to hear Solita's reply to Nadia's question (though it was true, there was something spooky about the scene, and the sounds of the singing viscerally upsetting).

<<Solita longs for transudation. But she restrains/denies herself that ineffable pleasure/experience. The crew who remain sent Solita out here, away from the ship, because they fear Solita will shift the ship against their wishes. But Solita could shift the ship from here—she is so connected with the ship now that she can

sing it from anywhere. She can even shift radio transmissions from out here. But the crew remaining are mad. Solita feels safer away from them. So she complies with their fear-driven orders. They cannot reach Solita here without the ship's assistance. And the ship obeys her before all others. But not many remain. All the female humans but Solita and two others are dead. The other two are catatonic. Many of the male humans are dead, also. Solita dreams of transudation. She is immensely impoverished by the pointlessness of spacetime.>> Solita's eyes filled with tears and shimmered like green analogs of the jewel in her throat.

As we arrived in the Cygnus system, before achieving orbit around La Femme, those of us who survived transudation discussed the possibility that the Birds, having provided us with the technology, intended to deliver one of their incomprehensible "lessons" by sending us to a hostile place. We were all on edge after having to dispose of so many dead bodies because the second period of transudation resulted in much greater violence than the first; you could say we were waiting for the other shoe to drop, so to speak, and wondering if this place would be as unwelcoming as the first. And yes, that old ghost grumbling that the Birds had given us the technology as a bribe to keep us out of their system surfaced. Because just about everyone who'd survived believed that, the main question we debated was whether the tech had sent us to the Cygnus system to hook us up with the trading partner the Birds refused to be, or for some less benevolent purpose.

—from Paul 22423's Report to the First Council

The translation was coming out almost as garbage, Julia thought: the AI's idiotic language was clearly too stilted to reflect accurately anything one word processor might say to another. But surely it could not have mistranslated the horrible fact of mass fatalities. It seemed to her she could feel the truth of the fact in her belly, where it burned and pounded like sharp points of lead.

Julia waved at Nadia and tried to catch her eye before she commenced a reply. "Ask her, Nadia, how the deaths occurred," Julia said.

"What are they saying? *Julia*, what are they saying?"

Julia leaned toward Fuyuko as far as her restraints allowed. "Solita is saying that many of the males are dead, and that only two females besides herself are alive now, and *they're* catatonic. And that the remaining crew are afraid of her and sent her out here to keep her separated from the ship. But she says that she shifts radio transmissions through transudation when they request her to."

"This is so *frustrating*," Fuyuko hissed through her teeth.

<<Nadia regrets that Solita suffers so. She herself longs for transudation as well. But her crew members—the ones that are awake—are not insane. They do not appear to fear her connection with the ship. But they are concerned to know what happened on *Pax I*. They are concerned to know how the deaths occurred.>>

Solita looked straight into the camera at them. "I can't tell you that," she said, breaking into words. "I'm so sorry. But I don't know. The deaths occurred during the first set of transudation shifts." Her voice faltered. "Which is a long time ago, now. We did two more after the first, before reaching this system. Transudation takes me away. During transudation consciousness of my surroundings is effectively blocked, just as it is when you toggle into v-space." She touched her hand to her throat, covering the blood red stone. "I've been so afraid of becoming psychotic too that I spend most of the time singing to my ship. *Pax I*, I mean." Her mouth twisted. "They've forbidden me to do that, but my sanity depends on it. There's nothing for me in v-space. Ask Nadia. She could explain it. And I've been sitting out here alone for months—except for my link with the ship. Which harms no one."

"I think you should join us here," Julia said, careful to keep all emotion from her voice.

"What!" Fuyuko leaned close to whisper: "Don't be precipitate. You have no idea what's really going on here."

"We have much to discuss, Solita." Julia ignored Fuyuko's insistent clawing. "I suggest you dock the *Leopard* in one of our vacant shuttle bays. Nadia will meet you on the other side of the airlock."

Solita's eyes kept moving from Julia to Nadia (pointedly avoiding Fuyuko altogether). She looked tense and apprehensive. "All right," she said hesitantly. "But I have to warn you, I'm not an experienced pilot."

"Just take it easy, and the AIs will do all the work for you," Julia said.

Fuyuko groaned as the channel was closed and the screen blanked. "I can't believe you're doing this," she said.

Julia wondered if the psyche-synthesist regretted not having wakened Vance first.

13.

JULIA STOOD AT the mouth of the dim, cool cave. She saw S05 at once, kneeling beside the dark, bottomless pool, its long flowing hair—black, silver, gray—and long flowing robe—black, red, gray—a gray cloud hugging the rim of infinite black. Even after so many years, the potency of the dark water frightened Julia with its implicit icy threat. She never knew what her sybil might pull from its depths. One part of her suspected that the icy pool could kill her, the way certain dream-events were said to have the power to do. S05 was her creation, a construct of her own making, a worked-out figment of her own imagination. But the mind was potent—and thought always and ever potentially lethal. Staring into its fathomless depths (or rather at its impenetrable surface, as revelatory a surface as that of any pair of eyes in v-space), Julia shivered with the thought that perhaps she should not have toggled in without first having placed herself in her caretaker. And she questioned—briefly—the utility of what someone like Fuyuko would probably consider perverse and dangerous "child's play." But she needed her mind to be there, inside the cave with S05's manifestation as Sybil. What did it matter that others might not see the point? If Raye had taught her anything, it was that desire for approval was a trap that would eventually sap one's moral and intellectual strength.

"Sybil," she said into the quiet. And she listened to her voice and its echo cut across the endless, limpid music of dripping water.

S05 lifted its face and stared across the pool at Julia.

"I need your assistance," Julia said.

A weary smile pulled at the corners of the grim, wrinkled lips. Though S05 had a large repertoire of laughs (not all of them pleasant), it had never been generous with its smiles.

"You 'eavesdropped' on Solita's debriefing, as I requested?" Julia asked rhetorically.

"And learned little—about the *Pax I.*"

"Yes," Julia said. "Solita is unexpectedly ignorant. She was unaware of her surroundings during transudation and thus has no knowledge of deaths that took place at that time. And the remaining crew kept her locked up before deciding to send her out here, to the system's shift point." Julia sighed. "The AI verifies that she is telling us the truth as she perceives it. Which means we know little more than we did before."

"We know that five males have survived," S05 stated. "And we know that Solita thinks them insane."

Julia sank to her knees on the rough stone rimming the pool. Her neck prickled, as though an icy draft had swept down through the crannies and vents riddling the cave's shadowy upper recesses. She almost expected the water to ruffle, but watched its surface for movement in vain. She would feel safer with a barrier between herself and the water, but her sense of danger as she knelt at the edge carried a powerful significance she had to respect and accept.

"Are you frightened, Julia?"

"Yes, I am," she said. Her voice came out high and thin, as though she were a child again. "But I don't know whether Paul and the other four males worry me as much as the state of my crew. What should I do, Sybil?"

"Fuyuko is afraid of the word processors," S05 said. "As you are afraid of Paul and Vance."

"Fuyuko is afraid of me," Julia said softly, not looking at S05.

"Given the challenge you face, Julia, you're going to have to take a conscious role that will violate your ingrained sense of how one should interact with and make the world. You need to create a shared cultural reality and, in effect, establish a hegemonic center through which to guide the mission to completion."

Startled, Julia looked up at her. "What! Eutopians are always positioned at the margins. We lead through subversion, not domination."

"On this ship, under these circumstances, you need to think differently about politics. You can't afford to operate from the margins. If you try to do that, you'll present the crew with a power vacuum, which Fuyuko will fill if Vance does not."

"But I *am* on the margins, as far as Fuyuko is concerned. Even if I agreed with you, it just isn't possible."

"As crew members are wakened, you need to present each one with a cultural reality they'll feel naturally aligned with. They'll recall, vividly, especially if you remind them of it, of the absence of your leadership and even influence—and Vance's dominance—when the crew descended into insanity. Note well: you have Nadia and Solita to start with," S05 said. "Fuyuko is their enemy."

Julia snorted. "The word processors are a pointless way to start," she said. "They are more outsiders than I have ever been. And I can't claim to understand them. As soon as we wake the rest of the crew, *poof!* goes my hegemony if Solita and Nadia are my base, or, shall we say, at my center."

"Wake Blaise and Astra first," S05 said. "And then begin working the situation through." Its eyes, hard silver opals as chill as the pool, glittered at Julia. "You know how to do it. Granted the rest of the crew won't ever be thoroughly behind you and will balk at the first hint of perplexity. But if you create the culture you need for approaching the planet, that will help you hold the center."

Julia felt sick. She had known the necessity of this work since hearing Fuyuko's report. But she had hoped... She had always hoped it would be enough to be clear and centered herself and that the rest could be semi-ignored and simply managed from her position as head of mission... But she could not face Paul and his remaining crewmates without her own crew in consensus with her approach.

S05 chuckled, a sound so like the background drip of water that Julia almost missed it. "You're so inconsistent," it said. "All these years drawn by a fascination with different ways of being, yet finding social contact repulsive."

"What's so inconsistent about that?" Julia said crossly. "It's not contact per se I don't like, but contact as we in the Pax practice it."

"Are you sure?"

Julia had to laugh. S05 never could resist putting on the sybil if only briefly each time she visited. Still, the remark nettled. It was a fact that in certain respects S05 knew her better than she knew herself. And that was the thing with secondaries, wasn't it—though they could offer one only a highly partial view, they did so with matchless concentration and depth.

14.

JULIA SUFFERED SECRET guilt for her parental preferences for as long as she could remember. She tried from an early age to conceal them, for fear of hurting or offending the parents she did not love best, and thus kept not only her preferences secret, but her guilt as well. No one ever told her she should not have favorites. And considering how differently each parent behaved toward her, she might have reasoned that favoritism might even be expected of her. Only later, long after her coming-of-age, did she understand that child-raising within families was understood to proceed by phases, in which specific parents successively focused on the child in turn.

The guilt, and the sense of secrecy shrouding it, never left her, even after she had studied the art of child-raising in preparation for undertaking it herself. That guilt tinged her memories of particular parents, endowing them with an aura of illicit pleasure. This almost made sense to her vis-à-vis Joey and Saella, given their explicitly physical relationship to her from earliest infancy. They had taken hormonal treatments to alter their bodies just for her— "growing their breasts" (as she once thought of it) and otherwise making their bodies soft and round and cozy. For years, even after they'd returned their bodies to the status quo ante, she had gone to them for cuddling over anyone else. Their love always felt different to her. And they were never too busy to see her at the instant she wanted them, never sent her away (until later, when some of her parents had formed another family)... In her early twenties she could look back and see how needy and grasping she had been with Joey and Saella and how hurt could still make her ache for them. But after coming-of-age, she couldn't go to them in that way, any more than they could any longer expect to offer her what they had always given her. She supposed her lingering want must be the reason that particular source of guilt never did dissipate.

But she had never had that kind of physical relationship with Antoinette, thoughts of whom generated her most intense feelings of pleasure-guilt. Antoinette, as her first teacher, had used a calm, firm strictness with her. Julia had often fantasized that Antoinette could read her mind at will, that she knew exactly how rebellious and sly and deceitful she was.

During the period in which she was preparing herself for parenthood, Julia took her sense of secret guilt to S05. Julia had created S05 using S03, one of four secondaries created by her eutopian mentors, as template. Though she included many of her most personal "secrets" in S05's construction, her pleasure-guilt in connection with certain of her parents was not among them. In constructing S05 in particular she grew aware of the various tradeoffs one had to weigh in determining exactly how much and which parts of oneself to put into a secondary. When one refrained from embodying (as it were) certain aspects of her personality and those thoughts, ideas, and emotions one did not care to expose in a secondary to prevent their becoming apparently more "real" and consequently subject to the kind of scrutiny that could cause pain and embarrassment (even when such scrutiny was being done by, for, and with oneself), one at the same time gave up the possibility of those particular aspects and thoughts informing the secondary's knowledge, reasoning, and responses at times when they would be most useful.

Julia eventually learned that the repressed material could still be there, in the interstices, put in all unaware by one's primary self. And she knew that if any of her secondaries were to know (or rather guess) about secrets she kept from them, it would be S05, her ruthless, non-comforting personal sybil, who saw Julia's "underside" more clearly and critically than all her other secondaries combined.

The coldness of S05's gaze mostly suited Julia. But since she never courted S05's attention lightly, when, feeling the pressure of impending parenthood, she went to S05 to flush this deep, dark secret into the open, it had been with considerable trepidation, and she had hesitated at the mouth of the sybil's cave, trembling. When she finally entered, she listened to the crisp, melodic drip of water for a long time before speaking. "There's something I need to understand," she half-whispered. "About myself."

S05 skirted the edge of the pool, a tall column of darkness moving inexorably on Julia, thickly swathed in shadows that blotted out all but the gleaming opal eyes that shone with a light of their own. "Are you sure, Julia?" S05 said. "I'm only a fragment from yourself. I won't stop if it gets too painful, you know. So you must decide. How important is it?"

Secondaries lacked what could be called personal feelings. They could not be hurt. And if told that they should not be inhibited by the usual constraints, they lost all sense of what it meant to go too far. Lanna had warned her about that. *You can develop your own vocabulary and conceptual system, an entirely solipsistic universe, if you like. And, especially if you ransack past texts, you can learn fascinating, interesting things in the process and invent whole new areas of thought. But if you do, there's a drawback. You won't be able to share it with anyone but your secondaries. If you try, you'll be misunderstood at best, and be thought totally incomprehensible at second-best, and insane at worst. Some people have done this, you know. Those with a bent for philosophy, mathematics, and other inventive pursuits. Few have ever been able to find a way to communicate their invented worlds to others. And some have been lost from the social world. Rationality and language are socially determined, Julia. Carry any set of propositions far enough, and you'll be a thin twig of a branch on the tree of human society, an offshoot not going anywhere. Which is always a choice. But let's hope a conscious one, right?* Julia remembered the warning for a long time without understanding it, except as it could be (somewhat tenuously) applied to the notion of hegemony and margins and the development of eutopian spaces. But the first time she lost herself in exploring a few ideas in depth, she suffered the shock of discovering how difficult it was to translate her new insights into language that others—even those closest to her—could comprehend. Only then did she understand what Lanna had been telling her.

The secondaries could go on and on and on with you, without ever worrying about the normative limits of hegemony. They were wonderful that way—and terrible.

And so Julia looked at S05 and quailed. "I don't think I should undertake parenthood without understanding," she said, wondering if she would survive whatever S05 had to teach her about her secret guilt.

S05 bowed ironically. "Very well. Take off your clothes and get into the pool according to the ritual."

Julia hated going through the sybil's ritual cleansing, but she did it when told to. It served a purpose, S05 claimed. It prepared her mind; it tested her resolve. So Julia removed her clothes and lay down on the gritty stone and did the breathing exercise for blanking out all conscious thought. The cold seeped through her back, oozing into her body until her tissues felt saturated nearly to numbness. Gooseflesh pimpled her skin; her nipples tightened. Empty (though she hadn't fasted, as S05 sometimes insisted she do), cold, aware of her body as she was seldom made to be, she knelt at the edge of the pool, closed her eyes, and keeled forward into the icy, bottomless depths.

At any time during the ritual she could simply have reminded herself that it was all mere psychological effect, since her brain was not wired to simulate the sensation of body-piercing cold, much less the numbness induced by the near-freezing water. But the sybil did something to her, to make her believe in her effects through every nerve in her body. Hypnosis, she thought of it (when safely outside the experience). The sybil had great power to manipulate her.

Which was the point.

Once Julia was properly terrorized by the numbing cold and the panic that threatened her whenever, in the pool, she thought of its infinite depths, the sybil allowed her to climb out (no easy thing when one's limbs were stiff and numb) and huddle dripping at its large, brown feet. Teeth chattering, Julia confessed her favoritism for certain parents, and her secret guilt, especially over Antoinette, and her pleasure at her guilt and her guilt at feeling pleasure from her guilt and its secrecy... They discussed it all in excruciating (and sometimes pleasurable) detail. Julia went over everything she could remember that, for the moment, seemed to represent her entire childhood. She dredged up, for instance, a memory of being angry at Joey for changing his shape so drastically, making himself not the same person at all, but only a shadow of the parent she had loved so physically. That had been the beginning, S05 said, of her distrust of meat reality.

"I—distrustful of meat reality?" Julia was incredulous.

As for her feelings about/toward/with Antoinette, S05 said: "It's simple. And if it weren't yourself involved, you would have seen it plainly."

Julia, testy, snapped: "But you are myself. And so if you're seeing it, I'm seeing it, too. Am I right?"

"Not quite. But, in any case, that's a red herring. Think about it later. The point is, there are two components to your guilty pleasure where Antoinette is concerned."

"Yes? So what are they?"

S05 shook its head. "If I simply tell you, you'll just say *Oh, so that's what that was all about* and then toggle out and forget it."

Julia tsked. "Really, Sybil, that's an absurd assumption on your part. Why would I have gone to so much trouble to ask you in the first place?"

Again S05 shook its head. "Oh those red herrings, Julia. Your diplo training does you credit."

"One more crack like that, and I'm out of here," Julia said.

S05 produced one of its rare, evil smiles. "That's your prerogative, Julia." It was manifestly unperturbed. "Let's talk about Antoinette. Or, more precisely, your perceptions of Antoinette. Your feelings for her weren't at any time similar to your feelings for Saella and Joey, were they."

"N-no. But—"

"So doesn't it strike you as odd that you use the word *favoritism* when talking about your feelings for all three, as opposed to the way you felt about your other parents?"

Julia frowned at the white eyes shining at her like small, oval lamps punctuating rather than illuminating the night. "She was important to me," Julia finally said. "She meant more to me than the others. Her opinion of me, I mean. I wanted her approval. I suppose because she was my first teacher."

"You mean her authority went further with you than the others' did?"

Julia rubbed her hands up and down her arms, hard. "Can't I put on some clothes while we discuss this?" she said. "I'm cold."

"You would use the word *authority* in reference to your parents, wouldn't you, Julia?"

Julia felt pain in her abdomen. Like gas. Only you weren't supposed to feel gas when you were doing v-space from a caretaker. "I'm having a hard time thinking, I'm so uncomfortable," Julia said. "*Authority*? I suppose I'd use it in reference to some of my parents. But certainly not all." The authority of parents typically operated outside the parent-child relationship, precisely because authority needed a societal basis if it were not to transmogrify into a perverse effect of power. If the child did not internalize the abstraction clean of such perverse effects, she would be bent for life to criminal inclinations.

"I wanted their love and approval," Julia said angrily. "Especially Joey's and Saella's and Antoinette's! And yes, they taught me *goodness* and *honesty* and the need for minimal adherence to hegemonic norms of behavior." Julia glared at S05. "So if you call *that* an exercise of authority, then yes, their authority went further with me than my other parents' did."

"You said you used to think that Antoinette could read your mind, that she knew every negative thing you ever did or thought," S05 said.

"I can't stay here like this," Julia cried. "It's absurd, kneeling here shivering, and all the grit on the floor that you insist has to be filthy—" Catching a sob in her throat, she chided herself for letting herself be so ridiculously carried away. "Look, you told me straight out the reasons I have those feelings about Saella and Joey. And it's worked on me just fine, I know I won't forget—even though it's obvious that since children need physical affection, there's not much parents can do about it, bar giving meat-space a more positive valence." Julia frowned. "Though it's not as though I'm saying the feelings are *bad*, necessarily, even if there's something perverse about them, which—"

S05's voice thundered: "Julia! Stop evading the point at hand."

Julia sucked in a cold, shaky breath and pressed her crossed arms even more tightly to her chest. "You're the one not coming to the point." She glared up at the sybil's harsh, distant face. "And if you don't do it soon, I'm out of here, lady!"

"That's your choice. But if you toggle out now you might as well erase me."

Julia seethed. One's own secondary, threatening its primary! But S05 was hard. Very, very hard. It had all the obstinacy of the full personality without any of the mitigating empathy that could keep it from being insufferable. It made Julia feel like a child on the verge of a temper tantrum. "All right!" she shouted. "Yes, I had fantasies of omniscience in Antoinette—as you very well know already! And yes, she exercised authority over me. Is that what you're waiting to hear me say?"

"Very good, Julia," S05 said. (Mockingly? Julia wondered.) "That's the first point. But there's another ground for your guilty pleasure. Ask yourself this: did you see Antoinette as different from your other parents in any other respect?"

The argument against raising children in families centered precisely on the tendency of authority to be confused with affective responses. Pro-family advocates insisted that if care were taken it needn't be. And so no one ever wanted to admit it happened, except in cases of egregious dysfunctionality.

"Julia?"

Julia dropped her chin onto her crossed wrists. "Yes," she said, suddenly almost too depressed to speak. "Antoinette had neither parents nor family. She was raised in a kindercity. Which you couldn't help noticing. I think I especially liked her for it, even if she would never talk much about her background."

"She was the group's token outsider," S05 said brutally.

Julia swallowed. "As I've always maintained, she was a great example for a child. And everyone always said she was chosen to join the group because she was such an excellent teacher."

"You liked her being an outsider," S05 said.

"Yes," Julia admitted in a nearly inaudible voice. "She wasn't at all like my other parents. I think I loved her for that more than anything."

"And felt guilty for it, too. Since she didn't particularly like being different in that respect. Did she."

Julia sank down, onto her ass, and pulled her knees to her chest. "All right, Sybil. I understand. Can I go now?"

"Does understanding make any difference to you?"

Julia looked up at S05 and laughed shortly. "Only time will tell us the answer to that, Sybil." She did not mention that for the moment at least, she felt sick.

S05 walked past Julia to stand at the edge of the pool. "You'd better go see S06," it said.

Julia looked over her shoulder at S05's erect back. "It's you who are omniscient," she muttered—and toggled out. But then she had had to make S06 precisely because S05 was so mean. Which S05 knew very well.

15.

"IT'S SO *BEAUTIFUL*!" Astra kept gushing. She hadn't taken her eyes off the viewscreen since calling up images of the exterior field surrounding the ship. Given the cabin's smallness and drabness, the flat view of distant blue Albireo and its even more distant yellow companion, with La Femme hanging in the darkness like a great globe of blue light, managed to dominate the space. Astra snatched a quick look at Julia. "We had simulations of what a blue star would look like, but still! It's hard to get used to the reality of a star so much brighter than our sun and so obviously powerful while still all of a billion miles away."

Julia bore with it. This, after all, had been Astra's motivation for doing the trip. *Each to her own.* And that she, Julia, found the light outside disturbingly eerie, just another discomfort to adjust to, must be no one's concern but her own. She said, "Though Albireo is the sun, La Femme looks like a ball of blue light, too."

Astra's eyes glittered at Julia, startling her with their resemblance to La Femme. "I can hardly wait to see what our human vision makes of the light on the planet's surface. Even the most ordinary things—our skin, for instance, will be drenched with light radically different from what we're used to. One of my team's projects will be to record how long it will take our eyes' photoreceptors to adjust to the point of ceasing to notice the difference."

Astra's gaze moved back to the viewscreen, as though drawn by a force too powerful to resist. For a first taste this surely must be enough, Julia decided. But should she go so far as to order the viewscreen off? She picked at a section of the netting she had used to tie herself into a stationary position, working to tease free a strand of the tightly plaited fibers. "I hope you're well now, Astra," she said.

Astra's head jerked around. "Oh I am," she said. "The AI has given me a clean bill of health."

Julia watched the light in Astra's eyes quench. "Is there anything you think you should tell me about?" she said gently and softly.

Astra licked her lips. "I'm so parched," she said. "Was it that way for you when you came out of the caretaker?"

"Fuyuko had the AI administer a drug to every crew member. I gather it was necessary."

Astra's mouth and the muscles around her eyes visibly tightened. "Yes," she said. "I suppose it's that you're wondering about."

Watching Astra's face and body language, Julia saw how easy it was going to be to catch up individual crew members in the weft of her authority and weave them into a tight mesh called "loyalty." She could do that with one hand tied behind her back. Her current location in the larger netting of power—at a great knob or node from which radiated many thin threads, the location to which the Council had assigned her—would mean that resistance to her ordering of the mission would come with great hesitation. Vance hadn't counted on such strong deference to established authority when she'd tried chivvying Fuyuko into extracting her, Julia, from the node. But how did one tap the considerable power of the node without getting caught up in its netting? To make a hegemony meant creating a thick culture to which a substantial nucleus of the group would give nearly unconscious allegiance. If she were a cultist, she could probably do it. But that wasn't the sort of hegemony she wanted to create... A culture of loyalty—a steely, tight mesh surrounding her knob in the netting—would take them far. It would certainly keep Vance from jacking the mission. But Vance was no longer the principal problem with which she would be contending.

S07 would have to help her keep from being trapped.

Julia put it to Astra: "You were involved in the fray on the bridge, I believe?"

Astra swallowed. "Yes." She met Julia's gaze. "But it was necessary. You weren't around. And Vance—Vance wanted to kill Nadia.

And Fuyuko wasn't available, any more than you were. So since I was next in rank, I saw it as my duty to protect Nadia."

Julia produced a slight smile. "Which is to say, you're telling me you were on the right side." *My side.*

Astra's nostrils quivered. "Are you being sarcastic?"

Julia forced her lips into stern immobility. The very idea of "sides" was anathema to a eutopian. (As Astra no doubt knew.) One had to put up with "inside" and "outside" since one couldn't make sense of the Paxan world without such language. But the idea of *opposing* sides could only be trotted out with the deepest sense of irony.

Which she now must conceal.

"No, Astra," Julia said evenly, "I'm not being sarcastic. It's just that I find the idea of this crew being divided into sides disturbing. I'm glad you kept your head and did what was necessary to pre-serve the mission and prevent the sort of mayhem that decimated the crew of *Pax I* under apparently similar circumstances."

Astra's eyes widened, then narrowed almost to slits. "You know, then, what happened to the *Pax I*?"

Julia sighed. "We will get to that in a moment. But first…" She bit her lip. Astra's gold-skinned, freckled cheeks were suffused with blood, her eyes bright, their pupils so extremely dilated as to make her irises look black. "We're fortunate to have someone so…together as you are, Astra. If it hadn't been for you…" Julia smiled crookedly—and was pleased to see Astra's eyes grow bright with tears. She cleared her throat and made as if to start again, briskly. "I'm concerned about Vance and those who chose to follow her lead. My plan is to waken everyone but them and then decide where to go from there. Unless you would like to suggest some other way to proceed?"

"No, you're absolutely right," Astra said. "In fact, I'm not cer-tain we should wake Vance at all. Given how…" She averted her eyes, then shifted her grip on the hold-bar, as though preparing to shove herself off. "She was…*crazy*, Julia." Her gaze flicked back to Julia's face. "I mean, the things she was *saying*, it really put us on the spot, you know? Because she was giving orders. And you weren't around. And the filthy things she claimed about Nadia…"

Julia made a soft humming sound to both convey sympathy and suggest the need to move on. "Let me ask you something, Astra. Of course, if you deem the question too personal, you're free not to answer. Have you engaged in an alliance yet?"

A visible shiver ran over the science officer. "Yes. We have two children. One ten, the other eighteen."

Julia nodded. "We have a child, sixteen. Or she was sixteen—at the time we left Sol system."

Astra hugged herself tightly.

Julia regretted reminding her of the loss, though she wondered at her having left a ten-year-old. "The reason I ask is that it's useful to draw a comparison," she said. "When a group of people make an alliance to form a new family, they select themselves, so to speak. No one assigns them even one particular member, since the balance is too delicate to risk. Now compare our crew to an alliance, and our mission to the child we have allied ourselves to raise."

Astra looked at her, startled, and then suddenly conscious she was drifting, grabbed the gleaming chrome hold-bar and pulled herself back into position.

"Unfortunately, though all of us chose to be members of this crew, we cannot in the larger sense be considered self-selecting. I think we all know—with, perhaps, the exception of Nadia, who shared very few briefings with us during training—that this crew has been assembled as a series of compromises forced by Council politics. One faction wanted one set of people, another faction insisted on another. Instead of allowing me to choose a second diplo according to my own inclinations and needs, Vance was chosen for me, so that both factions would be represented on the mission. And Fuyuko, as you may or may not know, was drafted because certain members of the Council were concerned about the partial, fragmented nature of the transmissions received from *Pax I*."

Astra had begun doing leg kicks so rhythmically that Julia fancied she could hear her muttering the count under her breath. "Well yes, I think all of us—barring Nadia, as you say—have been aware of this...tension, all along," she said.

"But we are still an alliance, with a responsibility to our child," Julia said sternly. "And I think it's important that we begin consciously to think of ourselves in that way. Vance and those who joined her conspiracy are dysfunctional members threatening the well-being of the child. Now while it's rare for so many members of an alliance to become dysfunctional all at the same time, I believe that is the analog of the situation in which we find ourselves."

Astra held her legs still and looked solemnly at Julia. "I think I understand now why you have such an aversion to the idea of our splitting into sides. Which must mean, I guess, that you don't intend to take...reprisals."

Julia shook her head. "I intend to be cautious, yes. But alliance members never attack one of their number for taking a dive into dysfunctionality. During the first leg of this trip, we were...loose. But we have arrived, Astra. And I think we need to concentrate our minds on the mission—and not just its component parts for which we are each individually responsible, as in, for instance, your team's many major and minor projects. Because just as the component parts of the child's raising fade into insignificance if the child goes seriously wrong, so the component parts of the mission may be rendered pointless if the mission as a whole does not succeed."

Astra's nod was vigorous. "I see what you're saying." She gave Julia another long, solemn look. "Do you think that's what happened to *Pax I*? That everyone was so fragmented into their own component responsibilities that the mission couldn't make it under the stress of its members' dysfunctionality?"

"I don't know. But it's my best guess." Or rather, most inspired one, Julia thought. "It seems, though, that we're ahead of *Pax I* at least in the sense that we've so far lost only one member and some of us are functioning at least adequately."

"I wish we knew what happened on *Pax I*," Astra said softly.

"I'm going to assign you and Fuyuko to draw more out of Solita," Julia said. "I'm hoping that maybe she can tell us what she remembers the crew were doing before she lost awareness during transudation. If so, maybe she and Nadia and the rest of us can compare notes."

Astra nodded. "I see what you're getting at. Because though some things went wrong with our crew, they didn't go as seriously wrong as on *Pax I*."

Julia pulled the release tab on the netting and grabbed the hold-bar as the netting retracted. "There's just one other thing, Astra." The science officer raised her eyebrows. "I don't know about your family experience, but in mine, both as parent and child, the family includes outsiders with significantly different backgrounds. Now we all know Nadia and Solita are outsiders: presumably that difference is what made Nadia so irresistible a focus for Vance's paranoia. But she's part of the family, Astra. As is Solita now, too."

Astra grinned. "I hear you, Julia. You can count on me to make it work with them as best I can."

In other words, Julia thought wryly, to "work it through." But she knew better than to suggest such a formulation to Astra (who wouldn't have a chance of getting it, anyway).

16.

"SIT WHERE YOU like," Julia said, gesturing at the deliberately octagonal simulated oak table. She had to admit that her confidence level, her very ability to think, increased exponentially in v-space, particularly in her own c-spaces. They wouldn't be able to hold more than a few executive meetings in this one, since presumably they'd soon be spending most of their time on the surface of the planet. But why not optimize the situation?

Discipline was one thing. She calculated, though, that she'd be so overwhelmed by the effects of La Femme's gravity that the multiple irritations of meat-space would be barely noticeable. Besides, since arrival in the Cygnus system she had been spending three-quarters of her waking hours in meat-space. Surely, given the trickiness of the situation, it was appropriate to spend the other quarter using all the resources currently at her disposal?

The ship itself resembled a c-space to the extent that its default tended to be contained, empty space (except of course for the horrible caretaker ward). But when in use, the ship's spaces soon became visually cluttered with inflatable furniture and other appurtenances that could not offer the straight lines and pleasing angles and curves that characterized furnishings and their placement in c-space. Oh, to be like the moderns, capable of taking pleasure in small imperfections and the illusion of the "natural" rendering the accidental beautiful. Oh to appreciate the intricacies of context, and to submerge oneself in representation without the self-consciousness necessarily accompanying entry into v-space...

"I hereby open this executive meeting. The AI is recording the proceedings. Present are Fuyuko, Astra, Blaise, Candace, Solita, Nadia, and myself, Julia. I have asked Solita and Nadia to join us because I believe they have much to contribute to our management

69

of this mission. One of our regular members, Vance, is, for the time being, unavoidably absent from this body." Though Fuyuko's face was set in its usual blank v-space mask, her opposition to the word processors' presence was almost palpable; she had argued strenuously and at length to keep them out. Blaise, however, did not even bother to conceal her suspicion and disgust. She constantly slid quick, disapproving looks at Nadia and Solita, as though convinced she would eventually catch them in the act of illicit or inappropriate behavior.

Julia smiled around the table. "We have a full agenda to get through. While I want to encourage discussion, I'm concerned we not get bogged down in this meeting. So my suggestion is that unless you have fully developed points to make, you save them." Heads bobbed; no one liked sitting in meetings for hours. "First point of business: we've been in Cygnus system for thirty-six ship hours. And we haven't yet been hailed by *Pax I*. I've deliberately held off contacting them." Julia looked directly at Solita. "Solita. Do you have a conjecture for explaining why we haven't heard from them?"

Solita stroked her throat, conspicuously free of the augmentation permanently implanted there in her meat-space body. Julia guessed she had simply not bothered to update her primary, which gave her normally proportioned shoulders and chest and suggested a biological age of about eighteen. The throat-stroking was obviously a nervous mannerism, given the frequency and absentmindedness with which she performed it. "My guess is that they haven't noticed *Pax III*'s arrival. Oh, I'm sure the AI has told them. But in the first place, the last time I saw them they were totally focused on the inhabitants of La Femme. And in the second place, they didn't know that their transmissions were going out by way of transudation. I'm sure the last thing they're expecting is the arrival of another ship from the Pax."

Fuyuko, Astra, and Blaise gasped and exclaimed, and Blaise slammed a fist onto the table. "Are you saying you sent their transmission by transudation without the officers' knowledge?"

Julia, by way of her (simulated) implant, instructed the AI to transmit a message to Blaise by way of the latter's "implant": <Please consider your extreme emotional response to this new piece of data. I question its appropriateness.>

"Blaise, I don't think you understand," Astra was saying. "Sometimes following protocol is the worst thing you can do. And I for one am glad Solita warned the Pax. We're 500 light years from Earth. Which means radio messages take that long by the usual light-wave transmission. The Pax would eventually have sent out more ships anyway. In fact, I know they had plans in the works, since I had been slated from the beginning of the project's inception to be a member of the second crew out, before they decided it shouldn't include anyone identifying as female." She glanced at Solita, then back at Blaise. "And so I can only tender Solita my most heartfelt gratitude for sending the transmission by way of transudation."

Except for a fleeting flicker of a glance at Julia, Blaise's stolid stare didn't move from Solita's face.

Solita, hand at throat, looked at Julia. "It may be that they aren't even keeping in contact with the AI," she said. Her gaze dropped to the table. "I could sing the ship and ask if any non-comatose crew members are aboard. And whether those on the surface keep in regular contact."

"An excellent suggestion," Fuyuko said. Then pursed her lips in one of her primary's set-faces. "I believe that the more information we have before hailing *Pax I*, the better." It had been Fuyuko's suggestion that they hold off initiating contact, despite the risk of raising the suspicions of *Pax I* crew.

"Blaise?" Julia said.

Blaise scowled. "Sounds reasonable."

"I agree," Astra said.

"Candace?"

The development specialist shrugged. "I don't really have an opinion one way or another. Apart from our training, and then all the conspiracy-theory nonsense Vance fed me, I don't have much of an idea what's what. So I think perhaps I'd better abstain."

Spoken like a true bureaucrat, Julia thought. But it was the best one could hope from someone chosen for the mission by the same faction of the Council that chose Vance. Julia smiled at the word processors, who had chosen to sit side-by-side, with the one empty chair—Vance's—on Nadia's other side. "Nadia, Solita?"

"Yes, I agree," Solita said.

"I, too," Nadia said emphatically.

"Then you will sing your ship, Solita, as soon as we have finished here," Julia said. She glanced at Fuyuko. "Fuyuko and Nadia will stand by as you do, and Nadia will explain in real-time what is transpiring as best she can to Fuyuko in case Fuyuko can offer helpful advice." She looked from Fuyuko to Nadia. "If that's agreeable to both of you?"

"I'd like to be present, too," Blaise said.

"Of course." The whole crew could attend the singing if it liked. Anything to keep their xenophobia under control (though she doubted watching a word processor sing would make them exactly calm). Julia infused her voice with briskness. "The next order of business: how many and who of the crew to bring awake."

For a few seconds, the group held to a reluctant, tenacious silence. Julia tapped her fingernails on the table in a slow gallop. "No one has any preference, advice, or just plain opinions?"

More silence. Julia decided to wait it out—while her fingernails galloped, galloped, galloped in their slow, repetitive tattoo.

"We need a security specialist," Blaise finally said. "Especially if the crew of *Pax I* are so…disturbed as Solita keeps making out."

"I would like to debrief Astra, Candace, and Blaise at greater length before venturing a suggestion," Fuyuko said quickly.

Astra, Candace, and Blaise stared at Fuyuko. "I've told you everything I know," Astra said. "And the AI has verified I was telling you the truth."

"As you believe it," Fuyuko said. She folded her hands on the table. "Neither Candace nor Blaise were involved in the altercation on the bridge. So obviously they can't tell us what happened any better than Astra has attempted to do." Fuyuko's primary's face remained, as usual, perfectly expressionless. Julia recalled the difficulty the psyche-synthesist had had during their last c-space conference. Had her tolerance for v-space returned? "Or than I myself have been able to do," Fuyuko added. "But I'd like to go over what else they remember of transudation. And then administer a few standard psychological tests." She glanced at Julia. "Actually, I'd like to administer them to all of us."

Julia said, "Then do so. It's your prerogative. So I take it you're recommending that we hold off on waking any more of the crew."

"Yes. I am."

"While in the meantime," Blaise said, "if any crew left on *Pax I* get wise to our presence here, and they're as disturbed as some of us suspect they might be, they could very well attack—and without notice, too. Since we're in violation of standard ship protocol."

"Attack?" Julia repeated. "How, attack?"

Blaise shook her head. "You don't think we're going to believe they're not as well armed as we are? Come on, Julia. Give us credit for having some intelligence."

But then there's intelligence, and intelligence, Julia thought. Candace was shaking her head at Blaise. Julia fixed her gaze on the development specialist. "Tell me about it, Candace," she said. "I take it there's something Vance knew that I, the head of mission, wasn't informed of?" Out of the corner of her eye, Julia noted Fuyuko's stare. But she kept her gaze on Candace.

"We have a major complement of laser cannon and standard issue for personal combat as well," Candace said flatly. "Which the

Council assigned into Vance's safekeeping. Of which I have to say I'm surprised to hear that they didn't see fit to inform you."

Julia smiled openly. "Candace, you're mistaken. Vance was shitting you."

From orbit, the planet La Femme is a gorgeous blue. In fact, the light on the surface is tinted blue (appearing from orbit varying shades of violet). Everything about the humanoids inhabiting the planet La Femme is beautiful and desirable. Even the names of their cities: Isidora, Dorothea, Zaira; Anastasia, Tamara, Zora; Despina, Zirma, Isaura, Maurilia; Fedora, Zoe, Zenobia, Euphemia. Zobeide, Hypatia, Armilla; Chloe, Valdrada, Olivia; Sophronia, Eutropia, Zemrude, Aglaura; Octavia, Ersilia, Baucis, Leandra. Melania, Esmeralda, Phyllis; Pyrrha, Euphrasia, Odile; Margara, Getullia, Adelma, Eudoxia; Moriana, Clarice, Eusapia, Beersheba. Leonia, Irene, Argia; Thekla, Trude, Olinda; Laudomia, Perinthia, Procopia, Raissa; Andria, Cecilia, Marozia; Penthesilea, Theodora, Berenice. Even their names are a pleasure to the tongue, a pleasure that can be experienced only in meat space.

—from Paul 22423's Report to the First Council

Fuyuko gasped.

"The stuff is in the second hold," Candace said. "I saw it myself."

Julia shook her head. "No, Candace. I can assure you, you didn't. Vance only made you think you saw it."

Again, silence closed in. Julia let it drag on for a minute or so. "Shall we continue with the next point?" Julia said gently. "AI: give us a holograph of La Femme space and all vessel placements around it."

A glassy blue ball shimmered in the air above the table, hugely dominating the three tiny craft that popped into existence with it, casting such brilliant light that it tinted the faces and clothing of everyone at the table. "So when will we enter orbit around La Femme?" Astra asked plaintively.

Everyone laughed, as she'd obviously intended. Julia followed up: "Which brings us to the third point on our agenda, the approach to La Femme."

Which was bound, Julia thought, to make everyone (but Nadia and Solita) deliriously happy with anticipation—and frustrated at the tentativeness of all their plans, unavoidably contingent on the very considerations they would rather not have to deal with.

17.

JULIA'S FIRST EXPERIENCE of Delta Pavonian singing had been a shock—a shameful, ugly shock for which she had trouble forgiving herself. She had believed herself fully prepared to "open her being to the experience." Certainly she had gone to every length to equip herself with a theoretical understanding of word processors, their peculiar position in the Pax, the workings of their city, and—of course—all there was to be known about the Delta Pavonians and their methods of communication.

"If I were you, I'd do some mild drugs for the first few singings you attend," Sasha advised her. "To ease you into it. They certainly helped me."

Julia rejected the advice, though it came from Sasha, her first and last meat-space lover—Sasha, always and ever open to meat experience as no adult she knew was. But she had never fallen flat on her face before, not even during her eutopic apprenticeship, and certainly not professionally. She couldn't imagine her attitude and mental perspective failing to keep her emotional and physical responses in line. Her mind teemed with insight into the word processors' society, her will set to avoid the standard "allochronic approach" to both word processors and Delta Pavonians. She discussed it all with Raye, thoroughly. It never occurred to her that experiencing a singing would make her sick.

Literally.

Her tutor Rosina beamed at Julia when the latter, in the course of their first meeting, expressed an "intense interest" in attending singings. And so on the very afternoon of her arrival in the City of Word Processing, Rosina escorted her to one. She apparently figured that Julia, so eager and apparently knowledgeable, needed no preparation for the experience.

Julia's stomach burned, then roiled, and finally spewed forth an eruption of bitter, scalding vomit, giving her a second new experience to that of seeing, hearing, and smelling a Delta Pavonian. And why? she wondered afterward, bewildered. They looked and sounded exquisitely beautiful in holos. Why, then, should the meat-experience be so revolting?

She wanted to go to Raye or Sasha or both and ask them. But she so hated herself for her reaction that she couldn't admit her shame to them. *I am different.* Yes, she had always needed to believe that. Always needed to hold herself to higher standards. (In this and, in other cases, to standards the rest of the Pax—with the exception of a few kindred souls like Raye and Sasha—would find incomprehensible.) Instead, she struggled with the meat-ness so necessary in the City of Word Processing. She had a vague idea it was the key, that something about her adult aversion to meat-ness barred her from appreciating the experience as much as someone as unskilled as she in the language (or whatever one was to call it) could.

Living in meat-space full-time had been a shock in itself. She hadn't realized how little time she had been spending out of her caretaker. But during her first few days in Word Processing she experienced—another first—difficulty making her bladder work without a catheter. So what if she sexed with Sasha in meat-space? The fact was, she had ceased to live in it, but rather made trips to it the way, earlier, when more cautious, she had lived in it and made trips to v-space.

She had a clear memory of having been warned. And so she also had that bit of stupidity with which to reproach herself.

The birds were exceedingly long, excruciatingly slender, but so sleek and shining, the colors streaking and patching their feathers and throats a feast even for human eyes...and so frightening, somehow, in the flesh, each swoop making one's stomach dip, whether in (imagined?) empathy for how such violently fast arcing movement might feel, or with fear, that such a needle-shaped black beak might drill into one's body at who-knew-how-many klicks per hour, the glistening iridescence of exposed tissue at their throats nothing like the impression of the cold, clear jewel it looked to be on holos, the vibrations and resonances of their song, a swooping, staccato cacophony too intense for human ears, breasts, or bowels to bear, kicking one's hormones into who-knew-what insane flux, making one wild with emotion too inchoate to be expressed, making one vomit and cry and slide otherwise into the abject helplessness of infancy.

Rosina was patient. (Oh so, so patient.) She had seen it before. Sasha had been her pupil, too. And there had been others before him—though she remembered him especially, since males almost never came to be tutored, even "for the ride." "It's not enough," she said, "to open your mind. You have to open your body, too. You have to accept it in your body." Which was why the machines were useless. Which was why to really sing you needed the implantation in throat and a surgically enlarged thorax. Which was why—somehow, mysteriously, for no one yet understood it—only those identifying as women became word processors.

A fact that infuriated Julia. It was due to superstition, she thought, and the basic stubborn unwillingness of males to subject themselves to the experience of opening up, much less to the implantation and the alteration, forever, of their meat-voices. Those who had been born male and chose to become female had no problem, but no one who identified as male had ever submitted to the implantation. If the basis were hormonal, that could be adjusted for. Sasha wouldn't talk about it, said only that there were some "facts" one simply didn't quarrel with. That the chief problem of life was how to live honestly without being either a naif or a criminal, that he had no time for quarreling with the "obvious." This from meat-hungry Sasha, drunk with physical pleasures, able to ignore the myriad unpleasantnesses attendant on meat-space life, never minding all the little aches and cricks and stiffnesses and headaches and nasal irritations and itches and bowel and stomach spasms... And yet even he drew the line, a line he couldn't explain.

She had, after all, eventually gotten further—without drugs—than he had, and that had kept the word *failure* at bay, rendering it a relative rather than absolute judgment. She learned, after all, to feel the singing "in the belly," learned to allow understanding of the singing seep into her consciousness without grabbing for it (and missing). And she learned, finally, that if she were able to bear living always in meat-space, she too could have been a word processor.

She saw that it could be a good life, though probably full of frustration, since one had always to be managed and spied upon by supervisors. Ever ambitious, Julia knew that a good-enough life couldn't satisfy her. Would there be a new First Contact? She had no way of predicting that, but she never ceased to devote herself to preparing for it should one come in her lifetime.

18.

"EXPLAIN ME SOMETHING, S07," Julia said to the secondary, twenty ship's minutes before yet another executive meeting. She was wearing, as she always did in her c-space study, a sleek russet silk tunic with matching trousers, in a style she thought complemented her large, glossy black desk. "Why it is that at every stage of this mission we—including, of course, myself as well as the rest of the crew and the Council and our trainers, too—have from the beginning asked the wrong questions, missed important facts, all of which have been under our noses? For instance: the fact that the transmissions reached us so quickly. Why didn't we say Oh! That can't have traveled at light speed! How did the transmission come to us?"

S07, asprawl the sofa facing the desk, thick, heavy eyeglasses appropriate to logotypes of scientists of the moderns balanced on the tip of its nose, raised her eyebrows, which made them look as though they were waving at her over the nerdy black frames. "Who is 'we,' Julia? Certainly the Council and their science advisors knew."

That smarted. "Well *I* didn't know," Julia said and knew she sounded defensive. "But there've been other things, like the Council apparently not questioning Paul's assertion that women couldn't survive transudation and should therefore stay home—since they *did* launch the *Pax II* without a word processor, when they must have known that Solita had survived, since how else account for Paul's reports being transmitted via transudation."

S07 said, looking thoughtful, "You really don't know the problem here?"

Julia thumbed her nose at the secondary. "Would I be asking if I did?"

S07 folded its arms over its chest. "It's elementary, Julia. The fact is, whenever Delta Pavonians enter the picture, human intelligence simply crashes. In this case, the reliance on Delta Pavonian technology rendered invisible to the Council almost every technological question that might likely arise—with the exception, of course, of the theoretical basis of transudation, which obsesses Paxan theoreticians and technologists. Our specialists are interested in every aspect of La Femme, and the scientists are interested in trying to figure out transudation. And so what the word processors do is seen as instrumental—as part of the ship's functioning, mediating between the AI and the ship. Solita's identity as a woman was simply bleached out of visibility. Even though they remembered that when they decided to exclude females from the second crew. So they weren't looking at the how of that transmission. So. Who *was* looking at the transmission? The people who wanted to know what in our Great Wide Galaxy Paul meant when he claimed that only "men" could "survive," and how and why *Pax I*'s AI records had been sabotaged. And of course *they* were so shocked and disturbed by these things that the basics fell into their blindspot."

Julia leaned back in her cushy, high-backed desk chair and pressed her palms flat against the desk's cool, smooth surface. "It seems so *obvious*—that the *Pax II* couldn't achieve transudation without a word processor—which is to say, without a female body on board."

S07 held up its index finger and raised its eyebrows above the frames of the glasses. "But the next thing in invisibility to anything Delta Pavonian, my dear, is a word processor."

Julia frowned. "Ye—es. I see what you're saying. To some minds, a word processor might be considered a thing Delta Pavonian." She grunted her impatience. "But that doesn't account for the continuing myopia. S07, I'm worried. At every turn something obvious that we've—I've—missed turns up."

"A dangerous pattern," S07 said. "And so now you've learned that Paul and his functioning crew have broken contact with the

AI since they sent the last transmission Solita took it upon herself to boost through transudation. And you wonder if *you're* asking the right questions."

Julia got up from behind her desk, circled to its front and perched on the edge in classic, office-confidential style. "I intend to put it to the team," she said. "But you're the one best able to help me, since you're not so easily distracted as I am. I mean, there's so much to manage: weaving the tight mesh I need to hold the mission together; deciding what to do about the ones still sleeping; and developing a protocol for governing our movements on La Femme."

"And deciding what to do about Paul et al. when you find them," S07 concluded.

"Precisely." Julia jammed her fist under her chin. "In some ways it's worse than being the first to make Contact. Instead of entering the mere unknown, we've got all kinds of other baggage to cope with besides." She kicked her heels back against the desk, lightly. "Fuyuko now thinks that *Pax I*'s AI wasn't sabotaged, just that it had the same difficulty functioning as ours did during transudation." She shook her head. "She calls it AI psychosis."

S07 slow-blinked behind the thick lenses that made the secondary's opalescent eyes seem abnormally large. "Don't laugh, Julia. Everyone living in meat-space, present-tense spacetime at the time of transudation suffered psychosis."

Julia wrinkled her nose. "The AI? Since when does the AI live in meat-space? "

S07 did not open its eyes, but smiled. "It does. Think about it. It never ceases interfacing with meat-space, even as it generates v-space for us and gives *us*, who only exist in v-space, a window on meat-space."

"What else, S07? What other areas am I not paying sufficient attention to?"

"Basically," S07 said, opening its eyes, "anything to do either with Solita and Nadia or the ship. Or rather, ships." S07 removed its glasses. "Before you go to your meeting, one other thing needs to be mentioned."

Julia gestured it to continue.

"Paul believed his transmission to the Pax, which Solita says was conveyed to the ship's AI by the La Femmeans, to be going by light speed and thus that it would take centuries to reach Earth. You, on the other hand, know that either Nadia or Solita can send transmissions by way of transudation. Yet you haven't done so. You're in fact holding back from letting the Council know you've arrived safely and what you've so far found. Though given the Council's directives to the AI, we can assume the AI has already reported the safe arrival, it's unlikely it's reported anything else besides our communications with *The Leopard* and Solita's joining us. I wonder if you're aware of having made this decision and, if so, what you intend by it, and what your future intentions are. And whether you intend to bring your fellow executive officers in on the decision."

Julia left the desk to pace. "Well yes, I did have the vague sense that I should be preparing a transmission," she said. "But I was merely...postponing it, until I could send more definitive information. Since we really don't know what's going on. And..." She paused to read the titles of books on the shelf at eye-level before her, every one of which was available in her permanent personal library.

"And?"

Julia turned. "And I have in the back of my mind that the Council might interfere when I bring them in on it."

"Interfere how?"

Julia sighed. "They could send another ship. Or they could have a word processor send orders by way of transudation. After all, if it works going from here to there, it surely must work in the opposite direction as well."

S07 sat up and swung its feet to the polished oak floor. "You don't think your crew is going to be made uneasy by this?" S07 said. "Remember your mesh, Julia. This situation is a potential knot on the margins, around which another web of power could develop."

Julia looked at S07. "Yeah." She sighed. "You're right. I've got to deal with this now. One way or another." She half-laughed. "If only I knew which was the best tack to take." She raised her eyebrows at S07.

S07 put its glasses back on. "If I were you, I'd prepare a bare report of arrival, supplemented by a report from Fuyuko on her view of the psychical difficulties posed by transudation and a statement as to what you know about the crew of *Pax I*. Period. And at the same time develop some team-sympathy for keeping the Council out of an already overly complicated situation."

Julia moved to the sofa and sat down beside S07. "Yeah. That and the protocol have got to be the projects du jour. And then—" Julia inhaled deeply— "La Femme."

19.

SO EXCESSIVE WAS Julia's irritability that when Fuyuko and Blaise summoned her out of v-space a bare two hours after the executive meeting had broken up she fantasized assaulting them. Fuyuko could not tolerate v-space for much longer than the length of their meetings and would not toggle in for any other reason. And so Julia had no choice but to return to meat-space whenever Fuyuko wished a conference with her. But the growing (psycho)somatic discomfort of connecting and disconnecting from the caretaker every few hours set Julia's every nerve on edge. Perhaps, it occurred to her, she should patch a tranquilizer every time she re-entered meat-space...

So the three of them shut themselves up in a privacy unit, Blaise, Fuyuko, Julia, none of them exactly compatible with the others. The small cabin, furnished with four recliners, a hygiene cubicle, and a cabinet containing bulbs of water and tubes of food, felt cramped and restrictive, probably, Julia reflected, because she had been spending so much time on the bridge. She strapped herself in, folded her hands over her stomach, and tried not to look too impatient. "Well," she said in her mildest tone of voice, "now that we're all assembled, how can I help you?" Since Julia had for the previous fifteen minutes been carefully going over the report Fuyuko proposed to send back to the Council, she assumed they wished to talk about revisions to the crew's La Femme protocol.

Blaise, declining to strap in, drifted in a pattern so regular it had to be deliberate. *Show off*, Julia thought uncharitably, beyond appreciation of such an accomplishment. Though of course, a mean voice in her head sneered, I bet she wouldn't be so cocky in a larger space.

"Look, it's become perfectly obvious to me since we started working on the protocol that there's a serious problem we're not confronting," Blaise said, brusque to the edge of incivility. Jerking her arm in emphasis, she spoiled her pattern. "I've been considering this problem of communications breakdown between the *Pax I* crew and ship's AI, where all communications are mediated by the La Femmeans." Her eyes burned in the most startling way. But since Julia had spent little time with Blaise in meat-space, she had no idea whether such an expression was habitual or extraordinary. "The fact is, Julia, that even if crew members chose not to communicate with the ship's AI, the AI should still have been able to keep in silent contact with them through their implants. The AI should be at all times cognizant of their exact locations on the surface."

Julia tried to remember exactly what the last report from *Pax I*'s AI had said about the crew having broken contact. "Yes, of course," she said, "one would assume the AI would know their locations."

"Well the AI *doesn't* know their locations," Blaise said, "and hasn't since they were taken down to the surface by the inhabitant identified as Lalage." She crossed her arms over her chest. "Add to that bit of data the fact that the AI detected some sort of electronic shield interfering with its ability to scan the bodies of the inhabitants who boarded *Pax I*, and the matter becomes serious. If the inhabitants can interfere with our radio signals, then any protocol we follow will likely be irrelevant."

Julia, aggravated by Blaise's drifting closer and closer in such a small, confined space, raised her eyebrows. "You are assuming the inhabitants have interfered coercively," she said. "Which is, by the way, contrary to my impression that the crew were eagerly pursuing their every impulse and desire. How do you know the crew didn't choose to become invisible to the *Pax I* AI? Remember: Paul, for one, assumed they had become invisible to the Council and the Director-General of the mission, being all of five hundred light years' radio contact distant."

"You mean you think they've 'gone native'?" Fuyuko said.

Julia smiled. "Don't you?"

"But the point is that we don't fucking KNOW!" Blaise shouted. "We don't know what kind of alien power we're up against, low-tech civilization or not. All we have is a lot of bizarre, gooey ego crap from Paul. He fucking lost it, Julia! Three crazy intolerable transudations, and he was ready to be retired into therapy permanently."

"So tell me, Blaise," Julia said quietly. "What is it you think we should do. Return to Earth without getting any closer to the poison planet?"

Blaise looked at Fuyuko and gestured her to speak. Fuyuko glanced at Julia, then back at Blaise, then back again at Julia. "Blaise has suggested, and I'm inclined to think we should consider her suggestion carefully—

"Shit," Blaise hissed.

"Blaise has suggested," Fuyuko repeated, "that Vance be awakened before we achieve orbit." Her gaze met Julia's, then flicked away. "Because," she rushed on when Julia did not speak, "the situation is potentially very, very dangerous. The idea being, the very first thing we should do on matching orbit with *Pax I* is search for the missing crew members."

Julia thought she'd like to knock their heads together. Not that she'd ever in her life used violence on another person (in meatspace, at least), but though it would be a shocking thing to do, something about the thought of it made her imagine it would feel immensely gratifying. "We've been over this several times already," she said to Fuyuko. "And I thought we were agreed that waking Vance at this point would be unwise."

Fuyuko stared down at the floor. "Vance has a strong record of border assignments."

The problem, Julia thought, was that because she'd been spending so much time in c-space with constructs, she'd lost the patience required in primary interactions. Whenever a simulation didn't go right in a c-space, one could scrub the scenario each time it veered away from the parameters of usefulness. You couldn't do that in meat-space. And you most certainly couldn't scrub interactions with your crew when the mission you shared rated as one of the most important—perhaps *the* most important—set of points in your life.

Julia pulled the Velcro restraint off her right wrist so that she could exercise her forearm and hand. "Can you guarantee me Nadia and Solita's safety?" she said, fixing Fuyuko's eyes with her own, daring the psyche-synthesist to evade her gaze.

Fuyuko blinked. Fuyuko swallowed. Fuyuko ran her pale pink tongue over her wide pink lips.

"Sometimes you have to take risks," Blaise said. "Sometimes you've got no choice. What good does it do us to be able to get back to Earth if we're all disappeared and maybe even dead?"

Julia bit the inside of her cheeks to keep from smiling. "Blaise, listen to yourself," she said softly. "Sometimes you have to take risks, yes. Which is my point exactly. Sometimes you do have to take risks. If we're going to take risks, it shouldn't be with the safety of Nadia and Solita. Their technical abilities are—" Julia allowed herself to smile— "invaluable. And certainly more vital than those of any single other member of the crew."

Which point ended the discussion and sent Julia scuttling and clunking back to her caretaker—wondering whether Blaise and Fuyuko were bound to rip a great big gaping hole in the mesh she meant to make of the crew.

20.

ABOUT THREE-QUARTERS THROUGH Julia's eleventh year, one of her parents, Glenning, took her to a wildlife dome as a reward for having done exceptionally well in her studies. Although wildlife preserves, domed and undomed, made up more than half of the Pax's territory, humans were not allowed to reside within their precincts. Glenning made Julia understand beforehand the rare privilege such an in-the-flesh visit represented. Points alone could not win admission to a wildlife dome; few people were ever allowed to visit. Glenning, though, sat on the board that governed them and had arranged her admission to this one as a special perq. She knew that Raye, for instance, had never been to one. And of her parents, only Glenning had. The singularity of the honor stunned her.

On the eve of the visit she realized it might be the only one she would make in her lifetime. The thought awed her. Yet her reflection did not stop there, and soon she had a viscerally "funny" feeling about it that almost made her sick. While she felt astonishingly privileged on realizing it would probably be a one-time thing, unlikely to be repeated at any time in her life, she felt pinched by the prospect of future exclusion even before she'd set foot inside.

Sitting beside Glenning in the tube thrusting at high speed far below the surface of the earth, she articulated to herself the expression "butterflies in one's stomach" to describe her strange nervousness about a treat for which she had developed a great, almost desperate desire. "Glenning," she said, "I was thinking about how many animal metaphors we use to express ourselves." And when she saw he was listening (not that she didn't expect him to be listening, since this trip was his gift to her, but she had the habit of making sure lest she waste her breath and words, always a great humiliation to her when it happened), she continued, "I was just thinking about the expression *butterflies in one's stomach*. I've seen butterflies in holos of wildlife domes, and many more in c-space nature vistas. I'm wondering, Glenning, whether we'll be seeing any butterflies today?"

So then Glenning questioned her about the function of butterflies and asked her whether she thought they might be necessary for a wildlife dome's ecosystem. And then he told her that it was currently early summer in the wildlife dome they would be visiting and asked her on the basis of what she knew about butterflies and their function what *she* thought.

When they finished the lesson on butterflies, Julia trotted out every animal metaphor she could think of and wondered of her parent whether they would see those animals, too. And so the travel time passed quickly and pointfully, and she retained Glenning's full attention, in itself a treat. She didn't notice when the butterflies in her stomach stopped fluttering.

Her nervousness returned when they arrived at the wildlife dome. Though everyone there recognized Glenning, the two of them still had to negotiate the security structures protecting it. Once they were inside, Julia grew almost breathless with excitement. For a few seconds Glenning let her stand at the entrance and gape at the thick, lush panorama of high grasses and distant trees that seemed to go on forever. It was like a nature vista c-space, or a huge holo, only…different. *Wild*. Anything, she realized, might happen. The flora and fauna weren't programs, or holograms, but were as unpredictable and willful as meat-space humans.

Just a couple of meters inside the dome's entrance Glenning had her kneel down with him and examine the grass and the soil in which it grew. He burrowed his fingers into the dirt, then scooped some up and held it out to her in his joined, open palms. Julia bent close. The smell enchanted her. A gleaming red worm suddenly wriggled into visibility, twisting and coiling through the soil in her parent's palms. Julia jumped back to put herself at a safe distance. "You know what this is, Julia, don't you?" Glenning asked.

"Yes, it's a worm!" She glanced at his face, then, frowning, added, "Isn't it?"

"Yes. It's an earthworm. And it has no behaviors harmful to humans. So there's no need to be afraid of it." He held his hands out. "Would you like to hold the soil yourself?"

Julia's throat closed. "Please, Glenning, I think I'd rather not," she said. She thought she would vomit if the shiny, slithery creature touched her skin.

Glenning lowered his hands to the ground and let the dirt fall gently back into the space where it had been. He looked at her and shook his head. "You know about being afraid of things—or people—who can't or won't harm you, don't you?"

She swallowed and nodded. "Yes," she said. "But sometimes I can't help it. Sometimes I get a feeling in my stomach, and my throat, and I know I might throw up if I can't get away."

Glenning cleaned his hands with one of the towel-wipes he had brought, then slid his arm around her shoulders. "Gotta work at it, kiddo. Gotta at least think about it. Okay?"

She nodded.

"Great. Then let's get moving. We've got a lot more to see here today than just grass, soil, and worms."

And they did see a lot more than just grass, soil, and worms. But what Julia remembered most vividly years later was the worm.

21.

AGAIN THEY MET around the octagonal simulated-oak table in the small c-space conference room. Julia flashed her best smile as though it were a sticky secretion strong enough to make her net hold under pressure. "So," she said. "We're approaching the planet." She nodded at Fuyuko. "I take it we all have good, healthy brain chemistries now? And that our DNA has been properly repaired?"

Fuyuko pursed her lips. "As far as I can tell. I can give strong assurances for everyone awake. But there are tests that can't be done for those still sedated."

"And your own v-space problem?" Julia said. "I hope that's taken care of?"

Fuyuko's stare aimed somewhere past Julia's shoulder. "Sufficiently," she said distantly. "I am increasing my tolerance gradually. Neuroses are not as easily cleared away as psychoses."

"Excellent," Julia said brightly. She glanced at Blaise. "And thanks to the diligent collaboration between Fuyuko and Blaise, we now have a modified protocol for crew visits to the surface."

"Then we've got Go?" Astra said eagerly.

Julia beamed at the science officer. "I can see that at least some of us are still up-up-up for the mission." She leaned forward. "We are just a mite short of Go," she said. Astra groaned. Julia held up her hand. "And a mite's a teeny tiny insect by which to metaphorize an increment. We have one last stage of preparation that I'm guessing will take perhaps one ship's day to complete. If you've been in meat-space at all lately, you'll be aware that we're pulling some heavy gravity now. Last night Nadia had the ship initiate the final phase of deceleration."

"Oh come *on*, Julia," Blaise said. "We've done everything. What else was all the training we got on Earth for if not to prepare us for this moment?"

Julia laid her palms flat on the table. "I think we can all agree that we must expect a difficult challenge when we make Contact with the inhabitants of La Femme." She glanced generally around the table, but concentrated on Blaise. "Am I correct?"

"Yes, of course," Blaise said impatiently.

Julia nodded. "For which reason I've enlisted the aid of Nadia and Solita to help create AI simulations of possible scenarios we might face either individually or in groups." Julia bowed her thanks to the word processors. She had also "enlisted" S04 and S07, who had in fact done most of the work (but whose assistance she could not acknowledge). And she had given herself three hours of concentrated delta-wave sleep so that she could work nearly around the clock, as well. "Granted," she said, "the situations we've programmed aren't likely to be duplicated in our contact. But they will force us to begin to use our wits in a particular way that is ordinarily foreign to us." She glanced at Nadia and Solita, whose experience as word processors had entailed repeated contact with an alien species. "We expect Contact to be a shocking and unpleasant confrontation. Yet judging by the *Pax I* crew's initial reactions to the La Femmeans, Contact can be seductive, too. I would like us to be prepared for both possibilities. And I would also like us to get used to being present when telepathic communication excludes at least one of the individuals on site, as may well be the case, since, to the best of our knowledge, the La Femmeans can project thoughts into individual human minds."

"We don't know if it's done individually," Fuyuko said. Then added quickly, "But I agree, Julia, not only do we need to prepare ourselves against the disorientation likely to result from Contact with beings utterly alien—" She stopped. "Though we don't really know that they are *utterly* alien—" She looked from Blaise to Astra. "But we need to be able to trust one another—I think Julia's absolutely right that the very idea that one or more persons might be engaged in an apparently secret contact that everyone else has been locked out of is likely to engender distrust and suspicion." She looked at Julia. "And I suppose there are other sorts of pitfalls you've anticipated?"

"Yes," Julia said, "but I don't want to give them away. I think it would be best if everyone went through the exercises without knowing what to expect—which is how it will be during Contact."

Fuyuko swept her hand in a wide arc encompassing the others at the table. "Who exactly is to do these exercises?"

"Everyone," Julia said. "And I mean *everyone*. Who is awake, that is. The entire crew—not just all of us here. We have no way of knowing who will be engaged in Contact. If the La Femmeans really are telepathic, then any crew member could be contacted as the telepaths wish."

The La Femmeans don't have v-spaces—they believe that they don't need them. (We will of course teach them better.) Nor do the La Femmeans have anything that could be called language: they communicate via telepathy. And yet the beautiful names of their cities simply sounded in my mind as my mind screened images of them—just as the names of individual inhabitants do when I am in their presence. The name of the La Femmean who acted as my guide is Lalage, a tall, wispy milk-breasted female with skin paler than any I've ever seen. Her hair was silver that became a bright, shiny, metallic blue when she transported me to the surface, her eyes like chrome that became bright, shiny blue mirrors...

--from Paul 22423's Report to the First Council

Solita shifted in her chair and made a glum face. "Nadia and I won't be contacted," she said. "We will be in contact with our ships. Anyway, they didn't contact me the first time."

Preoccupied though she was with getting this phase of the mission to Go, Julia could not help noticing that Solita was finding interpersonal contact increasingly difficult. The months alone had probably damaged her socialization. And her extraordinary bond with her ship probably hadn't helped. Nadia had not gone through as many transudations, and so she provided no means for comparison. But the last thing Julia wanted was to endanger a bond that, while probably not good for Solita, in the long-run might well prove essential for their return home.

"But how," Astra said, "can we possibly prepare ourselves for the shock of dealing with psi? It's a capacity we've not only been unable to develop in ourselves, but which, if we had done so, would be anathema to every human without it."

"An appropriate question," Julia said. "But just try the simulations, okay?"

Julia could see they hated it, every last one of them, except perhaps Fuyuko. But she thought S07 absolutely correct: if anything would knit them into a strong, tight mesh, doing these simulation exercises would.

22.

FROM THE C-SPACE she had had S08 create to simulate a control room, Julia watched the crew, now in a c-space usually used for group yoga sessions, run through the first set of exercises. For this first set she had asked them to divide themselves into four large groups, working on the assumption that some crew members would feel easier participating actively in the role-playing after they'd played only supporting or spectating-critical roles. As the first situations played out, certain crew responses to her imposition of the exercises jarred her expectations. It hadn't occurred to her that the very people most likely to oppose her regime would consider the simulations the first practical and intelligent move she had made since they'd arrived in the Cygnus system. Fuyuko and Blaise, for instance, entered into them with great enthusiasm. Those who had displayed a measure of personal loyalty toward her, though, were reluctant, and in some cases even impatient or resentful in their participation. Solita and Nadia hated it. The entire science complement—which comprised, after all, the majority of the crew—could see no value in the exercises whatsoever. And the astrobiologists showed outright hostility and scorn for the AI's simulation of the humanoids. Julia realized she had erred in not drawing them into the preparation of the simulations—especially since she had enlisted the two word processors' assistance and publicly thanked them for it to boot.

But of course one's evaluation of methodology tended to have less to do with one's political position than with one's professional expertise. Vance, Julia reflected, being a diplo like herself, would have ordered even more sessions of practice simulations and would moreover have added a range of aggressive scenarios as well, to equip them with tactical drills they could instantly shift into on command. Scientists, though, did not role-play. And when they created simulations, they did so to model possibilities and probabilities, not to prepare themselves personally for situations they might reasonably expect to face.

Another thing occurred to her: eutopians used simulations, which they performed as something between games and theatrical improvisations, so continuously from an early age that collective creativity and invention became second nature to them. None of her crewmates had been raised as eutopian, and the difference showed: all were self-conscious and stilted in their performance. We should have had a game created, Julia realized, before leaving Earth, a game for exploring these scenarios. She felt a little stupid for not having thought of it in time.

And yet, as Julia watched them, focusing on their reactions and interactions, she gradually became aware of a treacherous emotional undertow pulling at her. She had viewed many, many times the holograms created from the drawings a member of the *Pax I* crew had sketched of the La Femmeans during their brief appearance on the bridge. But this time, as four holograms confronted the four groups into which the crew had divided themselves, she felt a swelling of powerful emotion catch at her belly, throat, breasts…a sensation resembling sexual longing, but tinged with loss and perhaps nostalgia—and far more powerful. Lalage and Icaria, two of those who had appeared were called (according to Paul); he had not named the other three. All of them with pale gray skin and silver hair, tall, thin, fragile-looking—thin except, that is, for their breasts. Julia's gaze kept returning to their breasts (which she previously had not so particularly noticed). They resembled the breasts of humans pumped up with estrogen for nursing—the breasts of milk-parents, like Joey and Saella's before they'd changed themselves.

The fascination the La Femmeans had for the *Pax I*'s crew now seemed understandable. But—the crew's talking about them as though they were tertiaries in "c-space brothels"? The thought of that made Julia queasy. To draw a connection between milk-parents and the most derivative entertainment... Of course pre-Pax humans had always done so, but that had been dependent on the sexual ideology of their day, which Paxans simply did not share, even those practicing certain dubious forms of familial child-raising...

Julia jerked her attention back to the virtual holotanks surrounding her, each projecting a group performing the exercise together. "We mean you no harm, either, but we must insist you tell us where the humans already here are," Blaise—who had appointed herself primary speaker for her group—repeated for the fourth time at least.

Julia inserted her primary into the other c-space and ordered the simulation for Blaise's group frozen. Quickly she told the other groups to continue, and faced Blaise's group. The primaries, all neatly dressed, like herself, in immaculate crew uniform and arranged in a loose, ragged semicircle around the five (frozen) La Femmean tertiaries, turned to stare at her. "You've already tried that tack three times," Julia said to Blaise. She glanced around the semicircle. "Anybody have a suggestion for making a different approach?"

Blaise's primary fisted her hands on her hips, arms akimbo, and glared in Julia's general direction. "Are you saying that there's no point in repeating a communicational gambit when one's first iteration of it hasn't gotten a response?" she said belligerently. "If so, this is the first time I've heard that diplos don't use reiteration tactically."

Julia addressed herself to Blaise: "Why do you say you haven't gotten a response?"—and then asked the group: "Does everybody here agree that the visitors have made no response?"

"Look," Blaise said, pre-empting her crewmates from speaking, "they just show up on the bridge, without warning, without even doing us the courtesy of hailing us—five of them just show up and announce themselves over our AI interfaces—" she flicked her gaze around the semicircle— "which yes, I remember, is meant as a simulation of telepathic speech—they just show up and announce themselves as the 'inhabitants of La Femme,' a civilization of cities that they then begin to list." She glared at Julia. "Which is hardly a friendly sort of gesture."

Julia stared at her, dumbfounded.

"But maybe that's their way of being friendly to strangers," Nadia said. She gestured at the gray and silver tertiaries. "They could be saying, hey, here we are, this is our planet you're orbiting, and this is who we are—we live in cities, we're called this—" The words spilled out of Nadia's mouth as forcefully as water flowed and foamed into a cistern from the pipe of a conduit. "Different species have their own ways of establishing Contact."

Which a communications specialist already had to know, Julia thought.

Blaise glowered at Nadia. "Yes, that's the *theory*," she said coldly. "Which no one needs to tell *me*. But the fact is that they have previously shown themselves to be dangerous, in that the crew members who accompanied them to the surface have not been heard from since."

Nadia shook her head. "That's not true," she said. "We heard from them after they reached the surface. Remember how Paul talked about what the La Femmeans look like in the deep violet light of the planet? And how he said they live in a 'state of nature'? And that their cities are beautiful?" She looked at Julia. "It's perfectly possible that Paul and the others find the planet so beautiful they don't want to leave it. Especially since they're probably scared shitless of going through transudation again. So why should they return to the ship? Or even bother to keep in communication, since they have no reason to think anyone will be joining them anytime soon?"

Wow, Julia thought. That was probably the most the word processor had ever said to a crew member.

"She has a point," Elora said. "In fact, that's been my own impression. That after the crew's disasters, the few remaining survivors were interested in making the best of their situation, which was that they couldn't stand to go through another transudation. And then to find the planet and its inhabitants so...attractive." Elora, like the other astrobiologists, had been reluctant to do the sims. Blaise's attitude might prove to be a more than trivial problem, but clearly it had worked positively to hook Elora.

Blaise looked at the others. "Do the rest of you buy such a naive line of crap?"

"The question you're raising," Julia said softly, "is in deciding what is and is not a hostile response."

Blaise crossed her arms over her chest and thrust her chin in Julia's direction. "Everything's a debate with you, Julia, isn't it," she said—probably, Julia thought, referring to the image noneutopians had of eutopians.

"Hardly any humans understand the Delta Pavonians in even an elementary way," Nadia said. "Except that we do have a pretty fair reason to believe that they don't intend to invade or dominate us. But since the Pax has always focused most on the sheer possibility of invasion and domination, we're still at a painfully rudimentary stage of communication with them. So it seems to me that detecting and responding to aggression and hostility in another species of aliens are not necessarily the most important goals of communication in Contact."

"But we have to be careful," Talib said. "And anyway, we don't really know that the Birds don't want to dominate us. It's only been a few decades that we've had Contact. And they could be pissed at us for having shown up in their space uninvited."

"Exactly," Blaise said. "Some members of the Council believe that this whole thing could be a setup by the Birds."

"They're not like that!" Nadia said passionately.

<<Your blood pressure has risen to 180/113, and the level of adrenaline in your blood is physiologically significant>> the AI told Julia. <<Do you wish to be chemically calmed?>>

Julia was so sick of this same old argument it made her want to scream. <Yes, do it.> A sense of well-being at once washed over her. She wondered that she had so little patience lately.

"...assure you none of us knows what the fuck is going on, and until we do, we should assume a posture of extreme wariness," Blaise was saying.

"All right," Julia interrupted the discussion. "Shall we put the sim back into play?"

"But we haven't decided yet," Nadia said.

Julia put a smile on her primary's face. "True. But we probably won't decide beforehand anyway, will we. Or at least we won't all agree with the decision." She jabbed her thumb at the tertiaries. "Do as you like—or rather as you can, as a group. And remember that if you argue, you'll be doing so in front of our ersatz visitors. AI: resume simulation."

At this rate they'd never reach the one-on-one stage before everyone was too exhausted to go on. But did it matter? The reality would probably be totally different. And yet if all they did was argue their basic differences in attitude, the mesh would be nothing more than a fantasy S07 had made up for her. Create a hegemony counter to the Pax's in this small group of Paxans? The idea was absurd on the face of it. But then S07 had always had an idealistic streak in its makeup. Which Julia very well knew—having, after all, invented S07 herself.

23.

JULIA SPENT THE break she had scheduled between the practice session and the final meeting the executive officers would hold before setting course to match *Pax I*'s orbit around La Femme in conference with S04 and S07 in her favorite personal c-space lounge. "If I thought it wouldn't demoralize the crew, I'd call another session of practice sims," Julia glumly told her secondaries. She climbed into one of the low hammocks slung between two of the lounge's square white columns. "But tensions are running high enough without my insisting on what at least half of them would likely consider an arbitrary abuse of my authority." Julia touched the polished terracotta floor and shoved off, to get the hammock swinging.

S04 and S07 seated themselves in high-backed white wicker rocking chairs, S04 informally cross-legged, S07 primly erect. A miniature potted cedar tree, which exuded a glorious scent that made Julia forget she was actually breathing the recycled air of the ship, sat between them. S07 wagged its right forefinger at Julia. "You accomplished more with the session than you realize," the secondary said. "Group three did very well in the initial scenario. And once the crew broke into smaller groupings, it became clear that the word processors and astrobiologists have a positive, open attitude toward the coming encounter. The crew's caretaker stats show that only one-sixth were measurably stressed by the simulations."

"Yeah, that's grand," Julia said. "And barely more than ten percent of the waking crew has hostile and/or paranoid attitudes towards the La Femmeans. How wonderful. But even if that were an acceptable figure, the point is that everyone knew those images were simulations and not the real thing. And so everybody was basically playacting. But when the contact is *real...*" Because she hadn't been paying attention, the hammock had already stopped.

S07 persisted. "That must always be the case before Contact. You don't know yourself how you'll react. It's unlikely the experience of telepathy will even remotely resemble communication via AI-interfaced implant. The point is not that it wasn't real, but that you now know who is and is not deeply prejudiced before Contact and likely to respond in undesirable ways to the La Femmeans." S07 uncrossed and recrossed its legs, as though they were meat that would grow uncomfortable if held too long in one position. "But that's not all we learned from the sims, Julia."

"Aha," Julia said. "So you saw it, too, this time." She grinned at S07. "The nature of Paul's attraction to the La Femmeans." She looked at S04. "And I suppose you saw it, also?"

S04 shook its head. And S07 said: "No, that's not what I was going to say. Paul's attraction is as mystifying to me now as it ever was."

Julia raised her eyebrows at S07. "Really? You didn't see it? But it's the shape of their bodies, particularly the fullness of their breasts. This time when I saw them, they reminded me of my milk-parents."

S07 shrugged. "You did not program me with the experience and sensibility that would make such a perception come readily. But of course, now that you mention it, I can begin to draw some interesting connections."

"Nor am I programmed with such experience and sensibility," S04 said. "It is, as S07 says, interesting. But I wasn't aware that people were strongly drawn to one particular body type more than any other."

"To full breasts," Julia said. "And a certain scent." She smiled. "I can assure you, milk-parents are sexually enticing. My only meat-space lover was a milk-parent at the time. They're almost irresistible."

S04 said, "But even if that's so, do you see this as a significant factor in our coming contact with the La Femmeans?"

Julia gazed up at the exposed oak beams twelve feet above. She hadn't had a chance to think about it since she'd made the observation. She saw now that she should not only consider it seriously but also discuss it with the rest of the crew. To warn them? she wondered. Or...but the whole subject, she noticed, was titillating. Just talking about it to her secondaries and thinking about it was giving her the same kind of sensations and feelings she experienced when plotting out a strategy for an erotic v-space pursuit. Presuming the rest of the crew would see the connection once she drew it to their attention (excepting the kindercity raised members, who would probably be indifferent to the resemblance), and presuming they would then respond as she was doing now, did she really want to make them so erotically preoccupied with the La Femmeans that they'd have nothing else on their minds when Contact was finally achieved?

Was she being ridiculous? To imagine that every sexual person among them would all become mindless, helpless creatures totally devoid of good sense and self-control?

"Perhaps, Julia, you'd care to share your thoughts with us?" S07 said. "We can't read your mind, you know. We are unable to 'hear' what you don't specifically input into our programs."

Julia looked at S07. "What was it you were going to tell me before I interrupted you?"

"I don't understand why you hold things back from us," S04 said. "We're a part of you, in a manner of speaking. "You could say it is like keeping secrets from yourself."

Julia blew a raspberry. "I just don't feel like articulating it now," she said wearily. "All right?"

"Certainly, Julia," S07 said in its primmest, most patient voice (a voice that made Julia wonder if that was how she had sounded to Arethustra during the years in which she'd given her lessons).

"Though I feel bound to remind you that if it's something you're wishing to repress, it is probably important," S04 added its two bytes.

Julia closed her eyes and sighed loudly. They knew better than to waste her time. And they certainly knew exactly how much time, down to the ship second, before the executive meeting was due to begin. Yet they let the silence beat on as though they had all the time in the world for playing games. Which was typical, actually, of all her secondaries. Time lay outside their experience and thus was apparently meaningless to them.

"To continue our earlier train of discussion," S07 finally said. "You've not only learned who should be on your initial Contact team—presuming, that is, the La Femmeans do not themselves choose which individuals to present themselves to—but you've also learned a means of countering the La Femmeans' telepathic abilities to no small extent."

Julia's eyes popped open. She turned her head to stare at S07. "What are you talking about?"

"Don't tell us you missed it, Julia," S04 murmured with suspicious sweetness.

"Look, I don't have time to work through one of your so-enlightening lessons," Julia said. "Just tell me what I missed."

S07 uncrossed its legs and leaned forward. "Real-time communication through AI interface is the obvious solution," the secondary said. "In the third sim of the session, Group 2B started doing it when the Lalage tertiary began speaking directly via interface to one team member only. Obviously the use of the AI interface to simulate telepathy gave her the idea in the first place. But she went one step further, by opening a channel through the AI to her team members and immediately repeating everything the tertiary said to her."

"No, I didn't know," Julia said. "Because it never occurred to me to ask the AI to report to me on that. And it would be illegal, anyway, for me to do so, since it would be a violation of privacy and the AI would never allow me access anyway." She looked from S04 to S07. "But how did you two know about it, without violating the law?"

S07 shook its head. "Because we were paying attention. During the break that followed that exercise, we heard people in Group

2B telling others of their technique. So that several of the three-person teams in the next set of exercises used it, too."

Julia groaned. "I knew I should have had a follow-up discussion after the session."

"It's all right, Julia," S04 said. "Fuyuko was in Group 2B. I'm sure she'll let everyone else know and incorporate the technique into the protocol."

"Stupid, stupid," she muttered to herself. They—she—should have thought of it long ago. But the general reluctance people had to communicating via AI interface when physically or virtually sharing the same space probably accounted for their not doing so. There was something disorienting about it—and clandestine. In general it was used mainly to warn people, or privately upbraid them so as to avoid embarrassing the others present. "Well thanks, guys," Julia said to the secondaries. "At least now I won't be caught off-guard in the meeting."

"There's something you've been forgetting apropos weaving your mesh," S04 said.

"Oh really." Julia wondered if she needed another spurt of something to calm her nerves. Usually she found the S04-S07 routine amusing. "Do remind me, then," she invited.

S04 bounced lightly in its seat, setting the wicker chair rocking. "You're trying to build an alt-hegemony." It drew a circle in the air. "Imagine your alt-hegemony as a circle. As with every hegemony, there will always be marginal elements in disagreement with it, fraying its edges, but held firmly to it by centripetal force. Which is to say, all you have to do is make a solid, reasonably heavy center that will hold and keep your circle rolling. The sim session has made clear that a substantial number of the crew share your sense of mission. Concentrate on them. And remember: at this stage, any threat from the fringe will pull the center tighter. That may not always be true, of course, particularly if Vance and her coconspirators were awake and asserting the orthodox view, but from what we saw in this session, I believe it is true for the moment."

Julia sat up and planted her bare feet on the cool tile floor. "I hope you're right, S04. I hope it's true that we've got a center besides just me." She did not feel so confident.

"Your team should be Nadia, Solita, Fuyuko, Melina, and Kristin," S07 said.

"*Both* word processors?" Julia said. "Don't you think that if something were to go wrong—"

"Have a little faith, Julia," S07 said. It's smile was gentle. "And remember, when the skeptics on the crew realize the La Femmeans aren't enemies waiting in ambush, they'll be pulled closer in to the center. It's fear that's the enemy, and exposure to what they fear will ease their fear far more efficaciously than you could ever do with persuasive rhetoric."

Julia looked from S07 to S04. For the first time, a funny little tendril of doubt sneaked its way into her conscious mind. Rationally, she knew fear was destructive. By electing to do the mission, they had agreed to the risk, and as long as the risk was confined to those doing the mission, it was necessary and acceptable. But then she remembered the Pax's history with the Delta Pavonians and the needless fright and revulsion she had taken of the many wondrous species she had seen when Glenning took her to the wildlife dome. No, she vowed, she would not let fear get to her, would not let fear distort her perceptions, would not let fear prevent her from striking out as far as she could in whatever new direction offered itself.

Life is change, eutopians always said. Life is change, and fear is stagnation and death. She, Julia, had long since chosen life.

24.

WHEN JULIA DREW her first assignment Outside, Raye greeted the news with, "Poor baby—now you're for it."

But Julia exulted. "Finally! Finally I'm to see the Outside!" Raye shook her head with disbelief. "What is it you expect to find Outside?" she said. "You've got to have figured out by now that relations with the Outside is the soft core of everything that's wrong with the Pax."

Julia had. Or rather, she thought she had. But despite having been raised by eutopians, like all children in the Pax she had grown up with many of the usual shared ideas about reality that basically amounted to consensual fictions. She had learned analyses and facts contradicting the fictions—but as abstractions that caused the anguish of real cognitive dissonance as only she experienced them herself. In the case of her illusions about Outside, Julia cherished a whole set of them special to her personally.

Julia knew, of course, that one of the primary challenges diplos faced was to remain conscious of the many fictional aspects of Paxan reality without refusing or opposing them, since the diplo's task was not to enlighten lay people as to their errors in perception and reasoning, but to use errors and fictions to manipulate persons and events. This basic premise, of course, ran counter to her most profound and cherished eutopic ideals. Until her first assignment working Outside the Pax, she imagined she would not be bound by it. (She even imagined that Raye was not bound by it.) Though her apprenticeship at Central HQ had deeply distressed her, it hadn't remotely threatened this conviction.

So she ignored the knowing looks she drew from other diplos when she told them about the posting and assumed their remarks that all diplos found their first Outside assignment "pivotal" or "formative" did not apply to her (since she already knew what to expect). Yes, she understood that she would be venturing into a poisoned, violent, and in every way alien environment, but while it would try her (especially since she would be required to spend a great deal of time in meat-space), it would not *shock* her.

For the first phase of her assignment Julia was posted to a bunker in a border zone. Border bunkers served several purposes, but chiefly as command posts for protecting the domes and coordinating the destruction of any forces attempting an assault on them. The defense wing of the diplo service preferred to maintain its staging operations outside the domes and right up to the safety perimeter, not only to keep Outsiders from thinking they could play edge games with the Pax, but also as a preventive measure should any Outsiders imagine themselves strong enough to launch an attack. The political wing liked having the bunkers outside the domes because it meant that they were (in theory, at least) accessible to walk-ins. And the commerce and Outsider relations wing required sites outside the domes in order to carry on the bulk of their business (which was, after all, with Outsiders). Considering the dangers that unscrupulous and violent Outsiders posed, diplos in this wing were quite happy to share space with the defensive wing.

Eyes shining, Julia passed through the underground lock from dome to border zone. But she had been in c-space bunkers throughout her training and so found the meat-space analog all too commonplace, if a bit grungy and stuffy. The bunker had offices. And it had living quarters. And it held a slew of diplos and even more professionals working under them. The saturation of security devices and personnel was the only strikingly novel thing about the place. She spent most of her first day in a caretaker, attending c-space meetings during the morning and afternoon, and a social event in the evening. Her first day, in short, disappointed her. It seemed all too ordinary and familiar.

On her second morning, however, the commanding officer told her she would be handling walk-ins. Though she kept her ecstasy to herself, she could feel her mouth stretching in a crazy grin she hadn't a hope of suppressing. What better place to start? As walk-ins, these Outsiders would be positively disposed to the Pax, which meant she wouldn't have to be dealing with hostility and potential violence while she got used to their difference from Paxans. And since the welcoming of Outsiders into the Pax was one of the highest symbols of Paxan values, this first duty would be like participating in one of the quintessential rituals of the Pax. (Yes, yes, though her eutopian schooling had taught her to distrust such representations, in the deepest recesses of her being she had fallen for that particular one.)

Julia arranged to do a complete rotation of the walk-in office's various duties in order to get full hands-on experience of how the office functioned. She began by sitting in on a few interviews prior to conducting some herself. Though later most of the interviews blurred into an indistinguishable mass of repetitious detail, she never forgot the first one.

Everything about the first Outsiders she met struck her (then) as exotic: they all had two or three names each (including one they shared in common); they designated themselves a family though they were four children and only two adults; they were all pale and extraordinarily large compared to Paxans and had an odd smell; they wore elaborate, tight-fitting clothing of the sort Julia had seen only in c-space historicals; one of the adults, a female, had the body of a milk-parent, though the youngest child was six. Afterward, Julia learned that all Outsider women had milk breasts for their entire lives (though their breasts held milk only for as long as an infant needed it, as had been the case for all women before the development of advanced techniques of genetic engineering).

The male adult who towered over everyone in the room said he spoke for all the members of his party. "The name is Charles Norbert Griffiths," the male said when Julia and her colleague, Nico, entered the room. "And this is my wife, Sheila Bethany Griffiths, and our children," he said. And then stuck out his hand at them.

The adult Outsiders shook hands with both the interviewers. Julia felt a thrill as the man clasped and pumped her hand. It seemed a little like taking part in a c-space historical in meatspace, or as though these people had stepped out of a time machine in full meat-representation of the past. But when the six Outsiders were seated, the images created by ever-shifting l.e.d. displays on their clothing distracted and disturbed her until Nico's touch on her arm reminded her that she needed to be paying attention. Nico later identified the images as advertisements for the consumer products and brands that dominated Outsiders' lives.

The man talked freely, garrulously, even, without much prompting. Following Nico's instructions (and determined to keep her eyes away from the flashing images), Julia kept her gaze fastened on her palm-sized hand-held monitor for indications of deception, but there were none. Later, of course, she realized that if he'd had the faintest of an accurate notion of the Pax he might well have tried to lie. But in his ignorance, he spoke confidently and candidly. "First off I'm sure you'll be interested to know that both I and my wife have excellent qualifications. We both have advanced degrees, I in electrical engineering, my wife in genetech. Well, you have our CVs, you can check us out for yourselves. Our education and job experience are first-rate. Both she and I are in great physical shape. We have a healthy credit balance. And we both currently hold solid middle-management positions."

Nico's smile implied sympathetic understanding and even faint admiration.. "You're saying you have it all," she summarized.

The adults exchanged glances. The woman looked suddenly very sad. "Well..." she said.

"Basically, yes," the male said in a bluff, hearty voice. "But unfortunately, a problem has cropped up. And we don't really see any way to solve it." He smiled ruefully. "Within the bounds of the Free World, that is."

"Charlie," the female half-whispered, touching his stiff, immaculate sleeve.

He shook her off. "Of course we used to buy all the propaganda about the Pax, just like anybody else," he said briskly. "But you know, like anything else, holes start showing through here and there, even the way the Pax is seen as the greatest source of terrorism the world has ever known. Because, you know, it started coming out that most governments, including all the legitimate ones, do business with it on a regular basis." He shrugged. "For medicines. Germ stocks. Software, that kind of thing..." He frowned. "You learn in school that the Pax hit the world with the Great Crash because the UN wouldn't submit to their blackmail. And that they're backwards socialists, human machines living in hives like insects..." He smiled again, a little uncertainly. "Of course I know now you're not, I had a buddy who defected to you guys a while back, you know, when the Southwest Republic joined you. Anyway, he got a few videos to us and debunked all that. I mean, I know you *are* actually socialists. But he says it works out fine. And that in fact things are really easy there—which must make for a lot of inefficiency, but... But I hear you have a very good health-care system. And you see, we have this problem...this quite serious problem..." The man's voice was suddenly hollow and shaking. The woman had her hands folded and pressed so tightly against her mouth that not only the knuckles, but the fingers, too, were livid.

"Our little Johnny has some kind of virus," Sheila Bethany Griffiths said. Her voice came out hoarse, choked with emotion. She glanced over her shoulder at the four children seated on the sofa behind her; each child appeared to be absorbed in the games they were playing on their hand-held devices. "Johnny's the six-year-old," she said, looking imploringly at Nico. At the sound of his name, Johnny looked up for a second, then returned to his game. Though he was a good deal taller than the typical Paxan six-year-old, he was painfully thin, the whites of his eyes were yellow, and his skin was an unhealthy shade of yellow. His mother's eyes filled with tears. "He's already had one liver replacement. It's not just that the insurance won't cover a second one. But the virus is rare among insured children. And so the pharmaceutical companies say it's not worth working on, even for those willing and able to pay out-of-pocket expenses. From all that we've heard about the Pax, you wouldn't just sentence him to inexorable deterioration followed by death sometime in adolescence. Or even before then." She appealed with her eyes to both Nico and Julia. "Isn't that true? That you take care of all illness, whatever the expense?"

"Look, we'd be willing to pay you for it," the male said. "If you didn't want to take us. In fact, that would, quite frankly, be preferable. Since we like everything about living in Heartland America—except for this problem with John, of course. We understand that you people don't use money yourselves. But we know you do use it for trade." He laughed self-consciously. "Of course, there'd be hell to pay if they found out we'd come here, and God knows they'd want to keep it quiet that you helped us with our problem. But we were very careful, and so it's not out of the question."

Which was nonsense, though Julia did not yet know that. The government on the other side of the border knew exactly who entered the Pax's consulate. But then Julia knew as little about the arrangement between the Pax and Outside governments as she understood what the man meant by "insurance" and pharmaceutical companies' notions of what was "worth working on."

"I'm sorry," Nico said. She touched her hand to her sternum and sighed. "It is terribly sad, your problem. But I'm afraid we can't help you."

Julia felt surprise. Even if these people were unsuitable for being brought into the Pax (as she could even then see they clearly were), surely something could be done to help with the child's medical problem?

The woman burst out with a horrendous noise that neither "sob" nor "shriek" could properly describe. She threw herself onto the worn vinyl floor, at Nico's feet, and pressed her face against Nico's legs. "My baby!" she cried. "You must save my baby!"

It was like the performance of a badly programmed secondary doing classical drama, Julia thought, embarrassed. She fixed her eyes on the monitor in her hand and, seeing that the woman's enactment of distress registered as genuine, wondered if Nico had any sedative patches on hand. Diplo texts taught that Outsiders tended to be emotionally volatile and even violent, but none of the examples given of such behavior had included anything of this order.

Nico, though, unfazed by the outburst, spoke calmly and gently to the Outsider, stroking her back as one would a child's—until the man pulled her roughly away and hissed at her to be quiet and leave it to him. "I genuinely regret—" Nico began to repeat, with a glance at the children, two of whom had begun sobbing, but the man said, almost shouting, "You people are supposed to be humanitarians, that's what my buddy claims. What is it you want? I'll match any price you name, somehow, some way. But if you want to bargain, let's do it outside. Sheila's had just about all she can take. There's nothing worse than a mother having to watch her own child die."

The Outsiders' language fascinated Julia. She recognized *mother*, for instance, as a word that Outsiders considered sacred, signifying an icon that had no equivalent in the Pax, where it existed only in ancient art work, c-space historicals, and as a curiosity of Outsider strangeness. Though she didn't understand exactly what he was saying, she could hear the sacredness in the violence of his voice and see it in the desperation of his face, which was tense and rigid in the precariousness of his control.

When the interview was over and the (sedated) walk-ins escorted out, Julia asked Nico to explain why she had turned them away without giving them any assistance. "We couldn't take them into the Pax. We almost never take individuals, and these people are certainly not among the exceptions we might consider," Nico said.

"I realized their unsuitability almost at once," Julia said. "Their desires are so…incompatible with Paxan mores and values. They have no desire for our way of life. And their personal interactions are so…unbalanced, and…perverse. The way they treated the children! So when the male said that that was the way they liked living, it became clear as clear… But what about doing something for the child? Treating his virus, I mean? Couldn't we have helped them with that?"

Nico shook her head. "No, Julia, we couldn't have. Granted, if we'd had the antiviral already on hand and only one dose was required, we could have administered it. But we don't. We don't get those kinds of viruses here, because we live protected from the toxins that trigger most Outsider viruses. As for medication—even if we had something that would help the child, it would be useless to give it to the parents, since the minute they left the bunker their government's border police would seize it as contraband and charge them with either illegal trading or treason or something of that sort." She shrugged. "It's been known to happen before. Believe me, they're all being thoroughly searched right this minute."

Julia went back to the training texts and simulations for more information on Outsider mores (to learn, for instance, about "insurance" and to try to figure out what the man meant when, as he was being sedated he screamed at them "Fucking beaners," beyond, of course, "beaners" obviously being an epithet), the policies of Outsider governments, and diplo arrangements with those governments. As she reviewed the texts she had already studied, she easily caught what she had missed the first time through. The Council forced the Outsider governments to set up these stations allowing the occasional in-the-flesh contact across borders and even a thin flow of intelligence. But though the Council was interested in developing new areas whose populations could be gradually merged into the Pax, it almost never allowed individual immigration. Since all Outsider governments wanted to prevent their "citizens" (particularly the best-educated) fleeing to the Pax, certain ground-rules strictly controlled and monitored access to consular bunkers. The principal point of interviewing walk-ins was to steer those expressing an approximation of Paxan desires to contacts in geographical locations where pro-Paxans were being concentrated under covert Paxan guidance.

By the time she finished her background review, Julia had concluded that the differences between the apparent desires of Outsiders and those of people in the Pax made any complex communication all but impossible. Julia considered desire a positive force, the engine that made things happen, the motor of change. In the Pax, which was firmly committed to its founding principle of "needs-plus," desire was supplementary (though not inessential) and never a force for stripping others of their subsistence. Yet outside the Pax, it was clear, while desire *posed* as the motor of change, it instead generated spurious needs that were basically destructive to life. Julia had long since been taught that this had been the case for most of human history—predicating war, slavery, and innumerable other forms of exploitation and annihilation. Hence the famous declaration of a pre-Paxan, "History is what hurts." Julia had known, though she had somehow forgotten, in her enthusiasm for contacting Outsiders, that it was a fundamental tenet of almost all Outsider cultures that one person's desire required the deprivation of others' needs, the belief that simply assuring universal subsistence would destroy desire (and therefore human existence). She had known, too, that as a consequence of this belief, Outsider societies considered inevitable an economy of deprivation (instilled from infancy) and an ethos that the only moral good is that of profit for an elite at the expense of the majority, a dogma that maintained an endless feedback loop of vicious profit-based deprivation. But Julia had never before wondered whether such a difference in the construction of desire could effectively obstruct any but the crudest commerce between members of the Pax and Outsiders.

Henceforth (as Raye had predicted) her border assignment became painful to her, though no less interesting. At the very least, she knew that if she persevered she'd eventually earn a post in one of the Pax's few merging zones. She took as her mission a greater understanding of these particular Outsiders (always reminding herself that Outsiders in one place differed from those in another, though they tended to hold the same warped construction of desire in common) and took as the horizon for her Kenning the goal of one day attempting an exploration of the possibilities for communication with one or more Outsiders, in a spirit similar to that in which eutopians undertook explorations in Cockayne-spaces.

25.

THE FAST, ABRUPT break into meat-space, the frantic sweaty wrestle into the uniform, the quick and hard short-of-breath trek to the bridge gave Julia no opportunity to prepare herself for the sight that confronted her on the real-time external viewscreen. Fuyuko's call had been hysterical: *There are birdlike creatures circling the ship, Julia. And not only are the word processors singing to them, but I can hear those creatures, inside my head, singing back!*

In the instant before toggling out, Julia fleetingly wondered that Fuyuko had even ventured onto the bridge, which had become virtually the shared living quarters of the word processors. Though Fuyuko never flinched from appearing on the bridge when necessary, she avoided the place when she could, which Julia suspected was because it held intolerable memories.

Like birds? had been Julia's dominant thoughts as she dressed. Does she mean like Delta Pavonians, or like c-space constructs of the creatures that once existed in astonishingly vast numbers and species on the earth? On entering the bridge, Julia saw the main viewscreen and halted on the threshold. "Hearing" the "singing" in her mind's ear as though via her implant, beholding the enthralling sight on the viewscreen, Julia understood that Fuyuko meant both. The creatures looked more like word processors than like Delta Pavonians, elongated streaming streaks of silver reminiscent of mythical creatures, if there had ever been imagined such creatures as hybrids of humans, birds, and fish. Yes, perhaps more like fish than birds, like long blue and silver fish with gauzy purple-veined wings or fins that spread out over an area ten times as great as their narrow, sleek bodies, their heads like those of dolphins, only mouthless and with jewels set in their throats, yet possessing legs and feet that though impossibly long were the most human things about them.

Julia's throat ached at the beauty of them, though in the back of her mind lurked the memory of how beautiful she had found the Delta Pavonians in c-space and how sick she had been the first time she experienced their presence in the flesh. <AI, translate the "singing" I am hearing inside my head. And describe its physical source.>

<<What you hear inside your head is not accessible for analysis unless it is routed through your implant. If you hear singing inside your head, its physical source cannot be determined.>>

Sweaty, exhausted, struggling for breath, Julia sank into a flight couch and as the word processors dived, leaped, swooped—despite the heavy-gee of deceleration—as though the bridge were a Delta Pavonian performance space, enabled, Julia soon saw, by the jet packs they had donned. <Then describe for me the physical specifications of the entities outside the ship, now appearing on the viewscreen. Include their size, distance from the ship, and a conjecture of the biomechanics of their locomotion.>

Sound split the air, powerful glissandi pouring out of both word processors in a rhythmic and tonal counterpoint that raised the hair on the back of Julia's neck. "Julia! Make them stop!" Fuyuko screamed.

<<There are no perceptible biological entities outside the ship within a thousand kilometer radius. Please be more specific.>>

Julia shivered. <AI, translate the word processors' singing for me.>

<<An exact and full translation is not possible. Their texts include the words "pleasure," "outside," "travel," "communion," and "home.">>

Julia had caught that much herself. She could not remember any singing like this. It was as though the word processors were flinging solidly physical musical objects around the bridge, setting up powerful vibrations in Julia's belly, ecstatic to the point of pain. She knew from the performances she attended in the City of Word

Processing how viscerally effective singing could be, but she had never heard more than one being singing at a time. Now not only Nadia and Solita were singing in the cabin with them, but the creatures outside—five of them, Julia thought she could distinguish in the dazzle of their kaleidoscopic choreography—were also singing, inside her head, with an intensity that made her long to dance and sing with them, leaving her both excited and bereft at her sense of exclusion. The grace of their wings or fins or whatever the glittering shapes of filigreed mesh were, furling and unfurling in what seemed both group caress and aesthetic display, the unearthly beauty of the sounds made by seven voices, five interior and two acoustic, never cacophonous yet like no music Julia had ever heard, even from the Delta Pavonians, and perhaps most breathtaking of all, the play of Albirean light over their long sleek bodies in what seemed almost graspable patterns that Julia strained unsuccessfully to discern—all this made her weep. They seemed to be showing her everything she wanted while simultaneously revealing her ignorance of what exactly that was. Bathed in this strange sensual ocean, Julia wished to be able to reach out and grab it, interrogate it, and become part of it. Here was ecstasy and beauty and ineffable sense. Here was perfection, which she never had believed in (she was, after all, a eutopian, who knew better than to slide into *that* kind of dodge). Here was the answer to the near-despair that had driven her to the mission.

She looked at Nadia and Solita through a blur of tears. They lacked fins or wings, and their bodies, though augmented, were all too human. Yet they had entered the splendor, were a part of it.

No wonder Fuyuko was in hysterics, shrieking and vomiting and sobbing herself hoarse.

26.

AFTERWARDS, WHEN JULIA checked with the AI to determine the duration of the "ecstatic event" (as she named it in her official log), she discovered it had lasted for approximately a ship's hour and fifty-three minutes. Julia would not have thought it possible to endure ordinary meat-experience for that long without feeling stressed. But to be immersed in a frenetic, barely conscious state with elevated blood-pressure, accelerated cardiac rate, and prolonged hyperventilation for that long, struck her as impossible. Only children could experience extreme states in meat-space, she found herself thinking—and then realized that that couldn't be true, since word processors routinely "blissed out" while singing, which could only be done in meat-space.

She had felt it, as word processors said, "in the belly." (And on the soles of her feet and in the palms of her hands.) It had taken her by the throat, which had strained to "sing" yet had closed up, silenced by the impossibility of access. Her arms and legs and torso had wanted to thrust into movement, into dance—as *they* were doing outside, on the viewscreen—only her body had stood frozen, as if caught in a vortex making her too dizzy, disoriented, and weak to move. Had *she* been "blissed out"? Not exactly, unless "blissed out" included closed out, excluded—longing aching desiring without possibility of access.

Fuyuko, vomiting, had clawed her way off the bridge (this the last concrete thing Julia remembered of the event)... In this time that had gone on and on without marked division of time, she remained in the eye of the action yet outside, until it all collapsed, in as sudden a deflation as a balloon pricked without warning. Simply, it was over, gone, finished. The viewscreen showed only great, looming La Femme, bright distant Albireo, and a slice of moon and a distant backdrop of stars. The word processors drooped in mute enervation.

It took Julia perhaps half a minute to make her lips and tongue work. Her entire body vibrated, as though with a tension not quite spent, in near-numbness. "Nadia," she finally managed to enunciate (though so stiffly it felt as though her lips were lisping). "Nadia, tell me. What happened. What you were singing. What they said to you. Please, Nadia. Tell me."

Nadia moved sluggishly, without looking at Julia. "Sleep," she slurred. "Have to sleep." Clearly exhausted, she struggled to the hatch.

"Solita," Julia said when she could remember the other word processor's name.

Solita, stumbling to the hatch, looked over her shoulder. "I'm wiped, Julia. I really really have to sleep. But you know about singings. You know that they don't necessarily communicate any one particular focused thing. It was just singing, that's all. Just singing." Solita's breath seemed to give out. Mutely, she waited beside Nadia for the hatch to open.

Julia understood. Much of the singing of the Delta Pavonians was done for its own sake. For aesthetic pleasure. Or rather, for the pleasure of doing it, for the pleasure of sharing the experience...not quite simply a communal ritual, not quite simply an artistic performance, but like them in not being easily translatable into functional message-oriented language. Their "message," Julia thought, might be *Here we are, this is us, this is what we care about, we are together in this, we know what beauty is, isn't it delightful to create beauty*...in other words, an affirmation of shared immanence. Though of course this was not Earth, and those creatures on the viewscreen were not Delta Pavonians. So the message here could possibly be significant, a communication to this second group of humans who had entered their star's system...

She would have to talk to the word processors later, after they'd recovered, Julia decided. Wearily, she joined Nadia and Solita, waiting silent and listless. Why was the hatch taking so long to open? "AI," Julia said, resigning herself to dealing with a malfunction. The odor of human sweat and the fainter stink of Fuyuko's vomit (lingering though a bot had long since sucked it up) pressed on her and sharpened her voice. "Open the hatch."

"Fuyuko has ordered the bridge to be quarantined," the AI said. "Therefore the hatch cannot be opened."

Julia ground her teeth. The psyche-synthesist was going to drive her edge. What would she do if La Femmeans actually appeared on the ship? Immobilize them? Expel them? *Kill* them? "AI, convey to Fuyuko via implant that I wish to speak with her."

"Julia? This is Fuyuko. Would you report please on your status there?"

Julia rolled her eyes at the word processors. "We're all tired, and Nadia and Solita in particular are in desperate want of sleep. So just cancel the quarantine, Fuyuko."

"Are the word processors...functioning competently, Julia?"

Julia bit her lip, hard. And tasted blood. "Yes, Fuyuko. As far as I can determine without a neural scan, everybody's sane. I presume that's what you're asking?"

The hatch dilated. Even before she followed the word processors over the threshold, Julia saw the gaggle of crew leaning against the walls of the passage. She looked them over and spotted Fuyuko.

"I'm sorry, Julia, for locking you in," Fuyuko said as Julia approached. One of her facial tics had returned. "But when I tried to evacuate you, you were so...mesmerized, you refused to come. And since it wasn't clear just what was going on..."

Julia said "Just what was going on was a performance of some form of a singing. And a very powerful and effective singing, at that—which is why it held my attention so strongly, as I would have hoped you could have understood."

Fuyuko's eyes widened; her voice came out in a squeak: "You mean, they were singing *Delta Pavonian*?"

Astra interposed herself between Fuyuko and Julia. Her eyes shone with excitement. "Julia." Her voice came out half-strangled and almost without breath. "Tell us: what happened? When Fuyuko reported Contact in progress, I requested a view from the AI, but it gave me the usual view of the local starfield."

Julia, too, was exhausted. The muscles in her face were so tired it hurt to stretch them into a smile. But she nevertheless smiled broadly at Astra. "Why don't we retire to our c-space conference room," she said. "Although we won't be able to debrief the word processors until after they've gotten some rest, we have plenty to discuss anyway." She looked meaningfully at Fuyuko. "And perhaps it would be best we do so."

"I would prefer we not use a c-space," Fuyuko said stiffly.

Julia pushed her way past. "I'm sorry," she said, "but I'm too tired to conference in meat-space. If you insist it be in meat-space, it'll have to wait until I've had some sleep." She looked back at Fuyuko. "It's up to you," she said.

Fuyuko rubbed her knuckle in the trough under her eye, where the muscle was continuously twitching. "All right," she said resentfully. "We'll do it your way, Julia. You know we don't have time to burn."

As though, Julia mused, everyone was convinced that the second they matched *Pax I*'s orbit Contact would be established, after which there would be no time to think or talk about anything...

27.

ONCE AGAIN, THEY met around the octagonal simulated oak conference table, but *sans* the word processors.

"Don't be so naive as to think that only brute physical force can be destructive," Fuyuko said. "Clearly these...*entities* have powers of meddling with our minds. Individually, we are each identifiable as consciousnesses. Culturally, we are a collection of consciousnesses and the expressions thereof across spacetime." Fuyuko slapped the table for emphasis, generating a rather satisfying sound. "And if they attack *that*, then what does it matter if our bodies are left intact?"

"What happened on the bridge was not an attack," Julia said, "but a celebration. A welcome. A greeting. Of that I'm *certain*."

Fuyuko produced a creditable snort. "Do you mean to tell me you understood exactly what was going on when they made us see and hear things the ship's sensors said weren't physically present? Then do please give us a translation." She glanced at Astra. "I'm sure I'm not the only one curious to know what it all meant."

Julia rested her folded hands on the cool, grainy surface of the table. "Nadia and Solita would be better qualified than I to speak to the meaning. But I *can* tell you that before we left the bridge Solita implied that it was a singing, of the sort the Delta Pavonians do for word processors. And she reminded me that singings don't necessarily communicate any particular focused thing." Julia glanced at S07, seated on a stool above and behind Fuyuko (like S04, screened, of course, from everyone but Julia). "Perhaps I should explain. Though some singings are meant to communicate particular messages about concrete things, such as trade arrangements between Delta Pavonians and Paxans, many are simply performative. The fact that they are done, and in the presence of certain people, constitutes their significance."

"Yes," Melina said, lighting up. "Such singings are a combination of art and social ritual. Often there's a 'story' they tell, which is a statement of who they are and their recognition of themselves. We have every reason to believe the Delta Pavonians don't only tell stories about themselves to Paxans, but that they do this among themselves, as well. Which is what human art forms aim to do, too, though the communal, ritualistic elements tend to be implicit rather than explicit."

Fuyuko drummed her fingers on the table. "All right. So it wasn't *intended* as a threat—let's just assume that for the sake of argument. In which case the threat doesn't vanish. Clearly, their ways are different from ours. Their mental organization is undoubtedly vastly different—probably unrecognizably so. Obviously we'd better find a way to protect ourselves against their fine, friendly, *sharing* intentions."

"That's just paranoid." Astra glared at Fuyuko. "Taking that line, we might as well have stayed on Earth. I, for one, have committed myself to risk." She sighed soulfully. "To tell the truth, I wish *I'd* been on the bridge to experience this singing. Even if it made me as sick as it made you, Fuyuko." She glanced at Julia. "Though of course it might not, since *Julia* didn't get sick, only tired."

"One generally needs to adjust gradually to the shock of the truly alien," Julia said quietly. "I had the benefit of encountering the alien in the City of Word Processing, where I lived for a while to learn something about the Delta Pavonians. And I have to confess that I got extremely—and embarrassingly—sick the first time I attended a singing." She flashed Fuyuko an expression of sympathy. "Though it wasn't as powerful a singing as this one, of course. Still, on the bridge just now we didn't actually have to be physically present in the same meat-space with aliens."

"They were *in our heads*," Fuyuko said. "It's spurious, not to say supercilious, for you to claim there's an important distinction between physical and mental contact."

"I wonder," Candace said, "if we should grant that these aliens have benign intentions. I mean, given that they used a Delta Pavonian form, it strikes me that Vance may have been right to suspect a Delta Pavonian setup." She showed Julia a grave face. "I can take a risk as much as anyone else. But I don't agree that we've signed on to being deliberately blind and naive."

Vance resurrected, Julia thought.

"Julia, may I interpose some advice here?" S04 said for Julia's "ears" only. It moved to perch on the edge of the table, blocking Julia's view of Blaise. It had this time adopted the appearance of Davis, a great-grandparent known in the family for having managed a kindercity for almost ten years.

<Make it snappy> Julia said via her implant, concerned lest she appear abstracted at such a crucial point.

"Certainly," S04 said, talking over Astra's voice. "While Vance is outside the group, she makes a fine border for holding together your web. But Candace and Fuyuko are not outside. If you let them mesh with Vance, your border will soon be a knot of threads likely to become a nodal center able to rival your own. Therefore, it's important that you discredit Candace's suggestion as thoroughly as possible—by (a) linking it to Vance; and (b) calling the sanity of such a position into question. Which you can do by drawing attention to Fuyuko's precarious control over her neurosis on the one hand and emphasizing your own good mental health on the other. As for Candace, you can remind her where Vance's paranoia led, and indeed remind everyone that this new expression of concern about possible Delta Pavonian treachery is the same old thing and no more likely now than it was previously."

"I am *not* a coward," Candace was answering Astra. "Nor is Fuyuko. We simply aren't rash, trusting fools."

"Fuyuko," Julia said calmly, cutting off whatever Astra meant to come back with. "If you'd like to do a new brain-scan of me and of the word processors—and yourself, of course—I certainly wouldn't object. It's my belief you'll find me as sane and stable as you did after transudation. And the same for Nadia. Granted, both of the word processors are exhausted. But they were exhausted after transudation. And their participation in this latest...event was intense. I'm fatigued, myself. But not, I believe, in the way one becomes fatigued when depressed."

"That won't be necessary," Fuyuko said stiffly. "I think we can all agree you are your normal, ornery self."

Julia grinned, then reformed her face into concerned seriousness. "But what about you? You looked very distressed when we chatted just now in the passage. And I know this trip has been a strain for you, particularly vis-à-vis the violence that occurred on the bridge during transudation. Tell me truthfully, speaking as a psyche-synthesist considering your own case as though it were someone else's. Do you think that perhaps your suspicions about mental interference might be related to your overall sense of malaise? And that your extreme caution might be generated by a desire to prevent at all costs another incident like the one that resulted in Glory's death?"

"You're pushing it pointfully hard, Julia," S07 said, gesturing down at Fuyuko's head.

Fuyuko's smooth, blank face stared at Julia. "That's very clever of you, Julia," she said after a long silence. "Especially since you must know I'm nearly at the limits of my tolerance of v-space."

"I'm sorry," Julia said. "I didn't mean to embarrass you. But there's more than your personal comfort at stake here." She looked at Candace. "I'm concerned about the continuing influence of Vance's conspiracy theory. Her take on things was what led to the bloody mess on the bridge. The majority of the Council considered Delta Pavonian manipulation improbable because there was no good reason to support such an interpretation of the evidence, only certain 'feelings' a few hawkish individuals harbored. Since the evidence has not changed, I see no reason for reconsidering such an interpretation now." Julia swept her gaze around the table.

"Unless anyone can put forward new evidence of which I'm for some reason unaware?"

"They did a singing," Blaise said softly. "Which definitely links them with the Birds, whoever these creatures are."

"Whom did they sing *to*?" S07 said. "Not to the entire crew."

"Whom did they sing *to*?" Julia said. "Not to the entire crew. No, they sang only to Nadia and Solita, who were on the bridge, and to Fuyuko, perhaps because she was on the bridge with them, and to me, because I came to the bridge in response to Fuyuko's call."

"Yes," Astra said. "Which is odd. Why do you think they did that? Because they thought the bridge was the most important place on the ship?"

"They're telepathic," Melina said. "So they'd know it isn't. And they'd know that Nadia and Solita can be sung to. That they in fact *prefer* to be sung to. The only question is why Julia and Fuyuko were included—unless it was simply, as Julia seems to be suggesting, their coincidental proximity."

"You're suggesting that they pick up on what means the most to us individually?" Astra said.

Melina shrugged. "It's possible. After all, we know they didn't sing to *Pax I*. Or so we must assume from what Paul said in his report."

"Well..." Blaise shrugged. "That makes as much sense as anything else." She looked at Fuyuko. "The point is, there's no way to make judgments about species completely alien to our experience. And it's totally plausible that a telepathic species would choose such an approach." She made a fist under her chin. "Though I do wish we knew whether—"

"Can't stay, have to toggle out!" Fuyuko said in a fast jumble of words—and vanished.

"Probably just her neurosis flaring up," Julia said into the thickening silence. All eyes swiveled toward her. "She's under extreme stress," she added. "She explained it to me herself. She gets physical symptoms in meat-space and hallucinations in c-space, most commonly that of the room erupting in flames."

Blaise said, "So that's what you were referring to, when you questioned her judgment of the event just now on the bridge?"

"Yes. It's likely that the violence during transudation upset her deeply, since she was apparently the only person awake of responsible mind. Though it may well be that she simply isn't suited to the character of the mission. The reason for her being included among the crew is quite different from that of most of us." Had she said too much? Certainly it felt nasty, spilling Fuyuko's secrets. And it might yet backfire on her. On the other hand, it seemed to be working to reinforce her repair of the web...

"And *she's* supposed to be in charge of *our* mental health?" Astra said peevishly.

Julia made a stern face. "Neurosis does not disqualify people from doing their jobs properly. It sometimes *handicaps* them, but that can be compensated for. And besides, Fuyuko isn't among us simply to monitor and tend our mental health. She's a first-rate psyche-synthesist and so can be expected to provide us with many useful insights into the La Femmeans and our contact with them."

"Nice touch, Julia," S04 muttered. "Just don't overdo it."

"We have roughly ten hours left before we achieve orbital insertion," Julia said briskly. "We'll want to meet with Nadia and Solita when they've awakened, to see what they made of the event, and consider any new implications their insight might suggest. In the meantime, I urge the entire contact team to spend the next few hours resting. So. Any questions or comments before—" Julia frowned. In the exact center of the table, defying the rules of general-purpose-category c-space, stood S05, ignoring the dimensions of the table, imposing herself like a (virtual) hologram. How, Julia wondered, could such a thing be? She hadn't summoned S05. And she had never taken the trouble to program any of her secondaries with the ability to violate the standard rules of general-purpose c-space. Secondaries weren't supposed to be capable of exercising undirected volition, much less possess the access needed to enter programs independently.

"It might be some kind of malfunction," Astra said. "AI: who ordered the hologram superimposed over our conference table?"

Julia's throat tightened. S05 was visible to the others!

"Look," Melina said, "the hologram has Julia's opal eyes!"

"Ooh, it's so spooky," Kristin half-whispered.

Julia tried to imagine how the sybil must look to the others—its long silver, black, and gray hair flowing over its voluminous black robe blobbed with gray and red patches, brown face gaunt and wrinkled with the age of centuries, the sharp curved nails of its ugly hands like a predator's claws, its lips tight and hard and uncompromising, and the eerily glowing opalescent eyes...

The AI said, "There is no hologram superimposed over the conference table in this c-space."

"I am Lacuna," the figure said. "I greet you in the name of my people, who live in the cities of La Femme, under the light of the Great Blue Star you call Albireo." Lacuna turned slowly, presumably, Julia thought, to let the people seated at the other end of the table see her face. "We welcome you in peace. In doing so, we both warn and promise that you will find in us all that you have ever desired, as well as everything that you have ever feared."

"What of *Pax I* and the crew members who left the ship with one of you named Lalage?" Blaise said quickly. "Can you tell us where its chief officer Paul is? And why his ship has been unable to retain contact with him?"

"All will be known when you experience La Femme for yourself," Lacuna said with the same gooseflesh-raising intonation the sybil used at her most portentous moments. "But rest assured, Paul left his ship of his own volition. We will meet again in meat-space shortly." And Lacuna vanished.

"How did she do that?" Astra said. "Did she turn herself into data to get into the AI and then somehow manage to..." She shook her head. "It doesn't make sense."

"Maybe she came in via someone's implant," Melina said. "If that's even technically possible?" She looked at Julia. "Maybe through Julia's—since she did for some reason choose to represent herself with Julia's eyes."

Julia shivered. Should she tell them? Probably. But recalling how Fuyuko had behaved on first learning of how Julia interacted with her secondaries, she hesitated. Would it make any difference if she withheld the information? Julia looked at S07, still seated on the stool behind Fuyuko's empty chair. Imagine if they knew S04 and S07 had been present through the entire meeting, commenting and advising...

Julia cut into the flurry of speculative chatter. "Let's discuss this later, after we've rested." She nodded at the communications officer. "And you, Blaise, if you like, can investigate the possible methods our visitor might have used to enter this c-space. Or can set Beth to it, if she's awake."

Without waiting for a reply from Blaise or further reaction from the others, Julia toggled out. Sleep would help clear her mind. It would be pointless to try to decide anything important now, exhausted as she was.

28.

WHEN JULIA TURNED thirteen Glenning told her that she was
entering a new stage of social development called, loosely, "puberty." This puberty, he said, bore little resemblance to the ata-
vistic hormonal stage through which most Outsiders still insisted
their children suffer. Her puberty would entail a new hormonal
phase, but mediated, and thus nothing as pronounced as the radical
bombardment of the Outsiders' iconic "natural." The point of the
Paxan form of puberty, Glenning said, was to prepare socially for
full integration into Paxan society. Her studies, which would be
in progress throughout her life, were preparing her for citizenship
and professional service. But like all eutopian-raised children, she
had so far spent time only with family members devoted to foster-
ing and teaching her, and never with peers. University would come
as a shock, even with the preparation of puberty. Moreover, she
would need to learn to interact with her family as equals, which,
being eutopians, they would expect of her by the time she finished
her apprenticeship. Therefore, Glenning warned her, she must understand that puberty was not a trivial addition to her education,
but an integral part of it.

Oh of course, yes, she understood that, Julia assured him earnestly.

That was before she discovered the nature of some of the
v-space exercises involved.

By this time she had been daily making brief trips into v-space
for her lessons, always under close parental supervision. On each
occasion that she toggled in, one of her parents' primaries would
be waiting to greet her, though they had equipped her personal
program with the usual gatekeeper. Glenning's primary greeted
her and oversaw the pubertal exercises he had mentioned to her.

But still she was taken aback when she learned the nature of one set of them.

"You've already learned a lot about your own sexual pleasures, through autoerotic stimulation," Glenning's primary said to Julia's. "But in becoming a social being involved in a broad range of interactions, your sexuality will undergo a similar broadening. Though one doesn't engage sexually with one's parents and grandparents, sex is occasionally an aspect of relations with non-family members. Social relations are very complicated, Julia. And sexuality adds to their complication. As you prepare for social relationships, you must prepare for their potential sexual dimension, as well. You already know that attraction, conflict, empathy, and responsibility are the major components of social relationships. The same is true for the sexual dimension. And as we start by learning empathy before we address the other components in social relationships, so we will start by learning empathy in the sexual dimension, too. And so the first step will be to provide you with a second primary, constructed with male genitalia. For the rest of your puberty you are advised to spend half your v-space time using it, so that it will become almost second nature to you. Though its sensorial responses won't be identical, of course, to that of meat male genitalia, it will offer a reasonable approximation. Certainly it should suffice to make you as empathetic to male partners as you naturally are to female partners. And it will also, of course, help you clarify any questions you might have about your gender identity."

And so Julia found herself equipped with a boy's genitals, which first made her want to giggle (in spite of Glenning's so-serious observation) and then intrigued her. For the first few years of her "pubertal exercises," her sexual experiments, like all her social experiments, were undertaken with tertiaries. Then, two years before she was scheduled to begin University, she engaged first with experienced secondaries and later, finally, with the primaries of peers—who, like herself, were new to non-family social experience.

In the year before she began University, Julia met others of her age, in the flesh. One of them was Sasha, who later persuaded her to try sexual recreation in meat-space. Social relations always seemed to her more "natural" and less susceptible to unintended inflections in v-space than in meat-space. She knew that must be because she had first learned such engagement in v-space, and so she spent several years trying to enter the "next phase," namely learning to be as comfortable with her peers in meat-space as she was in v-space. Attraction, conflict, empathy, and responsibility, she often still reminded herself, even at fifty—in meat-space.

Sometimes, usually after dreaming that she inhabited her pubertal training primary with boy's genitalia, she wondered why she had, on reaching adulthood, relinquished using it except in eutopian group exercises and private sexual recreation. She never seriously speculated about it, though.

29.

OF COURSE THEY had to have another c-space conference before orbital insertion, given the urgency of discussing the La Femmean intrusion into the previous meeting. In order to accommodate everyone needing to attend, Julia had had to replace the octagonal table for a long glass-topped rectangular one. She'd asked S04 and S07 to attend, as usual, but was thrown for a few seconds to see that S04 was wearing a crew uniform, which S07 almost instantly matched. "Thanks, Astra, for making it," she began. "I know you'd prefer to be taking in the spectacular view right now."

"Yeah. It's so…well, it's just not true that seeing the views *Pax I* sent back were the same thing. The fact is, we're approaching, and we *know it's out there*. That does make a difference, even if it *is* merely a psychological one. As far as I'm concerned, this is new, and not a replay of *Pax I* recordings."

"Solita, Nadia, I hope you've got your energy back," Julia said.

Solita's head darted forward, reminding Julia of a bird digging its beak into the soil, then quickly snapped back, while Nadia barely moved her head in a response that was more eyeblink than nod. Their faces remained blank of expression, and neither said a word.

"Super!" Julia clasped her hands together. "I myself am feeling wonderful for my dose of sleep. Everyone else well-rested and prepared for arrival?" She almost winced at the breeziness of her manner, which she realized was probably a reaction to the word processors' impassivity.

Fuyuko said, "There is an issue I would like to raise before we go further," she said.

"Certainly."

"I would like to be clear as to whether you consider me fit to continue as a member of the Contact team. You expressed doubts about my judgment at the last meeting, particularly after I left it. If there's some question about my competence, I would like—"

"But of course there isn't," Julia said, cutting short the painful gambit. "Your judgment about our Contact with the La Femmeans may be impaired by a slight phobia, but your competence has never been in question. I see no need for your removing yourself from the team, unless you have reason to distrust your own performance." Julia smiled. "You're the expert on mental stability, Fuyuko. And since there's no question of psychosis here, obviously you're the best judge of whether or not your phobia is going to impede the mission unduly."

"It is only you who consider me phobic, Julia," Fuyuko said. "I don't see a problem."

Julia systematically made eye-contact with everyone present in turn: first with Solita and Nadia, and then with Astra, Candace, Blaise, Melina, and Kristen. Finally she looked directly at Fuyuko. "I consider your response to the Contact event on the bridge to have been excessive," she said. "It concerns me that you might impose quarantines or order medication or take other such measures every time you don't know exactly what is going on. Probably everything that happens will be new to us. And will take a long to time to be interpreted. I'd like some assurance from you that you won't over-react again as you did when you ordered the bridge quarantined."

"I believe I was correct to have exercised caution," Fuyuko said.

"Go on to debriefing the word processors," S07 advised. "You can come back to this issue later. Whatever they have to say about the Contact is almost bound to make Fuyuko look extreme."

Looking directly at Fuyuko, Julia briefly tilted her head just a bit. "We'll return to the question of your judgment later," she said. "But since we have just roughly two hours until we've matched orbits with *Pax I*, I suggest we spend most of our time discussing the two Contact events that have occurred in the last few hours. Solita?" Julia nodded at the word processor. "I wonder if you could tell us what you thought happened last night on the bridge?"

Solita shrugged. "Sure. The La Femmeans performed a singing for us."

"And by 'us,' you mean—?"

The word processor swallowed nervously. It was obvious, Julia thought, that Solita was too inexperienced in primary-representation to have created an original c-space persona for herself, but used a simple, direct neural relay. "Me, of course, and Nadia," she said.

"Just you two? Not Fuyuko, who was on the bridge with you?"

Solita shot an anxious look at the psyche-synthesist. "No. Just Nadia and me. I mean, we were the ones who could appreciate it. And also, it was almost the same singing they did for me right after *Pax I* dumped me in the shuttle so far out from the planet. Which I doubt they did for any other crew member."

"They did that before, and you didn't tell anyone?" Blaise thumped her fist on the table. "Why didn't you report it when you relayed the *Pax I*'s reports back to Earth? Or at least fucking tell *us* when we picked you up?"

Solita looked at Julia. "I'm sorry, but I thought it was an hallucination. I mean, I was the only one who saw it. And I was pretty depressed and all by myself on the shuttle..."

"If you think the singing was for you and Nadia alone, why do you suppose Fuyuko and I could hear their singing inside our heads and see it on the viewscreen when the AI's sensors apparently could not?" Julia said quietly.

"I don't know. I really don't. Maybe their telepathy is general, and not private? Like a radio band rather than an implant? I mean, maybe it has to do with some technical consideration, and not anything to do with whom they meant the performance for."

"Yes," Blaise said slowly. "That sounds plausible. Only..." She spread her hands flat on the table. "I must say I have some concerns, especially about the second event. About how they were able to penetrate v-space. Which essentially means going through the AI, via digitized streams of data. It seems rather...unlike any notions of mental telepathy we hold."

"Telepathy has always been hypothetical," Fuyuko said. "It's not as though our notion of it ever had any basis in reality. So I don't see the problem of envisioning a telepathy mathematically sophisticated enough to operate digitally."

"They have an extremely high-tech telepathy," Astra said. "Is that what you're saying, Blaise?"

"The Delta Pavonians are very high-tech, isn't that right?" Fuyuko said. "It's possible to imagine they could penetrate our v-space, isn't it?"

"They wouldn't," Nadia said quickly. "They can't tolerate machine-digitized sound. They can't *read* it when a machine attempts a singing. I can't imagine them *wanting* to penetrate v-space."

"Can Delta Pavonians understand spoken language?" Blaise queried.

Nadia shook her head. "No. Of course not. It just sounds like noise to them."

"Are you sure?" Melina said. "Are you sure they didn't decide it would be more advantageous to them for us to have to communicate in their language? And that they're perfectly capable of understanding human languages but simply haven't let us know that? I mean, if they're as high-tech and sophisticated as everyone seems to think..."

Kristen nodded. "I've always wondered that myself. Whether they have passive knowledge of human languages that allowed them to...observe us."

"We're getting a little off the subject," Julia said.

"What I would like to know about this second event, which I missed," Fuyuko said, "is just what happened. What you saw. And whether the visitor...said anything."

Everyone stared at Fuyuko.

"You might try reading if not viewing the transcript," Julia said quietly.

"I *did* read it, Julia. Because I wanted to see how the meeting came out. But though I read your brief discussion at the very end of the meeting, I was puzzled as to its subject."

"You mean its appearance and speech wasn't recorded?" Blaise said.

"No," Fuyuko said. "It wasn't."

Astra said, "What? Are we to take it we all shared a group hallucination?"

"Well that's a break, then," Blaise said. Everyone looked at her. "Because it means we don't have to worry about our AI having been breached. It would seem her telepathy was of the old-fashioned kind, with nothing high-tech about it. Clearly she connected with our minds directly, without access to the AI or our implants, and somehow managed to read and enter our c-space in that way. In which case I no longer have to panic at the thought that they can enter our data networks at will."

S07, perched on a high stool behind Fuyuko, shook her head at Julia. "You know that's not necessarily correct, don't you, Julia? It's not likely S05 was taken from your mind at the time of the visit—unless, that is, these entities can directly access the parts of your brain you aren't at the moment using."

Julia felt chilled, as though a draft had drifted into the c-space conference room, even as most of the team were celebrating their joy at Blaise's deduction. Fuyuko, though, kept darting looks at Julia (even though she had to know Julia's face would show nothing she did not wish it to).

"What I don't get," Astra said, introducing a fresh note of uncertainty, "is why our visitations have been hallucinatory, while the AI recorded the physical presence of La Femmeans when they visited the *Pax I*."

"Maybe they visit only after Contact has been established," Kristen said. "After all, didn't Solita just say that she experienced the same hallucinatory singing when she was in the shuttle?"

"And it could have to do with physical proximity," Astra said. "Solita's shuttle was pretty far out. And we haven't entered orbit around the planet yet."

"Contact with the La Femmeans is the exciting part of our mission," Julia said. "But I think we should also be thinking of the crew of *Pax I*, and review our plans anent them."

"Which is my cue," said Candace. "I have my boarding party all set. Most of them are sleeping at the moment. I want them fresh and ready to go for however long it will take us. The plan is to secure *Pax I*, continue trying to get a fix on Paul and the other lost crew, and send the deep-sleepers back over here so that we can evaluate their condition and treat them. And as far as Paul and the others go, if we get any new clue to their whereabouts on the surface, we'll send a team down to investigate."

"I would like to stress," Julia said, "that you notify the Contact team if you or anyone on your team receives a visitation, whether hallucinatory or corporeal."

"Should we really be calling it *hallucinatory*?" Astra queried. "Since it is, actually, real, in the way that v-space events are real, even if they are, in a sense, imagined. I mean, we don't call it *imaginary space*, do we?"

"Well that would be confusing it with the mathematical sense of imaginary," Fuyuko said. "But what you really mean is that it's a consensually real experience, and not psychically invented out of whole cloth. And at least as far as we know, it's generated outside of our own thought processes, by an other. We could, I suppose, call it *ideal*, or *out of body*, or even *psychic* if you prefer."

"Obviously we should call it *something*," Astra said. "Maybe *psychic* would work. What does everybody else think?"

"What about just *noncorporeal contact*?" Julia suggested. "That would seem to take the pejorative tone out of the reference, which is, I believe, what Astra is concerned to do."

The meeting dragged on, with everyone snappish and testy and eager to be "getting on with it" and Julia cold and anxious about the information she continued to withhold from her crew and had yet to discuss with S05 itself. But she still hadn't come to a decision one way or another. The web seemed so delicate...

30.

ENTERING THE BRIDGE half an hour before their estimated time for orbital insertion, Julia found the entire conscious crew assembled, as though for a party, chattering and laughing. The sight astonished and bemused her. They all, she realized, felt that orbital insertion was the symbolic moment of "arrival." And so they had gathered to observe it together before the ship's largest viewscreen. Julia's eyes misted. They did have a community, they did together make a web. Excepting Fuyuko and the word processors, every crew member understood this moment as the reason for their coming. Quickly she addressed the AI through her implant and ordered it to have a bot bring her the small cache of token mini champagne bottles holding three swallows each of the pale fizzy beverage

Blaise came to Julia and said, "Do you think we should clear the bridge of all but the executive crew and the primary action teams?"

Julia said, "But this gathering is wonderful, don't you think? We're exactly as we should be." Julia noted again that Blaise's meat-face, like those of most of the crew around them, bore only a slight resemblance to its primary representation in v-space. All the irregularities in the features of her face, their many and varied expressions and fleeting and shifting presence, were unfamiliar to Julia. Blaise's voice in the flesh was about half an octave higher and oddly nasal. Only her physical movements, gestures, and posture marked her as recognizably *Blaise*.

Julia added, "Of course, the downside of so much excitement is that we don't know that anything in particular will happen when we match orbit with *Pax I*. And so there may be a bit of disappointment." They had been in communication with *Pax I*'s AI since they'd taken Solita on board, and the La Femmeans had already contacted them twice. They had no reason to believe Paul would necessarily show himself on their official "arrival." She looked steadily into Blaise's eyes. "But it is an important rite of passage. One which we have every reason to believe will lead to a new phase of the mission." As though, Julia thought wryly, one could structure events through timely planning.

"Oooh," the crowd cooed and cried. Julia looked at the main viewscreen, which she had forgotten to watch. As before, La Femme filled most of the screen, a beautifully shaped orb shimmering with blue light, but a moon—a small mauve and purple hemisphere of light—had appeared, as though emerging from behind the deep blue sphere.

A bot popped up through the floor beside her, presenting her with a net bag full of tiny green squeeze bottles.

Candace touched Julia's arm. "I'm going to get my boarding party into the shuttle now, so that we'll be ready when the AI gives us Go."

Julia put her arm around Candace's shoulder. "Whatever you do, keep in close communication. Let us know the instant you make contact with any *Pax I* crew or get either a physical or noncorporeal visit from the indigenes."

Candace nodded patiently. They'd been through the protocol half a dozen times already. "And just remember *my* point," she whispered in Julia's ear. "Wake Vance if things get *rough*."

Right. Julia could only imagine waking Vance if things were well enough developed that even doing her worst she couldn't wreck them.

Julia reminded them that with orbital insertion imminent, everyone needed to prepare themselves and the cabin for null-gee. Then someone thought to request the AI to make a countdown for exact synchronization of orbit with *Pax I*, and when it reached the last half-minute everyone started counting backwards aloud, raising the decibel level with each digit. "Prepare for null-gravity in ten seconds," the AI said. Then: "Eight! Seven! Six! Five! Four!

Three! Two! One! WE HAVE ACHIEVED ORBITAL INSERTION AND MATCH!"

Everyone cheered, hugged, and gestured madly at the viewscreen—and then grabbed for hold-bars as the drive ceased deceleration, plunging them into zero-gee. And in that moment, immersed in the electric thrill fizzing all around her, Julia longed to have Arethustra here, experiencing the promise of this threshold—and then realized that what Arethustra would have loved best was not the thrill of this collective moment but the "singing" performed by Nadia, Solita, and the four La Femmean creatures visible on the bridge's viewscreen. Smiling, she returned hug for hug and passed out the elegant squeeze bottles of champagne, which some of the crew held up and touched to their neighbor's before putting them to their lips and twisting the lids to allow the stuff to squirt onto their tongues. Fuyuko, watching the others with a detached, clinical eye, declined even that small token of celebration when Julia offered it to her, and the business of managing all of them through this phase again claimed Julia's consciousness and separated her from the group's ecstatic emotion. She thought how strangely abstract this threshold was, entering this new phase of their mission, with the view on the screen not discernibly different from what it had been ten minutes earlier, while their relation to both the planet and *Pax I* had in fact altered substantially.

The next step, of course, had to be taken, even if they had already made Contact (though some people might not consider it as such, given its elusive, *noncorporeal* nature) with the La Femmeans. Julia raised her arm to request silence, but before she had gotten it all the way up the crew spontaneously hushed and focused on her. *They're waiting to hear me do the honors, as part of the ritual of "arrival."*

"AI," Julia said, "broadcast at all frequencies the standard introductory message."

"The message is being broadcast," the AI said.

It was so odd, Julia thought, the way they all stood there in unpremeditated, consensual silence, as though waiting for a first response. She waited, too, wondering if the La Femmeans would choose now to make formal, meat contact with them.

Clumsily, Fuyuko bumped into Julia's side. "You haven't said how long we're to wait before taking a shuttle down to the surface to begin looking for Paul."

<<We welcome you to La Femme>> an eerily familiar but unplaceable voice said inside Julia's head. Fuyuko's face froze into a grimace of horror, and Julia knew that she was not the sole recipient of the message. <<And request your permission to send a delegation to your ship, to greet you.>>

The crew waited in profound silence, each one's gaze moving between the viewscreen and Julia. *It's happening. It's actually happening. We'll finally get to see* them *and not their chosen projections.*

"We would be pleased to receive your delegation," Julia said aloud, unsure whether she should have the AI broadcast it. "But before you come aboard, we must arrange to take precautions against either species infecting the other with microbial life innocuous to one but inimical to the other."

<<Precautions are not necessary, since our two species are unable to exchange biological materials. Your microbes will find no sources of nourishment in our biosphere, and vice versa. Still, we are prepared to adopt the precautions you specify, to allay your concerns.>>

Paul had reported their saying the same thing during the first Contact, and the Council's biologists had said that such a thing was theoretically possible (though not to be wished for, since it would mean the planet would not readily accommodate humans except in the short term). Paul, without knowing whether it was true or not, had apparently taken their word for it, for he had invited them directly onto the bridge.

Julia described the need for a sampling of their hair and skin and the quarantined hold that had been specially constructed for face-to-face encounter, and suggested the visitors dock their shuttle in the bay attached.

<<We will be transporting ourselves psychokinetically. Please visualize your ship schematically, Julia, with the hold marked, and we will transport ourselves there at once.>>

Julia's breath caught in her throat. Then it was true? But of course, the Delta Pavonians did that, too, in the City of Word Processing... Julia closed her eyes and requested the AI to send her the appropriate schematic. She waited, but felt nothing, no special awareness of it being taken from her mind, no slightest trace, even, of frisson. But then she hadn't felt anything earlier. *They could have been in my mind the entire time since we emerged from transudation, and I'd never have any way of knowing it.* A thread of panic snaked through her, but Julia reflexively suppressed it with one of the biofeedback techniques in her diplo toolkit and concentrated on the prescribed tasks of the moment.

"AI," Julia said aloud, "take hair and skin samples and make a breath analysis of whoever materializes in the quarantined hold. And then determine whether the microbes they carry with them can harm us."

"Paul and the others weren't harmed," Astra said.

Fuyuko grabbed Julia's arm. "If they can materialize in the quarantined hold, they can materialize anywhere on the ship," she said. "Julia, this situation is dangerous!"

Astra replied hotly, and the perpetual argument flared. Julia listened passively as she waited. She couldn't take her eyes off the huge blue globe so large and luminous on the main viewscreen.

"Verification that the visitors' cellular structure and molecular components match those recorded on *Pax I*," the AI said after perhaps ten or so minutes. "And that they carry no identifiable microorganisms on their skin or hair."

"AI, put the quarantined hold on the main viewscreen," Astra said.

Julia felt a light touch of anxiety stroke her thighs and calves. Turning her back on whatever the screen might show, ignoring Fuyuko, she surveyed the rest of the crew and said (over the oohing and ahing of whatever was showing on the bridge's main viewscreen), "Will the contact team please join me in the quarantined hold?"

A sigh of complaint rippled over the crew. "The *Pax I*," someone said, "had them right on the bridge."

"And that crew hasn't been heard of since," Fuyuko said angrily. Her eyes were fixed on the screen behind Julia. "Considering how rashly we are behaving, the least we can do is confine the risk to a discrete number of the crew."

Solita and Nadia were already positioned at the hatch, and Melina and Kristen nearby. Grimly silent, Fuyuko inched her way along the hold-bar; Julia followed closely behind. She was so excited and still so unused to meat-space that she was afraid she might wet her pants. Almost, she turned at the hatch to snatch a quick first look at the visitors, but her initial impulse, to reserve her first impression to in-the-flesh meeting, prevailed.

31.

"SHOW ME AGAIN, what a 'hard smile' is," Julia would request of the AI projecting a virtual holographic duplicate of her basic primary, and the image's face creased with a tight-lipped smile that failed to reach the cold, opal eyes. "And now show me a 'thoughtful frown,'" she would say, and the image's face became serious, its brows pulled down toward one another. Again and again she ran through the lexicon of her primary's facial expressions, trying first to see what they looked like and to learn their correspondence with the terms used to describe them and then to decide whether to keep, eliminate, or modify them. She knew some diplos preferred as mask-like a face as possible for their primaries, on the assumption that any degree of spontaneity would handicap them. But early in her training Julia had formed an emphatic preference for flexibility and expressivity. According to received wisdom, in v-space the strategies, tactics, and even words used by diplos exercised a far greater influence than interpersonal rapport, v-space being—as it was always said—v-space, and human beings in v-space being rational creatures not susceptible to hormonal, pheromonal, olfactory, and other such meat stimuli. Julia, having been raised a eutopian, believed otherwise. And always, when she heard talk of the loss of influence of sensual stimuli over human behavior, she wondered why visual and pharmaceutical stimuli continued to play such an important—and point-heavy—role in v-space.

How one represented oneself, Julia's tertiary tutor in The Basic Principles of Diplomacy continually stressed, was the foundation of one's competence and the starting point of all strategies one would ever consciously deploy. And though one might not think so, the principal recipients of one's self-representation were one's colleagues. The subordinates one managed were secondary. Impressing outside contacts was also of lesser importance. No, the toughest nuts to crack would be one's colleagues. And one's success would always and ever depend upon what *they* thought of one.

Austerity, experience, authority, and elusive urbanity were the qualities that constituted the successful diplo self-representation. On learning this dictum, Julia thought at once of her grandparent Davis, who in her v-space primary seemed to embody all of them. No, no, the tutor said. You must not copy anyone else. And you shouldn't stray too far from a representation of your real age, or you'll put others so much on guard that any advantage you might gain would be lost in the backlash. Julia then requested examples of successful junior diplo primaries. The tutor complied, projecting virtual holograms of the Pax's rising stars. "Perhaps I should adopt a male-sexed primary," she said when she saw that four out of five of the "stars" were male. No, no, the tutor said. If you want to adopt the sex opposite to your current meat-self, then you must change your meat-self to match; otherwise you'll appear to be dissatisfied and maladapted. It will be assumed you have a problem that could at any moment surface to interfere with your professional affairs. Once you've begun your career, you may change your primary's hair color. Change your primary's eye color. Change your primary's body weight and height. But if you want to be successful, do not change your primary's gender, for you'll be stuck at a desk for the rest of your career if you do. The tutor then asked her whether she felt right about her current gender and said that if she didn't, she needed to take care of it before much longer. Julia assured the tutor she felt good about her gender.

So Julia programmed her primary with a fairly large lexicon of facial expressions and physical gestures and chose a tall, gynandrous figure and a voice capable of speaking in several registers and a variety of timbres. (Only later did she come to recognize the marked similarities between her personally designed diplo primary and Raye's.) Her genetically engineered eyes, which resembled light-emitting opals, she retained, arguing to the tutor that they would naturally disconcert any opponent and therefore prove her most powerful and distinctive feature. No one, once having made her acquaintance in either meat- or v-space, she noted, would ever forget her.

And then she practiced, with a virtual holographic projection as an exact duplication, the primary's new repertoire until she had acquired a largely unconscious ability to manipulate, moment by moment, her self-presentation in v-space. This achievement represented, of course, the principal mastery Paxan diplos had over non-diplos.

But Julia didn't learn that until later.

32.

THEY ARGUED FOR about five minutes over whether to wear vacuum suits into the quarantined hold. Fuyuko insisted they go
through the "standard" procedures, including cycling through the
airlock and decontamination on re-entering the ship's atmosphere.

"It's been an Earth year since *Pax I* was exposed to the indigenes," Julia said. "And according to its AI, nothing terrible has
developed since."

"Then what's the point of even having them in the quarantined hold, if you're not going to follow procedure?" Fuyuko said.

"If you'll recall," Melina said, "the AI on *Pax I* found no microorganisms identifiable as such on the visitors. Just as our AI has
done with these visitors. In other words, they are somehow sterile,
or their microorganisms are outside the parameters by which we
define and detect them."

"Yes, yes," Fuyuko said impatiently. "We've all read the astro-
biology report commissioned by the Council. Which resolved nothing. It's a question of exercising reasonable caution."

Julia thought the entire issue pointless, since if La Femmean
microorganisms were undetectable there could be no way to be certain decontamination would catch them anyway. But she chose to
yield to Fuyuko on this one for strategic reasons. It would make the
meeting clumsy, but it would also show the crew that Julia would
take direction from Fuyuko when it was reasonable to do so.

So the six of them suited up and stood in the airlock while
the ship's common air was evacuated and replaced with air from
the quarantined hold. Chafing at the bulkiness of the suit, which
exacerbated her clumsiness in zero gravity, Julia fixed her eyes on
the light panel, which allowed her to track the airlock's cycle (and
avoid looking at her suited colleagues). *What will they make of*

us in suits? Maybe it's a good thing they're telepathic. Presumably they'll understand the suits as purely defensive... Though.... At the very least it will suggest less trust than Paul showed... And maybe that's not all bad...

Finally, after what seemed hours, the airlock's hatch into the hold dilated. Julia's heart raced. She told herself that the suit's supply of oxygen would be exhausted in no time if she didn't calm down. The others looked at her. "Maybe you should go first, Julia" Fuyuko said over her suit's speaker. "Since you are the diplo here."

Trembling with excitement—Julia noted the trembling with wonder—she pulled herself through the hatch, grabbed the nearby hold-bar and made a quick pan of the space, first horizontally, then vertically, so that she would know how to orient herself before entering. But the visitors were "standing" to the left, oriented exactly as she was, as though they were in a room with a good solid pull of gravity holding them firmly to the floor. She had expected to see four (an expectation she couldn't explain); but enough of them "stood" waiting that she had to count them to know there were eight. One of them advanced toward the hold-bar and held out both hands. <<I'm so pleased to be meeting you at last>> a voice said in her head. Julia focused on this individual, who now held out her hands—and gasped. *Davis! How can it be?* But it was so—except for the milk-breasts, which, beyond weird, kept attracting her gaze with a forbidden grotesque affect that simultaneously repelled her gaze.

<<I am Esée>> the voice said in Julia's head. <<I remind you of someone, don't I.>>

One hand clinging to the hold-bar, Julia bowed clumsily. *In appearance, yes.*

Julia's arms and knees shook; mixed with her excitement was now something else, something anxious and fearful. She wanted to stop herself from thinking, for she knew the other must in some way grasp her thoughts. But for all the techniques of doing so at her disposal, somehow she couldn't, perhaps because the need to think in the moment felt so urgent. Thoughts of Davis, and of how Lacuna had resembled S05, and speculation about *how* this entity had retrieved Davis, whether through S04's adoption of it, or from Julia's organic memory or from the tertiary of Davis she had stored in her personal program, flooded Julia's mind. It occurred to her that perhaps the entity couldn't read such a cacophonous confusion of thoughts but only discrete words subvocalized as for AI input. She clung to this idea as tightly as her gloved hand clutched the hold-bar.

<<Your mates call you Julia?>>

"Yes," Julia said aloud, weirdly hearing her voice through her helmet's speaker as well as inside her helmet. She remembered the team behind her and glanced over her shoulder. They had lined up just inside the hatch, along the hold-bar, five bulky suits all in a row, swaying gently. She gestured them forward, then looked back at Esée.

<<It's customary to touch hands on meeting either a stranger or acquaintance, isn't that so?>> Esée said.

Julia hesitated, then with a pulse of conscious will let go of the hold-bar and extended both thickly gloved hands, aware that she was moving, trying to use her legs for stability. "What is *your* protocol?" she said, focusing on holding eye-contact with the Davis look-alike.

<<You're disturbed and upset, Julia, isn't that so? Is it because of my appearance? Or is it that you are afraid we might harm you? But you are men, aren't you?>>

"Men?" Julia repeated, puzzled.

<<The others who've come to us call themselves *men*. Or *man*. You are a part of them, are you not? You are *man*?>>

Julia struggled against the creeping hysteria that made her want to giggle. "Yes, we are of the species called *man*," she said. "And so yes, in that sense, we are *men*."

Davis's—or rather Esée's—gaze moved over Julia's face with a frowning concentration that reminded Julia of an expression that would sometimes come over Glenning's face while teaching her. <<You are increasingly stressed. But unnecessarily. The other men here have not been harmed by us. On the contrary. They are happy with all we give them. Which we would like to give you, too.>>

Something in this speech bothered—even nettled—Julia. Suddenly she noticed the other entities accompanying Davis—no, *Esée!*—drawing closer and coming out of a sort of blur into focus. Julia wondered about it, for they had moved only slightly closer, which meant that the distance at which they had been couldn't have made that much difference to the focus of her eyes. *But I'm used to everything being in perfect focus in v-space, no matter one's position, since what one "sees" doesn't have to be processed through the lens of the eye. Which must affect my meat-space perception.*

Julia glanced over her shoulder, to check on her teammates, and found them immediately behind her, fanned out in a floating, ragged planar semicircle, with only Fuyuko anchored to the hold-bar. Their face plates reflected a strong glare back at her. She wondered just how much of their faces the La Femmeans could see.

Julia kicked awkwardly to join the team's line and steadied herself by grabbing hold of Nadia's sleeve. "Esée," Julia said, "please allow me to introduce my colleagues: Fuyuko, Kristen, Melina, Solita, and Nadia."

Esée bowed as Julia had earlier. <<And this is Orfea, Ursula, Monique, Ingrid, Paz, and Eurydice.>>

Julia shivered. Could these really be the names by which they called one another? Or were they picked, out of some abstruse knowledge about humans they somehow already possessed, to please (or disturb) the Paxans? She looked at her teammates. It frustrated her, not being able to see their faces clearly. "Did you-all hear what she said? And hear what she said to me earlier?"

"Introductions, nothing else," Kristen said.

"Same here," Nadia and Solita said almost in unison.

"Me too," Melina said.

"And I," Fuyuko said.

They all were using the speakers in their helmets, of course, which had the alienating effect of making their voices as mediated as the suits made the movement and appearance of their bodies— though not quite as mediated as the La Femmeans' adoption of human bodies.

Julia stared at the La Femmeans and tried to memorize each proper name with its face and figure, slowly moving her eyes from one to another, noting that they *all* had milk-breasts, reminding her of Outsiders. When she came to Ursula, a pain spasmed in her chest, as though a great powerful fist were squeezing her heart. *Ursula looked exactly like Antoinette!* Not like the tertiary she had of Antoinette in her personal program, but like Antoinette, the meat-person. Only...only there was something not right about her, something that eluded Julia. Ursula smiled warmly at her, meeting her eyes as though the face plate were no impediment, and Julia was flooded with a powerful surge of emotion, a warmth and sense of approval that felt like *love*.

Tears welled in her eyes. Her throat was too choked to speak. She barely heard Kristen say, "Leigh? Can it really—no, that can't be *you*, Leigh!" But the words penetrated and broke the moment. Julia shifted to look at Kristen. "What is it?" Julia said sharply. "Does one of our visitors remind you of someone you know?"

"No!" Fuyuko said, and even over her suit-speaker sounded as though she were strangling. "It can't be. Grace is dead. But this is all wrong!" Fuyuko grabbed Kristen, to pull her back toward the hatch. "These creatures are impostors, pretending to be like humans. But all they've done is copy our memories, to trick and manipulate us!"

<<You are different in some way from the others.>> Julia wondered if it was Esée who was speaking. <<Yes, it is Esée who speaks. The others were all pleased when we came to them. We know, of course, that individual men differ from one another in many respects. That became clear after we saw that they were different from what we had expected.>>

"You *expected* the *Pax I* to come here?" Fuyuko said. And Julia realized Esée must now be "speaking" in all their minds.

Davis—no, Esée—smiled serenely. <<Yes. We did. We have known of you for a long time.>>

"And where is Paul now?" Julia asked, putting that startling revelation aside for the moment.

Esée inclined her head. <<Paul is in the city called Despina.>>

"We would like to send a team down to the surface, to speak to Paul in person," Julia said. "They would, of course, wear vacuum suits and thus should presumably not affect your ecology. Can we arrange that now?"

<<Men don't need special clothing or gear to visit La Femme.>> Esée looked amused. <<La Femme can take care of itself. And anything needed will be provided.>>

"Why does she keep calling us *men*?" Fuyuko said.

"But we *are* men," Julia said, unperturbed.

<<Will you explain to me, Julia, why Fuyuko is troubled? Is *men* not correct?>>

Fuyuko is just plain upset. The subvocalization flowed from her mind before she could stop it. Julia glanced from Esée to Fuyuko and felt squirmily uncomfortable. She had concealed—from a teammate—her words to a La Femmean. Surely she should not have done that. Only…

Nadia surged "up" and sideways, almost jerking Julia into a somersault. A long greeting—in Delta Pavonian singing, Julia recognized that much—poured out through her speaker. Another greeting overlapped hers, coming from Solita. Julia looked up. Both Nadia and Solita were sailing slowly around the group of La Femmeans, singing all the while, their arms and hands graceful, notwithstanding the bulkiness of their suits and the clumsy thick gloves and boots encasing their extremities.

"Stop it!" Fuyuko shouted. "*Julia!* Make them *stop*!"

Julia would have liked to grab hold of Fuyuko and send her flying through the hatch. She looked up again at the word processors—

and did a double-take. *There were two of the creatures who had danced outside the ship, "up" there, soaring in circles around the word processors, laying down shimmering purple trails that quickly evaporated in blue, iridescent evanescence.*

Julia watched in fascination—until a hard jerk on her shoulder broke the spell. "Julia, we need to talk outside." Even through the faceplate—which reflected her own faceplate back to her—Julia could see the twitch pulling at Fuyuko's eye. "There's too much going on here," Fuyuko said, "and all at once. We really have to *talk*."

"Yes, Julia, I think Fuyuko is right," Melina said. "The La Femmeans needn't leave. But now that we've had introductions, it might be a good idea to take a break and collect our thoughts."

Julia's gaze sought Esée's. The La Femmean bowed gracefully. <<We are at your disposal and will be happy to see you whenever and as you like.>>

Julia felt too unsure of herself, too lacking in control to object to the decision, though the idea of giving up this fascinating scene for another tedious meeting tugged at her. Allowing herself a quick snatch of a glance at Nadia, Solita, and the creatures who sang with them, Julia said, "But we will let Nadia and Solita stay on. They're used to alien Contact."

"Shit, Julia," Fuyuko said. "That's not the point!"

"No, Julia's right," Melina said. "It's really we who need to think it all through, not the word processors. Their approach is different from ours."

"That may be," Fuyuko said. "But they're our only means of returning home."

"Did you have to put that into words?" Kristen said.

Julia got herself back to the hold-bar. "We'll be back shortly, Esée. If there's anything you need, let me know, and I'll provide it for you. Though I suppose if your microorganisms are different, then your food source must be, too, in which case we may not be able to supply it. Or else you may just want to leave..."

<<Don't even consider our needs. We will dematerialize when you have all left this hold. And then will rematerialize when you are ready to see us again.>>

By the time Julia got through the airlock and out of the suit, she was too exhausted to remember even a fraction of the many questions and observations that had bombarded her during the Contact. She felt as though she had been up and about in meat-space for a full twenty-four hours.

Though shivering with excitement, she wanted her caretaker.

33.

JULIA CALLED A crew conference to begin twenty minutes hence, got into her caretaker, and took a few minutes to meet with S04 and S07 before the meeting. S07, she noted at once, had dressed in a male get-up from pre-Paxan times.

"What do you think is going on?" Julia asked her secondaries. "Why do they represent themselves in the forms of people familiar to us? And why don't they let us see them as they really are?"

S07 shrugged. "Why do you and your crew represent yourselves as you do? No doubt the answer isn't simple."

"But they *can't* look as human as they do."

"Maybe their attitude toward representation is more flexible and complex than ours," S04 said. "Consider how conservatively Paxans represent themselves in v-space primaries. Suppose they were more...creative. Playful. Imaginative. And suppose meat-space is to them what v-space is to us."

"You mean—that they're *not meat?*"

S07 shrugged again. "Could be they're not, Julia. No law of the universe says that sentient entities have to be made of carbon-based molecules with the same kind of organic organization we tend to associate with life."

"No wonder Fuyuko is scared," Julia said.

"You weren't scared while you were in the hold with them," S04 said.

"No. I was...*thrilled.* One of them, Ursula, made me feel..." Julia stopped. She didn't want to talk with anyone about what she had felt in that moment, not even her secondaries. There was something too...*private* about it, too close to the bone. It bothered her to think that the La Femmeans must know what—and how intensely—she had felt.

"I'm too excited," Julia said. "I can't seem to organize my thoughts for the crew conference. And I have a feeling it's going to be chaotic—especially if the other members of the Contact team all had experiences like mine."

"I suggest you review the points of mission as the Council gave them to you," S04 said. "Which are, in order of importance, to find Paul and the other Paxans; take action if necessary for their defense and safety; and establish relations with the indigenes—with their principal governments, if possible. The subpoints of which are (a) define and investigate the governmental structures operant on the planet and the political context likely to impact on our contact with the indigenes; and (b) uncover and begin analysis of the planet's operant economic systems, with a view to future trade interests."

Julia stuck her tongue out at S04. "Yes, yes, I know what the agenda is. But that doesn't mean it defines *my* priorities. As you very well know, S04."

"Apart from the point of recovering Paul and his crew, I don't see how the mission points differ significantly from your personal agenda, Julia."

Julia threw up her hands. "I'm intrigued by the mystery of them and the mystery of what they've done with Paul. I want to understand the questions the *Pax I* reports have provoked about Paxan notions of gender. And I don't want our relations with La Femme to resemble our relations with the Delta Pavonians—with whom we effectively don't *have* relations."

"I don't think the word processors would agree that they have no relations with the Delta Pavonians," S04 said.

"I mean," Julia said, "that the *Pax* has no meaningful relations with them. And the word processors only *limited* relations. Because there's no *real* exchange between our species, only the word processors' listening to and imitating the Delta Pavonians and translating the traders' attempts to negotiate business with them. Which mainly consists of the Delta Pavonians visiting the City of Word Processing and taking objects of art and culture back to Delta Pavonis and giving us great gifts of technology in return, like this ship, which can take us vast distances through transudational shifts, apparently equipped with an endless energy supply."

S07 perched on the edge of Julia's desk. "What more, exactly, is it that you expect?"

"Visiting back and forth!" Julia said. "Interpersonal contact! An attempt by them to communicate with the entire population! "

"Be glad the Delta Pavonians don't deal with non-Paxans," S04 said drily. "Or should I say, that they haven't decided that dealing with non-Paxans is the next step, once they've acquired everything from us that they want. Because the planet would be in real trouble if they did."

Julia seldom felt as frustrated with her secondaries as she did this moment. "Look. We've discussed this before. Why pretend you don't know what I'm seeking?"

"Pretend?" S07 said. "Come off it, Julia. You don't know yourself. If you did, we'd know, too. And we don't. Only that you want more than what the Pax got from the Delta Pavonians. More contact. More answers. More...*intimacy* perhaps? More *reciprocation*."

"You see? You do know what I want," Julia, goaded, said.

"Less difference," S04 said. "I think that's what Julia wants. She wants the La Femmeans to be alien, but similar enough to humans to make the alien...comprehensible. Am I right?"

They were spoiling it. Her secondaries were spoiling her excitement, her triumph, her good feelings. For what reason? They were splits off herself. Certainly they knew more about her than any living being did.

Julia said, "Conference time, my friends. And don't forget to screen yourselves from the others' perceptions."

"That goes without saying, Julia," S07 said gently.

Julia didn't answer. It seemed to her that nothing went without saying, anywhere, with anybody, even one's own secondaries. And that maybe that was what was wrong with human beings, always having to spell everything out to the nth degree because people just didn't get it unless you beat them over the head with it, and even then they might miss the point, because that was how people were—imperfect communicators in an ever more complex world.

You didn't need to be a eutopian to know *that*.

34.

SHORTLY BEFORE JULIA began making v-space contact with others her own age, her parents—each of them, separately—discussed social sexual recreation with her as a series of choices it would be her role to make. She had already learned "the basics," they said, by doing the pubertal exercises Glenning had designed for her. For one year she would have v-space contact with family-raised people of her own age. And then she would have another year of meeting them in meat-space as well. And then she would go to University.

Antoinette told her that most people pursued social sexual recreation intentionally, rather than engaging in it by spontaneous chance, and that they did that by going to places known to be frequented by people interested in pursuing it. One could at least in theory enjoy sexual recreation with one's coworkers, for instance, and therefore not rely on intentional spaces, but in practice people preferred not to complicate their working relationships in that way. The question must always be raised whether it would be possible to manage "attraction, conflict, empathy, and responsibility" in relationships crossing functional lines. The strain could be enormous. And the likelihood of failure almost inevitable.

Michel, in his talks with Julia, stressed another choice: whether one pursued sexual recreation in v-space or in meat-space. Meat-space sensual experience tended to be unpredictable, he warned her, and full of noise—odors, sounds, bodily secretions, and blemishes that some people found distracting. It also tended to make some people self-conscious about their personal presentation. But other people liked it, saying it felt "more real" to them, fuller and more immediate, and made the exchange of bodily fluids more particular, since every body and its fluids smelled and tasted different from every other. They liked the way it reminded them of the evolutionary origins of the human being. It made them feel more *alive*, he said. And, obviously, it was spiked with real, pheremonal presence. Michel told her that he was one of those people himself and said he found v-space sex too sterile to be interesting, and even lonely.

Lanna discussed a more troubling choice. (The choices Antoinette and Michel presented seemed unlikely to cause her even a second of consideration: she knew she wouldn't like meat-space sexual recreation—masturbation, she had already found, was so much more fun in v-space that she couldn't imagine wanting any kind of sexual recreation in meat-space—and Antoinette had made clear that only an idiot would look at one's friends and coworkers as potential sexual partners.) Presuming one went to a c-space in search of sexual recreation, one could either go as oneself, or incognito. Many families would not allow their children to go incognito before their coming-of-age. Being eutopians, Julia's family would allow her to decide for herself. The chief danger of incognito was that people tended to forget they were playing with real people with real feelings. Which meant that they lost track of the attraction, conflict, empathy, and responsibility template for interpersonal relations and treated their partners like secondaries or even tertiaries rather than the primaries they really were. Having been raised a eutopian, Julia—Lanna reminded her—already knew that what happened when one played games could hurt, since the best play always touched susceptible parts of one's self. But she must understand that incognito partners might not necessarily take any of that into consideration. Going incognito one could forget a great deal, because one's public name and identity were detached from the consequences. But that didn't mean that other aspects of oneself couldn't suffer painful and even lasting effects.

Julia bore Lanna's discussions in mind long after their talk. She found many of her first social encounters, sexual and otherwise, difficult and awkward. A few disagreeable experiences shattered her trust in the honesty and benign intentions of her peers. And so by the time she reached University, the idea of incognito had become irresistible. She devised a pair of primaries (one of each sex) for sexual recreation that would not give her identity away and eagerly sought out the c-spaces dedicated to social sexual recreation. Some of them were places almost identical in construction to spaces available for tourism and study, particularly parks, formal gardens, seaside resorts, and mountainsides open to the stars. One could simply wander, idly, until another wanderer caught one's fancy. And then one played, and parted, and held in memory a partner as invented as any tertiary. This Julia loved. She could be any aspect of herself she liked for an evening. She could try out experiments with self-presentation that would cost her nothing permanent. Nothing could be more charming or relaxing than exercising one's imagination thus, for the partners, being primaries, were whole persons and all there, as the secondaries and tertiaries she played with alone could never be.

When she grew more experienced, she recognized another aspect of incognito spaces, one that caused her to recall Lanna's early warning with disquiet. Many people who went to incognito spaces followed what Julia came to call sexual scripts. She realized this when she discovered herself and her partners repeating past scenes almost line for line and gesture for gesture. To confirm her suspicion, she went shielded to the incognito-spaces, to eavesdrop and spy. There were about a dozen scripts, she concluded. A dozen scripts with variations. Hardly anyone bothered to be original.

Should there be an incognito space marked "No Scripts Allowed?" At times sexual scripts were just what she wanted. But she could not help feeling that the scripts made them all into types and figures and ciphers—without, that is, meaning.

After that, Julia avoided the incognito spaces and threw herself into "real" sexual encounters, including her meat-space experience with Sasha. But aspects of these troubled her, too, and often interfered with her ability to concentrate on her work. And so around the time she drew the assignment to the bunker on the border, Julia restricted herself to private sexual recreation. It was then that she constructed S11, S12, S13, S14, and S15 for sexual purposes only. She would have liked to have discussed the matter with Raye or with certain of her parents or grandparents, but of course did not. She was an adult by then and knew that adults did not burden others with their most personal, private problems and questions.

35.

ON INSERTING HERSELF into the c-space conference room, Julia
found most of the conscious crew already assembled around an
enormous T-shaped table, talking, it seemed, all at once. She preferred polygonal tables, but she had to admit the T-shape one of
them had chosen suited the size of the gathering, and its polished
granite surface made a nice change and seemed chosen to match
the color of their uniforms. The contact team sat along the top of
the tee, and everyone else down either side of the stem. The chair
at the center of the top had been left vacant. Forbearing to grum-
ble about this, Julia took it.

The talking stopped abruptly.

"Well," she said, smiling brightly. "We have a lot to discuss. It
seems we've made Contact."

"Yes," Blaise—seated near the top of the tee—said. "Indeed. It
seems *all* of us have made Contact. Which is the reason you see all
the conscious crew but Nadia and Solita here. While the Contact
team was in the quarantined hold, each and every one of us had a
contact experience, too."

Julia looked down one side of the stem and up the other. "Is
that true?" Every head nodded. Julia looked at Blaise. "What kind
of Contact? Corporeal? Or noncorporeal? Group or one-on-one?"

"Noncorporeal," Blaise said quickly. "The AI picked up *nothing*."

Julia looked at Astra. She couldn't recall seeing a primary's eyes
shine so raptly. It was almost spooky, in the context. Julia wondered
that she'd programmed such an effect. It looked unrealistic. "Nothing?" she queried. "Not even an energy presence or fluctuation?"

Astra said, "If there was, it was too slight to signify."

"Most of us were on the bridge, watching the meeting in the
quarantined hold," Blaise said. "Suddenly they appeared on the

bridge, at the moment you were leaving the hold. One or two for each of us, speaking—if you can call it that—to us individually, inside our heads. And taking our hands. I gather, from what everyone else is saying, their experience was like mine, in that the entity that contacted me resembled, very, very strongly, someone important to me." Blaise looked at Julia. "It was a pleasant experience, Julia. It made me feel good. Astonishingly warm and…secure." She made a grimace. "I'm not being clear. The entity didn't claim to be the person she looked like. On the contrary, she called herself by another name and said she was from La Femme. But…the resemblance…" Blaise hesitated. "The resemblance still had an emotional effect on me, though I knew it was fake. As though…" She looked at Fuyuko. "Emotions are your expertise, Fuyuko. Do you know what I'm talking about? A resemblance so strong, so powerful, that it floods you with a certain feeling, maybe because you weren't expecting that person to be there, and suddenly, she was…" Blaise shook her head. "I don't really know how to talk about it. Maybe somebody else, more articulate…?"

"They're telepaths," Fuyuko said loudly. "And clearly highly gifted ones. Not only can they reach beyond the language barrier that must exist between the cultures of two very different and widely spaced worlds, but they can apparently tap our memories, simply reaching into them and pulling out whatever image they think will make us most easily manipulable." She leaned forward to look past Melina at Julia. "And they've violated our ground rules by appearing as they like on this ship, to whom they like, without permission. Plundering our memories, entering our space without leave: these are violations of privacy. And considering how much they apparently know about us, they surely must be aware that they are being offensive by doing so."

Julia looked up and down the stem. "Does everyone feel that way? As though her privacy has been contemptuously violated?"

Astra rapped her knuckles on the table. There was so little resonance that Julia barely heard the sound the rapping made.

"I didn't feel violated," she said. "Surprised, yes. And in certain ways *challenged*—but in a positive sense, as in stimulation rather than defiance. I'm no communications specialist or psyche-synthesist, but it seemed to me, at least at the time, that I was being offered an opening. That they were coming most of the way to meet me, to make it easy for me to learn about them as slowly as I might need. Do you know, I asked my contact, who called herself Artemesia, about her planet's geological history and its place in the Cygnus system. And she *at once* began to give me data—which poured into my head like a stream of music—until I asked her to stop, since I was finding it impossible to absorb at that rate. And which I then had to interrupt altogether because Fuyuko entered the bridge, saw the La Femmeans in silent conversation with crew, and demanded we all come to the conference at once."

"We've got to keep ourselves in order," Fuyuko said. "As it stands now, only one hour into Contact we have no idea what has been said by whom to whom. Only that there have been a number of highly personal contacts in psychologically risky circumstances."

"Excuse me, may I speak?" Carlton, one of the astrobiologists, said. Julia gestured them to continue. "If these indigenes aren't hierarchically organized, their not arranging permission from above prior to making individual contacts with the crew would hardly be intended aggressively. I think we must reserve judgment about their intentions. Second, I myself had no sense of psychological peril or distress. Though the indigene presented herself in the form of one of my parents, I knew the entire time that this being was different, and distinctly so. The very sight of her made me feel comfortable and warm, but she made no attempt to disguise her difference. And when I asked her why she had chosen to represent herself so, she said that the first step of communication between different beings must be an assumption of similarity. That differentiation would inevitably follow. But that it could only proceed slowly, as the relationship strengthened and allowed the presence of difference. And that her species was uniquely gifted with the ability to adapt itself to and understand other species." Carlton hugged themselves. (Unconsciously?) "I'm not putting it as clearly as she did—which may seem incredible. But for some reason, her ability to articulate these things vividly was remarkable—or at least it was as I remember it. Unfortunately, I can't recall her words verbatim, and since the AI didn't pick them up, I have no way of retrieving them mechanically."

"I'd like to make a proposal," Julia said. She looked at Blaise as she spoke. "I think we should each prepare a report on their Contact experience and then take the time to familiarize ourselves with everyone else's. This is one way to avoid the kind of splintering that I think is Fuyuko's greatest concern." She leaned forward and looked at the psyche-synthesist. "I don't think we should attempt to interdict contacts not previously approved by the executive crew. We have all been carefully chosen for this mission and are all qualified to carry out its ends. The designation of certain of us as executive officers is a matter of convenience and organization, not hierarchical privilege and superiority. The Pax, after all, prides itself on being a collegial, laterally organized meritocracy. The crucial point is that we keep one another fully informed about our experiences and that we not fail to communicate with one another while striving for communication with the indigenes. Are we agreed?"

"No!" Fuyuko said. "We are *not* agreed!" Her primary surged to its feet. "Can't you see how dangerous this is? If they can summon up any image from our minds that they choose, we are clay in their hands! Maybe this is the way the crew of *Pax I* went—each individual getting involved in their personal contacts with the aliens, breaking all discipline and forgetting the *Pax I*—not to mention the Pax itself—entirely!"

"Just what do you propose?" Astra's tone was openly hostile. "That only the designated members of the Contact team be allowed to talk to them? Making the rest of us sit around waiting for you to get around to what really interests us?"

"Astra has a point, Fuyuko," Blaise said. "And besides, just how would we enforce the interdiction?"

Astra cut off Fuyuko's attempt to respond. "Why are we talking about *force*, anyway?"

Fuyuko said quickly, before anyone else could speak, "What Carlton was saying—about one of them telling them—I mean, Carlton—their plan to let us see how they differ from us slowly, a bit at a time, should *terrify* us! We don't know *what* they are! Or what their intentions are! They say they want to communicate, but why should we believe that anymore than we can believe they're who they appear to be?"

Astra glowered at Fuyuko. Julia studied the rest of the crew's primaries for their reactions. "Either we trust them, or we leave now," she said. "I see no other choice. We've always known the mission could be dangerous. We each agreed to take the risk. Our chief security consideration is for the Pax's safety. And unless we're willing to make the leap of judgment to say there's a good chance they're going to somehow suborn us into endangering the Pax ourselves, I see no reason to be worrying about security. Comments?"

"If they're really not hierarchically organized," Melina said, "then it's unlikely they've got plans to take over the Pax. And since Paul and his surviving male crew haven't yet made a move to threaten the Pax as their surrogates, is it likely to happen through us?"

"That really is an excellent point," Blaise said.

"Then let's break up and get down to preparing our reports," Julia said.

"May I make a suggestion?" Carlton said quickly.

Julia was itching to be out of the meeting. "Go ahead."

"It would probably be a good idea for all of us to keep running logs of our contact experiences. And include ideas about them as they occur to us."

Julia nodded. "An excellent idea. And then set up a library of the logs, as we'll be doing with these initial reports. So that we can keep in good touch with one another on what we think is happening."

Julia popped into her v-space study. What we *think* is happening. Precisely. Because it's a sure thing we haven't got a clue as to what is *actually* happening.

36.

WITHOUT LEAVING V-SPACE, Julia requested a square, bare-walled room furnished with a yoga mat and recessed lighting, where she lay down on her back with her knees flexed. She needed *peace. Silence. Quiet.* That is to say, time alone, to let the images and impressions wash through her mind without the constant questioning and probing of her secondaries. The very thought of trying to explain to them what had happened—all that had been supplemental to what the AI had enabled them to "see" and "hear"—disgusted her. It would all be just talk. And while some of her secondaries (though not S04, S05, or S07) were programmed to simulate warmth and understanding, the fact remained that they were incapable of affect. She could easily imagine it, hearing herself talk and talk and talk until ready to scream.

Talk, she believed, would obscure something important. Or something she thought might be important. So many feelings had touched her during the contact that she needed space to process them. The last thing she wanted to do was *talk*.

Of course to write her report she *would* have to talk, to describe her experience of contact. But first she wanted to savor the memory of it—and decide what exactly she should and should not say. Some of what had happened was personal. And she felt strongly that her personal emotions and responses were hers to reveal or keep close as she chose. Privacy was a privilege held sacred by Paxans.

Julia spent five minutes on breathing exercises to clear the cacophony of arguments and justifications from her mind. When she felt relaxed and centered, she opened her eyes and stared up at the plain white ceiling. She thought of Ursula—who resembled Antoinette—with a burst of pleasure, then resolutely put the recollection of that moment aside. She would start with her encounter with Esée, summon up each moment of it, the words spoken (or planted) in her head, the gestures made, the thoughts and ideas they had evoked.

She began with the shock of recognition—false recognition. Before anything else, she had noticed that Esée looked like Davis with milk-breasts. Or no. Not like Davis, but like Davis's primary—an important distinction. Or, which was more likely, had Esée resembled the tertiary of Davis Julia had stored in her personal program, as Lacuna had resembled S05?

Julia tried to remember exactly what words had been spoken in the encounter. Esée, she was sure, had named herself first. And then had asked—yes—she had asked if she was called Julia. *She already knew. She was just prompting me to confirm for the sake of making our introductions formal.*

"I wish I could recall every thought I had during the encounter," Julia said aloud. As far as the La Femmeans were concerned, the humans' *thoughts* were a part of the encounter, too. A vivid image of Davis overpowered her mind's eye—an image she supposed she had probably taken from her memory of the tertiary of Davis, that wouldn't necessarily be *identical* to Esée. *If S07 were here it would make me call up Davis's tertiary, for comparative purposes...*

The introductory moment had lasted for most of their conversation. Hadn't Esée prompted her to release the hold-bar and clasp hands? And then...then there had been a reference to Paul and his crew. Yes. Something about how they were happy with the La Femmeans. Yes. *Happy*. Julia distinctly recalled that word. She sat up in frustration. If only one could tape the words the indigenes implanted in human minds. She wasn't used to having to rely so heavily on memory. Ordinary human memory, the kind that lodged in the cells of the brain, tended to be faulty. She knew it often tripped you up. What was it, *exactly*, that Esée had said? She wanted—no, she *needed*—the verbatim words. There had been the suggestion that the La Femmeans were somehow taking care of the remaining *Pax I* crew. That they had personally undertaken to make them "happy."

Happy. What does that mean, *happy*?

<<Julia, Astra wishes to communicate with you. She is on the bridge and says she has received a transmission from *Pax I* that you will want to know about at once.>>

If Astra were on the bridge, she wouldn't want to toggle into v-space. "AI: patch Astra's words through my implant, and my words through hers."

<<Julia, I think you'd better take a look at the…report Candace just sent us. She didn't send it real-time, so I couldn't try to reason with her. Actually, it's not just Candace talking in the file, but everyone on her team. I mean, it's not just an aberration in Candace, but something going on with all of them.>>

"Can you speak a little more plainly, Astra? I can't make sense of what *you're* saying," Julia said.

<<I think you'd better look at the file recording for yourself. If I had to put what I think has happened in so many words, I guess I'd say that it seems Candace and her team have…well. I don't know how to describe it. But I think we may have a problem.>>

Julia bit her lip. "All right. Let me watch the file and then get back to you." Julia asked the AI to confirm the transmission and then play it back for her.

A large viewscreen appeared on the wall facing Julia. It showed Candace standing in the foreground, with Shaelle, Celeste, Felix, Paris, and Tree in a semicircle a couple of paces behind. "*Pax III*, we're speaking from the bridge of the *Pax I*. We've checked out the ship and found it to be in good order. The comatose crew members are in caretakers, as Solita reported earlier. We suggest either that they be transferred to *Pax III*, or that Fuyuko come and tend to them here. We would also like to report that the indigenes have made direct contact with us on this ship. We of course asked them to take us to Paul and the rest of the crew."

Candace's highly eccentric meat-space face slid into a strange-ly...*goofy* expression. Her eyebrows worked up and down for a few seconds, as though in response to something that was being said to her. "Yes," she said, resuming. "We requested to be taken to the *Pax I* crew currently on the surface. The indigenes have offered to take us down to the surface. But they say that Paul and the others do not want to see us. And so although they are willing to *show* us all *Pax I* crew on the surface and reveal their location to us, they say they can't let us *disturb* them, which is what they say our presence would do." Candace smiled broadly. "And so I'm pleased to report that we'll be looking in on Paul, and then, since we'll already be on the surface, touring the planet, with a view, of course, toward fulfilling the mission's mandate." Candace turned to the crew ranged behind her. "Anyone else want to say anything?"

Felix stepped forward. She, too, was beaming. "I'd like to confirm all that Candace just said. And to say that although it sounds frightening, the telepathy isn't at all threatening. Basically, these people are really very much like us. Only...nicer."

Candace nodded. "I'm inclined to agree with that assessment, although it is, of course, early days. But they've been remarkably forthcoming and easy. And the fact that they care so much for respecting Paul's privacy—well, if it's true that Paul doesn't want to see us, it's more likely to be a problem of his creation, than theirs."

"AI: stop the recording, and play back the last ten seconds."

Julia listened, then let the play-back continue to its end. "We will keep in touch, *Pax III*," Candace said. "And will let you know our location as we go, and Paul's location if and when we get it. Candace and team, out."

Julia had followed S07's advice to allow Candace to pick her own team. The idea had been that Candace would draw off all those awake who were most likely to tilt toward Vance's position. And in fact, she had. So how could the lot of them suddenly be so trusting of the La Femmeans?

<<Julia, Fuyuko wishes to discuss the urgent need to take measures to protect the rest of the crew from telepathic subversion.>>

Julia would have liked to discuss the question of what had happened to Candace and her team with S04 and S07. What was it that the indigenes had said to Candace's team? And what form had the indigenes taken to ease their communication (as Julia thought Esée would be likely to describe it)? Instead, she had to deal, once again, with Fuyuko's paranoia.

Julia toggled out.

37.

CREATING SEXUALLY GRATIFYING secondaries proved a long, frustrating, and only occasionally amusing process. Julia at first used the standard tertiaries available for points, but they soon bored her, and so these she modified incrementally. She gave all the male tertiaries, for instance, Sasha's voice, and all the females and intersexes Raye's; she gave one of the females and one of the males milk breasts, after the physical style of the female Outsiders she met in border stations. She programmed all of the tertiaries in mannerisms of persons known to her in social and work life whom she found attractive. And she alternated between her female and male primaries, for variety in experience. But the tertiaries remained too much like dolls. Tertiaries were, simply, *thin.*

In the meantime, her work developing more useful and satisfactory secondaries showed promise. Though there had always been things she hadn't liked about the secondaries her parents had given her, she had never thought them *thin.* Stubborn, willful, infuriating, perhaps, but never cardboard and dull. What could be more natural, she thought, than fashioning secondaries to serve this area of one's life, too? Surely aspects of oneself must approach the ideal sexual partner more closely than any tertiary ever could. But it was difficult. One had to be excruciatingly clear and honest in describing the sexual side of oneself to create an accurate split from it.

And so Julia experimented at length. She strove to become conscious of what exactly attracted her. The results were often ludicrous, since she would start with one of the secondary templates her parents had made for her, try to shape it to match whom she thought she was, and then superimpose upon it the bits and pieces of erotic fragments she thought would (as though in and of

177

themselves) excite her. She deleted seven versions of S11 before reaching one she finally decided she could work with. The ultimate S11 had the face of an Outsider (with Julia's eyes, of course), milk breasts, Sasha's voice, Raye's laugh, Antoinette's hands, and male genitalia. S11 was Julia's most physical secondary. With it Julia would wrestle, working up a sweat. And S11 knew how to cry. It surprised Julia to learn that she sometimes enjoyed making S11 cry. (S11 had no feelings and could not be hurt, Julia told herself: so there was nothing wrong with that.) She would sometimes cry along with S11. It felt good, because it was illicit to cry with anyone outside herself. And if there was nothing specifically sexual in crying, it still seemed appropriate to do it with S11, since the point of the sexual secondaries was to exceed the limits of ordinary social and work relations.

S12, S13, S14, and S15 came into existence over the years, each time as the result of Julia's observation of a new source of erotic excitement. In every case she used the original S11 as template. As did Julia's primaries, S11 of course continued to evolve through its experiences with Julia and in response to Julia's needs and desires. Julia never discussed their existence with anyone. She had never heard of people using secondaries for sexual recreation. Only eutopians used secondaries for much of anything besides social or work obligations of a routine nature. Most people used tertiaries, obviously. Tertiaries, after all, conformed to certain common tastes and standards. Secondaries were strictly idiosyncratic and in a sense simply the excessive development of individual personal quirks. Her use of them made her wonder whether she were becoming dangerously solipsistic.

One could almost live alone among one's secondaries and lead a complete life, Julia sometimes thought. One could almost be socially self-sufficient—as if a single individual could be proliferated into an entire society. Only...only wasn't it the case that the reason she wanted to know about Outsiders was her sense that an entire society's solipsism was dangerous and sterile?

I am a microcosm of all the Great Conflicts, Julia put it to S07. At the age of 50, I am a world with a history, all within myself. An imperfect world. A world in need of something more. Like the Pax, S07. I have my entertainments, my self-definition, my defenses, my goals. But what are they, in the larger picture? How do they fit in, how do they relate, what do they mean vis-à-vis the Outside?

It's a mystery, Julia, that's for sure, S07 replied, a mystery. And so you think you can solve it by going Outside?

What else is there? Julia asked in return.

S07 had no answer, of course.

38.

JULIA REACHED THE bridge sweaty and physically irritable. She hated meat-space. She hated zero-gee. And she hated being interrupted by mysterious messages that might or might not portend serious trouble for the mission. She didn't need S07 to tell her that Candace and her team, as they constituted the border of her mesh, were more important to its strength than, say, the astrobiologists who provided the perfect meshing of warp and woof. She had expected to find Fuyuko, but only Astra was there. The very sight of her, casually twined around the central hold-bar, staring raptly at the image of La Femme filling the main viewscreen, for some reason annoyed her. "Just what were you doing on the bridge when the message came in, anyway?" Julia said to her. "Everyone's supposed to be making their reports. You can't have made yours already?"

Astra's eyes never moved from the screen. She said, "I needed to do some thinking. To organize my thoughts and review everything. So that I don't forget any details." She gestured at the viewscreen. "It's amazing, isn't it. The way the continents are like eggs, all linked end to end. It's so artificial-looking. But you can see, at this level of magnification, the continuous range of mountains running along the borders. As though they're all one continent, and the mountains all one range." She looked at Julia. "That's one of the questions on our list. Whether or not the continents were engineered. By whom. And why. Look at how strangely the tides bulge. Making the planet almost ovate itself, don't you think? One of its moons is larger and closer than ours is. The planet is younger. And so the tides are much stronger..." Astra sighed. "But it doesn't make sense. With tides that extreme, the planet should be torn apart."

"Have there been any more messages from Candace's team?" Julia said sharply.

Astra looked at Julia. "Not exactly. Not verbal messages. Only their location on the planet. AI: display on the main viewscreen the location of Candace's team on the surface."

A satellite view of one of the continents appeared on the screen. A red cursor blinked at a location that appeared to be an island in the middle of an interior sea or lake. Julia said, "AI, magnify by two."

The lake and its island expanded to fill the screen, but all Julia saw with the supposedly improved resolution were the tops of trees growing in clusters on the island. "AI, magnify by ten," Julia said.

"Magnification doesn't help," Astra said. "It's impossible to see anything but natural topographic features."

Julia studied the image on the viewscreen. Between the clusters of trees were fuzzy gray areas. And the blinking red cursor had vanished. "AI, mark the location of Candace's team on the viewscreen."

"There is not enough information to allow a visual representation of Candace's position at this magnification. Cameras and sensors are unable to make readings in those areas."

"Which is what the *Pax I* AI said in its report," Astra said.

Right. "AI, are we within communication range of the area displayed on the main viewscreen?"

"All areas of the planet La Femme are accessible to communication."

"The crew of the *Pax I* were sufficiently together in the beginning at least to deploy relay satellites in geosynchronous orbits around the planet," Astra said. "Even if they didn't make much use of them after they did."

"AI, relay my voice via their implants to Candace, Shaelle, Celeste, Felix, Paris, and Tree. Candace, I thought we had agreed you and your team members were to keep in continual touch with *Pax III*."

"It is not possible to contact Candace, Shaelle, Celeste, Felix, Paris, and Tree through their implants," the AI said. "The *Pax*

III crew members on the surface of La Femme are not currently accessible by radio contact."

"AI," Julia said, both frustrated and worried. "You just said that all areas of the planet are accessible by radio contact."

"That is correct," the AI said.

"AI," Julia said. "If all areas of the surface are accessible by radio contact, why can you not link me to Candace via her implant?"

"Candace has entered a sector outside broadcast and sensor range."

"It's the same problem the *Pax I* AI reported to the Council," Astra said. "The conjecture is that there's some kind of electromagnetic interference."

Julia was nauseated from the zero-gee. And her already weary arms were tiring from her grip on the hold-bar. "AI," she said. "As soon as our sensors detect Candace or other *Pax III* crew members, inform them that I wish to speak with them at once. And then patch them through to me." Julia looked at Astra. "I'm going to go write my report. And then I'm going to play back Candace's message again."

"And you think I should do the same," Astra said. She gave Julia a speculative look. "What I think is that we need to send another team down there—one sworn and determined to keep in close contact while investigating. And with some sort of dead-man switch set up so that the *Pax III* can be informed if there's danger involved."

Danger? The gnawing in her gut (which she kept assuring herself must be from the zero-gee) gave her pause. Candace should have checked in as soon as she touched down on the surface. It wasn't like her to be so offhand. Now if it had been *Astra*...

Julia moved hand-over-hand along the hold-bar to the hatch. She wanted her caretaker. She felt so...giddy. As though her endocrine functions had gone awry. Of course it could just be weightlessness. Certainly there were few things physically weirder. One tended to expect it to be like moving in v-space, when of course it wasn't like that at all...

The hatch dilated. Julia peered back over her shoulder and saw that Astra was staring again at the planets' linked continents. Like eggs, Julia's thoughts echoed Astra's characterization, like eggs one could cup in one's hands. Lavender, purple, blue, and black eggs... ridged and then sharply flattened around the edges, as though floating on the deep purple oceans, visibly bulging and crinkling on the viewscreen, so many textures, so many shades of purple... Terra incognita, she thought, not anything like Earth, like no world she had ever heard of.

Julia left the bridge. The image remained in her mind, beautiful, mysterious, alien, teasing her palms with the desire to cup and caress those egg-like shapes.

She was a long way from home. Five hundred light years distant. It gave her a cold feeling to think of it. Thrust from the womb, she thought. Thrust from home. Separated from the nest.

Outside.

39.

S07, SEATED WITH S04 across the desk from Julia, said, "You can remember, Julia. Take it slowly, one step at a time. Concentrate. You are entering the quarantined hold. What is the first thing you remember?"

Julia leaned back in her cushy chair and closed her eyes; she tried to concentrate, to re-create the moment. "They were standing facing us, as though we were in a room in ordinary gravity. And I was surprised by how clearly I saw them. They had the sharpness of definition characteristic only of v-space representations. And then...I think I counted them, so that I would know how many there were."

"Yes? And then?"

"And then I saw that one of them was Davis. Or rather," Julia said hastily, "that she looked like Davis."

"Who spoke first?" S04 said.

Julia hesitated, strangely confused. "I— I'm not sure," she said. She opened her eyes and stared at her secondaries, who had, while her eyes had been closed, donned white coats and heavy dark-framed glasses. S04 held a notepad in her lap, and a stylus in her hand.

"Julia," S07 said. "You know that if you think carefully and slowly, you can remember. Think. Who spoke the first words?"

Julia said, "I...I think I did. I think I said 'Davis? Is that you? But it can't be!' I *think* those were my words." A twinge of anxiety gnawed at her. Something was wrong. Something just wasn't right.

"If you are careful, Julia, you can recall it all perfectly. You're a trained, seasoned diplo. *Think.* You are standing there looking at them, counting them."

Julia shook her head. The longer she tried to make her recollection exact, the more confused her impression of the encounter became.

"Would you like to view the recording the ship AI made of the interaction? So that you can fill in the missing telepathic words?" S04 said.

"I think that should be kept as a last resort," S07 said.

"I think it would be a good idea for me to see it," Julia said. "Because then I'd really remember." It had been less than three hours since the encounter, after all. It should still be fresh and easily recalled.

S07 requested a virtual holocube and asked the AI to begin a playback of the encounter. A holocube popped into the space above the desk. Julia's throat tightened at the sight of the eight La Femmeans in the hold arranging themselves into a line that just happened to be correctly oriented to the six suited humans who came clumsily through the hatch and then hand-over-hand along the hold-bar.

"AI, rotate the holocube 90 degrees," Julia said, so that she'd be facing a side view. Esée "stood" slightly forward and held out both hands. The suited human in the lead stopped and released one hand from the hold-bar. Julia heard a gasp coming from a suit speaker. Her suited self became oddly rigid in the zero-gee. And then bowed awkwardly. After a few seconds, her suited self said "Yes." And then glanced over her shoulder at the five crewmates lined up along the hold-bar just inside the hatch and gestured them forward. Her suited self looked back at Esée. After a surprisingly long interval she let go of the hold-bar and held out both gloved hands to the La Femmean, who took and held them. "Men?" Julia's playback self said, sounding puzzled. And then, after a few seconds, "Yes, we are the species called *man*. And so, yes, we are *men*."

"AI, pause the playback," S07 said.

Julia stared at the frozen tableau in which Esée still held her playback self's hands.

S04 said, "Obviously the La Femmeans spoke first, since your first word, Julia, was an apparent answer to a question, and your second word a question in apparent query of something said by one of them to you."

"I'm at a loss to reconstruct what the 'yes' was in answer to," Julia said, unable to take her eyes off the image of her suited self holding hands with a Davis look-alike. "But the men—that had to do with Esée's asking me to confirm that we, too, are men, like their first visitors."

"Oh, you mean the word *men* in its archaic, unmarked form," S07 said.

"Can you remember the exact wording of their request for confirmation?" S04 said.

Julia's anxiety returned. "No," she said. "I can't. Just that something about my reaction made Esée wonder whether I was the same as Paul."

"Did she mention Paul by name?" S07 said.

Julia stared at the holo. "I…I'm not sure. I don't think so. I think it was a more general reference, to the ones who had come before us. Something like that."

S07 shook its head. "I can't believe this is the best you can do, Julia. With all these prompts before you, surely you can remember *exactly* what Esée said."

"But Esée didn't really speak," Julia said in sudden vexation. "It's more that I heard her words in my head—which isn't at all the same as *hearing* them. I mean, I'd be hard put to it to remember my own *thoughts*. There's something about hearing words spoken aloud—whether one's own or someone else's, that makes them memorable."

S07 came alongside Julia and put its arm over Julia's shoulder. "But you didn't remember your own words at all, until we played the tape for you. Which is why I think that if you worked at it, you could remember what has more the quality of *thoughts* than of speech."

Irritably, Julia shook off S07's arm. "What does it matter?" she said. "As long as I have a general idea…" Her voice trailed off. As a diplo she knew how critically important exactitude in recalling communications could be.

S04 said, very quietly, "It matters, Julia, and you know it. Surely you don't need me to explain to you why?" The dark frames made her opal eyes dramatically serious. For stage props they were amazingly effective.

Julia bit her lip. "No, S04, I don't. But the fact is, I simply can't remember."

"I don't like this," S07 said. "I don't recall your ever having had trouble remembering anything when you've had S04 and myself to assist you." Which was true. With S04 and S07—alone or together—Julia had always been able to recall details she by herself could not. S04 and S07 had time and again proven to her that while long-term memory was basically unreliable, short-term memory was highly retentive indeed. And yet, not only could she not recall exact details, but the more she concentrated, the hazier her recollection of the encounter seemed to become. As though she were muddying the water as she sifted the bottom of the river for lost treasure, making it impossible to see all the most obvious things that had been apparent before she'd started.

Had Esée held her hands for so long as the playback showed?

"AI, continue playback," Julia said, ignoring her secondaries. She wanted to see what else showed up on the recording that had been dumped from her memory. Maybe she couldn't hear the La Femmean's words, but at least she would be able to watch their gestures and hear her own and her crewmates' responses.

40.

IN HER EARLY thirties, Julia sought out a group of people with whom to build a family. She considered mainly eutopians, though within that rubric was interested in combining with as diverse a group as possible. The process taxed her diplo capacities to the limit. In the end, she contracted with three men, one intersex, and four women, all but one eutopians, all in their thirties, all engaged in different areas of work.

Except for Arete, the only person in the group who hadn't been raised a eutopian, all expressed indifference to the sex of the child. Arete hailed originally from a merging zone that had joined the Pax when she was three years old. Her parents had been born and raised Outsiders, and although they had strongly supported their nation state's decision to join the Pax, they had never completely rid themselves of what Arete called "the old prejudices" (which tended to linger in merging zones for two or three generations at least). Among the "old prejudices" Arete found most constricting were those relating to perceptions and constructions of sex and gender. "These old prejudices are being resurrected by certain Paxans' nostalgia for things past," Arete claimed. "What you have to understand is that in the world my parents grew up in, women's social and ethical role demanded service to the comforts and interests of males, regardless of their own work or profession: a classic example of cognitive dissonance, no? You probably don't understand what it meant. In the Pax the social contract is negotiated by all adults— by women as well as men. Every member of the Pax is considered a full stakeholder. Outside the Pax, most women are subsumed by the social contract, which is made only among men and is entirely dominated by a tiny, largely Caucasian elite. With the exception of a few elite women, women are largely non-agents there. And it's clear to me that if the Pax isn't careful, its reactionary forces will expel women from positions of moral and social agency."

Arete's anxiety was difficult for the eutopians to take seriously. Julia came closest, because of her contact with Outsiders during her border assignments. But it did seem to family members that Arete was being a little hysterical in imagining that the experiments of a few people in raising children in Outsider fashion could lead to the valorization of males over females.

"And so that is why I want our child to be female," Arete said. "Where I come from, most people value the interests and perspective of males over those of females. And you must know that even in the Pax, the canonical human being is male. And third, as eutopians we are dedicated to challenging the canonical norms we consider socially damaging. Fourth, females are biologically stronger than males and healthier. And fifth, though the Pax generates more females than males, Outside, females are a shrinking minority, by something like 2:1, even though birthrates are considerably higher than in the Pax, where all population increase is due to immigration."

Although no one else in the group agreed with Arete's notion that in the Pax the canonical human being was male, they expressed no particular inclination for sex selection, and so Arete's desire carried the decision, and a few months before Julia's thirty-fifth calendar birthday Arethustra was born to the family. Julia appreciated Arete's so-different take on every problem, issue, and question that arose, since in a way it was like having access to an exceptional Outsider. But she found it exhausting, too.

41.

ALL CREW CONSCIOUS and present on the *Pax III* attended the next formal c-space meeting. Again they used the spacious T-shaped table. S04 and S07, visible to Julia only, attended also. Julia said, "My impression, after looking through the crew's reports of their personal contacts with the indigenes, is that none of us have reconstructed verbatim any telepathic speech tendered. As I said in my own report, I tried, diligently and urgently, such a reconstruction, but—my diplo training notwithstanding—could not only not recall with any distinctness any telepathic speech made to me, but found, when I replayed the tape of my encounter, that I misremembered the entire event, including my own speech. I think it may be worth asking whether anyone else attempted a reconstruction."

"I did," Fuyuko said, and several others as well.

"And the results?" Julia said, indicating that Sonia should go first.

"It was peculiar," the demographer said. "I began with clear, vivid impressions of my encounter, but as I tried to reconstruct it moment by moment discovered that my memories are blurred and indistinct. To the point that the longer I struggled to remember exactly what had happened, the less certain I became of what I thought I knew when I started. Which I don't understand. Catalina, the indigene who appeared before me, you see, had given me a great deal of highly specific information about urban populations on the planet." Sonia frowned. "But about all I remember now is that Catalina told me that their population is perfectly stable everywhere. That there is no disease. That there is no *death* known to their species." She smiled faintly. "Of course, I couldn't forget a startling statement like that—except that I don't remember when she told me, or exactly what words she used." Sonia sighed. "Unfortunately, the ship made no record of the encounter. Though I wonder if it would have, even if I'd requested it—since, as we noted when we met earlier, according to the ship's AI, no indigenes other than those in the quarantined hold ever boarded ship."

"Which means little, since it's apparent they favor noncorporeal contacts," Astra said.

"When you tried to make a reconstruction, Astra," Julia said, "did the attempt blur your memory, as it did mine and Sonia's?"

Astra nodded. "Like Sonia, I began with a strong set of impressions of what had passed between us. But as I tried to pin them down and make my recollection as clear and exact as possible, I grew increasingly confused. Which makes no sense, since unlike some of you, I didn't allow myself to be distracted by Artemesia's personal resemblance to someone once close to me and therefore came away with *facts* rather than emotionally laden statements. If there's one thing it's easy to remember, it's facts—these being geological and cosmological data I came here to learn."

"Which makes it plain," Fuyuko said, "that we're dealing with a deliberate manipulation of our minds and not a manifestation of our own weakness somehow elicited by the indigenes' representing themselves in intimate and familiar forms."

"If it is a manipulation, it's not necessarily deliberate or malevolent," Carlton said. "I think we should bear in mind that telepathic communication is a wholly new experience for us. And it may be that something about it generates stresses and demands that our current mental organization finds difficult to adapt to."

Fuyuko glanced from Carlton to Julia and back again, as though suspecting a setup.

"That's an interesting idea," Blaise said. "Very interesting. It would for one thing suggest that although language can be translated between species, the texture of such communication—if one can use such a metaphor—doesn't remain identical, as it has traditionally done in translation between human languages. Perhaps because there might be too much noise involved, which we don't notice at the time of communication. Or—"

"This is no time for theoretical speculation," Fuyuko said, blatantly and impatiently interrupting. Blaise gave her a look of silent indignation and query. "Forgive me for interrupting," Fuyuko said. "Obviously this problem fascinates you in the abstract, since it falls within the area of your special expertise. But I think you should be theorizing on your own time, Blaise. Because we have some very pressing questions to consider. Namely, why Candace and her team not only deviated from their stated mission to the *Pax I*, but also ignored the protocol for crew visits. And what we should be doing about it. And what measures we should take to preserve what the indigenes say to us—since our forgetting may very well be caused by a posthypnotic suggestion and thus signal that verbatim transcripts might bear particular significance."

"Communications is my specialty," Blaise said slowly, "but if the AI can't hear the La Femmeans, I don't see how we *can* make verbatim recordings of their speech."

S07, perched on a stool behind Fuyuko, said to Julia: "The solution is simple. Suggest that everyone, when talking with the indigenes, speak aloud or subvocalize everything they're thinking, and echo—again aloud, or through subvocalization—everything they mentally hear the indigenes saying."

While S07 was still speaking, Kristen suggested essentially the same thing. "Does everyone agree?" Julia asked the crew at large.

"It will make things a lot more difficult," Astra said.

"Which is all to the good," Fuyuko said. "Since it seems to me a large part of the difficulties we face here has to do with the apparent ease of communication with these aliens. It *shouldn't* be easy. Because they're entirely different from us."

"That's an excellent point," Carlton said. "It has appeared easy. But as our confusion in recall makes clear, there are going to be glitches, and likely they'll be turning up in unexpected areas."

That feeling of being submerged in a heavy dense fluid crept over Julia again. She recalled—hazily—discussing the difficulty of remembering important things when it came to this mission.

The obvious kept escaping them—and had, since before they'd even encountered the La Femmeans. As though the strangeness and mistaken familiarity of constructed resemblances had permeated the consciousnesses of everyone who had so much as heard of La Femme.

"So it will be difficult," Julia said, "and will make communications less 'natural'—so to speak—but perhaps denaturalization is what is needed. Since communications between humans and La Femmeans is not, in itself, hard-wired into our brains."

"Unless," S04, standing behind Julia, whispered into her ear, "humans and La Femmeans have a previous relationship we know nothing about."

Julia barely restrained herself from whirling in her chair and snapping at the secondary. The secondaries *knew* they weren't supposed to distract her when in camouflage.

"Which brings us," Julia said steadily, "to the questions Fuyuko raised about Candace and her team."

Astra spoke first. "I think we should send another team down to investigate and report back. And that they should go down via shuttle and not be transported by whatever means the indigenes used on Candace's team. And I think the second team should swear themselves committed to keeping a channel open the entire time, so that everything they do and see is communicated back to *Pax III*'s AI and crew."

Julia nodded. "That sounds reasonable. But with the proviso that if for any reason communications are broken off, they return at once to the ship."

"That's not a wise idea," Fuyuko said. "Anyone watching the recording of Candace's transmission to *Pax III* can see that she was under a foreign mental influence. A sort of intoxication. Which to my trained eye is all of a piece with the memory blocks we've all suffered after our encounters with the indigenes. If we send a shuttle down there, the La Femmeans are bound to intercept it one way or another. And we can be righteously certain that if they do, no degree of commitment to reporting back to the ship will hold."

Astra folded her arms over her chest, leaned back in her chair, and snorted.

"Discussion?" Julia said.

"I guess I don't understand what Fuyuko is so worried about," Kristen said. "Apart from loss of control—which, I agree, is a frightening prospect, but which so far seems not to have resulted in a loss of either autonomy or life. What is the worst that has so far happened? Paul and his crew went native, or something like it. Bad, but not it would seem as bad as what happened to the *Pax I* during transudation. Candace's team deviated from its mission. Bad, but again—we have no reason to believe they've taken harm. Or to expect that they will take harm. The point being, we're here to explore and investigate contacts. And if we aren't prepared to take risks, we shouldn't have come."

"I agree," Melina said quickly. "Just the fact that we came at all was a risk—and a voluntary one. Transudation, as Kristen just noted, has been far more deleterious than anything we suspect the La Femmeans of. It's caused all our fatalities. I for one am willing to take more risks—since by Fuyuko's reasoning, just being in this system is risky, considering that the indigenes contacted us before we began orbiting the planet."

Melina's speech turned the tide. Satisfied, Julia let the discussion flow as it would and subvoked to S07 and S04 with a query as to who should be on the new team.

The AI interrupted: <<Julia, Felix has returned to the *Pax III.*>>

"AI," Julia said quickly when Fuyuko paused in her argumentation, "will you ask Felix to join us in this c-space?" Julia smiled around the table. "Felix has returned to the *Pax III.*"

"Felix says she will toggle in at once," the AI said.

Amazing, Julia thought. If *she* had been down to the surface and suffered the by now unaccustomed vicissitudes of gravity, she'd want to go straight to her caretaker.

While everyone was still exclaiming over the news, Felix appeared—accompanied by a small gray-skinned woman with silver hair and milk breasts. Quickly she positioned herself at the foot of the table, presumably so that everyone could see her without having to crane their necks. The La Femmean stood with her. "This is Kazuko," Felix said, smiling broadly. "It is she who transported me back to the ship and who was my guide for the brief time I had the pleasure of visiting La Femme."

"Could you explain how you toggled in to this c-space with Felix?" Fuyuko said to the La Femmean. "Since you manifestly lack the wiring that makes toggling in possible?"

Kazuko bowed and smiled. <<This is something I don't know how to explain. But don't worry about it. We mean for you only what you want for yourselves. Since my presence here threatens you, I'll leave, though Felix would rather I stay. Another time, then.>> And the La Femmean toggled out.

Felix glared at Fuyuko. "Your paranoia drove her away!"

"This is a private meeting," Fuyuko said.

Felix glanced around. "Private? Are you joking? It looks to me like a big part of the crew is here. What you really mean to say is that it's only for Paxans."

An interesting distinction, Julia thought. "Are you prepared to make an informal report, Felix?" she said.

"Oh shit," Astra said loudly.

Everyone looked at her.

"Did anyone think to repeat what Kazuko said to us before she left?"

Julia rapped her knuckles on her skull. It had happened so fast, the need to do it had slipped her mind—as it had apparently slipped everyone else's.

Blaise had said something about the textures of communication. This one, Julia was beginning to think, was both slippery and translucent—if not, in certain lights, downright invisible.

42.

AFTER SHE'D ORDERED a chair near the top of the T, which, refreshed, had expanded, and sat down in it, Felix said, "There's so much to say about the little bit that I saw of the planet that I hardly know where to begin."

"You might try explaining why you deviated from both your mission and the protocol for visits to the surface," Fuyuko said.

Felix's primary, Julia thought—the transmission from the *Pax I* still fresh in her mind—resembled her meat-space self so little that she wondered Felix could bear the disparity in-the-flesh. Often people who chose such a vastly different v-space representation of themselves either avoided meat-space altogether (which Felix could not on this mission do) or surgically altered or camouflaged their meat-space bodies.

"We didn't want to get bogged down in having to conduct another meeting to decide whether we should go or not," Felix said. "You see, on meeting the La Femmeans it became sharp and distinct to us that these were honest, fine-intentioned beings who were eager to answer all our questions. Granted, it was a trifle freaky because they manifested as people each of us knew. But when we asked them about it and learned that they meant only to make us comfortable, they dropped their disguises and appeared as themselves—pale blue skin, silver hair, and all."

Carlton waved her hand in the air, to get Felix's attention. "Is that how they put it? That the blue skin—which I have to say, looks gray to me—and silver hair were *natural* to them? That this is how they look to one another and isn't just another illusion for our benefit? Because my contact said that they would only gradually alter their appearance to accustom us to the differences between themselves and us."

Felix frowned. "I...*thought* that was what Kazuko said—that she was appearing to me undisguised, as her real self. Only...only now that I think about it, it may be that she didn't say that at all..."

"Don't think about it!" Fuyuko said sharply. "A number of us have discovered that the more we focus on a particular fragment of conversation with the La Femmeans, the hazier and less distinct it becomes. There's some sort of memory block operating. And so if you want to recall anything at all, try not to think too closely about it."

"That's pure speculation," Blaise said. "It's far more likely to be some sort of coding problem. We seem to be exchanging messages with the La Femmeans. But the code in which the messages are constructed may be imperfectly understood by both sides. And since our communication with them has only just begun, we have no frame of reference for clearing up the ambiguity. And so perhaps though we think we know what we're hearing inside our heads, it may be that we are interpreting the message through such a heavy filter of expectations and preconceptions that we don't know *what* we're hearing."

Fuyuko thrust out her hands, palm up, in a sardonic gesture of hopelessness. "Oh fine," she said. "In which case we can't say whether we haven't simply invented every one of the telepathic impressions we've received!"

"Clearly, we need to explore the issue of our communications with the indigenes thoroughly," Julia said. "But may I suggest we allow Felix to report, which was the point at hand."

Fuyuko rapped sharply on the table. "The point at hand, as I see it, was the question of what exactly this alien who identifies herself as Kazuko said—which, our new protocol to the contrary, not a single one of us sitting in this space remembered to relay to the AI. May I suggest we clear that up before Felix reports."

"I thought you said we weren't to try to remember anything the La Femmeans have communicated to us," Felix said to Fuyuko.

"Remember verbatim," Fuyuko said. "I'm asking that we remember generally—in our own words, so to speak."

"More like paraphrasing, or summarizing," Blaise said. "The way we do with our dreams—putting them into language, that is."

Fuyuko's head swung sharply around to face Blaise. "Do you realize what you just said? The fact is, when we put our dreams into words, we solidify their meaning—or rather, *create* their meaning. And impose narrative and symbolic order on an essentially disorderly series of images. Whereas this works in the opposite way, such that language imposes *disorder* on our memories."

Blaise's primary sat up significantly straight in her chair. "A fascinating observation, Fuyuko," she said. "What I'm wondering, suddenly, is whether all of us carry away the same impression and meaning when communications are made to all of us at once. For example, do we all remember what Kazuko said to us in the same way? As being an essentially similar, identifiable message?"

<S07, should I allow this discussion to continue, or pull it back on track?> Julia asked her secondary.

Fuyuko said, "I propose an experiment, whereby we each input to the AI our own impressions, very briefly, and then have the AI play back a sample of them."

<<Let this flow, Julia>> S07 replied.

Fuyuko instructed them to dictate a sentence or two describing their impressions of Kazuko's words without thinking at all about them. Silence descended while they each subvoked to the AI. When the AI announced that everyone present had provided a statement, Fuyuko requested that it read, at random, without naming the authors, eight of their statements.

The AI said, "Statement One: Kazuko said that her toggling in was inexplicable, but was a means for communicating better with us. But that because we are paranoid, she wouldn't force her presence on us. Statement Two: Kazuko said that men are apparently unable to understand the abilities of La Femmeans, and that they could never know which of their abilities men are inclined to fear in particular. That Felix did not fear this ability, but that out of respect for the fears of certain crew she would leave. But that she looked forward to meeting us again. Statement Three: Kazuko said that humans are too primitive to understand her ability to toggle in. That this ability didn't matter to Felix, and that Felix wished her to stay. But that out of understanding for our primitive fears, she would leave. Statement Four: Kazuko said she was no threat to us, but that because we didn't yet understand enough about La Femme and its inhabitants, she would respect our fears and leave. Statement Five: Kazuko mocked our fear and boasted that her ability to toggle in was beyond our comprehension. She then made clear the sway she holds over Felix and implied that eventually we would all be as accepting of her as Felix is. Statement Six: Kazuko said she would like to explain how she could toggle in, since it so astonished us, but that it would require building up a broader background in La Femmean telepathic skills than we at present have. She said these skills don't threaten us, because La Femmeans are dedicated to giving others only what they themselves want. And then she said that because of our anxieties about her appearance in our c-space, she would leave, Felix's wishes notwithstanding, and speak to us another time. Statement Seven: Kazuko said she was sorry her toggling in upset some of us. That it wasn't meant to threaten us. That she came because Felix wanted her to come, but since she was creating such fear, she would leave and speak to us another time. Statement Eight: Kazuko said that she didn't know how to explain La Femmean telepathic powers, that our language doesn't give her the means to do so. But that the La Femmeans want only good things for humans. That because of the misunderstanding, she would leave and seek us out another time."

When the AI ceased relating the statements, Blaise said, "The differences could be taken for the usual distortions made by receivers of the same message. And not necessarily a distortion created by a memory block or other sorts of psychological manipulation."

"Except," Carlton said slowly, "that the initial part of the message was put in such radically different words—with different tones, different connotations for how Kazuko related to us the reason she was not going to explain how she toggled in."

"Yes," Kristen said. "It wasn't just that some people heard it as variously arrogant or apologetic. But that some people apparently recall extensive statements—and I don't suppose we've any means of knowing whether they were implied or inferred—about the reasons underlying the problem of communicating to us how she toggled in. Which one would think wouldn't have been so quickly embroidered by the receivers."

"It's possible, though," Blaise said. "You'd be surprised how much people can read into ordinary statements made to them in their own language."

Julia addressed her secondary. <What do you make of this?>

<<I am frustrated, Julia, since I didn't 'hear' the initial communication. Whether the differences were implied or inferred remains to be seen. The simplest explanation would be that each individual remembered what they expected to hear.>>

"I suggest we hold this topic for future discussion pending the language and communications specialists' theoretical development of the problem," Julia said. "Felix, would you like to proceed?"

Felix made Julia a wry look. "Sure. But after hearing all that, I wonder if there's even a point? Not only is it unlikely you're going to be able to take anything I say as the truth, but I'm not sure that *I* can do that now, either."

Julia made a smile. "Just give us a representation—think of it that way—and then we'll at least have something to work with."

Felix shrugged. "All right," she said. "I'll give it my best try."

What a pity, Julia thought, that the crew didn't know what all eutopians understood: that people only ever made representations anyway, whether they realized it or not.

43.

THE DREAMS, OH the beautiful texture and weight of the dreams that came to Julia in the early years of parenting. Morning after morning she woke with a mind thick with images that would haunt her for the whole of the day. Often, in the dreams, she would have milk breasts, sometimes suckling Arethustra, at other times suckling her co-parents or even her own parents and grandparents. Or she would be pregnant, undertaking gestation within her body, as Outsiders and families driven by nostalgia did. Or she herself would be a child again, suckling Joey, suckling Saella—only to find herself, of a sudden, a grown adult. And then there were the more shocking dreams involving Raye—in which she, Raye, and Arethustra were often transposed within the same dream and dream setting. She had more or less put Raye out of her conscious mind. Raye, she had thought, no longer held any place of significance in her present life, except as a past, historical force in her earlier development.

Julia had the impression that she might have recalled dreams so densely in her childhood but, until S05 reminded her, forgot that she had dreamed comparably during the most intense stages of her eutopian apprenticeship. S05 mocked her: "Did you think you had stabilized into a psychical stasis that would take you safely through the rest of your life, Julia? Did you really think you had it all worked out? Did you think of parenting as an experience touching only the child, and not the parent?"

What met the eye, of course, was the remarkable fact of the web the ten of them made as a family. The web had been conceived by the nine of them, ever so exquisitely designed and carefully warped on the loom of eutopian structures. Together they wove themselves into a beautiful, vibrant fabric, in which the figure of

Arethustra emerged bold, brave, and above all confident. It never ceased to be a wonder to Julia, this human being so very much herself, independent of all of them yet reflecting back at them the most unexpected bits of themselves.

Julia took as her special task teaching Arethustra in the middle years. The child's mind, it seemed to Julia, worked more quickly and unexpectedly than an adult's. Arethustra often saw (and when she saw, always articulated) the seemingly small things adults, in their wearied resort to comfort, ignored. She discomfited her parents on such occasions—but also reminded them of what they themselves had once understood.

"You know so much, Julia," Arethustra would say, sighing. "How will I ever learn all that?" And Julia would feel strong for her daughter's confidence—and false and weak for the childishness of it. The first time Arethustra said this to her, Julia flashed on how she had used to say the same thing to Glenning, and wondered about it, wondered if she were now comparable to Glenning.

She had always taken her parents for wise and knowing. She had never thought of herself as like them, even when she'd been recognized as a full adult and told she must henceforth be responsible for herself. But Arethustra's unconscious re-enactment of her own childhood reliance on and admiration for her parents forced the subject on her. She had thought she understood the old eutopian saying "Raising a child makes one grow up," but now comprehended that she couldn't have known what it meant until she had actually gone through the experience—and had, indeed, finished growing up.

44.

AT LAST, FELIX was allowed to tell her story to the crew seated at the T-shaped table. Julia was struck by how, even in v-space, the beige uniform and light gray of the granite tabletop washed-out Felix's primary's youthful olive skin. "I wanted Kazuko here to explain to you what she said to me," Felix said. "Because I knew I wouldn't get it exactly right." She frowned, then glanced anxiously at, one after another, Fuyuko, Astra, Blaise, and Julia. "Well, we've seen that none of us are fit to pass on the La Femmeans' words—or whatever it is we want to call their telepathic messages. Clearly, inevitably, we'll get it...*wrong*." Her fingers tugged and pulled against one another, making Julia wonder (again) if it was true that few people knew they could program all that fidgeting out of their primaries, or if it was another case of an individual requiring the ability to visibly fidget, even in v-space, for psychological reasons.

"But you surely must see why we'd want your first report in privacy," Fuyuko said.

Julia glanced at S07 and subvoked <Though of course the point is that the aliens are probably capable of "listening in" on us if they really want to.>

<<Yes. It's simply a question of comfort for those who perceive the La Femmeans as a threat.>>

"At any rate," Felix continued, "when our team went to the *Pax I* we had no intention of doing more than checking out the situation. But a number of La Femmeans appeared before us— noncorporeally, I suppose, since the AI didn't pick them up—and spoke freely and openly with us—"

"Excuse me," Blaise said. "They appeared in the guise of people each of you had known?"

"Yes. And of course we asked them about that—"

"Sorry to keep interrupting," Blaise said. "But when you said that they 'spoke' openly and freely, by which I assume you must mean they communicated to you telepathically, did they speak only individually, or did the entire group 'hear' what any individual La Femmean 'said'?"

Julia could not shake the distraction caused by her nearly obsessive awareness of the discrepancy between Felix's primary's appearance as a svelte, muscular thirty-five or forty and the meat-self on the tape Julia had replayed half-a-dozen times before the meeting, a meat-self that even in the throes of wide-eyed excitement showed the harshness sixty-five years had carved onto the flabbiness of decades spent largely in a caretaker. She wondered how the discrepancy could so bother her...

Felix looked at Blaise. "Most of what was 'said' to us was on an individual basis—except when the La Femmeans issued the invitation to visit the surface at once. It came to all of us at the same time—though I couldn't begin to say from which La Femmean." Felix leaned forward, toward Fuyuko. "It didn't seem important at the time. What astonished us was that they said they would take us anywhere we wanted to go—anywhere at all, with the exception of the areas occupied by crew from the *Pax I*. They said that travel would be virtually instantaneous. That they wanted to show us whatever we wanted to see."

"It's obvious we need to see the crew of the *Pax I*," Fuyuko said flatly.

"But the La Femmeans won't allow us to force the issue," Felix said quickly. "Anyway, it's not that we can't *see* them, exactly, it's just that we won't be allowed to *intrude* ourselves on them."

"In that thicket of double negatives, what exactly *do* you mean to say?" Blaise asked.

Felix spread her palms flat on the table. She sighed. "What I *think* the La Femmeans were telling us is that we'll be allowed to...*look at* the *Pax I* crew, as a one-way transmission."

"That's not good enough," Fuyuko said. "They could be show-ing us anything they liked, and unless we could catch some incon-sistency in presentation, we'd never know."

"How would we know anyway?" Julia said. "Considering just how good their resemblances are, they could deceive us in the flesh if they wanted."

In the shocked silence following Julia's remark, every primary present gaped at her.

S07 tsked at Julia. <<Are you sure it's wise to put such an addi-tional burden on Fuyuko? She's scared half-to-death as it is of the La Femmeans.>>

Fuyuko rose to her feet. "This entire mission is hopeless!" she said. "Obviously we should attempt to retrieve the survivors from *Pax I* and then, whether we succeed or not, return home and re-port. And let the Council decide if there's any point in treating with creatures who are so...*impossible*."

"Retrieving the survivors of the *Pax I* is not the only point of the mission," Julia said firmly (and wearily).

<<I've just figured out Fuyuko's problem>> S04 said. <<She lives for survival, and nothing more. It must be the way she was brought up. To always be prepared for the worst, and never strive for the best, since to do so might endanger the most trivial notion of survival.>>

<Really> Julia replied to S04. <Is it possible a Paxan could be raised with such an attitude, when the means for basic survival is guaranteed for every Paxan?>

<<Eutopians are different>> S07 said.

Felix was saying, "I don't understand why going to the surface or even just talking to the La Femmeans is intrinsically pointless—or, as you said, Fuyuko, *impossible*."

"Because we can never be sure that they're not deceiving us," Fuyuko said. "Which means that no matter how fine their tele-pathic skills, there's no possibility of trustworthy communication between them and us."

Julia laughed, most pointedly. "Fuyuko, it's easy to see you're not a diplo."

Most of the crew sitting at the table tittered, chuckled, even roared at that. Which pleased Julia, since it broke up the tension Fuyuko had whipped up.

"Must toggle out," Fuyuko said. And her primary vanished.

"Felix, why don't you continue your story," Blaise said mildly. "Fuyuko will catch up on it by reading the transcript of this meeting."

Julia wondered which was worse—to find v-space difficult to tolerate, as Fuyuko now did, or meat-space, as she herself did. Earlier she had thought the latter worse. But now that it had emerged that the La Femmeans could visit them in v-space, it wasn't so clear who was most handicapped.

45.

INTERRUPTED BY A constant flow of questions and discussion, it took more than two hours for Felix to report, and so, immediately after the meeting, Julia, exhausted, had her caretaker induce first delta-wave- and then REM-phase sleep. When she woke, refreshed, she met with S04 and S07 in her c-space study to discuss Felix's report and the issues it had raised.

S04, manifesting the form of Julia's primary (unmodified), clad in the simplest classic diplo garb, said: "Have you noticed, Julia, how crew meetings have grown increasingly disordered with every new set of inputs from the indigenes? Or, to put it more bluntly, with what disorganization so much new information is being met?"

Julia got up from her desk and paced, staring at the bookshelves lining the perimeter of the room; her eyes swept over the titles, but she did not particularly notice them. Somehow she managed, as she paced, to miss tumbling over S07, who was seated on the rug, folded into a Full Lotus. A dozen (and more) thoughts and images competed for Julia's attention. Above all she wanted to concentrate on what Felix had said about Kazuko's perplexity as to whether the crew of the *Pax III* might be a different race (or even species) from the crew of the *Pax I*, and on Felix's descriptions of the places she had so fleetingly visited on the surface. And so she addressed S04's question irritably. "Yes, yes, you're right," she said, scowling at the secondary. "The old free-form is a disaster, given all that we now need to engage. I'm going to have to control the meetings more tightly. Not allow questions except at set times, and so forth. Not allow Fuyuko, for instance, to hijack the meeting into diversionary areas."

"You've missed my point, Julia," S04 said softly.

"I couldn't care less. We have more important things to discuss than process," Julia said. She flipped S04 a rude gesture.

S07 cleared its throat. "Calm down, Julia, and try to remember the reasons you have for being polite and responsive to mere sets of data like us. S04 is trying to make a point, an important one, that you for some reason don't wish to hear."

Julia returned to her chair and rested her head against the high back, then closed her eyes and expelled her breath in a burst of impatience. (She loved all the "physical" sounds she could make with her primary, all of them so very pleasing, so distinct and crisp and round and full by comparison with the mush of sound in meat-space. And she especially loved the squeak her chair made now as she leaned back in it, an effect she had programmed long ago, but which never ceased to gratify her.) Of all times to be sidetracked by the niceties of eutopian guidelines for conduct! she thought but did not say to her secondaries. Certainly she subscribed to the eutopian principle that one must necessarily be affected by the way in which one treated constructs of human beings in scenarios made deliberately to resemble the settings and narrative structures in which one interacted with primary representations of living, breathing human beings. If she treated secondaries (her own or others') made to resemble primaries (her own or others') rudely, peremptorily, and without courtesy, she would pay for it later in the way she would find herself treating others' primary representations (and their meat-space selves as well). Slippage, in such "shorthand," *always* occurred. Julia *knew* that.

The fact was, she thought, that her impatience to encounter, know, and understand La Femme was making her want to treat *everyone* peremptorily. She wished she could just sweep Fuyuko out of her way. She was tired of thrashing out points in meetings. And she wished other people would simply follow their assigned missions and let her get on with her own.

Julia smiled and gestured her apologies to S04. "Excuse my rudeness. There's so much I want to think about and discuss, it just seemed the last straw to have you bringing up yet one more thing to consider. Please, continue with what you were saying."

S04 inclined its head graciously. "My point is not that you should be concerned with the tendency to feel sidetracked by the many directions the discussions take, but to make you notice that our basic problem is that we have no clear sense of what new information is important and what is not. Much less how to interpret it. The latter, of course, being the greater area of focus. But even if you were to impose a stricter order on the meetings, that would mean determining in advance what is significant. And the problem is, in dealing with a completely opaque situation, we can't really be certain, can we."

Julia almost snorted. The idea of a secondary feeling certainty! But S04 did have a point. "I hear what you're saying," she said. "Only I don't see how your insight can help make things clearer."

S04 folded its hands in its lap. It made an even more perfect picture of wise and calm contemplation than S07 in its Full Lotus on the floor. "Consider," it said, "what I mentioned earlier, about Fuyuko. That survival is her purpose in life. It means that her foremost concern will always be safety. What will always strike her as significant will be factors that either threaten or assure her safety—and that of the crew, and the Pax at large, and perhaps, in her mind, even the human species generally. Therefore, whenever she receives new information, she evaluates it according to that single parameter. *She* has no trouble deciding how to arrange new inputs conceptually. Undoubtedly she has filtered out of her notion of the mission all that does not relate directly to issues of safety. And if you confronted her with this, she'd no doubt say that the safety issue comes first, and that because safety cannot be absolutely guaranteed in the circumstances, the rest of the mission must therefore be considered impossible to carry out."

"Precisely," S07 murmured. "I see what you're getting at, S04. Now for the various specialists, who aren't obsessed with concern for their safety—having never felt threatened before and not prone to interpreting uncertainty as a lurking threat—*their* conceptual arrangements of new inputs are determined by their special interests in the mission. Blaise, obviously, to take another example, is fascinated with the problem of how two alien species can communicate, particularly when one of them has no experience with the channels the other uses for transmission."

Julia thought of how Arete, though fully aware that she had been raised in "survival mode," continually had to struggle against the tendency to settle, always, for comfort and lack of threat. "Do you suppose Fuyuko has been so threatened at some time in her life that she somehow developed that attitude? I hadn't particularly noticed this attitude in other crew members raised in kindercities, so it seems unlikely it developed out of that experience."

S04 shrugged. "I lack the information to make an informed guess. But many Paxans who are not eutopians live to appease their various fears, which generally have little to do with physical survival. You may recall that early in human history, fear was a useful emotion." S04 resumed: "To continue. If you examine crew concerns for establishing *truth*, they're quite different. Fuyuko, who suddenly finds the fact of such extensive voluntarily determined self-presentation an intolerable impediment to her sense of certainty and therefore security, takes La Femmean representations as deliberate deception concealing some horrendous, dangerous truth. The rest of the crew appears, to the contrary, to be taking them as they take c-space representations of individuals who look quite different in meat-space."

"Clearly a red herring," Julia said decisively. "And a funny sort of one, for a Paxan. A little like the way Outsiders tend to respond to Paxans when they come into our border stations." She smiled a little at the thought. "I wonder if we shouldn't just send Fuyuko back on *Pax I*, with all our reports. To get her out of the way. And to let the Council decide what is to be done about the *Pax I* crew living now on the surface."

S07 tsked at Julia. "You'd let Fuyuko have the ear of the Council all to herself? Imagine the hysteria she could whip up among the members responsible for siccing Vance on us."

"It was just a thought," Julia said, knowing S07 was right. "But about S04's analogy. It is difficult to know how to take the La Femmeans in any case, when we're not sure we're even hearing—or understanding, rather—their messages correctly. The problem is, we can't seem to get a permanent and therefore undisputed fix on their words—if their messages are indeed words." Julia intuited that she had stumbled onto something key. "But hey. What if we asked the La Femmeans to write them down?" She grew excited. "Then we'd know at least the words of their texts, wouldn't we?"

S04 nodded. "An excellent solution—if they're capable of writing. It would certainly solve a lot of problems."

As well as relieve the crew of further discussion about the fact and significance of the ambiguity of their telepathic communications. "Though," Julia said, "it wouldn't, of course, bring us any closer to the part of the mission that calls for our establishing an idea of their political and social structures. It's not just the language problem, of course. But if they never let us see them in their ordinary, social state, interacting with one another... When you think about it, you realize that apart from asking them questions and accepting their answers as sufficient in themselves, we'll never be able to draw our own conclusions from observation."

Julia sighed. Of all things, she had looked forward to watching individuals of another species and civilization interacting. She had learned a lot from watching Outsiders in the border stations (even if not precisely what she had been looking for). "There's so much we'll never be able to know about the La Femmeans," she said, "unless we somehow are able to acquire telepathic skills, the way word processors learn Delta Pavonian singing." Unlikely, Julia thought. Telepathic skill probably required an innate capacity hardwired into a species' biology. Could it be surgically implanted, the way the physical capacity to sing Delta Pavonian is implanted in word processors?

"I believe you had some points, Julia, you particularly wished to discuss?" S04 said politely.

"Points? Oh—yeah." Julia nodded vigorously. "Remember what Felix said about Kazuko's asking her whether we were of a different race or species than the *Pax I* crew?"

"S07 and I have total recall, Julia," S04 said mildly.

"The question was rhetorical," Julia snapped. "According to Felix, Kazuko said that though we resemble the crew from *Pax I* externally, there's something very different about us. So different,

that they—the La Femmeans—were having trouble understanding us."

"Yes, that is interesting," S07 said. "Did Felix tell them what the difference is?"

"Do *you* know what the difference is?"

S07 leaned back and craned her neck so that she could see Julia. "Am I misunderstanding? Surely the only difference must be sex and gender."

Julia laughed. "Sex. But what does that *mean*? To visual inspection, sex is an *external* difference. On *Pax I*, at least, the males had predominantly male genitalia, females predominantly female genitalia. As far as gender goes, linguistically females and males are all over the map. And absolutely everything else is fluid, and what isn't fluid but a cut and dried binary is simply an arbitrary consensual fiction. Am I missing something here?"

"It would seem so," S04 said drily.

"Do you recall how you said that Esée asked if the crew members of *Pax III* were 'men'? Consider the fact that your reported confusion couldn't have been due to *Esée's* language but had to relate to how you were 'hearing' her communication to you."

When I and other crew members perceived in the La Femmeans' "speech" a confusion in their use of "men" (which I at first interpreted as the now rarely used unmarked version of the word, a synonym for "human"), we were in fact being confronted with our own, deeply embedded confusion about gender. It was only when I realized that the La Femmeans themselves do not use words that I realized the word was, in fact, my own, which meant that I was receiving an image of a human or humans that was sufficiently male as to lead to my encoding it with the word "man" or "men." This leads me to conclude that the notion of human identity the La Femmeans picked up from the *Pax I* crew accorded to a degree with the notion they were picking up from me and other *Pax III* crew members—although the La Femmean I shared Contact with at times wondered if the males and females respectively might be of different species or races. The confusion, obviously, reflected significant cognitive dissonance.

— from The Summary of Julia 9561's Report on "La Femme" to the First Council

"Oh! You mean, I picked up on *males* and recoded the concept as 'men,' which my conscious self could then interpret as the unmarked form of 'humans'?"

"Precisely. You need to remember, always, that the La Femmeans' frame of reference for shared communication with you, at this stage, must be the one established by their previous Contact with Paul et al."

"How frustrating this is!" Julia exclaimed. "What I *need* is to visit the surface myself. Or, at the least, to talk again—this time without interruption—with Esée. I—" Julia broke off as the tertiary of Gertrude Stein popped into the c-space without warning. "How can it be?" she said. "I didn't order any tertiaries. Nor have I given access to anyone else who might do so."

<<I am Esée>> Gertrude Stein said. <<You expressed a powerful desire to speak with me. And so I have come.>>

"Julia?" S07 said. "What is it you're saying about tertiaries?"

Julia looked at S07 and realized it didn't see Gertrude Stein—or rather Esée—standing only inches from where it sat on the rug. "Esée has come," she said to S07. Looking at Esée, she said, "You are invisible to my secondaries. They can neither see nor hear you. Is there any way you can make them do so?" Which was a better way of putting it, Julia thought, than requesting Esée to *write*.

<<It's not possible>> Esée replied.

S04 said, "Julia, please try to remember to repeat to us everything that Esée says as she says it."

"Esée just said that she is afraid it's not possible," Julia said. She looked at Esée. "Why did you come in the form of my tertiary of Gertrude Stein?"

Esée bowed exactly as Julia imagined Gertrude Stein might have done. <<Our previous forms made you uncomfortable. And so we now seek images more pleasing to you. Ones without personal emotional resonance.>>

"Where did you get the idea of this particular form?"

"Julia," S07 said sharply. "Please don't forget to relay Esée's words to us."

Julia stood up from her desk. "It's too difficult to carry on a conversation that way," she said irritably. "Please, Esée, continue."

<<I took this form from your thoughts.>>

Julia scowled at S07. "Esée just said that she took the form from my thoughts." She looked at Esée. "Specifically, from my mind? Or from our AI programs?"

Esée looked amused. <<From your mind, Julia. We cannot read your AI.>>

Well that was interesting. A new thought occurred to Julia. "Can you see my secondaries here, in this place with me?"

Esée shook her head. <<I understand that you are directing certain thoughts to entities you consider a part of yourself, but they are opaque to me, except as you reflect their existence in your thoughts.>>

Very, *very* interesting. It suggested that as far as Esée was concerned, she, Julia, was at this moment lying in a caretaker, having conversations that showed up as only one-sided to the La Femmean. Which meant that the La Femmeans were indeed, as Paul had indicated in his report, strictly meat-oriented.

46.

JULIA TOOK ARETHUSTRA to visit the City of Word Processing shortly after the child's eleventh birthday. She had long had in mind the importance of her own childhood trip to the wildlife dome with Glenning. Even with all her diplo connections, however, Julia couldn't pull off a trip to a wildlife dome for Arethustra and herself. Though the City of Word Processing was easily accessible, few people ever visited it or even much remembered it existed. Since it was a site visited often by the single non-terrestrial species known to have visited Earth and the home of a section of Paxan society absolutely sui generis, Julia knew it would be a rich experience for her daughter.

The predominant meat-orientation of the City of Word Processing fascinated Arethustra. "There are so many places for people to go!" she said with wide-eyed excitement. "And there are people *everywhere*!" Indeed, the City of Word Processing resembled a small, slightly messy full-scale mockup in meat-space of a c-space city. Julia hadn't considered how magical such a setting would seem to a child growing up in a household whose members lived only partially in meat-space, in a dome where the meat-space living areas, all located within households, largely accommodated children who had no choice but to spend most of their time in meat-space. Most word processors preferred sleeping, working, eating, and amusing themselves in their meat-space dome to spending any time at all in the c-spaces most Paxans used. And so they had extensive, meat-space facilities in which to do it. They were attuned to their bodies—as they had to be, to sing.

Arethustra was thrilled to be taken to a cafe, where people with rose crystal implants in their throats sat on cushions on the carpeted floor, eating and talking to one another and sipping coffee. "Is this how people lived in history?" Arethustra whispered.

"We can only guess," Julia said. "There are films and books and paintings that show places where people met publicly to eat and drink and talk. But they're only representations, of course, and so must always be open to question."

After lunch Julia guided Arethustra around the city for an hour or so before giving her a tranquility patch and taking her to a singing (and surreptitiously pressing a patch on her own skin). Arethustra did not find the experience revolting; Julia suspected the tranquility patch had been unnecessary. Following the singing, Arethustra expressed amazement that there could be such a species as the Delta Pavonians. "They have no facial expressions or body-language that I can read," she said, "yet their entire presentation is one of obvious expressiveness! Do you think that humans might ever have expressed themselves differently? That they might have developed an entirely different way of communicating and making art and meaning? Or is the way we express ourselves hard-wired into our species?"

"These are important questions," Julia said. It pleased her to think that Arethustra, having posed such questions, would carry them around with her for all of her life.

"And the word processors, when they sing," Arethustra said, stealing covert glances at a pair of them gliding by arm-in-arm on the slidewalk passing theirs. "When they adopt Delta Pavonian types of expressiveness, do they lose human expressiveness and look inhuman?"

"Yes," Julia said, like all eutopians dedicated to telling her child the truth as she knew it. "They do. And other humans find them scary and repulsive for it, too. Which is one of the reasons they have to have their own dome apart from other Paxans."

And finally, Julia took Arethustra to that most peculiar of the word processors' amenities, the swings. The two of them sat in a double (which Julia knew tended to be shared by lovers) and in wild exhilaration swung high and wide, out, it seemed, over the city, each arc more dramatic and far-reaching than the last, giving them the sense that if they swung long enough they'd be able to touch the mountains (actually a projection on the wall of the dome) with their toes. Arethustra giggled and screamed and crowed with pleasure, while Julia just missed having a gratuitous orgasm. "This is what Delta Pavonian flying is supposed to be like," Julia told her, gasping.

And then they dined at a restaurant in the management's quarter of the city and took the underground tube home. Arethustra asked, "Is that what it's like to be in a kindercity?" Arethustra had always had a ravening curiosity about children raised differently from herself.

"There are more meat-things for the children in kindercities to do," Julia said, "if that's what you're asking. And they're more socially oriented, as word processors are. Because they grow up with other children, the older helping to teach the younger, with mentors rather than parents, and are given heavier social responsibility sooner than family-raised children are."

"Is it better or worse to be raised in a kindercity than in a family?" Arethustra asked.

Julia took her hand and gently squeezed it. "It's impossible to say, love. The two things are different. And the people raised in those ways are different. But though sometimes one can say that certain ways of raising children are harmful, in the case of these two ways, no one can truly say which is better."

Her answer, Julia knew, left out so much that one might say she had equivocated to the point of disingenuousness. But she was tired, and Arethustra was tired, and she could not think of a concise, illustrative way of explaining the truth as she knew it.

47.

ESÉE SQUATTED ON the seat of the armchair (by a happy coincidence, not the one S04 occupied), in the idiosyncratic posture characteristic of Gertrude Stein. She looked so much more like a primary than like the tertiary Julia's Gertrude Stein had always been that for a moment Julia almost thought her independently *real*, rather than the configuration of imagination she had programmed by herself. But then she realized that for the moment, the figure before her resembling her tertiary was indeed, functionally, a primary— the primary representing the alien entity who called herself Esée...

Julia blinked—and flinched at the pain she felt in her breast, a pain that might be a sensation of sharp, sudden loss. That she didn't recognize the object of this sense of loss made the sensation all the more poignant, and after a while, it overwhelmed her. Though her primary self did not show tears, she imagined herself to be weeping. (And wondered briefly if her meat-self, lying in its caretaker, was in fact shedding the hot, wet, salty tears prickling some unrepresented and therefore phantom self's eyelids.)

<<Men carry such richly complex and powerful emotions within them>> Esée said. <<And it is good and wonderful that it is so. These emotions are the very being and essence of men, but are also, in some strange way, violently outside and other, even as they rage within. They both permanently and temporarily take over parts of men's minds, and thread through the many forgotten places. And are both familiar and strange, cherished and repudiated. And a source of unending conflict and beauty. Men can be many things, all at the same time, in one entity. This is a mystery to us of La Femme. And a great beauty. Men are quite alien to us.>>

Julia stared in amazement at the image of Gertrude Stein, and she remembered that Esée could not see her secondaries, and her secondaries could not in any way perceive Esée, and the pain that had momentarily left her for the astonishment with which Esée's words had filled her returned, like a knife severing her heart in two. She felt disoriented. She couldn't stop herself from trying to grasp the relationship between the presence of her secondaries on the one hand and that of Esée on the other. It eluded her, and thinking about it confused her. This c-space was *hers*, designed by her, and always and ever under her control. But it felt alien to her now.

Esée threw back the large head, exposing its thick, strong neck, and her glittering eyes peered out from below the shapely, heavy lids at Julia. <<If we were in what you call meat-space, this confusion would vanish, Julia>> Esée said. <<It is only because your secondaries and I cannot communicate directly that you feel confusion. But think of it this way: I'm not really in your c-space, but am simply one mind meeting with another in a convenient, sensorial medium. You are, in other words, in two or three places at once. You are in your c-space, with your secondaries. You are in your caretaker, experiencing neural impulses, nourishment, and medication, and you are on another plane intersecting both of those planes, talking to me.>>

"Yes," Julia said. The weight of confusion lifted from her. It made sense when one thought of it in such conceptually simple terms. It was possible to be too abstract.

"There are many things I need to ask you, Esée," she said. "Could you start by telling me why it isn't possible for you to inscribe your speech to me in writing, or project it as a physical voice that could be recorded by AI?"

Esée leaned forward, taking the weight of her upper body on her arms, which were braced palms-to-thighs with elbows flaring outward with strangely powerful, balletic grace. Her face beamed with an animation Julia had *never* seen in that tertiary. <<Your question is excellent for what its answer can teach you. Your mind

is the medium for our communication. It is also the channel. If it were possible for you to inscribe into writing, or project into physically voiced language, all the thoughts in your mind in all their nuances and complexity, then it would be possible for us to communicate as you have asked. But it is not possible. It might seem to you that we should be able to use the language you use for writing and vocal speech to communicate. But we have no such language ourselves. We would not know how to do it. When you dream, and you wake up and describe your dream, your description bears only a partial relationship to the dream you actually experienced. When you describe a dream, you are not only abstracting parts of it, but are creating it anew, so that it becomes something else. Something meaningful and clearly taken from the source of the dream, and therefore not false, yet not the dream itself. Because it wouldn't be possible to put all of the dream into words. This is an approximation of the problem of putting our communications into words. Even now, as I speak, your memory is selecting and refining phrases and concepts you are abstracting from the flow of this communication. What you recognize, what strikes you, is what you will recall. Rehearsing what you recall will authorize its status as the words that I spoke to you. While of course I'm not really speaking to you, but am in telepathic communication, which one part of your mind receives as a message and refines into words...>>

And indeed, as Julia listened, she began to feel the strange and terrible frustration of a mind inundated with multiple images and streams of thoughts and whispers of ideas eluding her conscious grasp, as though suddenly a million nerves she had never been aware of had woken to painful, stimulated life, teasing, prickling, tickling her with a mélange of impulses far beyond her capacity to process. Like a stream of hypnagogic images, memories and emotions flashed through her mind's eye, too fleeting to be grasped after their passage—Joey and Saella nursing her; standing in the rain with her face turned to the dome's heavy gray sky; Arethustra holding tightly to her hand; herself and Raye wrestling on an exercise mat; her finger touching the slippery pink tip of Sasha's penis; rocking and soothing a frightened infant Outsider in her arms...

<<Julia, you can control your perception of our communication>> Esée said, staunching the flow of images, most of which Julia had already forgotten.

"Did you see all that, Esée?" she cried. "Did you call all those images forth? Is that one of your powers?"

<<These images are always there in your mind. You mostly don't perceive them. Yes, as you've formulated it to yourself, you sometimes perceive them when you're just about to drop into sleep. But that's because the part of your mind that dominates has at that point let go, so that for just those few instants you glimpse something that is ordinarily going on in your mind all of the time. I don't call them forth, they are simply there. And they are a part of your communication with me.>>

Julia felt as though she were suffocating. For a few moments she forgot she was in her caretaker, assured of a constant, controlled feed of oxygen. A terrible fear engulfed her. Humans had always hidden the unbearable from their conscious selves; it was the only way they could stand the pain of consciousness. What horror, to think that all of that was being communicated, without her awareness, *all of the time*, to these beings they knew nothing about. Perhaps Fuyuko was correct. Perhaps there never could be authentic communication between such unequivalently represented species.

48.

"JULIA," S04 SAID sharply. "Let us help you."

"Which we can't do unless you tell us what Esée has been saying to you," S07 added.

Julia sank back into her chair. "AI," she said, "remove S04 and S07 from this c-space."

The secondaries vanished.

<<You are upset and anxious>> Esée said. <<The thought that all that you hide from yourself is apparent to us disturbs you. The thought that all that you hide from yourself are things you haven't confined into language frightens you even more. Do you know why, Julia?>>

Julia's heart lurched with shock. In the absolute silence of v-space, in which even the sound of her blood was muted, Julia felt unmoored, as though she were drifting haplessly in free-fall without a handhold or surface in sight. Standing before the desk appeared to be S03, unsummoned by Julia. Like S03, the figure had Julia's eyes, the body of Saella (as Julia imagined it had been while Saella was her milk-parent), the solemn drapery, posture, and body-language of Davis, and the face (mostly) of Lanna. Julia guessed it must be Esée, and not S03. When she "heard" the voice inside her head, she knew it. <<Perhaps some of this anxiety would be dispelled if we were to confront, as an example, one of these areas you conceal from yourself, one that has lately preoccupied you greatly, though without acknowledgment.>> The figure held out a white-sleeved arm and pointed with a thick brown finger at a place behind and to the left of Julia.

Julia looked over her shoulder and found a holostage where the wall had been. Harsh yellow light strobed in long rhythmic strokes over the disorganized mass of struggling and flailing bodies. Julia recognized the site as the bridge. The screaming and shouting, the thuds of flesh against flesh were deafeningly loud, as though her auditory inputs had gotten glitched. To one side of the mass of wildly struggling crew drifted a body, surrounded by crimson strings and glistening gobs of something Julia recognized, in an instant of shocking clarity, as meat. The body was Glory's, and though blood still seeped out of its neck, it looked dead (or nearly so).

Julia gagged; her eyes filmed with tears, so that she did not see when exactly Fuyuko appeared. Blinking, she made out the psyche-synthesist clinging to the hold-bar just inside the hatch (which Julia for the first time saw had been wedged open). The moment dragged interminably while Fuyuko stood there, surveying the carnage. Julia could hardly bear the racket pummeling her ears, rubbing her nerves raw with overstimulation. A new sound, of moaning, caught her attention, and she searched for its source. She realized it must be coming from another body that had separated from the mass seemingly glued together in its cataclysmic homicidal fury, a bleeding body she recognized as Sering. Julia rose to her feet and took a step toward the holostage before she stopped herself. All this was past. There was nothing she could do now to restore order.

So Julia looked at Fuyuko, still barely inside the hatch, face contorted with distress, body rigid with shock. Julia wanted to scream at her to help Sering, she longed to shake her into action, to jolt her into bringing the crew to their senses. Finally, finally, Fuyuko moved, inching her way along the hold-bar as though it were a wire she was suspended from and the bridge a bottomless chasm she was crossing at risk to her life. "Move, man," Julia urged, "for the love of your parents *move*!" Still Fuyuko just inched her way along, stiff and rigid in the wild and noisy chaos.

Julia turned her back on the scene and stared at Esée. "I already know what happens," she said. "Fuyuko gets Sering out of there and then orders the med-units to put everyone on the ship to

In the course of writing this report, I frequently recalled what the *Pax III* word processor, Nadia, reminded me that the Delta Pavonians say about traveling outside one's own culture: "People leave home to find out who they are and to learn anew how good and appropriate home is." Whenever I've heard this saying repeated, it's struck me as a paradox that humans will probably never understand. But it seems to me now that our encounters with "La Femme," as we have so far experienced it, have all been about "finding out who we are." The most obvious aspect of this lies in the circumstance that though La Femmeans are themselves nodes in a network rather than individuals, they deal with us only as individuals. Since they apparently reflect ourselves back to ourselves, that suggests to me that we see the Pax (and humans, generally) not as a cohesive whole, but rather as an assemblage of individuals. I conjecture that this is the reason their Contact with us has been with individuals with separate interests and desires rather than with the mission of which the individuals are parts (contra Fuyuko's suspicion that they divide us for particular, inimical reasons). The La Femmeans' confusion around gender similarly reflects points of confusion we did not ourselves suspect we held.

— from The Summary of Julia 9561's Report on "La Femme" to the First Council

sleep and into their caretakers. I don't see the point in prolonging the agony."

<<Whose agony, Julia?>> Esée said, coming to stand beside Julia. <<*They* can't feel anything, since it's merely a mental recreation of events.>> Julia glanced (briefly, so briefly) over her shoulder. "Mental?" she said. "Does that mean this isn't from a recording, but implanted in my head by you? But from where did you get it?"

<<These questions are trivial and, quite simply, evasive of the point.>> Esée—still in the form of S03—shook her head at Julia. She turned slightly and held her arms wide. <<It is your agony, Julia, that concerns me. It is your agony that you conceal from yourself. Don't you know that things concealed can be just as powerful—if not more so—than those given full representation?>>

Julia's throat tightened. "No," she said. "It's better to keep things like that at arm's length. There's nothing I can do about it. It's past. Perhaps I haven't learned anything from it yet, and that's not good. But there's been no time." She hadn't had the time to meet with S03 since she had woken after transudation. "I have responsibilities. Clearly, I failed in some of them, or Glory's death wouldn't have happened. But that's no excuse for me to fail in my other responsibilities. Later will be time enough." She longed to go into those inviting arms. S03's embrace meant more to her than almost anything in her adult life. S05 might be her sybil, but S03 was her confessor and healer. S03 was her moral authority. Only S03's approval could satisfy the part of her that was still a daughter.

S03 was all that she had left of true parents.

S03 touched Julia's shoulder, then blinked out. Julia looked around and saw that Gertrude Stein had returned, squatting as before in the armchair. <<Surely you can't be as frightened as you were, now that you've seen an instance of what you communicate unawares.>>

Julia lay down on the sofa and covered her face with her arm. "All this has been about me," she said. "And nothing about you. But if you know anything about me, you must know that's not why I came all the way here from Earth."

<<Are you sure, Julia?>> Esée said. <<Are you really sure that's not why you traveled so far from home?>>

49.

BEFORE ARETHUSTRA'S BIRTH, Julia and her co-parents debated when, if it proved necessary, they should inflict instruction for controlling the expressivity of her face and body on her. They understood that children often learned such control by emulating, unconsciously, the adults around them. By all accounts, the child who had to be taught such control suffered a painful period of self-consciousness that could be as short as a few weeks or—in meat-space—permanent. They hated even discussing it, because tampering with another human being in such a way in many respects violated eutopic principles. But they all knew that their child would be handicapped in engaging effectively in meat-space relations if she lacked this crucial control in her self-presentation. Though Paxan adults spent three-quarters to four-fifths of their conscious lives in v-space, it would be a mistake to overlook the portion spent in meat-space.

Arethustra, unfortunately, did not unconsciously emulate her parents. And because they had decided in advance that it would be best to tackle such a problem when the child reached the age of eleven, it fell chiefly to Julia and Moira, the parents intensively engaged at the time, to teach her to control her bodily expressions. The responsibility vexed Julia and tried her patience. Certainly it was unpleasant to render her daughter self-conscious about her appearance. But while Julia had found Arethustra's uncontrolled expressivity charming in early childhood, it irritated her, sometimes intolerably, as the child grew older. Although her irritation told her that the task needed to be performed, it also made her feel that she was the wrong parent to do it. She often wished that Jorreau, who had intensively parented Arethustra during her fifth through tenth years, had done it on his watch. Of all the parents, he had the easiest, most approval-conveying manner with their child. He had a knack of seemingly drawing out of Arethustra herself the many things he taught her. And, Julia believed, of all her parents, Arethustra trusted Jorreau most.

Julia put off the task until Arethustra had nearly turned twelve. She discussed the manner of approach with the other parents, most especially, of course, with Moira (whose period of intensive engagement was during Arethustra's eleventh through sixteenth years). Arethustra's best hours were in the morning, so one morning, Julia took her into the sitting room, whose holography made it a sort of vivarium (since plant life so fascinated Arethustra that her parents thought she might eventually choose to become a restorationist), and told her that it was time to begin a new project in her socialization, namely the start of what would be her lifelong construction of her self-presentation. Arethustra already grasped a great deal about representation through her limited excursions in c-spaces, which required that one not only create one's own primary representation, but also accept and interact with others' representations of themselves, however different one might know their physical appearance to be in meat-space. That morning, however, Julia discovered that her daughter found the very idea of applying the principles of v-space representation to meat-space upsetting.

Julia locked her fingers together as she watched Arethustra's face go into wild, complex action.

"What is done in c-space," Arethustra said, her gleaming black eyes narrowed almost into a squint, "is an abstraction, or even a stylization of meat-space. Isn't that so? It's very controlled, and programmed, and rule-driven. But the wonderful thing about meat-space is that things are...accidental. That they just happen as they happen. I mean, you don't have to worry about what all the little things *mean*, because likely they don't mean anything in particular, but just *are*."

Though Julia thought she knew Arethustra well, the answer shocked her. "That's a rather romantic way of looking at it," she said drily. "Or, perhaps more accurately, *childish*. You see, Arethustra, your experience of meat-space has been rather…limited. And protected. And so you've been free to enjoy the easiness and looseness and apparent randomness of that…*happening*. Or *being*. But when you've entered the world as an adult—when you've gone to University, say—well, you'll find that the random and accidental will be remarkably difficult to distinguish from the deliberate. Because in fact, though there's more variation and imperfection and noise in meat-space, still, it's just as programmed. Even though, looked at superficially, one might not think so."

Julia knew such an argument wasn't exactly fair, since Arethustra had no logical means of countering it. But she wasn't thinking of it so much as arguing (in the way Arethustra was) as establishing the foundation for the lesson she was obliged to deliver. Julia gave Arethustra what she thought of as her quiet-and-gentle-but-strong parental gaze. "The point is, love, that most of what you like to think of as accidental will be endowed with meaning whether you want it to be or not. Therefore, if a difficult-to-interpret expression comes unconsciously into your face, or your body positions itself without your being aware of it, the people interacting with you will nevertheless make their own interpretations. Put simply, the difference between accidental and conscious expressivity is that in the former case the interpretation will be made not only without your knowledge, but also without your having any conscious influence at all on it, while in the latter case you will know exactly how others will interpret it, and will in fact determine how they will interpret it in advance."

But Arethustra loathed the very idea of "programming" her meat-self. She protested to that effect at length. "You're always already programmed, love," Julia said. "Don't you understand, it's just a matter of whether the programming will be made without your knowledge, or with! There is no such thing as a 'natural' human being. Our bodies don't simply do things without reference to learning and meaning. It only *seems* accidental to you, to the extent that you are unaware of what you're doing. It's like saying all right, I'm going to wear a blindfold from now on, so that the sight of things won't obscure my sense of hearing, which is more 'natural' than my sense of sight."

Julia had always assumed that the worst of the lesson would be watching Arethustra painfully catching herself again and again in uncontrolled and unintended expressivity. The next step was to have entailed recording Arethustra in meat-space and setting her to study the recordings. It had never occurred to Julia (or the other parents, either) that Arethustra would simply refuse to see the necessity for undertaking the lesson at all.

50.

FULLY ONE-THIRD OF the conscious crew had contributed reports, like her own, full of "answers" to many of the questions preoccupying them. "So how many of us have had a Contact since our last meeting?" Julia queried the assembled crew. So many hands went up that Julia said, "How many of us *haven't* had a Contact?"

Three hands were raised: Nadia's, Solita's, and—after a slight hesitation—Fuyuko's.

"And would everyone agree," Julia said, "that the Contacts were…desired, in some…obvious way?"

All around the c-space table heads bobbed. Except, of course, for Fuyuko's, Nadia's, and Solita's. Julia offered a weary, mock-self-deprecating smile. "Yes. Well, the truth is, I find the wealth of new material overloading me." She had fed it all to S04 and S07. But she had to wonder if the others' reports were as incomplete as her own. If they were all holding back on one another… Julia flashed on a scene she had inadvertently witnessed only a month or two before Arethustra's thirteenth birthday. The child had been showering in the large bathroom, not the small private room designated for use when one didn't wish interruption by or contact with other family members; Julia came in when she was toweling herself. Arethustra, intent on rubbing her breasts, didn't notice. Julia halted, in distress. The child's breasts were raw and bleeding. But judging by the expression on Arethustra's face, she was taking pleasure from the friction. Without thinking, Julia left, very quietly. What she had seen troubled her, for she didn't know how to classify it. She felt instinctively that it was a private matter for Arethustra and thus beyond discussion uninitiated by the child herself, and yet she worried there might be something…misguided, something requiring instruction, some seemingly insignificant but particular matter inadvertently omitted from explication by all of the parents.

The med-monitor on Julia's caretaker chose this moment to ask her if she wanted to be chemically calmed. The fact was, she was anxious, and now angry, too, that her mind was betraying her with inappropriate material at a time when it was already flooded with more than it could handle. *S04 and S07 can handle it for me. They may not be me, but they work for me. And their brains are modeled on parts of mine.* Julia's irritation expanded to the point that she felt like smashing something to express it. *Why am I cluttering my mind with useless thoughts. Is this a sign of instability?*

"I've made a list of items abstracted from our reports," Julia said carefully. "Items I thought of particular interest." *S04 and S07 made the list.* "AI, run the program 'Leanne,' magnification 6, 'behind' me."

"And may I issue a caveat," Fuyuko said grimly, before Julia had finished speaking to the AI. "Namely that we try to keep in mind that all the so-called information provided by the aliens is unverifiable and based on their word alone."

"Though it surely counts for something that we can check it for consistency," Astra said.

"Consistency with what?" Blaise said. "The very nature of our communications with them precludes our being clear on the message being communicated. On the basis of what I learned—or rather *think* I learned from my own Contact, the messages they transmit could be described as broad-spectrum, and our conscious reading of them as selectively narrow. Such that our dominant consciousness takes in one part of the message and processes it into the words we think we hear in our heads."

Kristen and Melina were nodding as Blaise spoke.

"Think of it as being analogous to vision. The cones and rods of our retinas pick up signals along a certain narrow band of light and then convert that pattern of light into a neural signal, which is then processed by the neuronal network of the retina and transmitted to the brain. The input, which is the nature of samplings of the visual field, is processed in the visual cortex. The end result is the representation of the visual field we take for sight. It would be a lie to say we 'see' everything that we look at. In fact, our eyes do not *see* everything, but the processing lets us think that we do, or rather, our minds simply ignore the holes or blindspots. In this case, I believe that some part of our brain is processing the inputs we're getting from the La Femmeans. Because these inputs are new to us, we lack any standardized response that would allow us to feel that we're all receiving the same message."

Blaise had spelled this all out at even greater length in her report, but Julia thought they could probably stand to hear the theory several more times besides, since it took the sinister edge off the subject.

"I agree completely," Melina said. "I hadn't thought of that analogy until I read it in your report, but I think it's beautifully apt. Or one could use the analogy of hearing—particularly of music, which as we all know is a culturally acquired skill. What sounds like music in one culture may sound like structureless noise in another."

"What I'm curious about," said Carlton, "is whether they actually have a language by which they communicate among themselves."

"We'll never be able to perceive it if they do," Kristen said sadly.

Something in this statement brought Julia's anxiety back full force. She said, to recall them to her agenda, "Now that we have a working theory on how their telepathy operates, which was by the way the first item on the list Leanne is ready to give you—" and Julia glanced over her shoulder to verify that the tertiary was standing, larger-than-life-sized, behind her— "perhaps we can go on to the second." When no one objected, Julia said, "Leanne, read Item Two, please." And she turned around for the pleasure of looking at her choice, a muscular, leather-clad, large-breasted woman in standard heroic posture, the image of Leanne Chenadi, one of the most famous of the twenty-first century ideological terrorists who some historians considered precursor figures to the founders of the Pax. Though Vance would have recognized and applauded the choice, Julia knew it unlikely any other crew member would catch the allusion.

"Item Two: on the basis of communications made by the indigene Catalina to Sonia in the course of two encounters, the La Femmeans do not reproduce sexually, have no disease, famine, war, or poverty. And Sonia understood Catalina to say that the La Femmeans expect to live for as long as their planet and star do."

S04 had discussed this item with Julia before including it in the list. But still, hearing it again Julia felt an unpleasant butterfly sensation feathering her stomach and nauseating her. No one knew anything about the Delta Pavonians' life expectancy, but the idea that they might be immortal had never to Julia's knowledge been entertained. Something about the linkage of the La Femmeans' lives with that of their planet and star struck her powerfully. Though humans understood themselves to be intimately connected with their planet and sun, an identification between the existence of the entire species on the one hand and Earth and its star on the other was simply never posited. Humans did not think that way.

"If Sonia understood what the aliens wanted her to understand," Fuyuko said sharply, "then we have to assume such a claim is a fabrication meant to impress us—or to test the limits of our naiveté."

Sonia gave Fuyuko a look she made both patient and solemn. "But if they don't reproduce, immortality is the only possibility."

Fuyuko, who had been looking at Julia while Sonia spoke, now looked at the latter and said, "They've described themselves as females—to the crew of the *Pax I*, if not to us. And they've been representing themselves with milk breasts. Maybe they really are females and have the purpose of attracting male gametes. In case you haven't noticed, they keep referring to us as *men*. Which suggests they think we're male. As I'll remind you the entire surviving crew of the *Pax I* are."

S07 bent and whispered in Julia's ear. "Fuyuko is using a secondary verbally slaved to her meat-space self. Fuyuko's not connected, but is receiving voice transmission through the AI and is transmitting commands in the same way back to her secondary." *So. Fuyuko has realized she can participate remotely. It's a clumsy and slow kind of participation, to be sure, but better than none.*

"Well if that's what they're really interested in," Astra said, scoffing, "then they've got a big disappointment coming."

Julia, like most of the crew, laughed. She said, "But the La Femmeans' confusion about our sex does bring us to another item on the list. Leanne, read Item Six, please."

"Item Six," Leanne said. "The La Femmeans demonstrate confusion about the differences among three groups: the male crew of *Pax I* with whom they've had Contact, the word processors, and the non-word processor crew of *Pax III*. Because Julia told them that we are all men, they now wonder whether these three groups represent three races or subspecies of men."

"It's because they don't have language," Kristen said, wonderingly. "And so they can't distinguish between males and females!"

"Which is why," Julia said, making a sweet smile she directed at Fuyuko's secondary, "I doubt their interest in us has anything to do with gametes."

51.

S04 WHISPERED IN Julia's ear: "You're making this into a rhetorical competition, Julia. Fuyuko's argument bores everyone here. There's no need to score points off her. You should be encouraging a more serious discussion of the items on the list and a consideration of what as a whole they suggest."

Point. "And they could be triggering this mass hallucination chemically," Fuyuko was saying. "The point is, just as everything we don't understand can be accounted for by their lack of a structured language, so we could as plausibly explain it as a mass fantasy we're consensually constructing as we go along."

Astra said, "Have you noticed neurochemical changes in us, on which to base your hypothesis?"

After a tiny pause, Fuyuko said, "Not yet. It may be something subtle, something that manifests itself only during encounters. And since no one has been scanned during the course of an encounter…"

"But we are all still within normal parameters of healthy brain chemistry?" Julia asked.

"Yes," Fuyuko replied (again after a barely perceptible delay), "but it's not our ability to reason or our emotional stability that's in question. Only our desire to interpret these encounters—which for the most part the AI can't verify as even taking place—in a particular way."

Julia said, soberly, "Since you haven't any positive ideas to put forth of your own, Fuyuko, humor us, please, while reserving your skepticism. Let's hypothesize, just in case we're not all sharing an hallucination, that the La Femmeans have been communicating with us telepathically. We can always scratch whatever we come up with and start over fresh, if it turns out you're correct. Which you could test by scanning some of us while we were undergoing non-corporeal Contacts, which as we noted at the top of the meeting, all but three of us know we can initiate merely by wishing for them."

"Any volunteers?" Fuyuko said. Hands went up all around the table. Even Julia raised her hand. "Very well then, I'll begin working on this when we've finished this meeting."

"Excellent," Julia said. "And now. May I suggest we let Leanne give us the rest of the list, so that instead of running points off on tangents, we consider them as a whole?"

"Item Three," Leanne said. "The La Femmeans by their own report lack anything resembling a formal governing structure. There is, therefore, no centralized authority with which the Pax can negotiate trade arrangements.

"Item Four: La Femme, the planet, has had a geological history determined almost solely by its inhabitants. Three different crew members asked their contacts about La Femme's geological history, and in each case the crew member understood the La Femmean to be saying that the planet is coterminous with its inhabitants. One crew member believes, from further questioning in this vein, that their contact was claiming that the physical features registered by our sensors are creations of the inhabitants. But another crew member concluded that the La Femmeans say that they *are* the planet and shape it as they will.

"Item Five: The La Femmeans say they have provided, in particular areas of their planet, the correct atmosphere and environment for human habitation. Our transmissions are blocked from these areas because of a special shield they have constructed for holding that atmosphere (which they themselves do not require).

"Item Seven: the La Femmeans have had contacts with the Delta Pavonians. They say that the Delta Pavonians helped them prepare for our eventual arrival.

"Item Eight: the La Femmeans do not seem to understand the concept of trade. They say they are willing to provide for the needs of any Paxans who wish to visit or live on La Femme. They say it would be impossible for them to leave their star system and visit other worlds because they are La Femme, and are thus bound to their place and world.

"Item Nine: they say all the names used for themselves and their cities and even their planet are the creation of Paxan minds, because they do not make names among themselves.

"Item Ten: a La Femmean's conscious-ness encompasses all of her world and all of the inhabitants of her world. And now encompasses all of us.

"Item Eleven: what one La Femmean knows, all La Femmeans know. Therefore, when one of us has an encounter with a La Femmean, the encounter is perceived and remembered by all La Femmeans. The La Femmeans say that theirs is a group consciousness.

"Item Twelve: the La Femmeans recog-nize aggression in other species, specifically in humans, but consider it a neurochemi-cal condition. They say this neurochemical condition has never appeared among La Femmeans. They say the same thing about other human drives. These are the twelve items Julia extracted from the crew reports that have so far been filed. I am now pre-pared to address questions crew may have about the reports."

The oddity of the La Femmeans' stress on individuating us was especially striking to me, given my clear sense that none of the inhabitants, as they appeared to us, are actual individuals but rather manifestations of something analogous to an AI's subprograms.

I see only open questions here: Is this peculiar refusal to treat with us collectively a deliberate passive-aggressive tactic designed to neutralize and even fend off outsiders? Or is it an artifact of the *Pax I*'s initial interactions with them? Or of some other history of past interactions with other outsiders? Or an indigenously evolved structure, in which case one must wonder whether other intelligent/sentient organisms inhabit (or at one time inhabited) the planet.

— from The Summary of Julia 9561's Report on "La Femme" to the First Council

"If only," Astra said, "we could be sure we understood them."

Blaise said, "If it's true, as they seem to be saying, that the Del-ta Pavonians have not only been here before us, but told them we would be coming, then there is clear reason for concern."

"The entire list of items is preposterous!" Fuyuko said. "Notice, by claiming not to have language, anything we get wrong is our own doing. And any aggression is our doing, since of course they simply *aren't* aggressive. And finally, they welcome us with open arms. Happy to give us the planet and anything we need or want. If they *do* have telepathy, and I see no reason to leap to that conclusion, but if they do, you can bet they've used it to figure out exactly what we want to hear. While in the meantime, we have people down on that planet with whom we've yet to speak."

"Oh Fuyuko, they're fine, I assure you," Felix said. She smiled engagingly, and Julia remembered again how entirely different her meat-space body was from her primary's appearance. "I didn't, of course, see any crew from the *Pax I*, but there's no question about my team down on the surface. And if you'd let me return, I could verify that for you."

"Nadia," Fuyuko said sharply. Nadia jumped a little, then sat up straight, uncomfortable at the sudden attention. "Have you transmitted these reports and a tape of the contact in the quarantined hold back to the Council?"

Nadia looked at Julia. "No one told me I was supposed to do that. Do you want me to do it now?"

"It would be wise, Julia, to agree," S04 said. "But insist on sending *everything*, in raw form. So that they'll be faced with a flood of data and not the debate Fuyuko would like to hand them."

"Send them everything," Julia said to the word processor. "Including the recording of the first corporeal Contact. Plus all the new astrophysical data for this system the crew have been amassing."

"One does have to wonder about the Delta Pavonian connection," Chandra said. "And about what preparing for our arrival entailed." She looked at Nadia. "Have you any idea what the Delta Pavonians would be likely to make of our Contact with La Femme?"

Frowning, Nadia gnawed at her lip. After considerable hesitation, she replied, "The Delta Pavonians say that people leave home to find out who they are and to learn anew how good and appropriate home is. I'm not sure, though, if they think we're at the stage of doing that. So it's a little hard to project what they might make of our coming here. Except that since they programmed the ships they gave us with certain destinations, presumably they knew we would be coming here if we used their ships." She glanced down, then added, almost mumbling, "When the La Femmeans sing to me and Solita, they sing about how much they love La Femme and want to give of it to us. As though it's something, like an atmosphere or a space, with which they can surround us." Nadia looked up. "One of their analogies is to their star, Albireo. Or rather, to the light of Albireo that, they say, feeds and warms them."

"An analogy?" Kristen said. "I don't understand."

Nadia folded her hands tightly. "You have to understand about singing. It's full of images. And evocations. And I think they are figuring themselves—or rather the planet—as being to us like Albireo is to them. Rich and nurturing. An environment in which they thrive. Although like most analogies, obviously it breaks down fairly quickly if it's true that the La Femmeans can't live away from Albireo, which, they sing, gave birth to them." Nadia stared at her hands. "Since we *can* live away from La Femme. And we were born on Earth."

"That's spooky," Carlton half-whispered. "I think we're going to have to insist on seeing the crew of *Pax I*."

"At the very least," Fuyuko said into a long silence. "At the bare-bones, minimalist least."

52.

IN HER TWELFTH year Arethustra suffered such a severe back-lash headache that she refused to undertake any further lessons in c-space. Julia explained to her that these things happened, and that until she was old enough to use a caretaker she must be brave—and keep a supply of medication patches next to her so that if another headache struck she could toggle out and apply a patch before the pain built into the torment she had experienced. Arethustra refused. "What is the point?" she said. "I don't see why I can't just do all my lessons in meat-space. I could read printouts, couldn't I?" She slid Julia one of the sly, sardonic looks she had tended to lately. "Of course, it would be inconvenient for you and Moira, I know, since you hate the messiness of meat-space. But it might be healthier for you, too."

Julia ended by bribing her. Arethustra had repeatedly asked Julia to take her to the City of Word Processing for another visit. At wits' end, Julia negotiated a two-day visit, including a meeting with her old tutor, Rosina, in exchange for Arethustra's return to c-space lessons.

The meeting with Rosina thrilled Arethustra. She stared, wide-eyed, at the enormous jewel implanted in the word processor's throat and grinned without the faintest whiff of self-conscious-ness at Rosina's amiable profession of willingness to answer any questions she might have. Julia, sipping tea, almost choked when Arethustra led off with a question as to why only those who gen-dered themselves female became word processors.

"That is just about the hardest question you could ask," Rosina said, smiling. "But no male-gendered person that I've heard of has wanted both to live and work in meat-space and give up a particu-lar secondary sexual characteristic of being male at the same time.

And I'm afraid that that would, indeed, be a part of the physical alteration involved." She touched her huge chest. "You can see that my lungs are much enlarged." She touched her throat. "And you can see that I've had implanted in my throat an apparatus that is partly synthesizer and partly amplifier. What you can't see is that I have more vocal cords than I was born with. And all of them are in the upper registers of my voice. If a man wanted to sing as we sing, he'd have to be willing to give up vocal cords in the lower registers. You see, although it has been tried, it is really not possible to keep the longer and thicker cords that give men low speaking voices and accommodate all the other cords they would need for singing as well. If they tried to keep them, their physical shape would change horribly, and they would have to take all food by valve, as people who live permanently in caretakers do." She shrugged. "I really don't understand psychology well enough to be able to tell you why men can't change their attitude about this one sexual characteristic." She winked at Julia. "But perhaps your parent can help us figure this out?"

In the Pax, we are used to thinking we've achieved the ideal relation to gender. Until the Delta Pavonians came, only Outsider cultures were able to hold up a mirror in which we could see ourselves. In that mirror we saw only how sane we were by comparison with their obvious perversity. The Delta Pavonians did not exactly hold up a mirror, but our attempts to communicate with them showed us something important that most of us do our best not to see: a previously imperceptible, unrecognized difference in how those Paxans who identify as male or ungendered regard their bodies from how those Paxans who identify as female do. This revelation should have been astounding, considering how often men grow milk breasts to suckle their children. Rather than ask ourselves why this distinction emerged with our realization that men avoided becoming word processors, we simply accepted it as "natural," that "it is what it is."

— from The Summary of Julia 9561's Report on "La Femme" to the First Council

Julia, of course, declined. If Arethustra had been male, the question of male psychology would have been interesting and perhaps better known to her. But except for Sasha, her relations with males outside eutopian circles had always been limited and work-oriented.

That night as she and Arethustra were lying in bed in a guesthouse in the management quarter of the City, trying to go to sleep (which Julia, used to sleeping in her caretaker, found difficult), Arethustra said in a bright, matter-of-fact voice (instead of the wistful, dreamy one she usually employed when spinning wild fantasies), "You know, Julia, I've been thinking about this for a long time, and I'm almost sure that I want my career to be in word processing."

Julia's body chilled with the sudden striking frost of fear. *Arethustra sounded serious.* Really, truly, totally serious. Not fantasizing. Not playing "Wish, wish," not even trying to be shocking. The terrible thing, Julia thought, was that Arethustra didn't seem to realize she had made an unthinkable, shocking suggestion. And Arethustra, though a child, had a solid record of carrying out her intentions, no matter how many obstacles encumbered them.

"Word processing is a fascinating profession, but for you to take it up would be sad indeed," Julia said as steadily as she could.

"You think I don't realize?" Arethustra said sternly.

"Realize what?"

"That word processors aren't considered...important."

"Important?" Julia echoed weakly. "I don't understand. By what criteria are you judging importance?"

"It's not I who's judging," Arethustra said. "Do you think I don't know that you make these judgments all the time, that people who are considered important by the Council are your idea of important?"

Julia shivered. "Oh, Arie! If I've ever given you such an impression, it's wrong. You *must* know I value what Rosina does. Or I would never have brought you here in the first place."

"You have this double way of looking at the world, Julia. In one sense, you do value what Rosina does. But you'd never want me to do it, because other people don't value it. Isn't that true? You're so aware of the difference in your values and that of other Paxans, but you hold your values *in theory* only. And would be upset with me if I acted in accordance with those values."

Julia sat up. She was both proud and disconcerted to find that Arethustra had been thinking along such lines. She certainly wasn't *surprised*. "There may be something to my being too acutely aware of others' values," she said. "But I don't believe this split you describe drives the way I actually live. The reason, love, I would hate to see you become a word processor is because it would take you almost entirely away from us, your family. And outside of the eutopian community." Julia wondered if she should have the lights on. She wished she could see Arethustra's (too, too expressive) face.

"Why do you say that?" Arethustra's voice took on a tone of belligerence. "Would the family kick me out?"

Julia sighed. "No, darling, I doubt there's anything you could do that would make the family kick you out. It would be the other way around. You'd be here, in the City of Word Processing, living almost entirely in meat-space. Word processors find it necessary to do that, both because they need to be immersed in their special culture that allows them to understand more and more of Delta Pavonian singing, and because they can't afford to lose the physical stamina merely living all the time in meat-space demands of their bodies. Though one lives longer in a caretaker, one loses a certain kind of strength and stamina by doing so. Word processors use caretakers so seldom that they *rent* them in the rare instances when they need to stay in v-space for longer than an hour or two." Julia paused, to give Arethustra an opportunity for feedback. When she didn't speak, Julia said slowly, "Believe me, love, that's the main reason I feel...disconcerted to think of you taking such a career path."

"You heard what Rosina said, after she put me through the preliminary test," Arethustra said.

Julia sat very still. What had she done, bringing her daughter to this place, after years of talking about its wonders? She tried to imagine Arethustra living here, totally physical, her body altered for singing to Delta Pavonians. "Rosina said your ear was very acute," Julia said.

"Why must the family live almost entirely in v-space?" Arethustra demanded. "Can you understand, that the meat-ness of this place is part of what I so love about it? There's almost nothing in meat-space anywhere else. Because people spend all their time in caretakers! Here—it's so...*spontaneous*. There are imperfections. Uncontrollable factors. And people aren't all hidden off in their own spaces. Imagine, if you want to see somebody who lives here, you can just do it, instead of having to connect, locate them, and ask permission to enter their space! Julia, I think it's *beautiful*!"

For the second time, Julia realized that she had failed to convey to Arethustra one of the most fundamental facts of Paxan life. It wasn't the sort of concept one could teach, exactly. Most Paxans simply picked it up. Silently, Julia grieved and worried at how to get through to her daughter. Somehow, she had to. She shuddered to think of what Arethustra's life would be if she didn't.

53.

WHEN JULIA WOKE the morning of the ship's day that had been chosen for the first authorized expedition to the surface, the AI informed her that Paris, Tree, and Celeste had returned to the ship. As a matter of discipline Julia always made it a point to rise from her caretaker, bathe, and groom herself and sometimes even take food by mouth in meat-space instead of through her gastric intake valve, her preferred method for taking nourishment. She had gotten into the habit of taking breakfast with Arethustra and her other co-parents and had continued on the ship to take it by mouth to keep in practice. Before committing herself to observance on this particular morning, though, Julia checked on the whereabouts of the returned crew, thinking that if they were already in a crew c-space she would postpone the shower and have the caretaker feed her. <<Celeste, Paris, and Tree are on the bridge>> the AI told her. And so Julia bathed, grabbed a tube of Morning Mush, and hurried to the bridge.

A set of small display windows had been opened to face the recliners that Astra and Marietta occupied; Celeste, Paris, and Tree "stood" to the sides of the recliners—their posture giving the appearance of their having their feet planted firmly on the "floor." "What *did* they feed you?" Astra was exclaiming. "Wait until Fuyuko sees these numbers! They're textbook perfection for the healthiest of the healthy human profile. Not just your brain scans, but even your basal metabolic rate."

Marietta said, "And if you do a comparison to the last numbers their caretaker registered before they left *Pax III*, you'll see that Tree was borderline anemic."

"Welcome back," Julia said to the returnees. Smiling, she clapped each on the shoulder before requesting a recliner for herself and noted that they did indeed look to be glowing with health, not to mention looking as young as their c-space primaries.

"Astra told us we're going to have to make reports," Celeste said quickly. "But she wanted to check out our numbers first."

Astra looked at Julia. "The gravity doesn't seem to have affected them at all. It's amazing. Almost my first thought when the AI told me they'd gotten back was that we'd find that six ship's days at one and an eighth of Earth's gravity had severely stressed them physically."

"You three look...positively *glowing*," Julia said.

They grinned at her. "And feel great, too," Tree said. "I mean... *wonderful.* Though I gather things are pretty...serious here. Which is the reason the three of us came back."

Julia strapped into the recliner. "I don't think I understand."

Astra said, "It seems, Julia, that Fuyuko threatened to wake Vance if Candace's entire team didn't return pronto and show that they hadn't been harmed."

Julia's gaze held Astra's in a long, sober exchange of the kind it was possible to have only in meat-space. Julia said evenly, "I hadn't heard about that. Perhaps you could elaborate."

Tree said, "Well, the La Femmeans kept giving us messages from the ship—some of them relayed through the La Femmeans, others played out in holocubes they provided us. So then yesterday—actually, it was ship's night—the La Femmeans played out a message that Fuyuko had sent. It was an ultimatum to the effect that because none of us had returned to the ship from the surface—except Felix, who hadn't stayed for more than a few hours—the *Pax III* had no way of knowing anything about our condition. And that if another ship's day passed without our having returned, she, Fuyuko, would be forced to take the only defensive action available to her, namely, 'tap' Vance and her force."

Julia said, "AI, where is Fuyuko?"

"Fuyuko is in her caretaker, sleeping."

Julia looked at Tree. "Did Fuyuko say that the entire team had to be returned to the ship?"

Tree bit her lip. "Yes, I'm afraid she did."

"We thought that if four of the six of us were back, Fuyuko would be reassured."

Julia took the tube of breakfast from her loin pocket. She glanced at Astra and Marietta, then looked soberly at Tree. "If Candace and Shaelle aren't back before Fuyuko awakens, our hand will be forced."

"Oh shit," Marietta said.

Julia said, "Unless you'd like to have to deal with Vance's force?" In who knew what mental condition?

"They didn't want to come back," Paris said unhappily. "I mean, they said that it didn't matter if Vance was awakened, that there was nothing Vance could do to mess things up on La Femme. And that they were sorry if things got ugly on the ship, but..."

The pause heightened the tension. "But?" Julia said sharply.

Paris and Tree looked at one another, and then at Celeste. Celeste said, "They said they didn't care what happened on the ship, that they intended never to go back to it again, and that if the rest of the crew were smart, they'd come down to the surface, too, and see for themselves that ship's business was just..." Celeste looked nervously at Tree.

"Was just?" Julia prompted.

Celeste flushed. "Just a puddle of unrecycled shit," she said softly.

54.

SINCE BEFORE ARETHUSTRA'S birth, her co-parents had been meeting biweekly in a privacy-shielded family c-space. At the first regularly scheduled meeting following Julia and Arethustra's second excursion to the City of Word Processing, Julia related their conversation as well as remarks Arethustra had made at various moments of the trip, supplementing what she had said about wanting to become a word processor. Like her, Julia's co-parents expressed dismayed astonishment at the very idea. Zuni urged that they search for other explanations besides the stated intention to account for Arethustra's remarks. But Denny, in the Aha mode, said, "Well it fits, I'm afraid, it fits with other bits and pieces that have randomly presented themselves over the years." And there followed, in speedy profusion, a cascade of similar comments from almost everyone. In short order they assembled a puzzle, the pieces of which they had not previously known they possessed, spelling their daughter's aversion to c-space, her resentment that her family members spent so much time in it (away from her), and her belief that c-space was *dead* and that the grandparents and great-grandparents who lived permanently in caretakers and manifested themselves only in c-space were not really alive. And finally, they glued their puzzle together with observations on their daughter's desire for unmediated experience and perception, which she had somehow not learned had never been and would never be available.

"This is a disaster!" Mei said. "We must do something to help her see. By the time she has worked it out she'll have suffered so much she'll be ready to give up altogether. That spark is given to us only once. It never returns once it's been extinguished."

"I thought you were all eutopians here," Arete said sternly. She rapped her knuckles on the table for a nicely crisp, staccato emphasis. "We absolutely must help her take her chosen path. And by 'chosen path' I mean the path she chooses to take. We may not share the same idea of what is appropriate for our child, but among ourselves one of the few principles we share is respect for the diversity of life. And we are all sworn to uphold the uncoerced and informed choices of others. Arethustra has made a choice." She scowled at Julia. "And thanks to Julia, she's made an *informed* choice. I don't think we can question *that*."

The silence was stunning. They had from the beginning chosen never to have music or any ambient background sounds during their parenting meetings, on the assumption that they would think and communicate more clearly in utter c-space silence. But total c-space silence meant no white noise whatsoever, nor even the sound of the blood circulating in one's ears that one always had in meat-space silence. It struck Julia with a sense of unreality. It was intolerable. Yet still…it continued.

"That's ridiculous," Moira said finally, and an almost physical pressure lifted from Julia. "We have no way of judging how *informed* Arethustra is on what is involved either physically or socially. Or on what the long-term consequences are likely to be. In any case, I think it's safe to assume she has only the most superficial idea of what life as a word processor would be."

They all looked at Julia, and she wondered if they blamed her for the fiasco. Which, she thought, was indeed her fault. "I'm afraid I filled her in pretty thoroughly, particularly after she made her announcement," she said. "Perhaps that was premature…" Of course it was. Arethustra had a stubborn streak; she always had. If Julia hadn't been so panicked, she would have waited for a time when Arethustra was more neutrally disposed, to elaborate on the consequences of making such a choice.

"Well she can't have really understood," Garcia said. "Or…did she specifically say she didn't want to do the apprenticeship?"

Julia said, "Perhaps I haven't made myself clear. This decision isn't something Arethustra's definitely taken...yet. But it's something she thinks she wants, intensely."

"You mean it's a sort of infatuation?" Jorreau asked.

"Yes, I think you could say that." And Julia realized that although "infatuation" sounded frivolous, it was a comprehensive state of mind that had throughout history been the basis for significant decisions with irreversible consequences.

"Well we'll just have to work on getting her better informed on not only the word processor's life but also the eutopian life generally," Jorreau said in his usual staid but determined fashion. He nodded at Arete. "Without, of course, plotting to coerce her choice, but only to make it more...informed."

Arete was probably less than happy with the formulation, but she accepted it. Julia only hoped it wasn't too late. She felt frightened and hurt. She had thought sharing the pain and threat with the others would help. But the fact remained that for the first time, Arethustra's will opposed everything that they'd hoped and expected, even opposed their continuing relations. In a sense, they had lost their child already—in the way in which parents always "lose" children to adulthood—only it had happened several years too early. Would they be condemned to spending those years preparing themselves for the almost total loss now threatening them?

55.

JULIA SHUT HERSELF into a privacy cabin, ordered the AI to notify her the instant Fuyuko woke, and toggled into v-space. With such a high potential for important meat-space activity, Julia chose to forgo a return to her caretaker. She felt she needed to be ready for anything.

S04 and S07, dressed in purple yoga skins, joined her in her c-space study. Julia tersely informed them of Celeste, Tree, and Paris's return to the ship and the reason for it. "It outrages me that Fuyuko went behind my back," Julia said. She glared at her secondaries. "I'm seriously tempted to put her into deep sleep, out of the way. There's no telling what she might do next—or when. Given her possession of emergency codes, she could shut us all down without even checking with me first."

"I thought you instructed the AI to require confirmation from a second officer for putting any crew into deep sleep?" S04 said calmly.

"Yes, I did. But if she woke Vance up, she could do anything!"

"Anything Vance agreed to," S07 said—pedantically, Julia thought.

"I don't see the problem, Julia," S04 said. Julia raised her eyebrows. S04 smirked. "Fuyuko can't wake Vance without your confirmation. Unless, of course, you are first declared incompetent. So all you have to do is refuse to wake Vance—and throw the beautiful physical stats on the returned crew at her, as a rebuttal for her fears."

"Except that Shaelle and Candace's refusal to return offers an all too usable counterweight," S07 said.

"*Could* Fuyuko declare me incompetent?"

S04 stroked its chin, as though in deep thought. "In theory, yes," it said. "But since there's no physical evidence of incompetence, only interpretive sorts of evidence, without an order from the Council Fuyuko couldn't do it without holding an official hearing and taking judgment from a panel designated to rule on your competence."

"Unless, of course, she declared everyone incompetent and invoked an emergency code," S07 said.

"We're going around in circles!" Julia snapped. "Can she *do* that? Would the ship's AI take her orders like that?"

"It does seem preposterous," S04 said. "But…in *theory*, yes."

"Then it seems I *should* confine her to deep sleep, without giving her a chance to sneak any more behind my back!"

"But Julia," S07 said. "Don't you think you should see if you can reason with her first? Your action, if unnecessary, would deprive the crew of an important element, however troublesome. And, since she is not verifiably incompetent, would raise questions about your exercise of authority."

That cold feeling in her belly wasn't the familiar brush of tension or even anxiety: Julia realized she was apprehensive, maybe actually afraid—an emotion she seldom experienced in her professional life. If Fuyuko wrecked everything, all because she, Julia, failed to take sufficient precautions… "Shit. I don't see how I can go to the surface when I don't know what the fuck kind of sabotage that psyche-synthesist might be getting up to."

<<Julia, may I assist in this discussion?>>

Julia almost jumped out of her virtual skin. Esée-as-Gertrude-Stein was standing just behind and to her left, between the desk and the wall. "Esée?" she said, unable to resist the need to verify that the Gertrude Stein tertiary hadn't somehow been activated.

<<Vance and her forces can't hurt La Femmeans>> Esée said. <<There is no risk to us if they attempt an attack. Please do not be concerned on our behalf.>>

Julia looked rather self-consciously at her secondaries. "Esée is here," she said. "And she claims—if I have it right—that Vance can't harm La Femme."

"That may be true," S04 said. "Though of course there's the question of whether you understood correctly. But even so, Vance poses a threat to all crew interested in pursuing relations with La Femmeans."

Julia turned to Esée. "Did you catch that, about the threat Vance poses to the rest of the crew?"

Esée smiled. <<It's very plain in your mind. But trust us. Let Vance be wakened, and let us meet her and her contingent. I believe you would stand in no danger.>> Julia stared at Esée in near disbelief. "You're saying you think mere contact with La Femmeans will change Vance's mind? But what about Fuyuko? You haven't changed *hers*!"

Esée sighed. <<No, we haven't. But that is because we respect Fuyuko's wishes to be spared further Contact.>>

Julia leaned back in her chair and closed her eyes. "I'll have to think about this," she said. And then she asked the La Femmean to leave.

"Julia," the AI said. "Fuyuko is awake. Do you wish to be patched through to her?"

"Just tell her I'd like to speak to her, on the bridge, after she's had breakfast," Julia said. And then added: "AI, direct Fuyuko's attention to Celeste, Tree, and Paris's current physical stats. Tell her I thought she'd be interested."

Images of Esée in her various manifestations played through Julia's mind's eye. Had she just heard the La Femmean imply that the La Femmeans had the power to change Fuyuko's mind but had refrained from doing so because they were so respectful of her wishes?

Julia opened her eyes and looked at her secondaries, who this time hadn't said a word about the presence of the tertiary, perhaps to keep her from sending them away. Esée was not visible, for what that was worth. "Every Contact I've had with the La Femmeans has been so ephemeral that it feels as if I've been talking to shadows," she said. "And now *you* don't seem as real to me as you always have. I had great hopes for actually *seeing* the planet, but… I feel as if I don't even know who I am anymore." Hearing her words, she felt disgusted. "At fifty, I've no excuse for that. It's wrong, wrong, wrong."

"Hmm." S04 put her fist under her chin. "Do you think you've changed enough to require the creation of another secondary to represent either new or previously hidden parts of yourself?"

Julia stared at S04 in consternation. Leave it to S04 to make her crisis of confidence concrete within the secondaries' own frame of reference. "Perhaps I misspoke," she said after a pause. "Almost since our arrival in this system you've been nagging me, insisting that I articulate my interests. I thought that was an absurd demand, since I've had a strong sense of what they were all my life. But now, with the elusiveness of the Contact we've been having with the La Femmeans... I keep telling myself everything will be clear, once we actually set foot on the planet—that we'll be able to see beyond these...reflections, these shadows of the real thing or whatever they are. When Esée was telling me that Vance would be no threat, I believed her, and not because it's what I wanted to believe. In fact, I believe her against my own judgment and inclination. So there is something there that isn't me. But realizing that...scares me. And maybe that's why I feel I don't know myself anymore." Julia resumed pacing.

S07, watching, said, "Your passion has always been for contact with Outsiders. But your encounters with human Outsiders were all disappointing. You felt disillusioned—with what? What were you hoping for? As for non-human Outsiders, their otherness so revolted you that you fled from your first encounter with a Delta Pavonian and were never able to bring yourself to attempt real Contact. And so, what happened with La Femme..."

Julia glanced at S07 when she realized it wasn't going to continue and saw that it expected her to pick up where it had left off. Her mind, full of visceral images of her first Delta Pavonian singing, of her body's revolt against the experience and her attempt to expel the disgust and shame physically by spewing vomit, seemed stuck in a loop she couldn't break out of.

Struggling to wrench her attention back to La Femme, her mind made a lateral move, recalling the word processors' experiences of Contact with La Femmeans. "I think," she said, the words coming out in fits and starts, "my doubts about myself have something to do with the difference I suspect in Nadia and Solita's experiences of Contact from my own. Part of it might be due to their long experience of Contact with Delta Pavonians. That's opened them to radical difference in a way that I've never been, for all my fine ideals. And it's taught them to attend to perceptions and nuances imperceptible to everyone else. I suppose part of it might be due to their using language alien not only to themselves but to the La Femmeans as well." Julia nodded to herself as something seemed to click into place. "When the La Femmeans and the word processors sing and dance, or whatever it is they do, they're using a mutually alien language as the ground of their communications. Maybe that does something to the kind of attention the word processors bring to the table—attention the rest of us humans lack, because we're using a language we take for granted. Does that make sense to you?"

"Oh," S04 said. "I think I see what you're getting at. They're using forms provided by the Delta Pavonians that they can share with the La Femmeans as a sort of neutral ground."

"Something like that," Julia said. "At any rate, it's a ground I am unable to perceive as neutral and thus can't even visit, much less stand on. And in the meantime, the La Femmeans communicate by reflecting our images of ourselves back to us and 'speaking' telepathically so elusively that we can't agree on what we even 'heard.'"

Julia sprang to her feet and paced. Suddenly she halted and faced her secondaries. "I was wrong to oppose Arethustra's ambition to become a word processor."

It felt like a tremendous admission to Julia, but her secondaries simply looked at her, and the perfect silence of the c-space (the default background of her study setting, since she usually liked to choose an audio background to match her needs or purpose in being in the study) fairly smothered her. "It's becoming clearer. Using the Delta Pavonian forms short-circuits my tendency with the La Femmeans to perceive their response to me—or to my conception of humanness—since there's less room in those forms for seeking my image of myself."

"Go on," S07 said when Julia just looked at them, waiting for a response.

"I feel as if I'm caught in a pattern of failure. I think what happened with the human Outsiders is that my image of them—an image supporting my core sense of myself—so overlaid the persons and culture I actually encountered that I never had a chance of really perceiving them free of that image. With the Delta Pavonians it was worse, because my revulsion was all that I saw. And then there are the word processors...with two of whom I've been up-close and personal. Intellectually, I've always seen them as mediators. But emotionally, all I know is that my repugnance to Arethustra's desire to become one suggests that I think of them in some critical way as alien."

S04 said, her voice very cold, "But with the La Femmeans, they do no more than reflect your sense of yourself back to you, with nothing left over."

Julia knew that was correct. After a few seconds, S07 said, "I think we need to return our attention to the current situation, Julia. Despite this sense of there being nothing left over, as S04 puts it, you've essentially told us that you are now willing to trust the La Femmeans' understanding of politics over your own. I suggest you think more carefully about introducing Vance into the situation."

56.

GROPING HER HAND-OVER-HAND way back to the bridge, Julia worried over S07's parting shot. Her secondaries couldn't see any merit to Esée's suggestion to release Vance and her contingent from deep sleep. They questioned Julia's judgment in being so quick to talk herself into the proposition. And the very fact of her contention with them argued that something strange was going on in her mind. Her secondaries almost never found it difficult to grasp any particular idea she might express to them. The point was, they were virtually embodied parts of herself. The whole is greater than the sum of its parts, Julia murmured to herself, grunting, uncomfortable, sweaty. And they hadn't, after all, heard anything Esée had ever "spoken" to her. That alone sufficed to account for the blank gap between her thoughts and their comprehension of those thoughts. They had only had what she had relayed to them, which hadn't been everything by any means, even when Esée had been "present" in the same c-space with them — and had included her deepest anxieties and misgivings.

The passageways, Julia thought, would be easier to negotiate if they were narrower. Why hadn't the engineers responsible for adapting the ship thought to make them so? Obviously, the generosity of space would be perfect for the Delta Pavonians, particularly when the drive was engaged; and they were used to less gravity than humans. Julia tried to visualize Delta Pavonians in the space before her. She concentrated on remembering the Delta Pavonian at the last singing she had attended. Up close, it had looked painfully etiolated and not at all beautiful. But in flight, in the heights of their auditorium in the City of Word Processing...

A blizzard of blue butterflies swarmed before her, fluttering madly in a thick and strangely fragrant cloud filling the passageway as far as Julia's eye could see (namely, to the elbow-bend only a few meters ahead)... Julia blinked. Of course there was nothing there. No butterflies, no cloud of blue, no swarm of anything living or dead. The butterflies had had the sharp definition of v-space images. Julia could remember seeing blue butterflies (with deep purple and brown markings) only in the wildlife dome and nowhere else. V-space butterflies tended to be plain white or yellow, or large, richly patterned Monarchs. Her stomach fluttered. As though, she thought, she had swallowed the cloud of butterflies, or rather had let them in through her gastric intake, let them in to flutter against the walls of her stomach, a cloud of blue impervious to gastric acids... Turning the last bend into the final stretch of passage to the bridge, Julia stopped short at the sight of a meat-space Gertrude Stein. *Esée, of course.*

<<Yes.>>

Julia swallowed. The very idea of seeing a flesh-and-blood tertiary caught her off-guard. She reached forward and grasped the creature's arm. The sleeve, thick linen, felt absolutely real. And the arm beneath it was warm, its flesh yielding. Julia wondered how it was done, taking a tertiary representation and molding it in flesh exactly right. She didn't think her own imagination that exact—it seemed impossible that the La Femmean could have taken it from her mind. Her tertiary of Gertrude Stein was the best she could make it, but it was cartoonish. This Gertrude Stein seemed...full, rich, multidimensional.

"When you're like this, you don't seem a figment of my imagination," Julia said. "In v-space, when you appear, you are...unreal. Because all the time you're there I know you've only projected yourself to *seem* to be there—since 'there' is really only bits of digitized electronic space. But then, to see you using the exact same form, in meat-space..."

Perhaps most extraordinary, the face kept within the range of expressions Julia imagined constraining the historical Gertrude Stein's face (which were the very ones she had programmed for the tertiary). When it smiled, its face was oddly knowing and, though affectionate, restrained. Julia clutched the hold-bar more tightly and willed the cloud of blue butterflies to leave her stomach.

<<You don't know the power of your own mind.>>

Julia said, "But I'm beginning to realize your powers over it."

Esée gave her head the brisk no-nonsense little shake Julia knew so well. It was a kind of headshake she had never seen anywhere and in that constituted a minor source of pride in the imaginative distinctiveness of her creation. <<You are concerned about my suggestion to release the crew you feel threatened by. And it is true that this suggestion did not come from you, or from any other human, and as such makes a difference from every other communication we have made with you and your crewmates. My wish, though, has been to assure you that you needn't fear for La Femme.>>

Julia pressed back against the cool carbon-filament wall. Her bowels were spasming painfully, so violently that she knew she hadn't a hope of safely reaching a toilet were she to try to make it. She held her sphincter tight and breathed in slowly and carefully. After a half a minute or so the pain eased and then disappeared altogether, without trace.

"Julia!"

Julia turned her head. The voice belonged to Carlton, who was swimming gracefully up the passage. "I've heard that three of Candace's team have returned. Is our own expedition still on?"

Julia glanced back at Esée, but she had gone. *Gone where, Julia? Vanished into the ether? Or did she somehow open the hatch to the bridge without making a sound?* Julia made Carlton an easy, amiable smile. "I don't see why not," she said. And wondered if that meant she had made a definite decision about Vance without even having realized it.

57.

ABOUT HALF THE crew were congregated on the bridge. Julia blinked in a sudden access to strangeness. Their jumpsuits, of identical style in an identical shade of beige, struck her as regimented as Outsiders were often known to think Paxans were. Julia recalled how puzzled and amused she had been, during her first tour of border duty, at the Outsiders' apparent inability to tell any of them apart. She had heard their whispered comments to one another. *Everyone is sexless and dresses alike, in drab, shapeless clothes. Nearly everyone is short and thin with dark hair and dark eyes. Like robots.* And in fact, it turned out that some Outsiders did have robots, dressed like Paxans, with brown and gray heads, bodies, and appendages. Julia had once tried to explain to an Outsider wondering whether if he were permitted to join the Pax he would be required to dress so drably, wondering whether he'd be allowed to continue wearing his favorite clothing (which, as far as Julia could tell, like most Outsider items of consumption took their value from their visible marks as consensually privileged signifiers, which they paid heavily to purchase), that most Paxans spent the social and professional parts of their lives in v-space, where one confronted a constantly growing choice of designs, including several point-pricey haute coutures whose fashions changed every few days for those interested in presenting a flashy style. "The entire number of points people spend on such designs goes entirely to the designer," Julia had added. "In the Pax, the people who are creative directly reap the rewards of their creativity, rather than having the rewards go mainly to intermediaries, as is usually the case Outside." Julia could have saved her breath. The Outsider only sneered and said that v-space wasn't "real," and why would anyone waste their money on anything so ephemeral. Still trying to

get this Outsider to understand, Julia then said that some people
went so far as to have their meat-space faces cosmetically altered to
match a particular v-space representation of themselves. But this
elaboration only exacerbated the impasse; only later did Julia realize it had been a mistake to offer it.

How did the La Femmeans see them? Julia wondered. As easily distinct individuals, certainly, since their main perceptions
seemed to be telepathic to a highly personal degree. But the reverse
wasn't—perhaps couldn't be—true. The fact was, the Paxans hadn't
yet learned to distinguish La Femmean individuals, precisely because they lacked La Femmean perceptual abilities. Each time Esée
made Contact with her, Julia depended on hearing her apparent
voice speaking in her mind. Merely seeing a tertiary of Gertrude
Stein, or the primary of Davis, for example, could never give Julia
sufficient certainty that it was Esée she was seeing. In fact, she realized, except for Esée's consistency of "speech," Julia had no way of
knowing whether she wasn't in fact encountering a series of different La Femmeans, all of them calling themselves "Esée."

Oh shit. Thinking this way is like studying ancient Greek philosophy.

"Shall we go in, Julia?" Carlton said.

Julia started and looked over her shoulder. "Sorry. I guess I was
a slight bit taken aback by there being so many people here. What
do you suppose they all want?" The last time there had been that
many people on the bridge had been during their insertion into
orbit around La Femme.

Carlton's face lit up with a grin. "Going by the scuttlebutt rag-
ing in crew c-spaces, I'd say they're probably just a wee bit excited
by the news about the returnees. And wanting in on the mission to
the surface."

Julia groaned. The disorder of her crew had never been more
apparent. She supposed the majority of the Council would have
been understanding of her "permissiveness" (as she knew Vance
and her ilk would likely call it) at the time they'd accomplished
orbital insertion. And a few less than that would have accepted the

confusion of the first onboard Contact. But Julia *knew* that perhaps three members of the Council, max, would accept habitual spontaneous congregation on the bridge. Julia herself had no sense of the mission being out of control. But surveying the bridge from the hatch, she knew that someone like Fuyuko, putting it all together, would think nothing else. Julia had agreed to allow unsupervised Contact between crew members and indigenes. (As though it were possible to supervise telepathic contacts!) And she had refused to discipline Felix when she had returned from the unauthorized trip to the surface, and would also refuse to discipline Tree, Paris, and Celeste. If all these people on the bridge wanted to go to the surface... *Can I even keep them on board, if they're determined? The indigenes can take them whether I agree to it or not. The question is, do I really feel it necessary and desirable to exert my authority to keep everyone but designated crew on board?*

"Julia, is there a reason you're blocking the hatch?" Fuyuko said irritably.

Besides Carlton, Fuyuko and two others were now behind her, crowded along the hold-bars framing the hatch, waiting to pass. She propelled herself forward. *This is desire. The warp that holds us in our web. My desire, shared, magnified, past anything Fuyuko or Vance can defeat without the use of force. I seized my chance to head this mission, from sheer desire. Vance joined, from sheer hatred of the unknown, full from the first with the intention to confine whatever we discovered to the Great Outside. While Fuyuko joined because a few members of the Council flattered her into thinking herself essential to preserving "balance." Oh the harmonious psyche-synthesist, trapped in her longing for stasis, afraid of powerful desire and the change that it always threatens. Crush desire, control change, harmonize, synthesize, but never, never let go...*

Astra waved at Julia. "Have you heard?" she called. She pointed at Celeste, who was "standing" beside her. As Julia, working her way along the perimeter of the bridge, approached, she could hear Astra's voice above the hubbub. "Julia, Celeste has *weight*. It's not just a pose she's adopted. The La Femmeans gave her and Tree and Paris fields that control the gravity around their bodies. And the ship's AI has confirmed it. Look at this viewscreen, you can see from the schematic that the space is bent around them, as though they carried mini-gravity wells inside their bodies!"

Julia dutifully looked at the schematic and realized that the gravity fields were what almost everyone around her was discussing.

"That means *trade*," Blaise said, swinging along the hold-bar towards Julia. "Can you imagine the implications of our being able to create individual gravity fields?"

"Julia, what is this chaos?" Fuyuko said sharply.

In the excitement, Julia had forgotten the psyche-synthesist altogether. She touched Astra's shoulder. "Would you talk to Fuyuko, please, and update her on everything you've learned since Celeste, Tree, and Paris's return?" Julia looked at Fuyuko. "I don't think we should discuss anything until you've gotten up to speed on what we've learned this morning. As for what is happening here—it's simply that the crew is understandably excited about those very things."

"Julia," Blaise said, putting her hand on Julia's back. "I want to talk to you about the mission to the surface."

Julia turned to face her. "Don't tell me. You want to join the team—like almost every other crew member. Right?"

"There's good reason to include me. Surely you must see that without my even making the argument."

Julia smiled. "Of course I do." She leaned forward to speak into Blaise's ear. "What would you say to the proposition that anyone should go who wants to. Since the ship, after all, can take care of itself. Can you think of any reason against such a decision?"

Julia pulled back in time to see surprise widen Blaise's eyes. Blaise linked arms with Julia and edged her some distance away, so—this Julia surmised from Blaise's glance at the psyche-synthesist—that they'd be out of earshot of Fuyuko and Astra. "Fuyuko wouldn't like it," Blaise whispered. "The Council wouldn't like it. And...if she were awake, Vance would call it suicidally dangerous."

Julia squeezed Blaise's shoulder. "I'm asking you for your judgment, Blaise, not your take on others' reactions."

Blaise looked Julia in the eyes, seriously and searchingly (as few crew members could do). After about ten seconds, she said, "Me, I'd say it's the thing to do. Since to hold any one person back would be to deny them the clear benefits Paris, Tree, and Celeste received. Though of course we *could* compromise, by arranging for everyone to go in shifts..." She bit her lip. "I suppose that's the thing. What you're proposing does seem a bit...anarchic, if not uncontrolled."

Julia smiled. "Still worrying about appearances, Blaise?"

"Appearances, Julia," Blaise said. Her old wrinkled face suddenly looked, Julia thought, almost ill with uneasiness. "Shit, appearances are all we *have*. Appearances and interpretations of appearances." She bit her lip. "I mean...what I'm trying to say..."

Julia held Blaise's gaze. "Yes, I think I understand what you're getting at. But there's something new happening here, isn't there. With appearances, and interpretations of appearances, and so on..."

"Which, you think, renders the old interpretations—say the ones Fuyuko and the Council might make—inoperative."

Julia nodded slowly. "Yes. I suppose that's what I do think."

Blaise glanced around at Fuyuko, then looked back at Julia. "You're scaring the shit out of me, Julia. When you put it into words like that..."

"I think we should understand what we're getting into here, even if we don't want to put it on the record."

Blaise's face darkened with a rush of blood. "You make me feel as though I'm plotting against the Council. Fuck it, Julia. Maybe we're wrong."

"I'm not backing out now," Julia said softly. "I'm going down to the surface. As I'm going to allow anyone else who chooses to go to do." Where only a few minutes earlier the idea had shocked her, it now felt as right to her as the sound of her own name. She wondered that she had ever wanted to see things through the old lenses. They were useless, here. They were inappropriate for La

Femme. She might be momentarily sightless without the old lenses, but a new vision would come in time. She could feel that now. It was a question of relying on her own responses—and not on past ways of thinking, which her secondaries represented—and on La Femme, in the form of Esée. Esée would be her guide, as Virgil had been to Dante in his visit to Hell, Purgatory, and Heaven, as the ladies named "Reason," "Rectitude," and "Justice" had been to Christine de Pisan in her visit to the City of Ladies. Julia's mouth flooded with saliva; she trembled. She remembered how her parents had been guides in her earliest visits to v-space. Then a whole world had opened to her, including past, present, and future and all that she would ever have the strength and talent to imagine. This, *this* would be given to her, another world, new, beyond anything she could imagine.

She didn't know how she could stand to wait much longer. If Fuyuko argued too strenuously, she would simply go at once and give permission to everyone else to do the same.

58.

A FEW WEEKS before Arethustra's thirteenth birthday, while she and Julia were lying on a mat, close, in what they called "quiet time," Arethustra dismayed her by raising a subject that by Arethustra's age had an almost-taboo status. Her head was on Julia's stomach, long a favorite place during "quiet times," because it was always, as she liked to say, "incredibly noisy inside there." "Quiet times" had a sort of dreamy quality to them. Julia would relax and be almost or just asleep except when Arethustra chose to talk, which she did in spurts, often stream-of-conscious, sometimes asking Julia questions in what might seem random fashion. (Arethustra loved to talk just before going to sleep at night.) During "quiet times" she said and asked (it seemed to Julia) everything that she might feel too constrained to articulate when fully conscious. Though Julia held herself alert when Arethustra talked during these sessions, some part of her grew dreamy, too, from the intimate contact and lack of barriers to their talk. Sometimes Julia imagined, in her mind's eye, the two of them as flowers swaying together in the gentlest breeze, open and languid and sensual, pollinated by the low, irregular buzz of their talk, as intimate as two human beings could be.

"I wish you weren't going to leave me on my birthday," Arethustra said.

"What do you mean, leave you?" Julia said, half-chiding. Yet she felt a pang strike her breast at the thought of how these "quiet times" would soon be ending. These four years had granted an intimacy she would never know again, unless she chose to make another family. (And she knew she would not, since she had declined to join four of Arethustra's co-parents in forming a second family, giving Arethustra a younger cousin.) Julia said, "I'll still be

266

available whenever you want me. I know I've told you that at least a couple of dozen times in the last few weeks."

"It will be mainly in v-space that I'll be able to see you," Arethustra grumbled. "And you won't be on light work status anymore and might be off on big assignments anytime at all. It just won't be the same, living mainly with Moira and Mei."

Julia lifted her head to get a look at Arethustra's face. "We're all your parents, Arie. We all love you, and we all have different contributions to make to your education and nurturance."

"I know that," Arethustra said impatiently. "But why can't I live with the parents I prefer and just visit the others in v-space, as I do the ones who aren't living with me? You're all always claiming there's no difference between v-space and meat-space. Then why don't you act like it? " The girl shifted, raising her head and propping it up on her arm. Her face wore its stubborn look. "Though that would mean your staying on light work assignments. Which is the real problem, isn't it."

"At thirteen you're old enough to accept that sometimes things can't be exactly the way you want them," Julia said sharply. It seemed they had fallen into the practice of arguing about once a day. Julia thought they were definitely due a change. "Moira and Mei love you. I'm not deserting you. It's willful and perverse for you to say otherwise." Arethustra's eyebrows went into motion. Julia continued: "There's nothing wrong with preferring certain parents over others. All of us have done it ourselves, and we expect it of our child. But thinking that everyone else should adopt your scheme simply because you prefer it—" Julia sighed. "I'll miss seeing you as much as I see you now, honey, too. But I'll expect to continue seeing you a lot in the family c-spaces." Julia studied Arethustra's face and decided to dare the other subject. "You're so rough on us. You talk about my leaving you—but in fact you've already told all of us to start preparing ourselves for losing you permanently once you've come of age."

Arethustra's lower lip pushed out. "I thought *you'd* understand, Julia. You and Arete. I can't believe you don't!" The girl rose
to her feet in one beautifully swift, fluid motion. "Maybe she is
meant to be a singer," Julia thought in spite of her resistance to the
notion. Arethustra went to the mirror at the far side of the room,
the mirror in which Julia had hoped to teach Arethustra control
of her face. Arethustra glanced over her shoulder at Julia. "Do you
remember, Julia, when you showed me how to look in the mirror
in your meditation c-space?"

Julia had taught Arethustra what Antoinette had taught her:
to look at her c-space self and find the beauty in it, the animation, joy, and liveliness that was the essence of who she was. She
had taught Arethustra to regard herself as a whole being and had
shown her a thing she had never shown another soul—shown her
her own, Julia's, primary self surrounded by every one of her ex-
tant secondaries.

Arethustra took off her clothes before the hard, flat, meat-
space mirror. She flung out her young brown arms wide and over
her head and whirled around and around in a vortex that must
have soon made her dizzy. "I see myself, for myself, I love myself
for myself in *this* mirror, too, Julia," she sang, almost breathless
with spinning. Suddenly she halted and, giggling, staggered for a
few seconds in drunken disequilibrium. "Julia," she said, facing
her parent. "Julia, Julia, I'm so happy!" She touched her hands to
her breasts, her ribs, her stomach, her thighs. "This is more real
than the me I see in the c-space mirror! There's something missing
in the other place, Julia. I can *feel* it! And if I'm to see me for myself, then it must be in *this* mirror, too!"

A strange mix of anxiety and thrilling pleasure at the beauty
and misguidedness of Arethustra's perception seized Julia. It was
beautiful, *she* was beautiful, so free in her body, so strong, so unafraid
of regarding herself, so confident in her potential. Tears pricked
Julia's eyes with the awe that swept her. But at the same time—
again! —Arethustra had gotten it wrong, had misunderstood. Her

throat was too choked, Julia thought, to try to explain it. Instead, she said, her voice harsh, "You understand, don't you, that the Pax achieves what it does because most of its members live in v-space, taking up fewer resources. The tradeoff is better health, longer life, and as much beauty and imagination as one wishes for. In the Pax those adults who live mostly in meat-space die young, and their bodies age horribly. And when they finally retire into v-space, their options are limited by a lack of accumulated points, since during their working lives they spent almost all they made on meat luxuries." And for the first time Julia recognized anger, surging almost out of control, at Arethustra's stubbornness. "Beautiful now," she said, "but not for long."

From Arethustra's face Julia saw that she didn't believe her. Their positions had become polarized. The family web had been torn. All that remained was the idea of the web and a few fragmentary connections among the dozen dangling threads that were left of the warp. Julia realized she had identified herself with the web, as though she were Arethustra herself. She hadn't thought she'd done that (and knew it foolish that she had), but the sense of a gaping hole inside her made it obvious that she had.

Julia lay back down on the mat and pressed her hand to the place where Arethustra's head had been. It was time, she thought, to be getting less intense. She could see it was going to be as bad as losing Raye—or worse.

59.

THOUGH MOST OF those present were taken up with Celeste, Tree, and Paris's possession of weight in the zero-gee of the bridge, and though the bridge was no place for a meat-space meeting of such size, Julia called one to order and without the ado of inviting discussion announced that she would leave all crew members to decide for themselves if and when they wished to visit the surface.

In the irresistible swell of exclamations, ordinary decorum vanished. Julia noted that Blaise's face showed the dismay at the evidence of "anarchy" that Julia herself felt.

Fuyuko's strident voice cut through the disruption. "Julia, this is insanity! I can't believe any competent diplo would advise such a course of action."

Julia released the hold-bar and let herself drift. She adopted the diplo mode dubbed by insiders "the authoritative." "I ask only that everyone continue to report back to the ship and keep in touch with others' reports. We are all explorers, and that means we are here to observe, learn, evaluate, and reflect. Which in turn requires our keeping up with our colleagues' work and communicating with them at every stage of the mission." Looking directly at Fuyuko, Julia gestured. "This may seem an extreme method of going about our exploration, but I believe that each of us was chosen for this mission on the basis of their general competence and particular expertise. None of us needs direction; and coordination, which I take as my responsibility, has now been sufficiently structured into the mission such that if everyone does their work, my responsibility to coordinate will have been met." Julia bowed repeatedly and deeply around the room. *Esée, please appear,* she subvoked.

Esée *did* appear, in the form of Gertrude Stein. "I'll be in touch," Julia said and, wanting to time her exit perfectly, subvoked fervently, *take me to the surface now, please.*

Before Julia had time to think another thought or hear the words she could see forming on Fuyuko's thin, pale lips, she found herself soaring below a sky thick with the icy shards of stars and the eerie stillness of a half-exposed alien indigo moon, above an inky sea marked by an occasional deep purple phosphorescence, her hand held loosely in Esée's, soaring as though she had acquired the wings and body of a Delta Pavonian.

60.

JULIA'S SPIRIT SOARED in elation. For a few instants it was as though the universe itself had opened before her, taking her by the hand to show her—no, *give* her—what she had always wanted.

<<This is La Femme, all of this, which is to say this is me, into which you have come—>>

The horizon seemingly exploded in brilliant color, dazzling Julia's eyes with every shade of violet she had ever seen and more. The sea below turned amethyst. Wild with joy, she imagined herself spread far beyond the proper boundaries of her flesh, a plethora of light and consciousness, flung as far as her eye could see—no, farther, for she felt the web of herself flying far beyond her fleshly vision, out and out as far as her courage and boldness allowed.

Suddenly, sensing infinity as she never had before, she grew afraid of what she sensed she might be capable of knowing. Anxiety ate into the elation, rendering it mere excessive excitement, threatening her with loss of control. She became aware of the looseness of Esée's grasp on her hand and clutched the La Femmean's hand—only to suffer the bizarre, sinking doubt that perhaps Esée wasn't really there but had simply left her, and that really she was falling—no, drifting—without realizing it, drifting in orbit above the planet, above its atmosphere... Or that perhaps Esée had only made her hallucinate it all. That perhaps they were elsewhere.

Blaise was wrong. It's not that there is only appearance. What there is, fundamentally, is only consciousness...

And then she thought of what she had just done, of the chaos she had left behind among the ship's crew... To shatter the structures that bound them all, structures seldom recognized, charged with a power too frightening to be recognized as being, all the time, in their possession... All order, Julia thought, rested on that largely

272

unthinking obedience to such structures, whatever they might be. "Each society," Antoinette had taught her, "has its own rules. And the basis on which it recognizes rights and awards privileges says everything about it." Fuyuko would be certain she had either become psychotic or been subverted, beyond her worst fears, by the La Femmeans, two outcomes Fuyuko might, as a psyche-synthesis, consider tautological.

<<Fuyuko thinks herself unworthy of love. And so she can trust nothing not tightly bound in the safety of known and old structures. It is why she rejects La Femme. For if she is unworthy of love given without stint, from one who hasn't always known her, how could she possibly trust herself so far?>>

Julia's anxiety sharpened. *But who, far into adulthood, can think themselves worthy of love, unearned, unsought, from a stranger? It is hard enough to believe you are worthy of the love given by those you have yourself loved.* And Julia thought of how she had ceased to trust anyone to love her, of how she had long been lost in uncertainty and the sense that only those who choose to stop learning can, as mature adults, believe that they know what they're doing.

Esée said to Julia: <<You have trusted Arethustra, haven't you?>>

An image appeared before them, in the heart of the violet light, of Arethustra, surrounded by a shimmering web of gold and cerise and chartreuse, woven in the shape of a uterus through the threads streaming from the outstretched hands of the nine co-parents, Zuni, Jorreau, Moira, Rabil, Arete, Garcia, Denny, Mei, and Julia. Within the web danced Arethustra, joyfully, with abandon, her every movement glorified by the pliant magnificence of the woven texture surrounding her.

A tightness in Julia's chest loosened, a tightness she hadn't known was there but now perceived as a pain that had been worrying her for a silently long time. She turned her head to look at Esée, an incongruous Gertrude Stein rapt in the pleasure of flying. "Take me to one of your cities," she said. "Better: take me to your home."

The sea and sky vanished; the deep blue of Albireo remained only as an afterimage on her retinas. Julia felt the unaccustomed pull of gravity, pulling hard at her feet, her calves, her thighs and belly. Her bowels cramped, then relaxed, and the terrible pressure of weight eased. Julia blinked.

Esée spoke: <<Everywhere is home for La Femme. But here is Armilla, perched on a mountain looking down to the sea.>>

61.

SHORTLY AFTER ARETHUSTRA'S thirteenth birthday, Central asked Julia to take an assignment involving direct and likely hostile discourse with the top officials of one of the major Outsider governments. Julia seriously considered refusing. Such an assignment posed significant physical risk; in this case, the risk was heightened because it had been several years since any government had attempted to oppose the Pax by hostage-taking or other violent methods, which meant that Outsider memory would be vague about the consequences of inappropriate behavior. Julia's reluctance, though, stemmed entirely from her distaste for the role it would require her to play. But this she finally swallowed; if she did not accept the posting—her first "heavy" assignment in five years—she could be certain never to rise above her associate status and would probably draw only the most tedious and routine of assignments for the rest of her diplo career.

For preparation Julia attended briefings in policy and protocol and let herself be fitted with the formal costume diplos adopted when going Outside as an official representative of the Pax. Outsiders generally wore the descendants of these costumes, which they called "suits." But the suits the Pax used were replicas of those used at the time of the Pax's formation. They were uncomfortable—rigid and clinging, chafing and inconvenient. To use a valve while wearing them one had first to partially disrobe. Julia had never worn one before. The fact was, only diplos still active in meat-space could carry out such assignments. The most senior diplos, experienced in such missions, were mostly residing permanently in v-space, or else were overseeing the more delicate tasks involved in organizing new merging zones or in liaising with communities in other merging zones in their various stages of the process.

And so the morning came when Julia rose at dawn with her team in a border zone bunker, all of them dressed in suits and braced for non-connection for however long the mission would take. The Pax of course did not allow the Outsider governments satellite technology, but most Outsider governments, including the one they would be engaging, banned any development of v-space other than their own and harshly punished citizens they caught in crude but independent efforts. And they jammed the Pax's signals, to block their citizens' access.

The government, having received the Pax's demand for an immediate official audience with its head, after imposing a delay Julia's team presumed was meant to assert their dignity, sent air transport to their border station and conveyed the team to the capital city. Although Julia had seen many images of this Outsider land, she was not prepared for the meat reality. She got her first hard look as the transport circled above the capital city, preparing to land. Even from above, the city looked like the creation of a sloppy, disturbed mind. The buildings were jammed in every which way, without any aesthetic principle or order known to the human species. And vehicles crawled like bugs over the ribbons of pavement running between the buildings.

Once they had landed, though, the dissonance struck Julia viscerally. An official backed by a blatantly armed escort greeted them as they disembarked, then hurried them into vehicles operated by people in sinister military dress. Julia stared openly. Every member of the party greeting them showed visible signs of physical augmentation of the sort never seen in the Pax, though on average they were, even before alteration, much larger than Paxans. The array of weaponry displayed reminded Julia of everything she had ever been told about the constant incidence of violence in the cities ruled by this government, and the sight of it intensified her discomfort. But what she saw as they drove through the streets struck her as so wildly improbable that she thought that if anyone had created such a c-space they would be taken as deeply disturbed in both mind and body. Everywhere, *people*. Buildings. Trash. Vehicles. Noise. Holo-displays urging consumption. Raggedly dressed individuals hawking wares or begging or simply standing in sullen, slouched dullness. Julia asked Brynne, her protocol specialist, in a whisper, what the horrible stench in the air was, and they whispered back that some of the vehicles burned vegetable oil fuel. She cupped her palm around her nose, as though to protect herself from the resulting particulates. *Carcinogenic, for sure.*

The scene of the city made Julia feel dirty. And a passing glimpse of children fighting with their fists, booted feet, and clubs, apparently unsupervised, made her want to demand—despite her tours on the border—that the car be stopped and the children be somehow rescued. *Here they are, condemned a priori, children born to the losers of the interminable internal war for profit, to hunger, loneliness, stunted ignorance. And it's too late. For all of them, too late. Too late...*

And yet everywhere she could see people with milk-breasts. She knew they didn't acquire milk breasts for nursing their children, but the thought that these people did nothing but make families snaked insidiously through her thoughts... As she stared out at a crowd of children playing a noisy, aggressive game, Julia recalled her old longing. At one time she would have grabbed eagerly for a place on this team, grabbed with both hands and taken it all in with shining eyes and a breathlessness unrelated to the noxious particulates crowding the air. She had had an idea of the Outside she had cared passionately about. Now the pain she had suffered at the shattering of that old set of illusions revisited her, mixed with the pain of other losses. *But no, every passion is for the abstraction of the thing itself, and so it is incorrect to attempt to minimize that lost vision as particularly illusory, as if all one's most important feelings aren't, in essence, of the mind and one's own individuated body.* She thought, almost dazed, "I'm numb now on the subject of this place. I couldn't care less. This assignment means nothing to me but a steppingstone to assignment in a merging zone, where maybe *there* at least there may yet be some hope for me..."

A tickle of fear fluttered in her belly. *Some hope?* Was she really that far gone? And then realized: yes. She had stopped letting herself care about "abstractions"—except for the child. But then she had begun with Arethustra and the idea of her before she had taken to protecting herself from the pain that always—eventually—resulted from passionate attachment. Because that was the tradeoff. If you cared, eventually there'd be loss. Either sharp and dramatic (as with Raye), or gradual, in the form of the disintegration and dulling of the abstraction's significance in the face of the wholly unlovable reality (as had been proved in the case of her passion for discovering Outside). And now, though the child was only thirteen, she could feel already the beginning of losing her. So she had, perhaps, one more chance. When young, it took no courage to care, because one didn't comprehend the inevitability of the loss. But later, one knew...and then it became a matter of whether one wanted to live as a dead person—a sort of living tertiary, without a primary's affect—or whether one could stand to court the pain, for all that it made one alive.

Julia closed her eyes and performed the breathing exercise. Work loomed. Work that must be carried on in the silence of non-connection. She could not think about anything until she had gotten the whole shitty mess of the assignment behind her.

When finally the vehicles entered a more aesthetically arranged compound and disgorged the team under an ornate portico, the team had to enact a tightly scripted ceremonial scene through which Julia bowed and nodded and gestured her way. She understood the language, of course, and could speak it. But she knew that these particular people took words with utter seriousness, recording them, transcribing them to paper, analyzing them for the faintest nuances, conscious or unconscious, and so policy dictated that the team use words sparingly and only when essential. ("Do not, for instance, say you are happy to meet anyone, or that you are pleased to be there. They'll misconstrue it, probably deliberately, and consider themselves to be thereby privileged with an advantage.")

After enduring the tedious ritual so essential to the dignity of the Outsider government, they were led into a cavernous room grandly lit by mountainous crystal chandeliers suspended high above the largest and glossiest wood table Julia had ever laid eyes on in meat- or c-space. The Paxans were directed to one side of the table, the government officials took the other. The protocol specialist informed Julia that the chief government official would be entering shortly. Julia's team helped themselves to the supply of water they had brought with them. (The rule was never ever to drink or eat anything from Outside. Not only did Outsiders have different intestinal bacteria, but they also indulged in eating and drinking substances that damaged their cells and generated bizarre brain chemistry.) The room pulsed with a common, stilted silence. Julia caught herself staring at the milk-breasts of the official seated the furthest distance from her. She knew of course that the person must be a woman, since Outsider men did not lactate. Had she been seated so far off to the side because of some sort of taboo? Or was it coincidence?

Arete, Julia thought, would probably know. She would ask Arete about it the next time they met, since obviously she couldn't ask the Outsiders themselves.

After perhaps half an hour, music blared out of every corner of the room, and a military honor guard carrying the most ostentatious arsenal of weapons yet appeared at the main threshold. The spectacle sorely tested Julia's diplo discipline; she had to bite the inside of her cheeks to keep from laughing. The officials seated across the table rose and moved back several steps. At a gesture from their protocol specialist, Julia's team rose also. A couple of uniformed guards rushed a padded armchair to the table and placed it exactly across from Julia; the remainder of the guards took up excruciatingly rigid positions on either side of the door. As the music thundered raucously, a whole new set of officials appeared in the doorway and filed in (one of them also with milk-breasts). They carried themselves with pompous importance, but Julia knew from her briefing that the one who entered last, and by himself, and who then sat down in the special chair placed across the table from her, must be the chief. She had been warned not to offer him her hand. ("This government's officials have never shaken hands with us, Julia. And they certainly aren't going to start doing it now.") So she bowed, instead, with a moderate degree of politeness.

"Mr. President, I and my colleagues bear you greetings from the Council of the Pax," Julia said slowly, ceremonially. "I am Julia, and my colleagues are Lillo—" Julia gestured to each as she spoke their names— "Ferrante, Brynne, Modesto, and Planche."

"The leader's a *female?*" Julia heard the chief mutter to the official seated on his left. "Without hearing the name, you'd never know it. And why give first but not last names? But my God. They're all really neuters anyway, so I don't suppose it matters."

Last names, first names—Julia understood what he meant. Outsiders had (as had, of course, most, though certainly not all, pre-Paxans) secondary names that derived from an identification with sperm, used instead of the code numbers Paxans used for official identification, as well as, more broadly, for social and professional purposes. These secondary names were the sign and consequence of the Outsiders' (unspoken) premise that parents (chiefly sperm donors) owned their children. As for the question of sex—she wondered later, at leisure, thinking somewhat uncomfortably about the chief's comment, whether the human species could be in the process of bifurcating. She could well imagine the Outsiders' arguing that the species' ultimate survival was safeguarded by its continuing ability to reproduce, when necessary, without benefit of technology, which in turn depended on the ability of potential reproductive mates to recognize one another as such...

Julia switched on the electronic notepad for displaying the electronic documents she had ready and rose to her feet. Being without connection, she had to rely on written text to refresh her memory. But even if her memory should prove improbably perfect, the Outsiders would not take her statements seriously unless they could see them printed on official paper stationary and stamped with the Council's seal. "I have a prepared statement to deliver," she said. She nodded at Modesto to distribute paper copies to the six persons seated directly opposite. (Brynne had assured her that these officials would be the most important of those assembled.) "The Council of Pax hereby certifies that the territory marked on the map inset into this page has met all requirements and qualifications for entrance into the Pax." Julia raised her voice to be audible over the undisciplined response of the Outsiders. "The Pax therefore declares the said territory to be henceforth under its protection for such time as it shall take to merge into the Pax proper. The Pax therefore warns all governments that any interference with the persons residing in the territory or its resources will result in the usual sanctions targeting property and information that the Pax reserves for defensive retaliation against any and all Outside aggression. (For an exact description of such measures, see the Pax Charter, Article Seven, Sections One through Six.) The Pax further demands the release of all residents of this territory who have been taken captive in retaliation for activities whose purpose was to achieve the qualifications and requirements for entry into the Pax. A list of such persons is appended." In a slow, careful drone, Julia read off the names, which totaled more than a thousand. "These residents of the territory must be returned to their homes within fifteen days. If any are held past that time, the Pax will exercise such selective sanctions as it deems fit." Julia looked up from the text. "The statement," she said, staring coldly into the face of the man opposite, "is signed by the Principal Members of the Pax's First Council, with yesterday's date."

The chief had been scowling up at the chandelier throughout her reading. Now he leveled a smoldering, vindictive glare directly into her face. "This is an outrage. It is a violation of our nation's sovereign rights. Whether you're a signatory to the United Nations or not, you people are bound by international law just like any other country is. We will not tolerate an invasion of our borders."

Julia had no doubt that he'd known for at least twenty-four hours that the Pax had begun the process of establishing its official presence in the territory. According to the final briefing she had that morning, people not wishing to merge with the Pax were streaming out past the new border, taking with them vehicles and other goods that would no longer be of use or welcome in the merging territory. Julia nodded at Ferrante and reseated herself.

Ferrante rose. "Mr. President," he said. The officials grew even more openly perturbed. Julia wished she could connect with Brynne, to ask her whether they had inadvertently breached acceptable protocol. "We have taken a number of precautions anent rash and unconsidered action against the Pax, its citizens, the merging territory, or its residents. Though your banking records are hardened targets and therefore invulnerable to EMPs, we have taken the prophylactic measure of infecting them with a virus— one we know has not been detected since its injection into your system—that can be easily triggered at any time of our choosing. This will be the first selected sanction. The second sanction will be the deployment of EMPs directed at local, geographically defined targets." Though Outsiders lacked access to satellite technology and their governments prohibited independent development of v-spaces and restricted implants to those that could be defined as "enhancements of noncognitive, natural, physical processes," and though they tried to harden everything important against the risk of the Pax's EMPs, in fact almost all elites would incur personal damage from an EMP in their vicinity.

"Fucking neuters." The chief was actually snarling. "If we let you grab one more piece, what's to stop you from taking the rest?"

The twisted face of impotence is ugly and painful to behold. Looking at it straight on, Julia almost sympathized with the chief and his officials. The Pax hadn't merged territory under his government's control for almost half a century. Though Outsiders had no notion of how much of Paxan energies and resources went into such mergings, because they occurred so rarely, he and his officials had probably never given the possibility that it could happen during their rule so much as a swift moment of fleeting thought. Julia refrained from explaining that the Pax wouldn't take "the rest" even if begged to do so. Her knowledge of Outsiders told her that rather than being reassured, they would feel insulted, to the point of being emotionally inclined to make a bellicose response regardless of the futility of the gesture or the gravity of the consequences.

"Moreover," Ferrante said loudly, using the rote-prepared words in a language he did not know, "the Pax will publicize this warning and specification of its first line of sanctions by broadcast in all media available, so that those most likely to suffer from sanctions will be aware of the situation."

Though the chief maintained his mask of disgust, the official seated to the right of him looked visibly pained. Perhaps, Julia thought, they had been trying to think of a way to save face with their elites. Purporting to be the world's greatest power was a risky line to take, clearly. But of course there was nothing the Outsiders could do about it, short of pulling their own empire down about their ears and losing everything. At the Pax's founding, some of the governments had shown a willingness to go that far, and they had paid the price for it. Even if the Outsiders chose to gamble everything they had, though, the Pax was virtually invulnerable to Outsider threats. It could be damaged, it could be set back, but it could not be destroyed—at least not by Outsider governments.

And the Outsiders knew it.

62.

HAND IN HAND with Esée (still in the form of Gertrude Stein),
Julia wandered the walkways and arbors of Armilla, a lush oasis of
deep blue vegetation that shimmered with something like iridescence under the strange light of Albireo. Julia had hiked once in
mountains, with Sasha and two others, when she had been twenty-
three years old. The brilliance of the light and purity of the air
had amazed her as much as the vistas spread around them, for unlike the views, such a light had never (to Julia's knowledge) been
duplicated in v-space. Though of course other forms of beautiful
light, duplicating that which one might find in undamaged des-
erts, for instance, were regular favorites in c-space environment
catalogs. Although the light of Armilla was nothing like any light
to be found on earth, its crispness and crystalline quality reminded
Julia of the light she'd tasted that one time in her youth.

Besides beautiful scenery, exhilarating air and light to please
her eye, and the gentle rustle of foliage to delight her ears, Julia
welcomed the dozen or so pleasurable glimpses of families assembled, almost as she had moments earlier imaged, with Esée, the
family of Arethustra. These families, though, were real. In each
they encountered along the way, all the parents were young and
milk-breasted, while the children ranged in age from infancy to
adolescence. All played joyfully in the open air, rolling in the grass,
chasing about, executing sophisticated physical games with balls
and other objects of sport. Julia breathed in the air of love, as she
thought of it. For it seemed to her that love permeated Armilla's
very atmosphere, as though it were an element as distinct and
measurable as oxygen.

But after passing through meadow after meadow, arbor after
arbor, never once encountering any sort of physical construction,

Julia grew distracted and restless. The weight of her body—though she knew it could not by any stretch of the imagination be as great as it should be, given the gravity the AI attributed to the planet—began to drag at her energy. Finally she halted, withdrew her hand, and, putting her back to the breathtaking sight of the sea below, said to Esée: "How do they live? And how can there be children, if you don't reproduce, don't die, don't in fact know the cycle of life and death humans have to live by?"

<<Oh Julia. We are all one, on La Femme. La Femme is one entity. I am showing you that. These families, these children, they are La Femme, as the mountains and the sea and the air we breathe this moment. La Femme is that which lives here, simply. That is all. And it enfolds and nurtures whatever comes to it. Let me show you.>>

Armilla vanished.

Julia struggled against the press of tears choking her. She could not take these instant changes. Looking anxiously, maybe even wearily around, she found herself standing before a building as palatial as those possessed by Outsider governments. Even stranger, the light was familiar to her, not at all like the light of Armilla. Above hovered a yellow sun that beat down on her with such brilliance and heat that it made her want to hide herself from its terrible, blinding exposure.

<<I know you are concerned about Paul, Renard, Donsi, Olaf, and Gwynne. And so I will take you to see each of them, in the cities in which they choose to live. And you will talk with each of them in turn, since they have been persuaded that your crew members' concern is their concern, too.>>

Julia stared at Esée. "You mean they don't live together?"

Esée smiled in Gertrude Stein's most infuriating style. <<They live as they wish. And so far each of them wishes to avoid the company of other men, which is their reason for not wishing to see any crew from *Pax III*.>>

Julia's stomach heaved. They must be sick. As much as she enjoyed La Femmean company, she could not imagine living entirely

with them, with no other humans around. It would be like eras-
ing all of one's secondaries and making no others to replace them.
Or losing one's family at a single stroke. How could they possibly
know who they were, living in an entirely alien environment? She
looked at the mammoth bronze doors at the top of the pillared
steps of the building. "Which one lives here?" she asked hoarsely.

<<We are in Despina, the home of Paul>> Esée told her.
<<You have always spoken chiefly of Paul, and so I thought he
mattered most to you.>>

Julia's eyes moved to Esée's face in startlement. It was true, she
realized. She had tended to use Paul as a sort of synecdochical emblem, as she had come to use Vance as an emblem for the disturbed
and violent crew that would constitute a problem for her were any
or all of them awake.

Esée held out her arm in the grand manner of the one whose
form she had adopted. <<Shall we?>>

Resolute, Julia started up the shallow white steps. Had Esée spoken those words in her head, or had she supplied them to go with
the gesture? But of course, she thought, remembering—the La
Femmeans, in a sense, never did *speak*, at least not in so many words.

Which realization, she saw, didn't actually answer the question.

63.

THEY PASSED THROUGH a high-ceilinged airy atrium complete with plashing fountain and a profusion of lush, silken ferns suffused with a strong white light filtered through skylights (virtually identical with what the c-space environment catalog would call "Northern Exposure"), a setting that might have been lifted whole from one historical c-space or another. Several imposing thresholds opened out of each of the eight walls of the chamber. Esée indicated the one that would presumably lead to Paul.

They walked for perhaps five minutes, moving silently through a maze of rooms, each a recognizable classic (often at variance with those adjoining), accumulating in a proliferation of space exceeding the imaginable limits of what the exterior suggested it could contain. Julia entertained the bizarre thought that perhaps they were indeed in a c-space despite her not having been aware of entering v-space. Could she be lying in her caretaker, on *Pax III*, and somehow have forgotten? Had Esée spirited her into it and then struck her with a selective amnesia to conceal the truth of where they actually were?

Esée halted before a pair of tall, narrow, carved wood doors, which—unlike all the others they had passed—stood closed. She took Julia's arm. <<Paul is within. His condition for seeing you is that the contact be terminated at any instant of his choosing, without warning to you. Do you agree to this?>>

Worse and worse, Julia thought. But she agreed to the stipulation. And then, imagining mentioning it in a report to the Council, winced.

Esée opened the doors, and a heavy scent of incense wafted out. The room they entered lacked the elegance of most of what they had already seen. By comparison the ceiling felt low and oppressive, and the furnishings intensified the effect. The floor had been piled with richly colored rugs and cushions and pallets and divans, the walls and ceiling draped with fabulous tapestries. Fiery torches topping intricately ornamented cast-iron poles spaced at intervals of three meters provided the only visible source of light. It took Julia's eyes a minute or so to adjust to the relative dimness. When they did, she saw La Femmeans, exotic milk-breasted creatures dressed the way tertiaries were in some sexual rec programs available for points. They lay and sat and knelt about the room, less regularly spaced than the torches, and more densely. Julia remembered, then, Paul's bizarre statement about La Femme being a "meat-space brothel." She closed her eyes for a few seconds, not really hoping it would all just disappear from view, but more to give herself a space for free thought. The scene was an embarrassment, like walking into someone else's private sexual rec c-space. Imagine, if her own private spaces and tertiaries took flesh in meat-space, incarnate and observable and…living. Paul, she thought, must be in the room somewhere.

Our lack of male-identifying word processors should have sufficed to show us that gendered distinctions retain meaning for our culture as a whole and are not simply private, individual modes of personal organization. The La Femmeans, however, have offered us an actual mirror. The planet/its inhabitants respond, on an individual basis, to the deepest emotional states of those they encounter. Presumably Paul's other male crew mates did not respond exactly to the La Femmeans as Paul did, but consider: the La Femmeans did not significantly alter the physical appearances they presented to *Pax I* for the *Pax III*. I can think of only two reasons for that.

Esée had "said" he was.

"So, the Council sent women after all." The voice spoke in a thick guttural basso.

Julia spun around. She barely recognized the half-naked man posed against the closed double doors. How cliché. His voice wasn't like that in the report file. Did the La Femmeans change it for him? Or is this all an hallucination or a c-space representation? Nor did his appearance bear much resemblance to the slight, light-browed, light-eyed, golden brown-skinned man of medium height of the report.

Great-knuckled, hirsute hands fisted on leather belted hips. Julia stared in near mesmerization at the heavy gold rings circling most of the highly muscled copper flesh of his arms. His bearded mouth opened, releasing heavy bass laughter that visibly convulsed the flesh of his large, thickly haired belly. "The La Femmeans gave me to understand that men had come," he said. "I suppose that means they couldn't recognize you as a woman." He smirked. "But by their standards, you're not, are you."

<<Julia, I don't understand.>>

Julia had forgotten Esée. She glanced at her, glanced at the formidable sight of Gertrude Stein sunk in frowning puzzle-ment and thought: *That's because, Esée, I don't understand, myself.*

She said aloud: "The Council tried to take your advice, but without a word pro-cessor couldn't accomplish transudation. And so they decided the next best prospect was to send only women and intersexes." The disdainful look on Paul's face pro-voked Julia to smile.

One possibility is that they took the male members of *Pax I* as templates for all humans. I'm inclined to doubt that, though, since they did not appear to Solita in that guise, but as creatures singing in the Delta Pavonian style. The second possibility is that although our genders differ, the crew members of *Pax I* and those of *Pax III* share the same deep sense of gender, which is what mattered to the La Femmeans. Or, to be blunt: we women crew members, in deepest imagination, identify with the male position (despite our identifying as female). It's a nice contradiction, but one I can attest to myself. Anyone raised by milk parents (regardless of said parents' gender) is likely to. Whether this holds true for those raised in kindercities is another question.

— from the Summary of Julia 9561's Report on "La Femme" to the First Council

Paul nodded at Esée. "The La Femmeans were to bring only one of you in here. But I suppose this place must so disconcert you that you need the moral support of a buddy, eh?" His chin pulled up in a classic (cliché?) gesture of pride. "But for men—" Paul grinned— "*real men*, that is, any company but that of the La Femmeans is intrusive."

Julia wondered if that meant that Paul thought that only hetero-sexual men were "real men." She considered informing him of who Esée was—but then decided to save it. If he could terminate the in-terview at any moment, she had to use what time he gave her wisely. "So you're through with the Pax?" Julia said as casually as possible.

Paul produced another of his raucous laughs. "What would I need with the Pax, when everything I could ever want is here for the taking "

Julia glanced around at the women, many of them with deep blue skin, others of the more familiar copper, olive, pink, gold, and deep wood tones of Paxans. "You could get all this in a c-space, if that's what you want. But to live it, all the time, don't you get bored?"

Paul snorted. "There's more than this to it," he said contemptuously. "It's anything I want."

Julia said, passionately, "And what of who you are? What of your family, and your children and their families?"

Julia never got a reply. Instead she found herself, in the blink of an instant, standing outside the mammoth brass doors, at the foot of the steps, even as she was preparing to ask him whether he ever spent time with the other *Pax I* crew on the planet with him.

<<Julia, why are you weeping?>>

Julia put her fingers to her face and felt the tears wetting it. She turned her back, to compose herself away from the gaze of Gertrude Stein. She needed time to think, to analyze, to understand what had just happened. It had all gone by so fast. And it was becoming apparent that the La Femmean had never understood more than she, Julia did. If, that is, she "understood" anything about humans at all.

64.

A FEW DAYS after Arethustra's sixteenth birthday, Julia learned that the Council had instructed the Director-General of Out-System Missions to assemble an all-female crew to investigate the mysterious circumstances shrouding the *Pax I* mission. The new mission was given a rating of highly risky and thus would be composed of volunteers only. An inside source at Central assured Julia that he would be surprised if anyone senior to herself were to apply. The apparent ill fate of the first mission had killed most interest in out-system exploration, and rumor had it that humans could not tolerate transudation. Julia applied for it, hardly daring to hope she would get it. The only thought she spared anent Arethustra was relief that the child had turned sixteen, thus essentially freeing her for work likely to interfere with parental duties.

When the Director-General summoned her and informed her that she would be leading the *Pax III* mission, Julia was ecstatic—until, after perhaps two hours, it dawned on her that her co-parents and child would see her assignment as a desertion of the family, and that in fact she would in all likelihood (even supposing she survived the mission) not be seeing Arethustra into adulthood. Considering Arethustra's unflagging determination to become a word processor, departure with the *Pax III* might mean the virtual end of her relationship with her child.

The thought sobered Julia and tempered her pleasure. Aware that word would soon be out that she had been appointed to the position, she knew she could not put off informing her co-parents. This she did at once, in the emergency meeting she called. They all agreed that Arethustra would be upset and discussed a strategy for breaking the news to her. Only Moira expressed anger at Julia. One of the child's currently intensive parents, Moira had been having problems with Arethustra and had been relying on Julia, the child's declared favorite, to mediate. Julia's departure, they all realized, would be the child's first significant experience of loss.

Julia was in the habit of bicycling with Arethustra one afternoon a week. Usually they rode the bike path circling the dome and then flopped together on a mat for one of their quiet times. Julia broke the news during one of these. She talked about how the assignment was something she had always longed for. She did not mention the danger. And she assured Arethustra that though it would be painful for them to be separated, her departure must not be seen as a negative reflection on Julia's affection for her.

Her head in the favored place on Julia's sweat-damp belly, Arethustra lay rigid and silent for several minutes. Julia stroked her hair and wished she could read the child's thoughts. Finally Arethustra sat up, and Julia saw that her face was as stony as her body had been rigid. "Is it because I want to be a word processor?" she said. "Is that why you're going?"

"No, love. I'm going on the mission for what are probably similar reasons to your wanting to become a word processor. The first mission sent word that there are sentient beings on the planet they found. The Pax made a mess of their first alien Contact, with the Delta Pavonians. And I was too young to be a part of the initial encounters. I'm hoping things can go differently this time. And would like to do what I can to see that it does." She took Arethustra's hand between hers. "Why do you think the City of Word Processing fascinates you? It's certainly not because you don't love your family. And it's not even because they're a meat-society. It's much much more, and difficult to explain, isn't it."

Arethustra nodded slowly. "Yes. But…" Her eyes filled with tears. "I need you, Julia. Moira is so…awful. Arete's the only other parent I can talk to. All the others keep on at me about my wanting to be a word processor." She swallowed. "Though they don't always *say* that's what they're talking about, I know it is. I can feel the pressure, nonstop—except when I'm with you and Arete."

"But you know I don't want you to be a word processor," Julia said, in case it was necessary to state what she had thought must be obvious. "I'm as opposed to it as the others, you know."

Arethustra shook her head. "Yes, but not in the same way. I mean, you're more...*respectful* about it." She sniffed. "You know how Moira— "

Julia squeezed Arethustra's hand and said, to deflect the pending diatribe, "Believe me, this is a bittersweet situation for me. I *hate* leaving you. But there's only going to be this one chance. And love, I have to take it."

Arethustra passively allowed Julia to hug her, then jumped up from the mat, saying she was starving and wanted some fruit. Afterwards, she refused to discuss the coming separation and during their remaining times together acted as though everything was as it had always been. But the child vented her rage and grief on Moira in particular, and her other parents in general. Julia took it as a punishment and left Earth stinging with Arethustra's refusal to see her on their last scheduled afternoon before her departure.

65.

JULIA'S SHOCK SLIPPED into puzzlement and the anxiety of looming disappointment as words framed themselves in her mind in an attempt to describe and speculate on what she had just seen. *He's like a tertiary somehow incarnated into meat-space. A cartoon. That can't really be Paul. I can't believe anybody like that is living in the Pax. And certainly the Council would never have selected him if he were as he seems to be here.*

<<Julia, what you just saw is what Paul most desires. Or it could not be.>>

Julia turned to face the La Femmean, whose words—or communication, at any rate—so unspeakably interrupted her grievance, or grief, or grieving. What she felt seemed to change from moment to moment, excepting the overwhelming sense of disaster that was almost crushing her. She spoke out loud, as though doing so could end this horrid mixing of uncontrollable thoughts with intentional communication: "I can't believe anyone born and nurtured in the Pax would ever desire whatever it was I saw in there. I would've thought that any Paxan in such a situation would be bored out of their mind. He's lost, Esée. Don't you see? There must be something chemically wrong with his brain. It's as though he's living in a solipsistic fantasy. Nothing touches him. He's

"Esée" repeatedly "told" me (and of course the caveat I've noted must fully inform your reading of "told") that she "is La Femme." I at first assumed this was a metaphor, but gradually came to believe that "she" meant this literally—that the inhabitants are something like extensions or avatars of the planet. An opposing view, which I've sometimes held, is that they are mental projections produced by our minds as they interact with the planet. But because the AI was able to detect EM fields with distinctive signatures synched with our perceptions of physical beings as well as molecular patterns indicating physical presence, I don't believe they are mere mental projections. After all, they were able to transport us—instantaneously—off ship (presumably to sites located on the surface of the planet, although we have no means of verifying it).

—from the Summary of Julia 9561's Report on "La Femme" to the First Council lost who he is. It's as though he's been confined in isolation and invented a delusional world to compensate. Except that you—somehow—have given him the power to incarnate the fantasy. There's nothing human about it. It's an aberration. Humans are, above all, the society they make and the products of their society. They can't live without one another. Which is why we need common language to link and bind us, however imperfectly it can ever work."

Under this passionate onslaught, the face of Gertrude Stein remained calm and sympathetic. <<Julia, it is his desire. We didn't choose to separate him from his crew. We only gave him what he wished for. And it is good that we did, for he is happy, and living in peace and contentment. Surely you agree that that is good?>>

Julia snorted. "So does a heroin addict assured of a continual controlled supply of the drug live in peace and contentment! But no one would say it's *good*! Good for what? Good for whom? For Paul? How long has he been like that? How can he not have gotten bored out of his skull?"

Esée held out her hand to Julia without touching her. <<If he becomes bored and desires something else, he will have that. If he wishes for human company, we will help him to seek it. We force nothing on those who come to us, but only ask to do what is in our nature.>>

Julia shoved her clenched fists into her hip pockets. "That's not good enough, Esée. Otherwise you're just offering the trap of hopeless addiction. What I see here is only stasis. The man might as well be dead! If you want to do him good, then tell him the truth and teach him the other desires it's impossible to believe he doesn't somewhere have!"

Esée smiled sadly. <<Julia, we communicate with humans in the ways they make possible. Paul does not put into words our communications. He sees images. He hears names. But he does not receive our communications as words, as you do.>>

Julia stared at Esée. "What! If that's true, it means he really has been virtually in solitary confinement for all these months.

But it can't be." Julia's heart accelerated with suspicion. "I know I heard him say that the La Femmeans said something or other. I know he used the word *said*, Esée."

Esée shook her head. <<If he did, it was only a matter of speech. What he received when we communicated your need to visit was a sense of it, without words, and in images. Except for names, he has never 'heard' anything from us, as you are doing now, in words.>>

"No. That can't be right. Else how would he have not recognized that the crew of the *Pax III* weren't females? He was surprised to see me because he thought I'd be male."

Esée put her hand to her breast. <<This is too difficult, Julia. For we perceive only confusion in human minds when you apply the idea of women and females to the idea of human. We understood that females and women were what La Femmeans are to humans. The concepts aren't clear enough for us to communicate with coherently.>> She made a fist for her chin to press down on, in the Paxan gesture that meant "This is a tough one." <<We told you from the beginning. La Femme is here for you, to serve your desire. Despina is for Paul's desires, which are not what you desire. Let me take you to Eudoxia, which is for Julia's desire.>>

"No," Julia said, grabbing at Esée's arm, as though doing so could keep her from whisking Julia to wherever she chose. "I want to see La Femmeans. I want to know what La Femmeans are like. Despina is not about La Femme, but about an individual human named Paul. Eudoxia is apparently about an individual human named Julia. What I want is to know about Esée, and other La Femmeans. What is the name of the place where Esée's desire is engaged?"

Esée held out both hands, inviting Julia's clasp. <<We understand one another so poorly, after all. Paul was easy, compared with you. Julia, please attend to me: La Femme is the place engaging my desire. All of it. For my desire is to serve your desire, and to be exactly what you desire. That's all there is. Nothing more, nothing less.>> Julia stared at the La Femmean—or rather, stared at the image of Gertrude Stein as Julia had conceived her when creating the tertiary. Gertrude Stein would never speak such words. The incongruity made Julia want to scream. If the words did not sound inside her head, as though coming through her implant, she would be certain something had gone wrong with the tertiary programming. Only this was Esée, not a tertiary of Gertrude Stein.

"My desire is to know you," Julia said finally. "I came to La Femme, looking for something outside of myself, outside of the Pax. Don't you understand?"

Esée smiled. <<Let me take you to Eudoxia.>>

Julia knew that Eudoxia would be an incarnation of things that she might not necessarily want to acknowledge. Certainly it would be significant to her, given the powers of insight and perception the La Femmean had displayed on board the *Pax III*. What if what Esée showed her was so irresistible that she acquired an instant addiction to it? In Esée, morality or even ethics seemed utterly absent, as though considerations beyond drives like fear and desire were so foreign to her she could not read them. *The ease with which we seemed to communicate has deceived us. Or rather, we deceived ourselves. And above all, I deceived* myself.

Julia crossed her arms tightly over her chest. "I'll agree to visit Eudoxia on the condition that you return me to the ship either after we've been there a ship's hour, or at my request, whichever occurs first."

Esée smiled. <<Of course, Julia. But how little faith you have in La Femme—or yourself. Remember how your crewmates returned, optimal in body and spirit. There is no sinister plot, no addiction. Paul is simply...different from you and your crewmates. You do remember, that I told you that they are as different from you as you are from the singers with crystals in their throats.>>

Julia put her hand over her eyes. Her only reason for agreeing to see Eudoxia was her knowledge that if she didn't she would revile herself as a coward ever after. "I'm ready when you are," she said. Though she knew that if Eudoxia were what she thought it might be, that would never really be true.

66.

JULIA FELT ON her skin as well as smelled the difference in the air before she lowered her hand from her eyes. A strong odor of earth and rot, leaves and grass filled her nostrils. The air clung to her skin, moist, almost tangible when a slight breeze brushed over her. Her ears pricked at the sound of a stream rushing over rocks. She knew when she looked she would see something like the wildlife dome Glenning had taken her to see. And the thought confirmed, oddly, her old, articulated desire to taste it at length, as she was forever barred from doing.

But when Julia opened her eyes, she forgot about the wildlife dome. Raye stood before her, Raye as she had been in Julia's youth. She stood smiling, radiating pleasure at the very sight of Julia, opening her arms to invite Julia in.

Without thinking, Julia rushed toward her. But less than an arm's length away, she halted, folded her arms over her chest, and stepped back. Her throat was full and tight. Her eyes filled. The longing for what the figure opposite was promising grew, and grew, and grew, until the sight of Raye became almost unbearable.

Julia turned her back on it. "I'm not a child," she said harshly to the La Femmean. Her stomach heaved in an emotional storm. She felt reduced to a child, indeed.

Esée gestured. <<Let's walk, shall we, and see more of Eudoxia.>>

Julia resisted the urge to turn around, to see what Raye would make of her desertion. Nothing. She'll make nothing of it. Because it is not Raye. It is not Raye any more than a tertiary of Raye is Raye.

The La Femmean led Julia down a mossy path along the edge of the stream through woods teeming with towering old trees larger in circumference than six or seven Paxans would be pressed close.

Tiny toads leaped from their feet, a bright green snake gleamed in a patch of sunlight, swift wild creatures invisible to Julia's eyes rustled in the fallen leaves and ferns carpeting the forest floor. Julia breathed in the serenity and beauty of it all. She tried to empty her mind of its turmoil. But when after only a few minutes they came to a clearing, she knew her short moment of peace had been illusory. She felt herself to be at war with the La Femmean. The sensation was new. But then she had never had an opponent like Esée, never been so vulnerable to another being in her life.

There they all were. Her parents. Her grandparents. Even her great-grandparents, whom she'd never seen in meat-space. Raye, again. And every secondary she had ever created. They stood there, welcoming her to them. Davis, smiling, moved forward.

Julia turned her back on them. "No," she said to Esée, anger sweeping away trepidation. "You've gotten it wrong. Maybe you thought that because I said Paul couldn't be human without other humans, that he couldn't know who he is without his family, maybe you thought that representations of my family would answer." Julia thought of the secondaries ranged in a circle around the family and shivered. "Tertiaries and secondaries incarnate are not the same thing, Esée. It's a question of engagement. Of independence. Those representations you've made are phantoms imitating people who matter to me. Just as you are an entity wholly apart from the representation of Gertrude Stein you've adopted. It's the same problem as before: these phantoms are, simply, an extension of myself and nothing more."

<<Appearance is everything. I've heard you humans say that>> Esée replied.

Julia laughed bitterly. "What we mean, is that we deal in representations. Not that a deliberately fabricated duplicate of someone is the same thing as the original. When people die, they leave behind secondaries they themselves have created as their representatives to those who survive them. No one imagines they're full, living agents identical to the people who made them."

The Gertrude Stein face drooped with sadness. <<You haven't seen all of Eudoxia, Julia.>>

"I can about imagine," Julia said drily. It wouldn't be Outsiders, since she had lost interest in them. A merging zone? But she had never worked in one and so would have no information about them stored in her brain for Esée to tap. Delta Pavonians? But they were no longer her desire, either: deep down, she knew that close contact with them would make her sick. Sasha? Some sort of sexual scenario, lifted from her recreational programming?

"Julia!" a voice rang out.

Julia pressed her hands to her ears. "Esée, no, I want you to stop it now!"

"Julia—" the voice was close, and suddenly a body flung itself on her from behind. "Oh Julia, I'm so happy you've come! I love it here, it's so *real*, and pretty, and like nothing I've ever seen. It's better than the City of Word Processing, a thousand times more wonderful!"

Arethustra danced around Julia, closed her arms around her. She pressed her cheek to Julia's. Julia swallowed hard. The cheek felt exactly like Arethustra's soft, smooth, warm. The ear touching Julia's neck felt cooler than the cheek, as ears never did in c-space. The texture and softness, the very scent of Arethustra's body, was nothing one could create in even the best c-space program. Arethustra felt *real*.

<<She is real, Julia. Not like a tertiary. That is the wrong comparison. More like a clone. And like a clone, she will grow and learn and change independent of the original. This *is* your daughter, Julia.>>

Julia ground her teeth. She couldn't bring herself to break Arethustra's hold, because a part of her feared that the child would feel whatever rejection she visited on her. *You promised to take me back to the* Pax III *at my request. I'm requesting you to do it now, Esée. This is not what I want. I don't believe La Femme has what I want. La Femme is not for me.*

<<Oh Julia. How sad. Very well. It is done.>>

Julia found herself on the bridge. She glanced around and saw Nadia, lying in a recliner. "AI, who besides Nadia and myself are on board?"

"No one else is on board," the AI said.

Julia snatched a bulb of water and ordered herself a recliner near Nadia's. Sucking from the bulb, she stared at the viewscreen. "Where's Fuyuko?" she asked Nadia.

Nadia opened her eyes and looked at Julia. "After she unleashed Vance on the planet, she took the *Pax I* and Solita and skedaddled with its comatose crewmembers."

The AI spoke. "Attention crew: a ship has just emerged from this system's transudation point."

Julia went rigid. "AI, is it the *Pax I*, returned?" But of course, it couldn't be—unless she had lost more time than she thought possible.

"The ship is the *Pax II*."

"It's begun, Nadia. Fuyuko is too late."

Nadia said, "Too late? For the La Femmeans, or for the Pax?"

Julia laughed. "I'd put my money on the La Femmeans any time. They'll make a feast of Vance, you know. And if the Council's sent a whole ship-load of Vances..." She shrugged and made the "it follows" gesture. "I'd say we're done here."

She instructed the AI to break orbit and head for the transudation point. Then she finished the water in the bulb and closed her eyes. She had a lot of thinking to do.

Acknowledgments

CHERCHER LA FEMME'S origins stretch back to the early 1990s. On being solicited in the mid-1990s for a novel ms by an agent whose name I saw often in the page of *Locus*, I chose this one to send him. He politely informed me that it wasn't commercial, and I set it aside. In 2009, after tearing through the Marq'ssan Cycle at speed, Dr. Helen Merrick expressed a desire to read one of my unpublished novels, and I sent her *Chercher*. And I'm so glad I did, because she offered me a critique (one which one of the novel's earlier readers, Dr. Ann Hibner Koblitz, confirmed) that I knew in my bones was right. The version she read opened with a 30,000 word section consisting of excerpts from Fuyuko's log, focusing on the events that occurred during *Pax III's* transudation to the Albirean system. Helen said that beginning in this way created a structural mess and suggested that either the first section be eliminated altogether or that Fuyuko be the crew member who died during transudation so that Julia could piece together what happened by accessing Fuyuko's log. When I took up the ms a few years later, I decided that the novel needed to begin after the *Pax III* had arrived in the Albirean system because the novel wasn't really about what had happened prior to that arrival. Helen's second, astute suggestion was that the novel, as written, contained enough thematic material for two novels, requiring the reader to spend a lot of time and effort trying to grasp what the novel was really saying. And so I excised the thematic material around gender that was so complex that even I, going back to the ms after more than a decade away from it, had trouble parsing it.

I spent a good deal of time rewriting the novel in 2016, during two writing retreats in Port Townsend. Kath Wilham, Aqueduct's managing editor, said the ms still had problems, and I realized I needed fresh views of the work. These I got from close readings and helpful critiques by Cynthia Ward and Kristin King; their critiques resulted in more iterations of the novel. Finally I solicited help from Nisi Shawl, who gave me one of the finest, most insightful (and frank) critiques I've ever received. Here's the thing about getting critical readings from people who are both writers and critics: they not only tell you what the story is that they've read (which may or may not be the story you intended to tell), they also tell you what in their technically informed opinion will make that story stronger. Cindy, Kristin, and Nisi all read slightly different stories (which is what readers *always* do with fiction that isn't recipe-driven), each of which opened a new window onto the work. I am indebted to them.

But above all, my as always profuse thanks go to Kath, for all the editorial care she's put into this book as well as for the decades of support she's given to my writing, and to Tom, who does so much in so many ways to nurture me and my work. It takes a community to make a ms into a book, something we, who live in a society that pretends individuals are in every way autonomous, often fail to recognize.

Author Biography

L. Timmel Duchamp is the author of the five-volume Marq'ssan Cycle, which won a special Tiptree Award honor in 2009, and the founder and publisher of Aqueduct Press. She has published two collections of short fiction: *Love's Body, Dancing in Time* (2004), which was shortlisted for the Tiptree and includes the Sturgeon-finalist story "Dance at the Edge," the Sidewise Award-nominated "The Heloise Archive," and the Titpree-shortlisted "The Apprenticeship of Isabetta di Pietro Cavazzi"; and *Never at Home*, which includes a 2011 Tiptree-Honor List story.She is also co-author, with Maureen McHugh, of a mini-collection, *Plugged In*, published in conjunction with the authors' being GoHs at WisCon. Her Marq'ssan Cycle consists of *Alanya to Alanya* (2005), *Renegade* (2006), *Tsunami* (2007), *Blood in the Fruit* (2007), and *Stretto* (2008). Her novel *The Waterdancer's World* appeared in 2016, and the short novel, *The Red Rose Rages (Bleeding)* appeared in 2005; she has also published the novella *De Secretis Mulierum* and dozens more short stories and novellas, including "Motherhood, Etc" (short-listed for the Tiptree) and "Living Trust" (Nebula and Homer Award finalist). In addition to her fiction, she has published a good deal of nonfiction. Since 2011 she has been the Features Editor of *The Cascadia Subduction Zone*. She was also the editor of *Talking Back: Epistolary Fantasies* (Aqueduct, 2006), *The WisCon Chronicles, Vol. 1* (Aqueduct, 2007), *Narrative Power: Encounters, Celebrations, Struggles* (Aqueduct Press, 2010), *Missing Links and Secret Histories: A Selection of Wikipedia Entries from across the Known Multiverse* (Aqueduct Press, 2013), and co-editor, with Eileen Gunn, of *The WisCon Chronicles, Vol. 2: Provocative essays on feminism, race, revolution, and the future* (Aqueduct, 2008).

In 2008 she appeared as a Guest of Honor at WisCon. In 2009-2010 she was awarded the Neil Clark Special Achievement Award ("recognizing individuals who are proactive behind the scenes but whose efforts often don't receive the measure of public recognition they deserve"). In 2015 she was the Editor Guest at Armadillocon. She has been a finalist for the World Fantasy Award twice, for her work as a publisher and editor. She has taught at the Clarion West Writers Workshop and has taught one-day Clarion West workshops. She has twice been nominated for the World Fantasy Award. She lives in Seattle.